I0650842

The Wild Adventures of Doc Savage

Please visit www.adventuresinbronze.com for
more information on titles you may have missed.

PYTHON ISLE
WHITE EYES
THE FRIGHTENED FISH
THE JADE OGRE
FLIGHT INTO FEAR
THE WHISTLING WRAITH
THE FORGOTTEN REALM
THE DESERT DEMONS
HORROR IN GOLD
THE INFERNAL BUDDHA
DEATH'S DARK DOMAIN
SKULL ISLAND
PHANTOM LAGOON
THE MIRACLE MENACE
THE ICE GENIUS
THE WAR MAKERS
THE SINISTER SHADOW
THE SECRET OF SATAN'S SPINE
GLARE OF THE GORGON

Also from Altus Press

The Wild Adventures of Tarzan

RETURN TO PAL-UL-DON

SIX SCARLET SCORPIONS

A PAT SAVAGE ADVENTURE

BY WILL MURRAY & LESTER DENT
WRITING AS KENNETH ROBESON

COVER BY JOE DeVITO

ALTUS PRESS • 2016

SIX SCARLET SCORPIONS copyright © 2016 by Advance Magazine Publishers Inc.

© 2016 Condé Nast. The Doc Savage character is © Advance Magazine Publishers Inc. d/b/a Condé Nast. "Doc Savage" is a registered trademark of Advance Magazine Publishers Inc. The Pat Savage character is © Advance Magazine Publishers Inc. d/b/a Condé Nast. "Pat Savage" is a trademark of Advance Magazine Publishers Inc. This book is published under license from Advance Magazine Publishers Inc.

Front cover image copyright © 2016 Joe DeVito. All rights reserved.

No part of this book may be reproduced or utilized in any form or by any means, electronic or mechanical, without permission in writing from the publisher.

First Edition — October 2016

DESIGNED BY

Matthew Moring/Altus Press

SPECIAL THANKS TO

James Bama, Jerry Birenz, Gary A. Buckingham, Condé Nast, Jeff Deischer, Norma Dent, Dafydd Neal Dyar, Elizabeth Engel, Mark Lambert, Dave McDonnell, Matthew Moring, Mel Odom, Ray Riethmeier, Howard Wright, The State Historical Society of Missouri, and last but not least, the Heirs of Norma Dent—James Valbracht, John Valbracht, Wayne Valbracht, Shirley Dungan and Doris Leimkuehler.

COVER ILLUSTRATION COMMISSIONED BY

Dave Smith

Like us on Facebook: "The Wild Adventures of Pat Savage"

Printed in the United States of America

Set in Caslon.

For Maureen Angela Murray,

1928–2016

Six Scarlet Scorpions

Chapter I

CRACK-UP

THE LITTLE CABIN monoplane was in trouble.

It was a high-wing job, a two-seater that had seen better days. It swooped around the spidery pipe derricks of a modest oilfield south of Seminole, Oklahoma, evidently seeking a suitable spot upon which to alight. Yellow wings flashed in the early morning sunlight as the pilot banked the trim ship in preparation for landing.

Unexpectedly, the motor began missing and sputtering. An experienced pilot would have recognized the unpleasant cacophony as the first warning sign of imminent engine failure.

The warning turned out to be not much in the way of advance notice. After a few more sputtering coughs, the engine quit entirely. The propeller abruptly stopped spinning, becoming fixed, and consequently about as useful as an auxiliary nose on an elephant.

The pilot did the best that could be done under the sudden circumstances fate had thrust upon the struggling aircraft. As the ship fell into a flat glide, the pilot gave up all thought of making the dirt airstrip west of the congress of unfinished derricks, and fought to keep the yellow monoplane level.

There was sufficient space between the scattered derricks to put the aircraft down safely. Sufficient, that is, if the gleaming wings did not clip any of the newly-built wildcat wells.

The pilot struggled with the pitching plane. But there was a steady wind coming off the prairie wilderness of red-oak brush and rolling tumbleweeds. It whistled and whined among the derrick interstices, and blew up dry red dirt in whirlwinds that looked like rusty dust devils. The wind pushed at the hapless monoplane. The pilot fought back.

The wind won.

Slanting toward level ground, the monoplane managed to scrape a looming derrick with one canary-colored wing. The wingtip only nicked the steel tower, but the result was disastrous.

The high wing came off, and went whirling away. The aircraft fuselage was flung about as if an invisible hand had reached down to give it a remonstrating bat.

Now the pilot was truly helpless. There was nothing that could be done but to ride the doomed ship to the ground and pray for the best possible outcome.

Not that there was any time for prayer. Not even a quick one.

The aircraft slammed into the red dirt, tail striking first. This freak of landing no doubt saved the lives of those trapped in the cabin. Had the monoplane nosed in, the impact would have driven the failed engine into the cabin, crushing out all life. Fortunately for all concerned, that particular calamity did not happen.

The tail of the tiny ship cracked, but did not separate. Neither did the aircraft catch fire, which would have been calamitous. Exiting a wreck is not easy for the stunned occupants, and fire moves swiftly, especially where aviation fuel is concerned. And the hour was so early that no workers were present in the small oilfield as yet.

The craft came to rest upon its side, and the high wing which had been jarred loose landed several yards distant, rendering the monoplane permanently worthless.

An awful silence followed the crack-up. Red dust was thrown up by the impact, forming a rusty shroud over the wreckage. Now it swirled in the steady wind, thinning and separating like infant clouds being torn apart by unseen imps.

Presently, the pilot's door lifted. A slim brown arm pushed it up, and sent it crashing back against the fuselage.

A hesitant head lifted, and looked about.

Had there been any witnesses of the male persuasion, doubtless they would have whistled in amazement.

For the hapless private pilot proved to be a young woman. She was a tall, sinewy, athletic girl in her twenties. She wore no pilot's helmet, and her wealth of bronze-colored hair showed in abundance. An attractive face, dominated by clear golden eyes, frowned like a brazen thundercloud. Her outdoorsy tan was a wonder.

"Rats!" she fumed. "Doesn't this beat everything?"

A squeaky voice from the passenger's seat beneath her asked, "Are you gonna climb out, or not? You're standin' on my arm."

"I'm climbing out, all right," the girl snapped. "And I'm going to get to the bottom of this!"

Suiting action to words, the bronze-skinned beauty clambered up, walked the crumpled fuselage and dropped to the dusty ground.

She was dressed like a cowgirl, minus the hat. Whipcord breeches, riding boots, and a crisp white short-sleeved shirt that showed off her delectable shape to perfection.

Reaching the ground, she stormed for the engine cowling, found the catch, and threw it open on the side pointing skyward. There was something electric in the way she moved, as if she might shed sparks at any moment. It was not merely the vitality of youth, but a quality that might never depart her.

The squeaky-voiced passenger emerged next. He was a sight. But not the way the girl was.

Had someone captured a gorilla, and shaven him to resemble a human being, he might have achieved something like the result that nature had made of this man. The hulking fellow stood five foot, five and he looked almost as wide. His arms were long and covered with rusty red hair, as was the top of his simian skull.

Using his overlong arms, he leveraged himself out of the slanting cockpit. When the apish fellow stood on the fuselage, it could be seen that his legs were short and bowed and he possessed practically no hips. His upper body, however, was ferociously muscled. This fact was especially evident since he was wearing a short-sleeved jersey.

Walking toward the nose, he came upon the girl fussing with the engine.

"What gives?" he squeaked. "We gassed up before we left Tulsa."

"I know that!" snapped the girl. "It wasn't a broken fuel line that caused the engine to conk out."

The girl had the cap off the oil reservoir, and from a pocket she produced a yellow pencil. She dipped this inside, brought it out dripping with oil that was suspiciously grayish.

Taking the oily end of the pencil between thumb and forefinger, she squeezed off some of this black stuff, rubbing it between thumb and forefinger.

"This oil," she pronounced, "is as gritty as sand."

The apelike individual had a very low forehead, and this wrinkled up, practically shrinking it in half.

"I filled the oil myself."

"Better check the container, Monk."

Monk did just that, crawling back into the cockpit and fishing around. He came up with the container of oil, and began doling out the remainder onto the side of the plane.

Getting down on one knee, he began wiping the oil around with a gaudy handkerchief pulled from a pocket.

"This stuff is full of grit!" he exploded.

"Sand?"

Monk shook his head. "Too fine for sand."

"What is it, then?"

The homely individual named Monk frowned with his entire unlovely face. "Wish I had my portable chemical laboratory with me, Pat. I'd find out darn quick."

The girl stood up and walked over, taking care not to step into the pooled oil. "What are those dusty-looking marks on the side of the container?"

The homely Monk hoisted the container, and saw what appeared to be the smudges of fingerprints.

"I think I smell rodents—and I don't mean the four-legged kind," he grumbled.

Holding the container higher, he brought his tiny eyes to bear. He used the clean thumb of his other hand to smudge one of the prints, and when he looked at the ball of his thumb, it was gray.

"Emery dust!" howled Monk. "Some joker poured emery dust into the oil container, and like a dope, I used it to fill the reservoir."

"Sabotage!" snapped Pat. "That could only mean one thing. That sneaky Grabber Daly is trying to beat us to that oil lease."

Turning about, Pat scanned the dusty field in which the oil derricks were being erected. To the south, she saw a line of red dust boiling up where the highway ran.

"Use your long arms to fetch me the binoculars, Monk," she requested.

Pivoting only to stoop, Monk reached down into the askew plane cabin to retrieve the binoculars. He tossed them over.

Applying the smaller lenses to her eyes, Pat studied the highway.

"Someone is driving up in a swanky roadster," she proclaimed. "Do you know what kind of auto Grabber Daly drives?"

"Not me," admitted Monk, "but I'll bet my last dollar that's Grabber Daly. He's the dog-eat-dog type. And if he figured out you're in Oklahoma to pick up some oil leases cheap, he'd be bound and determined to beat you to the punch."

"Since he's driving and we're on foot, it looks like he might win, after all." Pat's golden eyes narrowed in the morning sun and she showed every sign of thinking swiftly.

"Monk," she said slowly, "I believe I have hatched a scheme."

Looking around forlornly, Monk said, "It better be a dang good one, because the stew we have found ourselves in is pretty much dry-gulch stuff."

"This scheme of mine may save our bacon, but I'll need your cooperation."

Interest made Monk's eyes shine like those of an eager hound dog. "Whatcha got in mind, Pat?"

The red roadster was fast approaching and pretty Pat trained her binoculars on it steadily. She was able to distinguish the man behind the wheel. He was a pinch-faced sort who wore a Boss J. B. Stetson hat that was a size too big for his head.

"It's Grabber Daly, all right. Listen, Monk. This is what I want you to do."

Leaning in, Pat began to speak conspiratorially and, as the words filled the hairy Monk's ears, his pleasantly homely face became positively gleeful.

When Pat was finished, Monk said, "I was all set to hand that Grabber Daly a haymaker or two, but I like your idea better. Count on me."

Jumping off the plane, he scuttled behind a nearby sand hill, disappearing from sight.

While he was doing that, Pat pulled a clasp knife out of her whipcord breeches, and separated the gas feed line to the engine. Pulling a matchbook from another pocket, she stepped back, lit a single match, and got the entire matchbook blazing. This modest firebrand she tossed at the engine.

The engine went *woof!* violently, and was soon ablaze.

Retreating to the tail of the aircraft, Pat lay down as if she had been flung there.

As the flames bundling the engine crackled merrily, Pat lay doggo, feigning unconsciousness. Direct sunlight striking her bronze hair brought out coppery highlights suggestive of electrical wire carrying current.

The red roadster soon pulled up, kicking up a cloud of dust as it did so.

TWO individuals emerged from the roadster, and the pinched-face fellow with the oversized hat ran up to Pat and began talking to himself in an agitated voice.

"Look, Collins! She was thrown clear."

"Is she injured, Mr. Daly?"

Kneeling in the dirt, Grabber Daly looked Pat over and began moaning, saying, "I cannot tell. She may have a concussion, or worse. But she appears to be breathing."

"What if she dies? There's no doctor for miles around."

Grabber Daly looked stricken in a guilty way. He said, "You should never have put that emery dust into that oil container. It was a terrible mistake on your part."

Collins looked beside himself. "But Mr. Daly, you told me to do it. It was your instructions to do so. It was the only way to beat Miss Savage to the punch."

Standing up, Grabber Daly looked at his assistant and said fiercely, "If it ever comes to a courtroom hearing, I will deny ever giving you that order. Do you understand me? Your salary is at stake. No one told you to put emery dust into the oil container. That was entirely of your own initiative."

Collins looked abashed. "If you say so, sir. But—"

"No buts! Now help me pull her away from the wreck. Those flames are spreading fast."

The two lease brokers fussed about, trying to figure out the best way to move the seemingly unconscious woman—who incidentally had heard every word.

"Should we drag her by the heels?" asked Collins.

Daly shook his head violently, saying, "No, no. If she has a concussion, we can't be dragging her head across any stones lying in the dirt."

"What if her back is broken? We can't safely lift her, can we?"

"I do not know, I do not know," Grabber Daly exclaimed in a mounting panic. "I am no doctor. I'm an oil man!"

"Not much of a one," murmured Pat Savage in an undertone that no one could hear above the moaning of the wind.

In the end, they found a board which they slipped under Pat's back, and used this to drag her away from the flaming wreckage.

The burning crate kept burning, but it did not further explode. Its supply of aviation fuel was soon exhausted. After a bit, only boiling smoke emerged from the open engine cowling. Fire had gotten into the cockpit and the fabric seats were ablaze, adding to the malodorous smoke.

"What about Miss Savage's passenger?" Collins suddenly exclaimed.

"That's right! She was traveling with that Doc Savage man, Monk Mayfair."

The two men looked to the burning cockpit, and their faces grew pale and slack, eyes going sick.

"If Mayfair was inside the cockpit, he's a goner," said Collins thickly.

"We have no proof of that!" snapped Grabber Daly. "No proof at all. Look, we're here to acquire a lease option. Let's finish that."

"What about this poor girl?"

"You mean this claim jumper, don't you?" said Grabber Daly savagely. "Maybe she got what she deserved, not being from around here. I've been optioning oil land since I was of age. She's a carpetbagger. When we get to farmer Allison's place, he's sure to have a telephone. We'll ring up the authorities. It will be their job to sort matters out."

Collins appeared reluctant to leave the girl, but when his boss snapped his fingers impatiently and pointed to the roadster half obscured by the smoke coming from the burning crate, he reluctantly followed, casting a last backward glance at the supine form of Pat Savage lying in the red dirt of Oklahoma.

After climbing back into their seats, Collins started the engine and drove off. The new tires rolled over a set of footprints that were larger than either of theirs and which, had they noticed them, they could not account for here in the desolate oilfield.

Dragging a rusty worm of dust behind it, the roadster soon disappeared from sight.

AFTER a bit, Monk Mayfair crept out from behind the low sand hill and went to Pat Savage's side. Pat's eyes were still closed.

"They hightailed it out of here," he told Pat.

The bronze-haired girl sat up abruptly, eyes flying open to reveal tiny golden flakes suspended within. "But not before they confessed in my hearing!" she crowed.

"I overheard, too," said Monk, putting out a long hairy arm to assist Pat to her feet.

Pat was smacking the red dirt off her clothing when she asked, "Did you do what I asked?"

"Sure," grinned Monk. "I potted that sap's gas tank while you decoyed him with the fire. It'll leak until it runs dry."

"Swell! That'll buy us a little time."

Frowning, Monk looked around, saying, "We'll need more than a little time. We're on foot practically in the middle of nowhere."

"You could say the same for Grabber Daly in about fifteen minutes," reminded Pat.

Monk's grin widened alarmingly, making him look like a gorilla about to take a small coconut into his capacious mouth.

"Then it's a race!" he exclaimed.

"One that I aim to win," remarked Pat, adding, "I spotted a pipeline pumping station not far from here. Let's start walking in that direction."

Chapter II

SCHEMERS

OF ALL OILFIELD personalities, lease brokers, or "lease grabbers" as they are less politely known, probably lead the most hectic and unenviable existence. They keep their ears to the ground, and when they hear of a likely oil strike, they rush to the spot and grab options to lease for oil company production purposes all of the best land in the vicinity, paying as little as possible. Then they peddle the leases to big concerns for as much as they can get. A number of big shots in the petroleum business got started in this fashion.

Neither Patricia Savage nor Monk Mayfair were particular wheels in oil.

For Patricia was the owner of a high-class beauty establishment back in New York City, and had managed to make a fair wad of dough for herself catering to rich clientele.

But Pat, as she was best known, had a hankering to make a fortune. On what, she did not particularly care. Pat would have liked to dredge up sunken treasure, or possibly make a killing harvesting alligator hides down in South America.

She had tried both enterprises, tooling around the Florida Keys in her yacht, *Patricia,* but no sunken treasure did she raise. Shooting alligators down in Venezuela proved to be a bit more exciting, and she brought back a boatload of the valuable skins. They fetched her good money, but not as much as staying home and running her beauty salon emporium. Pat had become tired of plunking alligators, which are plentiful in Venezuela. But they had a bad habit of biting back if you got too close to them, and after she lost a perfectly good boot to one pair of snapping jaws, her interest had cooled.

Then Pat heard about the oil leasing business from Monk Mayfair, who was formally known as Lieutenant Colonel Andrew Blodgett Mayfair, one of the foremost industrial chemists in the world. He was also a member of the Doc Savage organization. Pat was Doc Savage's cousin. That was how the two of them came to know one another—although Doc refused to permit Pat Savage to join his band of adventurers.

Doc Savage was one of the most outstanding men who would ever be born into the 20th Century. Much has been written about him. Innumerable journalists and other scribes have attempted to condense into a few succinct paragraphs the breadth of accomplishment that was the Man of Bronze. None, however, ever succeeded. There was simply too much to Doc Savage to limit to a few orderly paragraphs.

There exist newspapermen who specialize in writing advance obituaries of living notables so that when the day of death arrives, all that is needed is to update certain details and go to press.

Although he had been a public figure for somewhat less than a decade, all attempts to pen an obituary for Doc Savage had failed spectacularly. For despite his long list of deeds and accomplishments, little was known about the man personally. So newspaper editors around the world had resigned themselves to publishing an obituary that would certainly run at least a full newspaper page—some six columns wide—and they hoarded all details uncovered of this amazing man of mystery.

Suffice it to say that Doc Savage was the premier scientist of the age, as well as a noted adventurer, surgeon and a fellow who followed the unusual occupation of helping those in need without taking any pay for it. It was responsibly asserted that the people of the 21st Century would recognize the name of Doc Savage—just as those of this present era know of George Washington and Abraham Lincoln—long after his eventual passing.

To be sure, Doc Savage was a great man, whose greatness was still being built. He was also known as a generous philanthropist, one whose wealth was considered fabulous—even as its source remained obscure to the general public.

The same could not be said of cousin Pat. So when Monk happened to mention a fresh oil strike in an area of Oklahoma that the homely chemist knew well, Pat had expressed keen interest.

"Do you mean to tell me that you can just buy up a hunk of land from somebody on the blind prospect that oil will be found in it, and then turn around and sell that patch of earth to a big petroleum company for a profit?"

"That's about the size of it," Monk had confirmed. "There ain't much more to it than that."

Pat had eyed Monk skeptically, almost closing one tawney orb when it narrowed.

"There has to be a catch," she insisted. "There's always a catch. What is it?"

Monk shrugged his burly shoulders and replied casually, "The catch is whether or not there's any oil. It's educated guesswork. Sometimes, you hit a gusher and other times when you sink a well, it's a duster."

"A what?"

"Dry hole."

"You seem to know a lot about the subject," Pat probed.

"I was born in Tulsa, and come up smellin' crude and playin' around the derricks. When I grew out of short pants, I worked some as an oilfield roustabout, in Cushing and Seminole, at Three Sands and Bowlegs. I was still a kid back then. Just a lease monkey with a violent itch in both feet. Because I could push a string of tools, and knew a crown block from the Sampson posts, I was able to make enough dough to come east and go to college. Get my chemistry degree. Of course, the war kinda got in the way for a while, but after that, I never looked back much."

"If we find a likely patch," Pat had wondered, "could you tell whether there would be oil or not?"

"Maybe. If we did it on the sly. But if the owner caught us pussy-footin' around, he'd likely run us off—maybe with a shotgun. You kinda want to cozy up to a landowner out there, and take a flyer for a small amount of money. It doesn't hurt a hard-up owner to take loose cash, and once you turn around and sell it, he's out of luck. That is, if there's oil."

"That sounds like a lot of money for not a lot of work," mused Pat.

"It's good dough on a short investment," replied the gorilla-like chemist.

Pat and Monk had huddled, hatching a partnership. They would fly out to Oklahoma, scout around and, if they found something promising, they would take a flyer on it.

Since Monk knew Oklahoma like the back of his hairy hand, Pat agreed to cut him in for a ten percent commission on any land he'd help scout.

SO they had flown to Tulsa, and fell to scouting.

It was tiring, tedious work driving around the sand hills and tallgrass, but they stumbled across a cluster of wildcat oil wells that had that not started production yet, for some derricks were still under construction. They took this as a promising sign.

Near this oilfield was a farm belonging to a man named Bill Allison. It was a big farm. Alfalfa and oats. A great deal of the land was not in use, crop prices being what they were.

This land was a fair hike from the new oilfield, but where there was one pool of black gold, there might be others. Sometimes it was the same pool. Big enough so a man could sink a well at one end of it and take out as much crude as his pump jacks could handle while another outfit was draining the opposite end.

The problem was that the oil industry was full of people with similar intentions.

One of them was Alec "Grabber" Daly, one of the most notorious lease brokers out of Tulsa.

Daly knew who Monk Mayfair was, and knew that he was a famous trouble-buster. So he began nosing around town to see what kind of trouble Monk was intent upon busting.

Some newspapers employ a creature called an oil editor. An oil editor makes it his business to know what is up in the petroleum business. Grabber Daly talked to two oil editors on two different Tulsa newspapers, and learned from them that there was no known business in Tulsa for Monk Mayfair.

This news made Grabber Daly suspicious. "If he is not here on behalf of Doc Savage, I'll bet my bottom dollar he's after oil. The fellow is a world-renowned chemist."

So Grabber Daly had put his man Collins to shadowing Monk. When Monk and Pat Savage arranged to rent a small airplane at the Tulsa municipal airport, they were forced to file a flight plan. Collins got hold of that flight plan by offering one hundred dollars—which was a substantial amount to the operations manager.

When Collins had called in the news to his employer, Grabber Daly had instructed his stooge to put emery powder in the oil can, and to swing around and pick him up.

There followed a mad dash across half of Oklahoma as Grabber Daly and Collins drove well in excess of the speed limit over hot tar highways and dusty back roads, with a map spread out between them.

"They're headed for that new oilfield out Tumbleweed Station way," Daly had mused. "The only land nearby that might be available is the old Allison farm. We've got to beat them to it, Collins."

"We will, boss," said Collins, pressing the gas pedal to the floor and practically lifting the seat of his pants out of the driver's seat cushions in his urgency.

They made it as far as a mile outside the oilfield. Now the burning aircraft was still smudging the sky in the rear-vision mirror as they fled the scene of their crime.

Collins was sweating. "God, I hope that girl don't die. It would be a tragedy if she did."

"A tragedy for *you*," Daly said coldly. "They'll electrocute you if they do. Remember that. Keep driving! We got to make it to the Allison farm."

They were proceeding at a fair clip, when suddenly their motor began to sputter.

Collins' eyes went to the gas gauge, and alarm lifted the skin of his forehead into worried gullies.

"Empty!" he yelped, pulling over to the shoulder of the road.

"What! What!" bleated out Grabber Daly. His thin voice was full of disbelief.

"The gas tank! The needle reads empty."

"Is that possible? We topped it off at the last filling station."

Coasting to a stop, Collins got out, went to the back of the machine, and saw the thin line of gasoline that had turned into thin oily spots on the pavement.

He opened the gas cap, peered inside, and perceived only gleams of gasoline.

Then he noticed the bullet hole.

It was a small-caliber hole, but it had punctured the gas tank, allowing precious fuel to leak out in a steady stream.

"Dammit!" Collins grumbled. "Dammit all to hell!"

Stepping out of the roadster, Grabber Daly demanded, "What is it?"

Collins looked about ready to cry. "Remember that popping sound when the plane was burning?"

"It sounded like firecrackers. Probably pieces of the engine exploding."

"Firecrackers sound like gunshots if the caliber of gun is not large."

Collins was pointing at the bullet hole. "That looks like a twenty-two caliber to me."

Daly bent over almost double to examine the puncture and said, "Who could have done that?"

"Sniper with a squirrel rifle maybe," Collins suggested. "But it doesn't matter at this exact moment. What does matter is that we're unquestionably stranded here."

Grabber Daly looked as if he wanted to remove his dentures and stomp on them. That is how deep his frustration ran.

Looking to the east, he saw seemingly endless prairie quaking in the summer heat.

"The Allison farm lies in that direction," he announced. "We will walk, pretending to be stranded motorists—which in truth we are—and I will strike up a conversation with farmer Allison. I will compliment him on his land and point out that there was a great deal of it not in production. Then I will offer to buy a parcel or two, take it off his hands, offering spot cash from my wallet. The odds are he will be sympathetic. We will have our deal, and if he has a telephone, a wrecker will be summoned to tow the roadster."

Collins looked as if the prospect of walking several miles in the morning heat did not much appeal to him. Doubtless it did not. His salary was the same whether he drove or walked.

On the other hand, Grabber Daly was motivated by the prospect of a fast dollar. He started off in the direction of the farm, snapping his fingers impatiently for Collins to follow.

As they walked along, the flunky fretted.

"Who would have shot up our gas tank, and more importantly—why?"

"Never mind that!" snapped Grabber Daly. "We must be thankful that we were not hit."

"I'm still worried about that girl," Collins intoned dolefully.

"Think about yourself first," Daly retorted. "Always put yourself first. Except when you are on my clock, then you must put me first. Always remember that."

"Yes, boss," Collins said miserably.

Chapter III

TREED

THE TELEGRAPH SOUNDERS seemed to snicker at Johnny Deal when he arrived at seven a.m. sharp for his day trick in the wire room of the Tex-Ok-Kan Pipeline. The busy instruments were laughing with sassy brass tongues.

As Johnny walked to the wire room, Mr. Swingles, the oil dispatcher on the southwest string, came sloping out of his office.

"Call for you, Deal. Take it in my office. But hurry it up. Personal calls on your own time in the future."

"Yes, sir," said Johnny.

Joe Troller, the early trick, stuck his head out of the wire-room door. The rattling of telegraph instruments and chuckling of teletypes became louder.

"Ponca is calling you for his seven a.m. stock," Joe hollered. "Get a move on, Johnny!"

"Open the key on him," Johnny called back. "Make him think it's wire trouble."

"O.K., but hurry it up. Day's a-wasting."

Stepping into the office, Johnny picked up the telephone headset lying on the desk.

"Hello, who is it?"

"That you, Johnny? This is Bill. Looks like there's trouble over at that new oil patch north of my farm."

"What kind of trouble?"

"Explosion. Lots of black smoke curling up. Can see it all the way from my farmhouse."

"That don't make a lick of sense," said Johnny. "They ain't started serious pumping operations yet. Story is their first drilled hole was a duster."

"Well, I saw a yellow plane buzzing my land pasture before it happened. Maybe it cracked up. You never know. Since you boys are closer to the spot than I am, you might want to take a run over and see."

"Thanks, Bill," said Johnny, hanging up with a bang.

Turning to Mr. Swingle, Johnny explained, "That was Bill Allison. Thinks a plane might have gone down at that oilfield that's just been set up. Maybe I should take a look-see."

Joe Troller had his head out of the wire room and was bellowing. "Hurry up, Johnny. Ponca is raising Cain about his stocks!"

Swingle said, "Attend to that first, then head over to that field. But I'm docking you, Deal. Rules are rules."

Johnny scuttled into the wire room. It was roaring like a pleasant beehive. The other operators were busy moving business to the refineries, the field offices and the other pipeline pumping stations.

The place was divided into two sections. This division, where Johnny worked, was called the message section. The oil dispatchers were at the other end behind a glass partition, like royalty. The dispatchers directed the movement of oil from the pipelines in much the same way that railway dispatchers handle trains.

Johnny took his chair. The sounder snarled brassily at him. It was Ponca and Ponca sounded quarrelsome.

"U TR, U LID?" snarled Ponca City. Meaning was Johnny there, you lid. Lid was a fighting word one called another telegrapher on the wire. It implied a reliance on the dubious practice of placing a lidded tobacco can on the sounder as a makeshift amplifier. This enabled a lackluster operator in his copying of Morse code dots and dashes to avoid hasty mistakes.

Johnny grabbed his bug and made some exclamation points. They were about the most violent noise you can send over a wire.

"GA STOKS," Johnny ripped. Meaning, "Go ahead stocks."

For ten busy minutes, Ponca City sent stocks. The tank numbers and how much oil and basic sediment measured in each tank. The Ponca operator made the sounder almost smoke. It was like hail on a tin roof. Ponca poured it on, shaking the tobacco can out of the resonator box. Johnny's hand ached and he wore the points off four pencils, but he didn't go under the table once.

"O.K., you combination-sender," Johnny keyed angrily. Telling another operator that he sent combinations—ran his letters together in a jumble—was a kick in the teeth. Combinations made it more difficult to take down the normally orderly flow of dots and dashes.

"WO TS?" asked Ponca belligerently. Meaning, "Who is this?"

"J," replied Johnny. "J" was his personal sign.

"Who's a lid?" demanded Ponca.

"You are, you lid!" Johnny hammered.

Came a short, ominous silence.

Then the sounder gobbled at Johnny.

"This is S," it said.

Oh, Gabriel! Johnny's hair stood on end. S was the Old Man, the boss. Mr. J. K. Seems, Communications Chief, bull of the woods. Bull of the woods in every sense.

"Report to my office at ten in the morning," ordered Mr. Seems so violently that the tobacco can fell out of the resonator.

"Yes, sir," Johnny sent, closing the key weakly.

Visions of his good Morse job sprouting wings and departing, Johnny hurried out of the wire room and shot a pained salute to Mr. Swingle. He hated to lose the hour or so of pay, but people's lives could be at stake. Now that seemed like the least of his worries.

Reclaiming his battered roadster, Johnny started the engine and sent the machine racing off. He could see a grayish smudge on the horizon, which appeared to be the ragged remnant of a heavier cloud that was dispersing. It suggested an oil fire, if a small one. Hard to say at that distance.

THE PIPELINE pumping station sat baking on the flat Oklahoma prairie this Saturday morning. It was hot. On the lease across the paved highway from Tumbleweed Station, the roughnecks who were goosing dry, inflammable grass from around the pumping wells were hitting the shade often. Now and then a tired Indian would struggle past the station, going or coming from town. About every second Indian would stop and listen to the *rum-rum* of the pumps for three to five minutes, then plod onward.

Away from the station, the road ran six miles as straight as a string, and passed the big north pasture of the Y-Cross ranch.

In the vast pasture was a sizable tree.

As they progressed through the pasture, Monk Mayfair was saying, "We might want to mosey over closer to that tree."

"Why?" asked Pat Savage.

"On account of there's buffalo yonder."

Pat had noticed the small herd of buffalo. But they seemed far away. Also, they were placid-looking creatures, like shaggy brown clouds that huddled close to the earth.

"They don't look like they would bother us," Pat offered hopefully.

Monk grunted. "You don't know buffalo. I grew up in these parts. Take it from me, if they start movin', we want a tall tree handy."

"What about your supermachine pistol? Could you knock one out? If you have to, I mean."

The homely chemist shrugged. "Hard to say. I've never shot a buffalo with mercy bullets. Buffalo hide is pretty dang thick. Slugs might not penetrate. Even if they do, it takes a lot of dope to stop a buffalo. He might not get around to stopping until he trampled us."

That sobering thought caused Pat to wander toward the substantial-looking tree.

Pat was complaining, "The pumping station doesn't look like there's anybody manning it."

"There oughta be a watchman of some kind."

"Well, there wasn't at the oilfield, was there?"

That was not a pleasant thought. But no more was spoken.

The big tree was a red oak, common in Oklahoma. As they neared that, Pat and Monk heard a sudden snort behind them.

In unison, they turned their heads and studied the herd that appeared to be listless in the heat, grazing peacefully.

One specimen in particular was eyeing them in round-orbed annoyance, his tail flicking like a whip.

The bull in question started to trot in their direction, and the trot turned into a gallop. Then the ground took to trembling.

"Let's go!" Monk yelled.

They raced for the red oak, which Monk reached first despite his bandy legs. Kneeling, he made a cup with two hairy hands. Pat stepped into the joined fingers. Monk boosted her up into the lower branches smartly.

When Pat was safely in the leafy crown, the simian chemist raised his incredibly long arms, grabbed a branch, and swung himself up like a baboon. It was almost a circus somersault the way he did it.

Perched in adjoining branches, they watched as the buffalo tore up to the tree, and began battering the trunk, dislodging bark and shaking them where they sat.

"I will never look at a buffalo the same way again," murmured Pat.

The buffalo seemed to enjoy his head-butting activities, for he kept them up for over a dozen minutes. Eventually, he settled down. Unfortunately for his treed captives, he settled down on the grass at the base of the red oak tree.

His tail switched lazily and it did not appear that he was in any mood to return to the herd.

Pat and Monk watched the buffalo bull switch his dusty tail. The thing went around like a balky propeller. Pat squirmed on her tree limb. The bark was rough and hard.

Monk broke off a dead limb and pitched it toward the buffalo. The beast only twirled his tail more rapidly. Monk scowled.

Pat groaned, "I wish I had my six-shooter, but it's kind of heavy to tote around on a hot day, and I was not expecting any trouble—never mind having to shoot wild buffalo."

Monk said, "You can't shoot that buffalo even if you had your old hogleg."

"Why not?"

"Because the local sheriff would clap you in jail for killin' somebody's buffalo. This pasture probably belongs to some farmer or rancher."

"Oh," said Pat in a deflated tone. She went silent for a bit, then offered dejectedly, "We're not doing very well in the leasing business, are we?"

"It's early yet," grumbled the frowning chemist. He clambered over to another limb where he could see the asphalt highway. There was one car on the road, about a mile distant. The Oklahoma prairie was limitless to the horizons.

The hairy chemist observed the car on the highway. It was coming their way. That was something.

"How do you tell a bull buffalo to get lost?" Pat asked suddenly.

"Vamoose is as good as any word in that department," suggested Monk.

Pat began calling down through cupped hands, saying over and over again, "Vamoose! Vamoose!"

The stubborn buffalo failed to vamoose.

"He's not vamoosing," Pat complained.

"He'll get around to it," squeaked Monk. "There's just no telling when. Buffalo are ornery critters."

"We can't be up here all day, can we?"

"When a buffalo trees you," sighed Monk patiently, "you stay treed until the buffalo takes a notion to wander off."

The hairy chemist was watching a roadster come bouncing over the pasture. It rolled up, then stopped under their tree.

The buffalo paid the car almost no attention, merely pivoting one sullen orb in its direction and then looking away. There must have been one of those new gadgets on the roadster, because the top folded down neatly.

Eventually, it revealed a smiling young man with a galaxy of freckles parading across his open features.

"One of you can climb out on that limb, and drop into the passenger seat," the young man at the wheel said. He was grinning now.

"Don't mind if we do," said Pat brightly.

The bronze-haired girl went first. She landed lightly, and sat herself down in the passenger seat beside the driver.

"Not bad," she decided. "My name is Pat."

"Call me Johnny. Johnny Deal." Then he tore his appreciative eyes off ravishing Pat, reached around behind him and unlatched the rumble seat. Throwing this up, he urged Monk, "Come on, Buffalo Bill."

Swinging out with simian agility, Monk dropped into the roadster's open rumble seat. "The name is Buffalo Monk," he said grudgingly.

Johnny was a young man with an engaging smile. They could see he wouldn't be afraid of buffalo.

"Good thing I happened by," Johnny said as he piloted the roadster headlong onto the highway. "You could've been up there 'til sundown. So what are you doing out in the middle of nowhere?"

"We cracked up our plane," Monk told him. "We were headed for the pumpin' station to get help."

Johnny shook his head sadly. "Tumbleweed Station isn't operating right now. I work at the telegraph office beyond it. We got a call that maybe a plane went down at the new oilfield. What were you two doing out there?"

Pat took that. "We flew in to see a farmer about purchasing a patch of land, but our plane went down. It was sabotage."

"Sabotage! You don't say?"

"I do say."

Monk inserted fiercely, "A no-good skunk of a lease grabber named Alec Daly filled our oil container with emery dust. And, like clowns, down we went."

"You don't mean Grabber Daly? He's just about the most notorious lease hog in these parts since the heyday of the Osage Indian headrights scandal about a dozen years back. Folks say he's so crooked he could swallow nails and spit out corkscrews!"

"Exactly who we mean," affirmed Pat. "The last we saw him, he was tearing up the road toward the Allison farm."

"So he's going to beat you to it?"

Monk grunted, "Maybe. Or maybe not. We managed to puncture his gas tank. Kinda like a return favor."

Johnny Deal laughed uproariously. "Don't that beat all! I'd like to take you up to Bill Allison. I know old Bill. But I'm on the clock. Going to take you back to the telegraph office."

Monk reached for his wallet and opened it. "What do you make in a day?"

"Ten."

"Is a hundred enough to change your mind? Tell your boss that you got a flat tire. Take us to Bill Allison and let's see if we can't make a monkey out of Grabber Daly."

Johnny Deal accepted the greenback with a wide grin. "Now that's something I would give you this hundred dollar bill back to see."

Turning about, the young telegrapher tore headlong up the blacktop highway. He needed no instructions. Before long, they were racing up a long stretch of dirt road leading to the Allison farm.

When they passed Alec Daly's abandoned automobile, Johnny remarked, "Kinda looks like your trick worked."

"Pull over a sec," directed Monk.

Johnny obliged. Climbing out of the machine, Monk reached into his rather loud coat, which he had salvaged from the plane wreck, and from an underarm holster he removed an impressive-looking pistol. This looked like an oversized automatic except that it was infinitely more complicated.

Methodically, Monk walked around the automobile and shot each tire in turn. The weapon made a single report that was answered each time by the sharp explosion of the inner tube letting go. Hissing snakily, the machine sunk on its springs at all four corners.

Returning to the roadster, Monk climbed back in and said jauntily, "Carry on."

"That was serious business back there," Johnny remarked uneasily.

"Alec Daly tried to kill us both, even if he didn't intend to," reminded Pat. "He's got a lot of ruction coming to him."

Suddenly, Johnny Deal got the idea that the young woman and the apish fellow were not ones to fool with. This impressed him.

Before long, they came upon Grabber Daly and his assistant, Collins, who were perspiring profusely as they trudged along.

The two men turned in unison, saw Pat Savage seated beside an unfamiliar driver, with Monk Mayfair sprawled in the rumble seat, and turned jackrabbit.

Breaking in opposite directions, they disappeared into the prairie grass, not by sprinting but by crawling like snakes, keeping low to avoid possible bullets.

"Roadrunners got more backbone than those two," remarked Johnny Deal.

"Keep driving," suggested Pat.

Johnny was only too glad to oblige. As the roadster whined past, Monk called into the tall grasses, "We'll look for you hombres on the way back. But don't let us catch you."

The rest of it was a simple affair.

THEY arrived at the farmhouse, were properly introduced, and told their tale.

William Allison the farmer listened intently in a tight-lipped but patient way. The sun-seamed scowl did not leave his face until the subject got around to selling a patch of his land.

"What patch are you interested in?" he wondered.

Pat said, "South forty. Nothing much going on down there. Unless you're growing weeds for market."

"You think there might be oil?"

"It's only a guess," inserted Monk. "But I won't lie to you, it's a good guess."

Rubbing his lean jaw thoughtfully, Bill Allison murmured, "Ever since that oilfield started going up, I harbored a notion someone would swing around and start asking to buy some of my useless land. So I already have a price in the back of my head. What would you offer me?"

Pat quoted the figure, and the scowl on Bill Allison's face lightened only slightly.

"It's more than that crook would offer you, Bill," inserted Johnny Deal. "And these two are square. They paid me a hundred shekels to run them up here, just to beat out that over-hatted chiseler."

Farmer Allison took a little more time to consider the matter and added ten percent of the price.

Pat Savage didn't blink. She said, "Sold."

They shook hands and that settled the matter.

"I will have a Tulsa lawyer draw up a contract and we'll be back tomorrow," said Pat. "Thank you for your hospitality."

"Any friend of Johnny Deal's is a friend of mine," said Bill Allison.

On the ride back, they saw no sign of Grabber Daly or Collins. Nor did they expect to.

"Probably hightailed it into Osage country," suggested Monk. "That's where the bad desperadoes go to escape the law. Old Grabber's an owlhoot now."

Johnny Deal wanted to know, "Are you going to file charges against those two varmints?"

Monk nodded. "I know a police sergeant from the old days. I'll tell him the whole story, and those two will be in handcuffs when they show their faces in the city."

Johnny grinned. "It's been a pleasure making your acquaintance," he said broadly.

"Same here," said Monk.

To which Pat Savage added, "You're a lifesaver, Johnny Deal."

The young telegrapher suggested, "Thank me by letting me take you to dinner."

Pat smiled back. "We have to get back to Tulsa, pronto. But if my wildcat well strikes oil, I'll swing by and treat you to that thank-you dinner!"

"I call that a deal!" exclaimed Johnny.

They shook hands on it.

Monk regarded the bronze-skinned beauty with his jaw seemingly sagging at its hinges.

"What's this about a wildcat well?" he asked.

"I am considering going into the wildcatting business," she told him.

"You," grunted Monk, "have been half-wildcat ever since I met you that time in the North Woods."*

Pat's grin of acknowledgement was a delight.

"And don't you ever forget it!"

---

* *Brand of the Werewolf*

Chapter IV

THE SCORPION BRAND

IT WAS THE noon hour in the city of Tulsa, Oklahoma. Office workers were out and about, seeking a quick bite to eat or relief from the oppressive heat of their offices.

In front of a white lunch room, an Osage Indian wearing a vermilion poncho was seated cross-legged on an equally vermilion horse blanket.

He fingered a flute, which consisted of a long tube of cut reed, whose upper surface was perforated by numerous holes. Bony fingers capping and uncovering these apertures, the Indian was blowing into the mouthpiece, producing a series of sounds that were not quite melodious, but were occasionally pleasant. Only the most generous critic would call the product of his manipulations music.

The red man was very serious about his endeavor. His features were a sandstone mask. One eye—the left—drooped as if from an affliction.

It was difficult to tell if the Osage was just practicing to warm up for the lunch crowd, or was sincerely endeavoring to be musical. On the blanket by his left knee was a woven basket, containing three shiny quarters and a rumpled dollar bill. It was the bait. The Indian was piping for loose change. He was unlikely to receive a dollar in these hard times, but Tulsa was an oil town, and some of its inhabitants were unusually well-heeled.

At the corner of Fourth and Boulder, a newsboy was hawking the morning paper.

"Extra! Read all about it! Alec 'Grabber' Daly wanted for attempted murder! Reported fleeing toward Chickasha!"

Pat Savage and Monk Mayfair were walking by the bank building at that corner. They stopped directly before the white lunch room.

"News travels fast," Pat observed. She had changed from her outdoorsy outfit to a summery sports dress and matching shoes which showed off the perfection of her girlish figure. Her bronzy vitality made a very striking portrait of young femininity.

Monk told her, "This town has two papers, the *Morning Trumpet* and the *Daily Globe*. They're always trying to out-scoop one another. As soon as we gave our story to the police, a little birdie flew to the telephone and got the word out to his favorite reporter. Sounds like the *Trumpet* got the news first."

It was late morning now. They had rented a car in Seminole, and made it to Tulsa in time for the noon hour and a quick change of clothing.

The Tulsa police had taken their statements and warrants were issued for the arrest of Alec Daly and his assistant—now officially termed his accomplice—Finbar Collins by name.

The police had assured Pat and Monk that everything would be done to apprehend the fugitive duo.

"You'll have to stick around town in case further statements are needed."

"We have business here," Pat had told the police official, "and we are in no hurry to leave."

The lunch room looked inviting, and they were considering its window menu when a bluecoat strolled by. He was wearing a crooked grin on his lean features.

"Well, well, well. As I live and breathe. If it isn't little Andy Mayfair."

Hearing the challenging voice, the apish chemist turned around and his eyes got truculent.

"Ain't nobody called me by that name since I left this burg," he growled.

"I've been reading about you in the papers, Andy," sneered the cop. "Looks like you made the big time, Andy. And look at me—just another flatfoot pounding a city beat."

"Fat head is more like it," returned Monk with absolutely no warmth in his squeaking voice.

The cop had a hardwood billy club and twirled the baton as if wishing to use it.

Pat Savage appraised the officer and asked, "Who is this fellow, Monk?"

"That's Jim Dandy. We went to rival high schools here. Played football against one another. He was a big booster of mine—not."

The cop's crooked grin straightened out. "Back then, I liked to say that Mayfair should've been disqualified, being more ape than man. But the coach wouldn't hear of it. Andy here made a pretty fair halfback."

"Trampled your thick skull into the gridiron more than once," snorted Monk. "Say, football hero, remember that time when I gave you a hotfoot in the middle of the final game?"

"Yeah, my big toe still gives me a pain from time to time. I ain't forgotten that."

"I laughed my head off for a week," chortled Monk.

Officer Dandy grew serious. "Listen, I hear you're going to be in town a while. Make sure you keep your nose clean, you hear?"

A scowl made Monk's face look like a cross between a gorilla and a bulldog. "You threatenin' to run me in?"

"Not before I bounce this baton off your skull, you bandy-legged baboon."

With that, the police officer continued on his rounds, whistling and twirling his baton.

Pat eyed the apish chemist and remarked, "Friendly rival or bitter enemy?"

Monk grimaced, saying, "Both. Him and me have been kinda antagonistic since the tenth grade. I thought it was all in the past. Except it don't sound like he ever got over it."

Pat was fanning herself. "Say, are we going to have lunch or not?"

"Sure. And after that we're gonna hunt us up a lawyer to draft your contract. Maybe by the end of the day, the cops'll have Alec Daly behind bars. You can pay him a nice visit in the hoosegow."

Pat frowned suddenly. "Speaking of paying, we're going to have to settle with the company that rented us that plane. That's going to cost a pretty penny."

Monk grinned carelessly. "Take it out of your oil profits. You'll have plenty to spare—now that you went and changed your mind about sellin' your land to an oil company for a quick profit."

Pat smiled like a cool ray of moonlight that had wandered into the heat of the day. "Why should I let an oil company make most of the money?"

The homely chemist reached out a long arm and opened the door. "Pat Savage, wildcatter. Wait'll Doc hears about this!"

AROUND the corner, lurched a man. The newsboy hawking his late morning edition failed to take notice of him. The man stumbled around, as if he had lost a great deal of his muscular strength. What could be seen of his muscles brought to mind animated beef jerky.

This wasted stumbling bundle of bones wore work clothes and dungarees, which were stained by crude oil. Face and hair were also stained, but even so, the paleness of the man was astonishing. He looked as if he had not seen the sun in a very long time; furthermore, there was something about his pallor that was unnatural and bloodless.

In contrast, his unruly hair was reminiscent of the dark parts of a pinto horse's coat. His staring eyes almost matched his unkempt thatch of hair. Over cheekbones that stood out grue-somely like those of a flesh-coated skull, the eyes were sunk deep in their orbits.

As he crept around the corner, he moaned. These were painful moans. They came from deep within him. Agony wracked his oil-smeared features.

"Help," he bleated. "Oh, please help me."

With one hand, he clutched the rough brick of the corner building. The other fist gripped something tightly.

Pat Savage noticed him first. Turning, she gasped once.

"Monk!" she cried out. "Look at that poor fellow."

The hairy chemist did. His small eyes almost bugged out of his head.

Together, they rushed for the unfortunate one, and just in time, too. As he struggled around the corner, one knee gave out, and he crumpled to the ground.

"What happened to you?" cried Pat, bending over the fallen fellow.

"I… escaped," he gasped out.

"You escaped?" blurted Pat.

"From where?" demanded Monk.

Instead of replying directly, the stricken man lifted one trembling arm and drove his fist toward Monk's homely features.

Thin fingers uncoiled, revealing a stubby cylinder of alumi-num. Monk snatched at this, studied it in his broad palm.

"What is this jigger, here?"

Pat looked into Monk's palm and frowned prettily.

"I don't recognize it." Kneeling beside the man, Pat asked urgently. "You say you've been held prisoner. What is your name?"

"Ben," he said weakly. "Ben… Nansen.…"

"Who held you?" Pat pressed.

"I stole that from… them," Ben Nansen gasped out.

"From whom?" asked Pat. "Tell us."

Ben Nansen endeavored to shake his head in the negative, and the word that escaped his lips was a hissing blur.

The breathy exhalation sounded like "vinegar."

"The person who abducted you, his name is Vinegar?" demanded Pat. "Does he have a first name?"

The man repeated his utterance, and Monk Mayfair, listening carefully, said, "He didn't say vinegar. He said 'vinegarroon.'"

Pat looked perplexed. Before she could press the hairy chemist for clarification, Ben Nansen gasped out more of his story.

"They held me for weeks. I can't remember how many. They kept taking blood out of me. Used it to nourish something. They were feeding my blood to the thing in the other room—the horrible thing."

"Blazes!" exploded Monk.

"Where were you held?" Pat asked.

"Ozarks. Deep in the Ozarks. But I got out. And I grabbed that thing as proof. Proof of what is coming. The terrible thing they plan."

A crowd began to gather and even the noisy news butcher had turned around and was absorbing the tableau in open-mouthed silence.

Among the onlookers was the Osage Indian wearing the vermilion poncho.

He had ceased playing his instrument, but as the scenario unfolded, he began fiddling with his flute. No one paid him any heed.

The stricken man, Ben Nansen, lapsed into a kind of babbling incoherency. He was trying to make words, but these syllables were not distinguishable one from another. They ran together in a gasping, bubbling confusion.

"This man is very weak," Pat was saying to Monk. "We have to get him to a hospital pronto."

Ben Nansen evidently heard those words, for he lifted his head painfully. His sunken eyes went to Monk Mayfair—and then they went wide.

He attempted to lift one spindly forearm, and extend a bony forefinger. That forefinger trembled in shock, swayed this way and that, as if he could not control it.

As the finger weaved about, pointing in Monk's general direction, there was a sudden soft sound, and then Nansen's head jerked backward. The back of his skull struck the sidewalk pavement, and all the animation that struggled to rouse itself in his gaunt form seemed to dissipate like so much smoke.

Monk lunged forward, dropped down and took the man's head in his paws, lifting it up.

Nansen's watery eyes were wide and staring and there seemed to be no life in them.

That was not the detail that caused consternation to roost upon Monk's and Pat Savage's strained features. For on the fellow's right cheek there was a sudden blotch. It was scarlet. It sprawled longitudinally, and from both sides spidery appendages were forming, and from its lowermost segment, a long, thin whip of a tail wound.

Pat's golden eyes went wide with shock as she saw the image burning against the bloodless features of Ben Nansen.

"That," she said, "looks like a scorpion!"

Monk corrected, "A whip scorpion. Another name for it is vinegarroon, on account of it ain't got a stinger but releases a vinegary acid the way a polecat sprays skunk stink."

Suddenly, they smelled a whiff of vinegar. It was simply in the air, coming from no particular spot. Bitter and astringent, it invaded their nostrils and made them look around for its source.

The gathering crowd was pressing close, forming a ring of gesticulating humanity.

At the spot behind where Monk Mayfair's bristled skull had been when Ben Nansen had been pointing in his direction, the Osage Indian retreated to his blanket, apparently to gather up his basket of loose change, for he had neglected it during the commotion.

He did not attract any particular attention as he shed his vermilion poncho and quit the vicinity in his faded cotton shirt and worn dungarees.

Chapter V

TROUBLE

THE SIGHT OF the scarlet scorpion splotch spreading out from Ben Nansen's cheek to discolor his gaunt features brought horrified exclamations from the gathering crowd.

A woman shrieked, "How horrible!"

A young girl of about fifteen tender years fainted dead away.

This caused someone in the crowd to cry out, "It's spreading! Run for your lives!"

Exactly what was spreading was unclear. But the crowd broke and ran, pelting off in all directions.

"Oh, for heaven's sake!" exclaimed Pat. "What's got into those people?"

"Panic," squeaked Monk.

The commotion naturally attracted the attention of the local constabulary. Shoving in against the tide of humanity, Officer Dandy made his way to the corner of Fourth and Boulder.

When he pulled up, Dandy found Monk Mayfair and Pat Savage hovering over the stricken man. The patrolman put his fists on his hips, and his wind-burned face got hard.

"What is it now, Mayfair?" he challenged.

Monk stood up, squaring his fists. "So it's Mayfair now, is it?" he growled.

"What did you do to that poor fella?"

"Not a thing," Monk flared. "We were walkin' into the lunch room when this fellow came stumblin' around the corner, talkin' a wild streak."

36

"What's that on his face?"

Monk said, "It's a whip scorpion—a vinegarroon."

Patrolman Dandy cocked his head to one side and then the other, studying the bloody splotch.

"You might call it that, I guess. But it looks like a splash of blood to me. How did it get there?"

Pat answered that. "He said his name was Ben Nansen. And he was trying to tell his story when his head rocked back. That red mark simply appeared there."

"Like magic, eh?" the cop said doubtfully.

"That's what happened," insisted Monk. "Take it or leave it. We got witnesses."

Officer Dandy looked around and saw only the newsboy who was standing on his corner, looking ashen.

"What did you see, Orrie?"

"It-it's just like what they said. The poor fella collapsed and then something happened to him. That's when the bloodstain showed up on his face. Those two were the only ones near him when it happened."

"Is that right?" Officer Dandy was on one knee now. Touching the bloody blotch with one finger, he lifted it to his nose, and sniffed slowly.

"Smells of vinegar."

"That's what we smelled, too," Monk told him. "But the odor isn't as strong now."

Dandy stood up, and grated, "Vinegar and vinegarroon may sound alike but they aren't the same thing. You know that, Mayfair. You been around scorpions, haven't you?"

Monk grunted carelessly, "Seems to me I went to school with one or two way back when."

The officer walked up to the hairy chemist, towering over him, and put his sharp nose almost against Monk's blunt one.

"Care to name any names, would you?" he asked belligerently.

"That was a few years back," said Monk, shrugging negligently. "My memory's gone kinda foggy on me."

Officer Dandy stuck the round end of his nightstick against the homely chemist's barrel chest and prodded it slightly, saying, "See that it stays that way."

Monk growled. It was a low growl, and it seeped out menace.

Pat stepped in and scolded, "You boys knock it off. This is serious business. We have to get this man to the hospital."

Officer Dandy pointed at the unconscious man's feet with his night stick and said, "You two stay right here. Don't move. I'm going to the call box."

"We're not budgin'," said Monk.

"We're sticking," added Pat. "This looks like excitement, and it came calling on us. So we're seeing it through. Whatever it is."

Officer Dandy turned to go, growling, "Well, see that you do."

He had hardly popped around the corner when a maroon sedan moaned up, and pulled sharply to the curb.

The driver was a young woman, perhaps twenty-five years of age, whose oval face displayed prominent cheekbones. She had hair that looked like honey suffused with sunlight. Her eyes were a deep brown, the hue of dark chocolate. They went to the stricken man and tightened.

"Oh, my goodness!" she exclaimed, "What happened to him?"

Pat offered, "We have no idea. He just collapsed. Do you think you could take us to the hospital? He needs urgent assistance."

The young woman stepped out from behind the wheel, and opened the rear door, saying, "Put him in back. The hospital isn't far away."

Monk reached out to gather up the gaunt victim, but Pat said, "We should wait for your friend in blue."

"This guy could die on us if we don't get a move on," Monk growled. "I'm puttin' him in back. Dandy can catch up with us."

The apish chemist lugged the unconscious man and deposited him in the back seat, placing him in a seated position so there was room for Pat in back.

"Get in," he invited.

Pat obliged, commenting, "Officer Dandy will have you in handcuffs if you're not careful."

Monk shrugged off the warning. "Handcuffs don't come that big. I got thick wrists."

The hairy chemist walked around the sedan and got into the passenger seat, saying, "My name's Monk Mayfair. That's Pat Savage. Maybe you heard of us?"

The blonde reached for the clutch, saying, "I have not. But I'm pleased to make your acquaintance. My name is Vina Hawks."

She was turning the front tires away from the curbing when Officer Dandy came charging around the corner, saw an empty spot on the pavement and then the newsboy pointing at the maroon sedan.

Dandy's face grew red. It grew even more crimson when he began blowing on his whistle, calling, "Stop! Halt!"

Monk stuck his head out the passenger window and yelled, "We're headin' to the hospital. Hop on the running board." To the girl, he said, "Put her in gear."

Vina Hawks did not hesitate. The car moaned away from the curb and Officer Dandy started running, his whistle forgotten. He was in good shape and managed to jump onto the running board on the driver's side, taking firm hold of the doorpost with both hands.

"Mayfair, I'm going to settle with you for this!" he roared.

Monk said nothing. He was growling again. Pat knew that was not a good sign.

Officer Dandy was looking down at the blonde, and asked, "What's your name, toots?"

"Vina Hawks."

"I don't remember seeing you around before," he said suspiciously.

"I hail from Oklahoma City. I don't get over to Tulsa much."

"That so? What are you doing in town today?"

Vina Hawks hesitated. "Nothing much. Just visiting." Her voice was crisp, unafraid. The way she enunciated her words showed intelligence and good breeding.

In the rear seat, Pat Savage asked, "Why the third degree, officer? She's just a good Samaritan."

"I'm paid to be suspicious of folks."

Vina Hawks said nothing as she piloted the maroon sedan toward the hospital.

Officer Dandy was holding on without difficulty and leaned down to examine the woman's profile.

"You got a nice face," he remarked.

"Thank you," Vina said politely. She refused to meet his suspicious gaze.

"It looks a little familiar to me. But I can't quite place it."

Silence from the girl.

Twisting about, Officer Dandy looked at the unconscious Ben Nansen, rocking back and forth in the rear seat where Monk had positioned him.

"Do a copper a favor," he requested of Pat. "Take hold of that man's head and twist it around so I can see his profile."

"Why do you want me to do that?" demanded Pat.

"Never mind!" snapped Dandy. "Just do it."

Shrugging, Pat complied, taking hold of the man's lolling head and angling it about, taking care not to touch the disfiguring splotch on his face so suggestive of a sprawling scarlet scorpion.

"Right there," Dandy said sharply. "Hold it right there."

He studied the unconscious man's profile as the car whirled around corners and shot through broad intersections.

"I'll be damned!" he exploded.

"What is it?" asked Pat.

Before the officer could reply, there was a screeching and squealing of brakes, and suddenly they were all thrown about the interior of the careening machine.

Except for Officer Dandy, who was flung off the running board.

He went rolling toward the curb, coming to a rest with his head against the granite curbing. He failed to move after that.

Eyes filled with fear, Vina Hawks clutched the steering wheel as she wrestled the machine around. The sedan reeled, nearly tipping over. At the last possible second, the lifting tires slammed down onto the road with teeth-rattling force.

The automobile came to rest against a parked taxicab and its nose crumpled, causing the doors to spring open.

Pat and Monk were accustomed to taking sudden action. So they popped open their respective doors without delay, stood poised to evacuate the damaged machine.

It was prompt action, but a bit reckless.

Blocking the intersection they had failed to clear, a dark touring car jounced to a stop. Four doors opened and hard-faced men sprang out. Their faces were not only sunburned red as brick, but they had a quality that was stony, expressionless in a determined way.

The men produced a collection of guns and opened fire without so much as an announcement of their murderous intentions.

Pat gave a yelp, ducked back inside and pushed the unconscious Ben Nansen off his seat and onto the floorboards, then hunkered down on top of him, hoping that flying lead didn't reach either of them.

Likewise retreating into the sedan's interior, Monk Mayfair drove a huge paw into his coat, and yanked free his supermachine pistol. Pointing it out the window, he opened fire. This frantic action didn't accomplish much. So he hauled back his feet, lifted them and smashed the side of the divided windshield behind which he sat.

The windshield section dropped out of its frame, and Monk began firing through the cavity thus created.

The bullfiddle bawling of the compact rapid-firer was intimidating. One man went down and another scattered, retreating to the opposite side of the touring car, where they began sniping purposefully. Their weapons barked and snapped like vicious animals.

Monk sprayed bullets liberally, but the touring car proved to be bulletproof. Aside from that fact, Monk was firing mercy bullets. They were no good against automobile steel.

"I'm pinned down in the rear," Pat was saying. "Are you making any headway?"

"None of us are," howled Monk. "Gonna switch to honest lead."

While the apish chemist was fishing out a spare ammunition drum from one capacious coat pocket, Vina Hawks snapped out of her spell of fright, and attempted to back up the automobile.

A violent fusillade of bullets chewed up the right front tire, putting a definite crimp in that maneuver. Another caromed off the automobile's roof, making it ring.

Monk finished affixing his ammunition drum into the receiver, and commenced shooting out the windows.

More bullets arrived, knocking off the side mirror, and battering the front fenders. One headlight, then the other, jumped off its mounting, and strew shattered glass about. None of the slugs seemed to strike anyone, which might have been due to poor luck, or even poorer shooting.

They traded bullets for a minute, and when Monk took one in the shoulder, all it did was make him grunt and yell, "*Ye-e-o-o-w!*" By habit, the simian chemist wore a bulletproof undershirt. It stopped the bullet cold, but there would be a nasty bruise visible later.

Monk was eyeing the touring car's profile, and started to consider dropping down onto the sidewalk and shooting at the feet of the gunmen huddled on the other side.

Suddenly, the girl did an unexpected thing. She stepped out of the vehicle and raised her hands. Her voice lifted. "Stop shooting! I surrender."

"What!" Pat yelled from the back.

"We are outnumbered," said Vina Hawks. "There was no point in resisting."

"There's always a point in resisting," yelled Monk, taking a wild shot at a dark hat that was coming up around the trunk. The hat went flying. The owner of the hat ducked back with appropriate alacrity.

"Somebody will get killed if we don't stop this wild shooting," Vina pointed out firmly. "And I am not interesting in dying today."

The girl promptly advanced into the teeth of the fray. There was nothing Monk could do—not without stepping out of the machine and exposing himself to at least four very active guns.

"Dang!" he ripped out.

Pat was saying, "If only I had my six-shooter."

"We're still outnumbered," said Monk. "We gotta figure a way out of this."

The hairy chemist looked over to the curb and saw that Officer Dandy was lying completely immobile. His uniform cap had tumbled off his head and the back of his haircut was resting against the granite curb. A slow worm of blood was emerging from under the man's skull.

Monk moaned, "That don't look good."

"What doesn't?" asked Pat from the rear.

Before the homely chemist could respond, another head popped up behind the long sinister hood of the touring car. Shoulders became visible and the snout of a Thompson sub-machine gun came to rest on the hood.

"That's a blamed Tommy gun they're pointin' at us," said Monk thickly.

The submachine gun commenced chattering with vicious intent, tearing up the sedan's hood and engine block.

"Out!" Monk yelled out. "Make a run for it! It's our only chance."

The gorilla-like chemist popped out of his side of the machine, firing wildly, but hit no one.

Pat pushed open the door on the driver's side, tumbled out, and scooted around behind the trunk.

By this point, police siren wail was filling the air, and that familiar caterwauling spooked the gunmen crouched behind the touring car.

Monk managed to reach the opposite sidewalk and threw himself behind a parked auto, whose window glass had collected stray slugs with distressing results.

"This way!" he yelled to Pat. "I'll cover for you!"

The superfirer started bawling again, and the machine gunner prudently dropped down behind shelter. In the now-deserted street, the bellowing blare of the compact machine pistol was an awesome thundering.

Then the Thompson began chattering and gobbling again. Under its noisy cover, two men rushed forward, grabbed hold of unconscious Ben Nansen by the ankles and hauled him out.

One threw the frail individual over his shoulder, while the other took snap shots at Monk and Pat hunkered down behind their automobile shelter.

Hot lead smacked and splashed all around them, so they kept low.

"Is Oklahoma still a dry state?" moaned Pat.

"Naw. Why do you ask?"

"All this typewriter racket," complained Pat, "reminds me of the Prohibition days of yore."

As the sirens increased in volume, they could hear the doors of the touring car clap shut and the engine get back in gear. Tires barked like snapping dogs.

After the long machine had screeched around a corner, Pat and Monk stuck tentative heads up and took stock of the situation.

"They got Vina!" squeaked Monk.

"And Ben Nansen," added Pat miserably.

Cautiously, they stood up, and Monk ran over to fallen Officer Dandy.

It took only a moment of examination for the hairy chemist to stand up, his broad face going to ashes. "He's a goner."

His voice was twisted strangely, causing Pat to remark, "I thought you didn't like him."

"One thing ain't got nothin' to do with the other," yelled Monk hotly. "He was killed in cold blood. No one deserves that. Not even a flatfoot like Jim Dandy."

Monk stood rooted for a moment, his smoking supermachine pistol gripped in one hirsute fist. For a moment, he looked as if he wanted to spray hot lead in all directions out of sheer frustration. He was growling again.

Monk got hold of himself finally. "Come on," he muttered. "No sense waitin' for the cops. They'll lock us up as material witnesses, or worse. We gotta get to the bottom of this."

Firming up her strained mask of a face, Pat Savage said, "Now you're talking my language. Lead the way."

They ducked down a side street, and found an alley that ran behind the business block. The pair navigated this, trying not to look suspicious.

"And to think," muttered Pat Savage, "all I wanted to do was strike some honest oil."

"Black gold and trouble sometimes congregate together," observed Monk in a tight voice. "Kinda like alley cats and junkyard dogs."

"Monk! You don't think this has anything to do with the charges we lodged against Grabber Daly?"

"I don't think nothin'," growled Monk. "I just wish trouble hadn't found me before I had my dang lunch."

Chapter VI

ALUMINUM PRIZE

EVENTUALLY, THEY REACHED their hotel, one of the best hostelries in Tulsa, a sixteen-story establishment known as the Metro, whose motto was "Your Home in Oklahoma."

Pushing into the large lobby, Pat and Monk attempted to look casual.

No sooner had they entered when an unfamiliar voice called over, "Monk Mayfair! Is that you?"

Monk practically jumped out of his hairy skin and Pat stopped stock-still.

"Are we in hot water?" she said out of the side of her grim mouth.

"I'll tell you in a minute," muttered Monk.

A rangy, well-muscled man stood up from a lobby chair, folded a newspaper and tucked it under one elbow. His hair was the color of freshly-cut carrots.

Monk studied him suspiciously, but failed to recognize him.

"Hotel detective?" undertoned Pat.

Monk shook his head briefly. "Don't look the type."

Walking up jauntily, the man put out one hand and said, "Allow me to introduce myself. Harold Manton. Oil editor on the *Tulsa Trumpet*."

Pat Savage had been holding her breath. Now she released it and offered her own hand, saying, "Pleased to meet you, Mr. Manton. I'm Patricia Savage, of the trouble-finding Savages."

Releasing Monk's hand, Manton shook Pat's politely and said, "I understood you registered at this hotel. My paper is anxious to get the scoop on your brush with Grabber Daly."

Now Monk's face relaxed.

"We just got in," grunted Monk. "It's been kinda a hectic day. Stick around and we'll talk in about an hour."

Manton shrugged agreeably. "O.K. by me. I'll just plunk myself down here in the lobby and await your convenience. Pleasure to meet you, Miss Savage. I've heard a lot about you."

Pat smiled with relief and they made their way to the elevator.

As they rode the cage to their floor, the simian chemist thrust one hand in his pocket as if making sure his wallet was still on his person, and gave out a gusty sigh of relief.

Witnessing this, Pat asked, "What is it?"

"Later," said Monk, eyeing the elevator operator.

Alighting on the seventh floor, they paused. Monk's room was at the opposite end of the hall from where Pat had secured her room.

"We never did have lunch," Monk muttered.

"I'll have sandwiches sent up. Join me in my room and we will try to sort out this mess."

The suite was a good one, consisting of two spacious rooms, but it was no luxury suite. It was air-conditioned and therefore cool enough that the windows did not have to stand open to capture cooling breezes.

Looking it over, Monk remarked, "The tradition in this town is when you strike oil, you rent yourself a full suite on the upper floor. Kinda like announcin' to the world that you made good. If that farmland you bought pans out, that's the first thing you want to do."

Closing the door, Pat said urgently, "Out with it! What was that noise you made in the elevator?"

Reaching into his coat pocket, Monk produced the short aluminum cylinder that had been handed to him by the unfortunate Ben Nansen.

Snapping her fingers, Pat exclaimed, "I nearly forgot about that! What is it?"

Monk shrugged. "Search me, but that Nansen boy thought it was important. Let's look it over carefully."

Monk set the cylinder on the writing table and they examined it from all sides.

It was short enough to fit into the palm of the average man's hand, but on the fat side in terms of circumference. No markings adorned it, and there was no indication it was anything other than a solid cylinder of aluminum.

Pat picked it up and commented, "Heavy for aluminum."

Monk nodded. "I noticed that. Give it here."

Before the bronze-haired girl could comply, she was twisting the aluminum at either end. To her pleasant surprise, one end rotated after some resistance.

It was a cap that could be unscrewed, but so cunningly contrived that there was no indication of a seal or joint.

The tube proved to be hollow, but inside there was a small hard object, wrapped in oilskin. The wadded stuff kept the contents from rattling inside the aluminum tube.

Monk put out both hands, and Pat emptied the contents into them.

Unwrapping the oilskin, they discovered a round bottle, not much larger than a vial of perfume. It had a cap, but they didn't open it.

Monk held it up and shook the bottle experimentally, but the contents appeared to be nothing more remarkable than clear water.

"Looks like plain, ordinary H_2O," muttered Monk.

"Do you believe that?" pressed Pat.

"Not for a minute. It's gotta be somethin' else. Somethin' important."

"The mystery deepens," frowned Pat. "Ben Nansen thought this is important enough to hand over to us. Dare we open it?"

Monk shook his head violently. "Not without knowin' what it is first. Could be a poison. Maybe the kind of stuff that, if you get a drop of it on your skin, will kill you in a flat minute."

Pat frowned. "Might be acid," she suggested.

Monk allowed, "Could be, could be. That vinegar smell we got a whiff of is an acid produced by whip scorpions. But there's no sense in foolin' with it. Later, I'll get out my portable chemical laboratory and maybe we'll see if we can test it without riskin' sudden death."

"If that's how you feel about it," said Pat in a chilly tone, "let's put this bottle of possible doom back where it belongs."

"I got me a better idea," Monk returned. "Got any perfume with you that comes in a bottle anything like this?"

Pat said, "I might, at that."

The bronze girl went into the wash room, rattled around for a minute, then came back holding a small vial of perfume. "This ought to fit. Try it."

Taking the vial, Monk inserted it into the aluminum tube. It was a tighter fit than he would have liked, but he used force, and the bottle went in and stayed there.

Pat took it back, and did the honors of screwing the shiny lid back on. When she was done, the fat aluminum tube once again looked seamless.

Their food arrived not fifteen minutes after they ordered it, and they ate in silence, punctuated by the occasional comment or question.

"Do you think this Ben Nansen business is tied in with our brush with Grabber Daly?" wondered Pat.

The last of a ham sandwich disappeared into Monk's rather large mouth, then he said, "It don't tie up in any way that I can see. But you never know about these things."

"What about what Nansen said? That stuff about his blood being drained out to feed something." Pat shuddered slightly.

Monk said, "I don't believe in vampires, do you?"

"Can't say that I do. But Nansen sounded like he had been through something horrific. And the look of him. Emaciated and bloodless. A victim of Count Dracula would probably look pretty much the same way, wouldn't you say?"

Monk made thinking faces. "Maybe we ought to call New York for help."

Pat arched her eyebrows violently and flared, "Don't you dare think about ringing Doc Savage in on this! This is our mystery. We found it, or should I say it found us. It's ours. To do with as we see fit. And I'll have a hopping fit if my big-shouldered cousin barges into any of it!"

"Doc's up at his Fortress of Solitude near the North Pole. There's no gettin' hold of him. I was thinkin' of callin' Ham."

"Why do we need Ham Brooks?"

"Well, for one thing," said Monk, "there's the minor matter of Officer Jim Dandy. If we get tied into that shootin' ruckus, we could be in a heap of trouble. Legal trouble. Ham's the best lawyer that there is."

"Don't let Ham hear you say that," warned Pat. "You'll never hear the end of it."

"Just the same, we could be in legal hot water any minute now." The hairy chemist sounded worried. "Tulsa cops are tough. Plenty hardboiled."

They finished their meal in silence while considering their next move.

Pat's facial expression began to look complex.

"Your brain," Monk observed, "is makin' your face do things. Peculiar things."

"I was just thinking back to what Officer Dandy said before we landed in this mess."

Monk looked at her. It had been a wild afternoon, and his brain was still in a bit of a whirl.

Pat continued, "Dandy thought he recognized Vina Hawks, and then he wanted to get a good look at Ben Nansen's profile. Why do you suppose he did that?"

"You got me," shrugged Monk. Then a light came into his tiny eyes. "Maybe that oil editor downstairs might recognize those names. Let's ring him up."

"Good idea," said Pat, jumping to her feet and striding to the room telephone. Calling down to the front desk, she requested, "Could you inform Mr. Manton, who is seated in the lobby, that he may call upon me at his convenience?"

The desk clerk assured Pat that the message would be conveyed. Not five minutes later, there came a knock on the hotel room door.

MONK let Manton in, and waved him to a chair, saying, "You got questions for us, and we've got some for you."

Manton grinned agreeably. "Sounds like a fair enough swap. Who goes first?"

Pat answered that. "We witnessed something strange this afternoon. A man named Ben Nansen collapsing on the corner of Boulder and Fourth telling a strange story. He was carried off to the hospital."

This was not a lie exactly, but it was not full of details either.

"Ben Nansen, you say?" Manton mused. "Seems to me I've heard that name somewhere. Of course I could be thinking of another fellow entirely. But there's a Ben Nansen who works as a tool dresser for one of the big oil companies around these here parts. I don't know much about him. Young. Unmarried. Loner type of fellow."

"No enemies?" returned Pat.

"Does that sound like it?"

"No, it doesn't," admitted Pat. On a hunch, she added, "A good Samaritan happened along and took him to the hospital. She gave her name as Vina Hawks."

"Vina Hawks?" exploded the oil editor.

Monk blurted, "You know that name?"

"I should!" Manton returned nervously. "She's engaged to my boss. The publisher of the *Tulsa Trumpet*, Morgan Marrs."

"You don't say?" mused Pat. "How intriguing."

"More intriguing than you can imagine," returned Manton thoughtfully. "You see, Vina Hawks isn't her full name. That's the name she uses when she writes her stories. Miss Hawks is a newspaper columnist. Not on our paper, by the way. She works for a sheet over Oklahoma City way. The *Advocate*."

"What's her full name?" pressed Monk.

Harold Manton hesitated. "I'm not sure I should say exactly."

Pat looked puzzled. "Is it a secret?"

"No, no secret," Manton said slowly. "I guess I can't keep it to myself. But her full name is Vina Hawks Nansen."

Monk and Pat exchanged startled glances. On Pat, it made her look even more delectable. On Monk, it gathered his homely features together in a knot that quickly went loose and slack. His blocky jaw sagged.

"Blazes!" he exploded. "They must be related."

"If they are, I don't know the particulars," admitted Manton. "But it sounds as if they must be."

Pat stood up and began pacing. "This is not coming together properly. The woman calling herself Vina Hawks just happened to be tooling by when Ben Nansen was stricken. She offered to take him to the hospital. And then—"

"Then what?" wondered Manton.

Pat bit her tongue, not wishing to divulge the rest. She went over to the room radio, and turned it on.

She dialed around until the hillbilly music went away and she came into the middle of a news bulletin.

"Homicide detectives are scouring the city for the assailants. Officer James Dandy was pronounced dead at the scene, and the driver and occupants of the bullet-riddled maroon sedan are nowhere to be found. Police do not believe this is a gangland slaying, but they admit that they do not have any other concrete information at present."

Pat inquired, "Did you know that Vina Nansen drove a maroon sedan?"

Harold Manton jumped to his feet and gave out a startled yell. "Do you think that's the same car?"

Pat Savage could be foxy at times. "A call to the hospital will tell the tale. Vina Nansen intended to take Ben Nansen to the hospital. If he didn't make it, then he wouldn't be a patient there, would he?"

"Do you mind if I use your telephone?" Manton asked urgently.

"Be my guest," invited Pat, waving to the instrument.

The oil editor practically leapt on the telephone and got a connection to the city hospital. He was not on the line long.

"Are you certain—that you have admitted no one by that name?"

After listening to the curt reply, Manton hung up.

"Yep," he said tightly. "Ben Nansen is not a patient at the hospital. Look, I want to get your story about Grabber Daly. But it sounds as if something happened to Vina Hawks Nansen, whom you say was driving that maroon sedan. My boss is going to want to know all about this."

"He probably already does," growled Monk. "Sounds like it's a big deal in town."

Throwing on his hat, Harold Manton said, "I'll be in touch," and went out the door like a human hurricane.

After he was gone, Pat turned up the radio once more and they listened for further news bulletins.

An announcer was saying, *"Reliable reports say that Officer Dandy was shot in the head by persons unknown."*

"That's not what happened!" squeaked Monk.

"How do you know a stray bullet didn't finish him off?" Pat wanted to know.

"It's possible one did," admitted Monk. His voice was once again hollow and the expression on his face was loose and full of grief.

"You look," observed Pat, "as if you lost your only brother."

Monk grumbled, "I had no love for that guy. But I don't like seein' cops killed."

"Let us hope," said Pat, "that we are not dragged into this by our hair."

"We've been dragged into it feet-first," grumbled Monk. "What difference does it make?"

"You may be right," admitted Pat. "I suppose we will have to lay low for a while. Until this blows over."

"Cop killin's don't blow over," said Monk flatly. "Not in this or any other town. If we're drug into this, we'll be squattin' on the hot seat in no time flat."

Pat's delectable mouth fell open. "You don't mean the electric chair, do you?"

"No, I mean the hard stool where they give you the third degree. The electric chair comes later."

Pat hugged herself and her bronze skin shivered slightly. "I don't think I've ever been in this kind of trouble before."

"That's why I think we oughta bring in Ham Brooks." Monk strode over to the telephone, but before he could capture the receiver, it began shrilling at him.

Picking it up, he asked, "Hello, who is it?"

A muffled voice said, "Manton. I got a hot scoop. I'm on my way up to spill it."

Before Monk could reply, the line went dead.

Monk turned to Pat and said, "Guy said he was Harold Manton, but I don't like the sound of his voice. He didn't sound like Manton. Says he's on the way up."

Pat raced for a suitcase. Flinging it open, she brought out a six-shooter that looked as if it had been constructed around the time of Buffalo Bill. She checked the action, opened the loading gate, gave the cylinder a brisk spin, snapped it closed again.

Satisfied, she went to the door and waited, gun in hand. The hammer sported a fanning spur that was well-worn with use.

Taking a position on the opposite side of the door, Monk unlimbered his supermachine pistol. They waited.

The wait grew protracted, and they began to fret.

"What's keepin' him?" mumbled Monk.

Pat lay a shushing finger over her lips and put one ear to the panel to listen for footfalls.

The window of the hotel room overlooked an iron fire escape, and they were so focused on the hallway on the other side of the door that they failed to notice a figure creeping up the fire escape ladder until a broken brick came sailing through the window, shattering it with a noisy jangle.

A gloved fist thrust through a jagged hole in the broken pane. From it, a .44-caliber revolver fitted with a long barrel gleamed bluely. In the other was gripped a similar pistol. Fingers constricted on twin triggers.

The cylinders began turning as the guns jerked, spitting out fire and smoke in the approximate direction of Pat and Monk, who were caught entirely unawares.

Chapter VII

OSAGE AMBUSH

THE GUNMAN AT the broken hotel room window emptied both cylinders of slugs into the room in a furious fusillade.

By all rights, he should have gunned down both Pat Savage and Monk Mayfair before they could react to the violent intrusion.

A small but significant detail preserved their lives.

That is: the gunman was not shooting at them, but in the direction of the writing table.

His two-gun fusillade knocked over the telephone, chewed wood from the writing table surface and with the fourth shot sent the aluminum cylinder resting there flying off and into the washroom.

The gunman cursed in frustration, and began using the barrel of one pistol to smash out the remaining glass. It was evident that he was determined to bust into the hotel room to finish what he started.

Monk and Pat lined up on him, opening fire simultaneously. Pat shot only once, but Monk drilled the assailant with a half-dozen mercy bullets.

The burst sent him flying backward, arms windmilling, and he lost his grip on the now-empty matched revolvers. The railing of the fire escape was not high; it came up to the man's waist. As he stumbled backward, his spine encountered it.

A look of surprise came over his rough face as he fell backward—and disappeared from view.

It is common to assume that a man falling several stories to the ground would emit a screech of horror, or vent some similar strong emotion.

This individual did not. He simply fell. And the next sound they heard was the ugly thud of his body landing on hard pavement below with its suggestion of finality.

Passersby noticed the sudden arrival in their midst, and their excited screams and sickened outcries rose up to the broken hotel room window.

There was no need to rush to the fire escape and look down.

"No one could've survived that," muttered Monk.

Bronze face growing pale, Pat Savage looked at her six-shooter with stupefied eyes. "I fired a mercy bullet. Not lead."

"I fired plenty," said Monk, "so it was my slugs that drove him backward. If anyone is to blame, it's me."

Pat continued to look horrified. Like her famous cousin, she abhorred killing. Monk Mayfair was considerably more sanguine, but he did his best to avoid excessive bloodshed whenever possible.

The fact that their would-be assassin lay crushed and broken on the sidewalk alongside the hotel was a sobering thought.

"Now we got a definite body to our credit," mumbled Monk.

Pat looked to Monk and asked, "What do we do now?"

Monk's simian features grew fiercely determined. "Get to the bottom of this. Let's see who this guy is before the cops show up. That might tell us something."

Concealing their weapons, they took the elevator to the lobby, and joined the crowd congregating around the body.

The dead gunman had worn a hat—one of those flamboyant things with a broad brim. It had fallen off and now sat rather forlornly beside him. He had landed on his back, and was sprawled out like a starfish on a beach. His rough features were drenched by midday sunlight.

A round-faced man was asking, "Does anybody recognize him?"

No one did immediately, but after studying the dead man's rather reddish countenance, someone ventured, "That looks like Joe Cloud."

"You don't mean 'Thunder' Cloud, the Osage bank robber, do you?" questioned another.

"That's the guy. They call him 'Two-Guns Big Thunder.' He's wanted from Kansas City clear down to the Texas border."

"Well," a plump man drawled casually, "desperadoes like him always come to a bad end, don't they?"

Monk hung back at the fringes of the crowd as he and Pat listened, managing to avoid attracting attention despite their striking and distinctive appearances.

"Let's skedaddle," Pat said to Monk.

The gorilla-like chemist nodded. "Yeah, we seen enough. I think we gotta find us another hotel, though."

Fading back quietly, they walked away. The pair did not progress far. Up the street, a touring car pulled up beside them. The doors popped open.

THREE very tall individuals stepped out. They were hard men with the kind of reddish faces that made them think of the dead man lying not a few hundred yards away. None of them stood less than six feet in height, and one had a good five inches on his companions. They wore Western-style hats with black-and-vermilion-beaded bands into which were worked Navajo designs in which scorpions stood out.

"You boys look familiar," commented Monk.

"That's because we are," said one of the trio. He was waving a short-barreled pistol that had been bulldogged after its manufacture in order to throw tumbling and destructive lead.

"We made room for you in the back," another added laconically. "Get in."

"Nice of you," quipped Pat.

One of the group waved the bronze-haired girl toward the open rear door. "You could take Joe Cloud's seat, girlie. I guess he's not using it."

Pat paled slightly. Suddenly, she didn't want to enter the touring car—not that she had been enthusiastic about the idea in the first place.

Gun muzzles pressed into her ribs convinced her otherwise.

Along with Monk, Pat was hustled inside, where they were relieved of their weapons. There had been no opportunity to use them without suffering numerous gunshot wounds.

"What's this all about?" asked Monk, settling into the back-seat cushions.

"Unfinished business," snarled the driver, taking off.

"Yeah? Who?"

"We don't mention names in this outfit," Monk was told.

"Sounds smart," the apish chemist allowed.

"It's wise—wise as the old brown owl," the driver clucked glumly.

Hands began investigating Monk's pockets and he asked, "What gives? You got my dang gun."

"You got something that belongs to us."

Shrugging, said Monk, "If I do, you'll find it."

They didn't. So they looked in Pat's direction, saying, "Don't make us get fresh with you, girlie."

Sighing, Pat produced the aluminum tube, which she had collected on the way out of the hotel room.

"I guess I have to give this up now," she said forlornly.

"That you do, girlie, that you do."

Smiling thinly, Pat tossed the thing out the window, and it landed with a distinct sound. It happened to come to a rest on the other side of the road where a passing truck rolled one of its fat front tires over it, flattening it.

"Sorry," she said sheepishly.

To her surprise, the driver said, "Think nothing of it. We didn't really want it back. We wanted it smashed. You did that for us."

"I guess I did," said Pat wonderingly. "I don't imagine that you're going to let us go now."

One of the gunmen laughed shortly, and received an elbow in the ribs from the driver, saying, "None of that. This is serious business."

"Sorry."

"I don't suppose you boys are willing to drop us off at our hotel?" suggested Pat demurely.

"You suppose right. We got something else in mind."

The driver settled down to his driving and the interior of the touring car went quiet.

Pat broke the uneasy silence. "You lads know I'm a cousin of Doc Savage, don't you?"

"Doc Savage is tall trouble," admitted one, "but he doesn't get out to Tulsa much."

"Only about every other year," interjected Monk hopefully. "But he'll make a special point of showin' up if anything happens to us."

"If anything happens to either of you," predicted the driver, "by the time Doc Savage hears about it, the deed will be done, the subject dead and buried."

"I don't like the sound of that," admitted Pat unhappily.

"No one ever does," said the driver in a doleful voice. It sounded as if he had no appetite for what lay ahead.

The touring car made its way out of the Tulsa city limits, and behind them police sirens caterwauled on and off.

"Cops are anxious to find the one that killed Officer Dandy," Monk observed. "I know them, and they're never going to give up."

Pat added, "They're sure to find the culprits."

"On that," said the driver laconically, "you and I are in complete agreement."

Pat and Monk exchanged blank glances. They did not know what to make of that comment.

They soon entered another town. Peering out the window, Monk recognized landmarks. "Sure looks like Broken Arrow to me."

"That's because it is," advised the driver.

The automobile tooled around a disreputable neighborhood. They seemed to be going in no particular direction and, after a bit, the touring car pulled over and gaudy neckerchiefs were produced.

Pat and Monk were blindfolded. The engine mutter of the touring car lifted anew, and the machine lurched back into motion.

Afternoon sunlight was strong, so they could still see filtered light until the machine pulled into a dark area that they assumed was a garage or some other large enclosed structure.

Doors were opened, and they were ordered out of the automobile.

One man got hold of Pat by the arm and assisted her out, as polite as could be.

Monk unfolded himself from the back seat, found his feet, and immediately felt several gun muzzles digging into him.

One gunman made the mistake of using his pistol to make a point.

Prodding Monk's barrel chest, he said, "No funny moves now. Make a reckless move and I'll hand you a lead pill. Get that, Monkey-face?"

"Do I still look scared to you?"

The gunman grimaced. "You look dumb. I don't know about scared."

"Well," said Monk, "I ain't neither one."

The gunman prodded Monk again, which began to get his dander up.

Possibly emboldened by his bulletproof vest, Monk abruptly brought his hairy hands up and clapped the gun between them. He didn't need to see to accomplish that swift feat.

The gunman was caught entirely by surprise. His hand was caught in the vise made by Monk's crushing fingers. They squeezed the cylinder, preventing it from revolving. The gunman didn't even try. The simian chemist's fingers had the feel of iron bands.

Emitting a yelp of surprise, he released the weapon, and Monk whirled around, reaching for his blindfold so he could start shooting if necessary.

The barrel of a different revolver came crashing down on the back of his bullet head, and Monk was driven forward.

Before he struck hard concrete, the homely chemist heard a voice say raucously, "Haw! The dumb ape fell for it! It couldn't've been easier."

"While he's down, fetch the branding iron," another said hastily. "We'll fix his ugly face before he comes around."

Chapter VIII

STANDING SCORPION

PATRICIA SAVAGE WAS no shrinking violet. Far from it.

She had been raised in the wilds of British Columbia and had learned to shoot at the age of eight. By fifteen, she was a crack shot. She could swim raging rapids, ride a horse and live out-of-doors for weeks at a time, relying entirely on her wits and her woodland skills. Pat was a modern cowgirl of the Calamity Jane variety.

The gun barrel striking Monk Mayfair's thick skull made a distinctive sound. It brought forth an explosive grunt from the simian chemist as his knees buckled and he crumpled to the concrete.

Another female surely would have screamed. Not Pat.

She did, however, yell after a fashion. "Monk!" she burst out.

Then Pat turned, and delivered a resounding kick to the gunman standing directly behind. She had no time to aim. But luck was with her. Her heel encountered a kneecap, and made it pop.

Screaming, the gunman went stumbling backward, and when his back impacted with the ground, the breath came out of his lungs through his open mouth and both nostrils. He laid there, stunned, hands waving feebly.

Pat was struggling at her blindfold as she turned once more and lunged in the direction of Monk's grunting.

"Stop that squaw!" a man yelled. Grasping hands reached out for her.

But Pat was too nimble. After she got the blindfold off, she fell upon Monk, who was on his hands and knees, the revolver still clutched in one gorilla paw.

Pat made a grab for it, twisted it loose from his hairy fingers, then snapped erect. She pointed the barrel at her kidnappers, made sure they all got a good look at it.

"If any one of you so much as flares his nostrils," she warned, "I'll perforate him where it will hurt the most."

The gunmen arrayed around the bronze girl regarded her for a moment in shocked disbelief. They had not expected such confident action from a woman as feminine-appearing as this entrancing creature.

Then a man laughed shortly. Another joined in. The third chuckled to himself.

"I mean it," Pat warned. "I've shot men before. Plenty of them."

One of the Indians grinned and said, "Why don't you add to the count?"

Pat looked momentarily perplexed, and her arched eyebrows crowded closer together. She wasn't sure why the gunmen were not afraid of her. Some men are overconfident in the face of a woman, even an armed one.

She directed her attention at the revolver in her fist, gave it a little heft, and decided that it felt lighter than it should.

Directing the muzzle in between two men, she squeezed the trigger and fired once.

The gun made a disappointing *click*.

Frowning, Pat tried again. This resulted in another *click*. She didn't need to make the cylinder revolve all the way around to understand the truth.

"Empty!" she murmured.

The lead gunman barked, "You can drop it or keep it. It's all the same to us. But you're going inside with us."

"I'll keep it," said Pat defiantly.

"Suit yourself." Men got behind her and prodded Pat in the shoulder blades with their weapons.

"What about poor Monk?" she asked.

"We'll drag him in after branding time; don't worry about it."

"Branding time?"

A man reached around and pulled Pat's blindfold back into place, then she was urged forward.

A creaky door opened. She was walked down a corridor that echoed, was made to turn left twice, and then placed in a room that smelled of stale air.

Dragging sounds accompanied by Monk's snuffling breathing indicated that the apish chemist had been deposited behind her.

The door was locked and Pat took off her blindfold.

She stood in what appeared to be a storeroom. It had no furniture. The floor was poured concrete. A single droplight hung from a frayed electrical cord. The bare bulb shed a pitifully inadequate illumination.

Monk lay in one corner like a sack of oddly-shaped grapefruits—or at least that's how the bulging muscles under his clothes made him appear.

Kneeling beside him, Pat began slapping his face lightly, saying, "Monk! Wake up! Can you hear me?"

A low growl like ripping cloth seemed to suggest that the homely chemist had not completely lost consciousness. Possibly, he had a concussion.

Pat had set the empty revolver on the concrete floor and kicked at it in frustration. "If only you had been filled with lead," she said bitterly, "I would've filled those crooks with their fair share."

The gun went skittering off into a far corner and came to a rest.

Monk Mayfair took his time climbing back into consciousness. He groaned and snorted a time or two, but only after he rolled over as if in restless sleep did Pat begin to have hope that he would come to.

The hairy chemist's eyelids rolled up. His dazed eyes peered about without his head otherwise moving. Then, with a groan, he levered himself up into a sitting position.

Monk blinked rapidly. "What happened?"

"They let you get hold of an empty gun," Pat said flatly. "Then they brained you."

"How do you know it was empty? I never got off a shot."

"I grabbed it after you fell and, believe me, it didn't even have any blanks in it. The cylinder was empty."

Monk frowned like a fist clenching and muttered, "Why would one of them be totin' an empty gun?"

Folding her arms, Pat asked, "Want to bet that that was the gun used to shoot that police officer?"

Monk's frown went in the opposite direction. His face became slack and loose.

"It's a theory," he admitted thickly.

"It's a frame," insisted Pat. "They let you grab it so you could put your fingerprints on it."

Monk's jaw sagged in alarm. "They're tryin' to pin that cop killin' on me!" he roared.

"Probably," said Pat. "But you're not alone. Since I handled it, my fingerprints are on it, too."

Monk tried to stand up, but his short legs weren't cooperating. So he continued to sit with his head in his hands, groaning, "I got a ringin' in my ears that won't quit."

"The gang said something about branding you," revealed Pat, examining Monk's simian physique, "but I don't see any marks."

"I don't feel nothin', except my face sure hurts."

"No wonder. You fell flat on it." Pat was looking around, murmuring, "If only there was a drain or someplace we could dispose of this gun."

"Good idea," said Monk. "Because if the cops get their mitts on it, it's enough to send the pair of us to the electric chair."

"Only one person could've shot that police officer. They couldn't convict both of us, could they?"

"When it comes to police killings, the cops aren't very fussy. They'll see that we fry, and let our next of kin worry about the sorting out."

Pat paled slightly under her bronze tan, and her golden eyes got a little frosty. Methodically, she began wiping the weapon on her skirt, and did not stop until she had rubbed every spot clean.

Finally, she dropped the revolver to the floor and murmured, "I'd like to know what this is all about...."

"If they ever open that door," muttered Monk, "be sure to ask the first guy who sticks his head in. But don't expect a straight answer."

It was another hour before the door—a ponderous affair of planks fitted with wooden dowel pins—swung open. They were ordered out of the room at gunpoint.

After they filed out into the corridor, one man came in, and used a yellow pencil to lift the incriminating revolver up off the floor by its trigger guard. He grinned as he did so.

"Evidence?" asked Pat archly.

"Don't worry about it," sneered the gunman. "You'll both be dead before the police get their hands on this hunk of iron. It's just sort of a ribbon to tie things up in a nice neat bow."

PAT and Monk were escorted along twisting corridors, and finally came to a dark door that was of veneer.

"Inside," a man directed. "The Chief wants to pow-wow."

Pat and Monk entered, not knowing what to expect. The sight of the room caused their eyes to widen and their expressions to take on slow lines of amazement.

In contrast to the rude storeroom and plain walls they had thus far experienced, this chamber was something out of a storybook.

The walls were a hot scarlet. It hurt the eyes to look at them. There was a raised platform, and on this was set a low dais that stood about three feet off the floor, its flat rim decorated with the black-and-vermilion scorpion symbols that had adorned the hatbands of the gunmen who kidnapped them.

On the dais, towered a striking figure.

He wore rich purple-black robes that fell to his feet. Peeping under the hem were beaded moccasins, red as new brick. Upon his head was some kind of matching hood. The hood concealed his features, of course, but even the eyes were covered. Red lenses sewn into the hood defeated any attempt to discern their color.

Worked into the front of the sable regalia was the vertical silhouette of a scarlet scorpion, which extended from the lowermost ribs to the concealed throat of the apparition, its exceedingly thin tail coiled tightly, lobster-like pincers spread out just below the robed shoulders.

The scorpion motif was carried out in the way the top of the shapeless sack of a hood hung back, forming a fat tail contrived to resemble a scorpion stinger.

Behind this fantastic apparition hung a blood-red curtain, and affixed to its crimson surface, a war bonnet of magnificent eagle feathers made a fantastic decorative fan. No doubt by design, this barbaric headdress framed the unusually tall figure, suggesting a war chief of the plains.

Pat was not ordinarily impressed by display. And she made a comment which proved that.

"Who are you supposed to be?" she asked. "Sitting Bull?"

"Call me Standing Scorpion," said the fantastic figure in a sonorous tone.

"O.K., Standing Scorpion. What's your racket?"

"Standing Scorpion is war chief of Vinegarroon tribe."

Monk snorted at that point, "There ain't no such tribe in these parts. I know. Cherokee and Choctaw and Chickasaw and Osage inhabit Oklahoma. But there's no Vinegarroon—except what you can find crawling out from under rocks."

The purple-and-scarlet apparition intoned, "The tribe of Standing Scorpion is older than any of those. The Vinegarroon people dwell in caves, out of the sight of the white man."

"Hooey!" snorted Monk. "Lay off the locoweed, guy!"

"What do you want with us?" interjected Pat.

"Heap talk."

"You want to palaver?" countered Pat.

"You catchum idea. Standing Scorpion does not like white men, or even bronze girl. White men must stay out of business of Vinegarroon tribe."

Pat flung back, "We didn't butt into anybody's business. Someone brought trouble to us. Put that in your peace pipe and smoke it. Better yet, why don't you let us go? Surely you savvy who we are?"

The concealing hood nodded, producing a rustling of fabric. "Bronze girl belong to Savage clan. Plenty bad medicine. Monkey man is allied with bronze chief. More bad medicine. Trouble for Vinegarroon tribe."

"Now you're talking," said Pat. "So let us go and save yourself a pile of grief. Doc Savage has more powerful medicine than you can shake a stick at. Trifling with us is the same as courting dire calamity."

Standing Scorpion's sonorous voice took on an edge. "What did pale white man tell you?"

Monk responded to that. "You mean Ben Nansen? He could barely talk. We didn't get anything much out of him, except some wild talk that sounded like vampires had got hold of him."

Standing Scorpion absorbed this in silence. Throughout, he loomed over them with his arms folded, and now he unfolded them, revealing again the gory red scorpion design worked into the front of his robe in all of its garish ugliness.

While he stood there, Pat asked, "I don't suppose you would care to explain what was in that aluminum cylinder that got flattened?"

"Medicine," said Standing Scorpion. "Powerful medicine. But it is no more."

"I'll take your word for it," said Pat diffidently. "What do you say? Let us go and spare us all a lot of trouble."

Standing Scorpion did not respond at once. But after a time, his robe shifted and rustled and he said in his muffled voice, "Standing Scorpion will consider your words." Lifting his voice, he said, "Remove them. Tribal council will decide their fate."

"Thanks for nothing," said Pat, as they herded her and Monk Mayfair back through the twisting corridors, where they were locked up in the storeroom again.

Monk's first words after the door shut were, "We're in a heckuva fix."

Pat spun around and made defiant fists, saying, "Well, we're not dead. At least not yet. What do you think of old Chief Standing Scorpion?"

"He's a phony," snorted Monk. "And that war bonnet he's got hangin' behind him for show ain't even from around here. It's Sioux."

"You don't say," remarked Pat, pretty brow wrinkling.

"No self-respecting Indian would dress or talk like that character," asserted the apish chemist. "He may have a mob of Osage braves. But all that talk about a Vinegarroon tribe and him bein' their chief is so much spangles and fancy buckskin fringe. Take it from me. I was born in Oklahoma when it was called the Indian Nations. You can pitch that yarn out the window. If there was a window, that is."

"He *did* talk like a comic strip Indian, didn't he?" allowed Pat. "Why do you suppose he did that?"

"Beats me, but it looks like you got your wish."

Pat arched a quizzical eyebrow. "What wish is that?"

"That wish you been harboring for a long time to grab yourself a hunk of excitement you could call your own. This kinda looks like it. But it'll turn out to be the end of us if we don't figure a way out of this tangle."

"Do you think they're going to kill us?"

"Probably. Unless they decide to vacate the joint, call the cops, and have them find us with the murder gun, all in one nice tidy bundle."

"Ham will probably get us off."

"Ham might be able to get *you* off, on account of you're a female," countered Monk, "but I'm liable to land in the hot seat before the month is out. They cook 'em quick here in Oklahoma."

Pat moaned. "Suddenly, I feel as if my hankering for black gold was the same as eating rat poison."

Having nothing better to do, and no furniture to take advantage of, they sat down on the rough floor, their backs on opposite sides of the storeroom, and silently contemplated their fate.

Hours passed. Nothing seemed to be taking place, and the only sounds that came to their ears were minor scratchings, suggestive of mice and not human activity.

From time to time, Monk complained that one side of his face ached, but no bruise bloomed upon it.

Since they had but one light, and a feeble one at that, the passing of day into night was not something they perceived. But the slow dragging of time made them realize that night was surely upon them, for Monk's expensive wristwatch continued to tick off the minutes.

Abruptly, Monk spoke up. "I'm hungry."

"You would think of your stomach at a time like this," Pat said crossly.

"I'm not thinkin' of my stomach. My stomach is doin' the thinkin' for me. We never did get to eat a fillin' lunch, did we?"

Pat moaned, "That was so long ago I can hardly remember."

After a very long time, there came a scratching on the door followed by the grating of a key. The heavy door started to open very slowly—so slowly that the rusting hinges creaked and groaned in a kind of metallic agony.

Their eyes shifting to the opening portal, Pat and Monk lifted themselves to their feet. They never got all the way up, because the head that popped around the opening door took them by surprise.

Had the hooded countenance of Chief Standing Scorpion regarded them with his hell-red eyes, they could not have been more shocked. It was not Standing Scorpion, or any of his minions.

Instead the pale features of Vina Hawks Nansen peered around. Setting a slim finger to her red lips, she made a slight hissing sound for silence.

"What are *you* doing here?" demanded Pat, suspicion coming into her tone.

The blonde woman slipped in, closed the door behind her and said simply, "Prisoner. Just like you."

Pat and Monk quickly scrambled to their feet and were crowding close to the woman, studying her face with suspicious eyes.

"If you're a prisoner," muttered Monk, "what're you doin' loose?"

"That is a very good question," added Pat. "Do you mind answering it, Miss Nansen?"

The woman shook her head violently. "No time. I know a way out of here. If we are quiet and careful, we could escape— all three of us together."

As a proposition, it was a hard one to resist, even if the circumstances were unusually suspicious.

Pat and Monk exchanged skeptical glances. A silent nod passed between them.

"Lead the way, Miss Nansen," invited Pat. "That way we can keep an eye on you."

"Ditto," said Monk.

The fact that Pat Savage had twice called the blonde woman by her correct last name seemed not to have made much of an impression upon Vina Hawks Nansen, alias Vina Hawks.

Chapter IX

DYNAMITE BLAST

AS ESCAPES WENT, this one was surprisingly smooth in execution.

At least, that was what Pat Savage thought as Vina Hawks Nansen led them through the twisting hallways of their unknown prison, coming finally to a rickety set of plank stairs that led to a cobwebbed basement.

As the blonde woman eased open the door, Pat Savage started to object. "Hold your horses. Where are you leading us?"

The vehemence with which the woman turned and hissed for silence took both Pat and Monk aback.

Vina Hawks Nansen gestured for them to follow, then disappeared down the stairs, moving so stealthily they couldn't detect the sound of her careful creeping tread. But they also knew that this was a sign that these sounds would not carry far to betray them.

Pat looked to Monk. Monk looked back, shrugging as if to say, "What do we have to lose?"

"Plenty," Pat said with her lips. Monk was an expert lip reader, and understood.

Pat was hinting that they could lose their lives, which appeared to be hanging by some very thin threads at this exact moment.

Monk went first, sniffed the air like a gorilla entering the den of an unknown animal, and ambled down the stairs, while Pat took up the rear. She carefully shut the door behind her.

The absence of illumination that followed was utter. But in the impenetrable darkness a tiny thread of light showed—a flashlight of some type. It beckoned like a spectral finger. So they followed it.

The beam raced around the cracked concrete basement floor until it came to rest on a dull disk of metal that shone slightly from the moisture of long years.

They crowded around this and the dime of light created by the tiny flashlight showed that it was a manhole of some type.

"Sewer?" Monk muttered.

In the wan back glow of the light, the blonde-haired woman shook her head vigorously. "Secret entrance and exit."

"How do you know about this?" asked Pat suspiciously.

"Later," breathed the woman, swinging the flash ray about searchingly. "They use pry bars to lift it open. But I don't see them around."

"Don't need 'em," grunted Monk, stooping to insert hairy fingers into the apertures of the manhole cover. Straightening his legs and broad back, he exerted almost inhuman pressure on the steel plate, which lifted up.

Vina Hawks Nansen's chocolate brown eyes widened in wonder. The homely chemist looked as strong as a bull gorilla. This feat of strength proved that he actually was.

Monk moved to one side and did his best to drop the manhole cover quietly. The steel rang. But that only gave them added motivation to enter the darksome hole without delay.

Taking the flashlight from the woman, Monk jumped down first, landed in soil that was surprisingly dry, raced the beam around and saw that the tunnel led in only one direction.

Monk called up. "C'mon. Let's make tracks."

Pat dropped next, saw that she stood in a tunnel of concrete with a dirt floor and said with suspicion, "My hackles are rising."

"I didn't know you had any," clucked Monk.

"This escape is a little too easy, if you know what I mean."

Monk nodded, saying, "Let's finish the escaping part before we wonder about that too much."

Vina dropped down next, and pointed in the direction where the tunnel seemed to run. "That way," she urged.

They moved quickly, Monk taking the lead, using the flashlight liberally and not encountering any obstacles or guards. The hairy chemist didn't expect any.

The tunnel ran along for several hundred yards, and the longer they followed it, the more impressed they became.

"Tunnels like this don't build themselves," Monk muttered.

"The leader of the gang whom they call their chief," inserted Vina Nansen, "has resources."

"You mean Chief Standing Scorpion?" asked Pat.

"That is one of his names. He has others. 'The Ozark Ogre' is another one."

Monk wanted to know, "Ever see him without that scorpion-tailed sack on his head?"

Vina Hawks Nansen seemed to hesitate. She bit her delicate lip. Finally, she breathed, "No. Never."

Her tone of voice was unconvincing. But they had no time to interrogate her now. There was an end to this tunnel somewhere and they were determined to get to fresh air as soon as possible. Tunnels are bad places to be caught in, and they had no desire to tarry.

Some twenty minutes of walking brought them to a ladder composed of pipe. It had been painted blue, but seepage of water from above had brought out the erosion of rust.

Carefully, they climbed out. It was sturdy enough. Monk, of course, went first, and when his nubbin of a head bumped the roof, he pushed up a mighty paw and a square trapdoor gave upward.

Although Pat and Monk had had an inkling of the passage of time, it came as a shock to find their faces full of moonlight.

Right now, Monk stood on firm ground and took stock of the immediate vicinity.

All around him, trees stood like shadowy sentinels. They were red oak trees, common to Oklahoma. Buckbrush also covered the ground in bristling patches silvered by lunar light.

Leaning down, Monk offered an overlong arm to assist Pat up, and when the bronze-haired girl was standing beside him, he performed the same courtesy for Vina Hawks Nansen.

"What woods are these?" asked Pat, staring about.

The blonde woman answered, "Just a patch of woods outside of town. Perfect for entering the tunnel unseen."

"I gathered that," said Pat frostily. "What I don't gather is how you come to know of this tunnel."

Instead of answering, Vina said, "You can never know when they come and go. We shouldn't linger here."

Pat looked as if she wanted to give the woman an argument, but Monk interjected, "She's right, Pat. We gotta make tracks. If that murder gun falls into the hands of the police, our gooses are cooked. Maybe literally."

That sobering thought seemed to take the fire out of Pat Savage's tawny eyes and she said, "We can't very well go back to our hotel room."

The blonde woman said, "We should split up. I will rent a hotel room under an assumed name. Natica Hawks. Go to the Gusher Hotel. It's a place where up-and-coming oil men stay. Come by no later than midnight. I will tell you everything I know there and then."

Pat Savage looked as if she was of two minds about going along with the plan.

The explosion altered her focus.

It came so unexpectedly that they didn't comprehend its meaning even as its searing blast tore through the woods in which they stood huddled. Swinging toward the hot flash of fire, their eyes took in the sight of the climbing cloud of fire and boiling black smoke that was punching skyward in the approximate direction from which they came.

Monk had previously dropped the trapdoor back into place, but now it jerked up of its own accord, and the hot blast of air that impelled it blew upward and caused them to stagger backward before its sudden heat.

Monk kept his feet. Pat Savage was knocked over, landing on the seat of her dress, and began sputtering inarticulately.

"I know what you're tryin' to say," said Monk. "The place we were held in just blew up."

Vina offered, "Chief Standing Scorpion is covering his tracks. He must have discovered that we were missing."

It made perfect sense, but it was also rather pat. The glance Monk and Pat exchanged told the blonde that they both harbored the same thought.

Despite that, they had no inclination to stick around and argue the matter. Pat got to her feet, brushed off her sport dress and informed their rescuer, "We will rendezvous with you at the Gusher then, Miss Nansen."

Without a word in response, Vina Hawks Nansen melted into the shivering trees and disappeared from their sight.

As soon as she was gone, Pat snapped her fingers angrily and said, "Darn! I meant to ask her about her brother."

"We'll pump her tonight. Let's skedaddle."

They faded in the opposite direction.

Pat wanted to know, "What will we do between now and midnight?"

Looking to his rather garish wristwatch, Monk said, "We've got three hours. Let's look up that reporter, Harold Manton. He may give us a line on something."

Pat considered. "I think we should find ourselves some dinner first."

Rubbing his ample stomach, Monk Mayfair said, "Now that you mention it, I could eat about three steaks and a steaming pile of mashed potatoes with gravy."

"Only three?" chided Pat.

"I didn't get breakfast this morning," returned the simian chemist, grinning.

As they worked their way out of the forest, they watched the aftermath of the tremendous blast in the center of town.

It was impossible to tell in what type of building they had been held, but it did not appear to be a conventional residence. Nor could they tell if other buildings had become involved. The scream of fire trucks was already in the air, and the smell that came to their nostrils was pungent with gasoline.

"Somebody," mused Pat, "didn't want anybody backtracking them."

"Mebbe," said Monk. "But that same somebody owned that busted building. That's another line we might wanta investigate."

Chapter X

COMPLICATIONS

IN SHORT ORDER, Patricia Savage and Monk Mayfair picked their way out of the forest—which was hardly even that. Simply a patch of red-oak scrub at the edge of the town of Oil Hill.

After walking through a pleasant residential area, they found the center of town and a homey diner that was open. The eating establishment called itself "OWL LUNCH." A window placard boasted that it was open 24 hours a day, which explained the first part of the name, but not the last.

There were no problems securing a table, for most of the town populace was out on the sidewalks, gawking and rubbernecking in the direction of the raging conflagration.

As they were being seated, Monk asked the waiter, "What blew up over there?"

The waiter evidently had already given that matter some thought, for he replied instantly, "Looks like that old storage building that's been empty since the bust."

Pat remarked, "The owner is probably out a pretty penny."

"Probably," agreed the waiter. "Not sure who that is though."

Monk ordered three T-bone steaks while Pat simply settled for fried chicken. When Monk finished his third steak, he ordered a fourth, and managed to consume half of it, finally pushing his plate back, grunting, "I think the old furnace is full now."

"Full to bursting!" declared Pat. "I've never seen you pack away so much food."

"I don't like to miss meals," said Monk, polishing off a cold glass of milk.

After they paid their bill, they went searching for a taxicab. These proved to be scarce, but finally one happened along, and they flagged it down.

"Tulsa, driver," directed Monk.

"Any spot in particular?"

"Trumpet Building."

Dropping the flag, the driver tore off, and took them to the city as rapidly as practical.

"Shame about that big building," he clucked. "But nobody's been using it for years. I think the owner must've gone bankrupt after the last stock market contraction."

Pat asked, "Ever hear his name?"

"No, can't say that I have," admitted the driver. "Just talk. Rumors. I think a bunch of those Osage Indians that got rich off of oil a while back may own it. There's a lot of rich Indians in these parts."

"And other kinds, too," said Pat darkly.

"What's that?" wondered the driver. "I didn't quite catch that."

"Never mind. Just drive. We have an appointment at the *Trumpet*."

They were there in less than fifteen minutes. Monk paid off the driver, their captors not having bothered with appropriating his wallet. That fact by itself suggested that they were not common gunmen.

Entering the narrow brick Trumpet Building, they went to the reception cage and Monk asked, "Harold Manton in?"

"Who is calling on him?"

"Tell him it's Monk Mayfair and Patricia Savage."

"One moment, please." The woman at the reception window picked up a telephone instrument and spoke into it briefly.

"Take the elevator to the third floor," she directed after hanging up.

"Thank you kindly!" said Patricia brightly.

As they strolled to the elevator, Pat asked, "What should we tell him?"

"Leave that to me, unless you get a better idea," suggested Monk.

Pat made a disapproving face. "Whose mystery is this, anyway?"

Monk shrugged. "Right now, it's up for grabs."

The elevator whisked them up to the third floor, and they found the door with Harold Manton's name on a frosted glass panel.

Pushing ahead of Monk, Pat knocked once, then entered.

The big rangy newsman waved them in, saying, "What can I do for you folks?"

They took chairs. Having been stung by Monk Mayfair's insistence upon leading the discussion, Pat Savage said quickly, "We'd like to unload some questions upon you, if you don't mind."

Dropping into the well-worn swivel chair behind his desk, Harold Manton literally swept the loose papers cluttering his desktop to one side and gestured magnanimously. He was wearing the green eyeshade common to those who toiled in the editorial trade and it clashed with his carroty hair.

"I just made space," he laughed.

Patricia Savage was a direct sort of gal. She began by saying crisply, "Tell us everything you know about Vina Hawks Nansen."

Manton seemed to hesitate briefly. Rearranging his fingers on the desktop, he began, "I don't know a powerful lot about her. Hails from Oklahoma City, made a name for herself on a newspaper over there. Established a reputation as a cracking good reporter and columnist. Already told you she's engaged to my boss."

"Golddigger type?"

"Never heard that said about her," Manton said sharply. "Miss Nansen comes from a good family. Her daddy is rich, by all accounts. And yet she is making her own way in the world." A cloud of concern passed over his face. "Not sure I much care for this trend of questioning."

"Let it pass," said Monk. "We're just trying to get to the bottom of something."

"Point me to that bottom; maybe I can help."

Frowning, Pat indicated the floor. "The bottom is so far down, even we can't see it." In order to convey the gravity of the situation, the golden-eyed girl left that statement hanging in the air a bit.

A quizzical expression roosted upon Harold Manton's muscular features and he eyed them both seriously.

"What sort of trouble is this? If you don't mind my asking."

"It's complicated," replied Pat. "Believe me."

"We may be in Dutch with the Tulsa police," added Monk.

"From what I heard, you were a sort of a hellion in your day, Mayfair. Does this have anything to do with the police officer who was killed today?"

"It might," allowed Pat, taking the reins of the conversation once more. "The weapon used to kill the officer fell into our hands by accident."

"You have it!"

Pat shook her head vigorously. "No, it got away from us. But not before acquiring our fingerprints."

Manton's ruddy face grew a bit ashen now.

"Where is the murder gun now?" he questioned.

"We don't know," confessed Pat.

"But we think it's on its way to the police, one way or another. Along with a note implicating us."

"Where does Miss Nansen figure into this?"

"Up to her eyebrows," grunted Monk.

Pat shot the simian chemist a withering look, and asked, "Has Miss Nansen been reported missing?"

"Not that I'm aware of." The editor reached for the telephone instrument on his desk, saying, "I can ring up my boss."

"Please don't," implored Pat. "We have nothing solid to go on. It appears that the persons who waylaid Ben Nansen on the way to the hospital may have abducted Miss Nansen. But she escaped subsequently."

"That's quite a ring-around-the-rosy you are describing," suggested Harold Manton tightly. "If I were a police reporter instead of an oil editor, I would be taking copious notes right about now."

Pat ignored that pointed remark and asked instead, "Have you ever heard of a local Indian chief or medicine man called Standing Scorpion?"

"No, I can't say that I have. Of course, there are lots of Osage and other red men around this neck of the woods. I don't know but a few dozen by name, and that's only the rich ones. The ones that got lucky with oil."

Pat eyed the oil editor steadily, then asked, "I'd like to ask a favor. Do you think you can find out who owns a certain storage building over by Oil Hill?"

"The address?" asked Manton, picking up a pencil.

"I don't have the address, but it won't be hard to determine it. It blew up over an hour ago."

"Oh, *that* old storage building," said Manton. "That one came in over the teletype—not that I couldn't hear it rattling my windows all the way here in Tulsa." He made his lips firm. "You two have been in and out of mischief all the livelong day."

"We," announced Pat Savage, standing up abruptly, "have hardly gotten started getting into mischief. Now if you'll excuse us, we have rounds to make."

Monk got up, grabbed hold of the doorknob, and said, "We'll be in touch. Mum's the word."

Harold Manton showed his open palms. "I'm a newspaperman. I can't promise anything. But good luck to you both."

TAKING the back stairs down to the lobby, Monk caught up with Pat Savage and remarked, "That was a pretty swell third-degree you pulled back there. Where'd you learn to do that?"

Pat smiled archly. "When I first came to New York a few years back, I set my cap on becoming a private investigator. I took some detecting courses, but obtaining a license got kind of complicated, I discovered. You had to be over twenty-one, and I had a few years yet to get there. So I went into the beauty business instead."

"Doc would've skinned you alive if you popped up as a private peeper," observed Monk.

"Why? Because I would have been stiff competition?"

"No, because you'd be dragging the Savage name into all sorts of mud and notoriety. Doc wouldn't stand for that."

"Well, Doc Savage doesn't own me—or our family name."

When the unlikely duo reached the lobby, they spotted a police radio car parked out in front, and decided to take the back way out. It's a peculiarity of Tulsa business blocks that most have back alleys running behind them, and these passages connected to one another. That made it easy for the pair to slip away in the darkness, unseen and unsuspected.

"The police machine might have been parked there for any number of reasons," suggested Pat.

"Includin' lookin' to nab us on sight," snorted Monk.

The pair kept to the back alleys and side streets as they wended their way around town, moving in the direction of the Gusher Hotel, which was located on a somewhat seedy side of the city of Tulsa.

Along the way, they passed a brick apartment building in which many windows were raised in order for the inhabitants to tolerate the summer heat.

From one window, dance music was playing intermittently, but the strains were interrupted by the strident voice of an announcer, issuing an important news flash.

"This just in, folks! The Chief of Tulsa Police has just issued a warrant for the arrest of Patricia Savage and Andrew Blodgett Mayfair, otherwise known as Monk, two associates of the famous adventurer, Doc Savage. The pair are wanted in connection with the slaying of Officer James Dandy, earlier today. This is startling news, folks, and we await further developments."

Pat and Monk froze in the darkness, looking at one another.

"Blazes!" mumbled Monk.

"Blazes doesn't begin to describe the temperature," declared Pat. "We're sunk!"

"Not if we reach the Gusher without being spotted."

Mouths grim, faces showing strain, they crept along the littered pathways and byways of Tulsa until they reached the Gusher Hotel, slipping in the back way.

"You ask for her at the desk," suggested Monk. "With these long arms of mine, I'm kinda conspicuous."

"Your gorilla arms," retorted Pat, "are the least of your worries. All right. Go hide in that phone booth over in the corner."

Monk ducked into the booth and closed the wooden door, hunkering down as if making a telephone call. While Pat inquired at the reception as to the room occupied by Natica Hawks, the hairy chemist suddenly realized where he was, and began dropping nickels into the pay-telephone slot.

"Long-distance operator," he requested.

"Number, please."

Monk gave the number of a private apartment in an exclusive club in downtown Manhattan.

The voice of a somewhat snooty valet announced, "Mr. Brooks' residence."

"Tell Ham to come to the phone. This is Monk Mayfair. Callin' collect. But don't tell him that until after he hangs up."

"One moment, please."

A cultured voice came on the line and asked rudely, "What is on your mind, you brainless baboon?"

"Listen up, shyster," growled Monk. "Pat and I are out Tulsa way, and we landed in a pickle."

"What sort of pickle?"

"It's the biggest jam you ever heard of."

"Which is it?" retorted Ham Brooks superciliously. "A pickle or a jam?"

"Pat and I are both wanted for the murder of a police officer out here. Our fingerprints got on the murder gun."

"How did you allow that to happen, you beetle-browed caveman?" Ham asked acidly.

"We fell into a trap, but good. Look, we're tryin' to sort things out, but if we get pinched, we're gonna need your help."

"I will be on the next plane to Tulsa," promised Ham.

"Do me a favor?"

"What is it?"

"Go around to my digs and pick up my pet pig, Habeas Corpus. Bring him along."

"What good will he do?" exploded Ham the lawyer.

"Well, just in case you can't get me off, I want to say goodbye to Habeas."

Losing his indignant ire, the attorney said, "I will see what I can do. Try not to get yourself in any deeper a hole than you already have," added Ham tartly, hanging up.

Muttering to himself, Monk dropped the receiver on its hook, and waited impatiently for Pat to return. Despite their sharp trading of insults, Monk and Ham Brooks were fast friends, in and out of their association with Doc Savage. Ham was by reputation one of the most accomplished attorneys who ever matriculated from Harvard Law School.

Before long, the bronze-skinned beauty knocked on the door, and Monk threw it open.

Pat hissed. "She's on the third floor, Room Three-ten. We had better take the stairs, otherwise the elevator operator is going to recognize you."

"The papers haven't hit the streets yet, so it might be safe."

"Have you looked in a mirror lately?" retorted Pat.

Monk grunted. He had, but he was so accustomed to the sight of his gorilla-like physiognomy that he often failed to realize how much he stood out in a crowd.

Together, they crept up the stairs, not encountering anyone along its winding stages.

Chapter XI

STRAINED MEETING

PAT SAVAGE KNOCKED on the door of Room 310 and, when no one responded, Monk stepped in and applied his hairy knuckles. The panel rattled under his relentless drumming.

A female voice asked anxiously through the veneered wood, "Who is it?"

"We're early," advised Pat, "but you know who this is."

They allowed themselves to be scrutinized through the peephole. Then there was the rattle of chain, followed by the turning of a doorknob.

The portal opened just a crack and the chocolate brown eyes of Vina Hawks Nansen regarded them with trepidation.

"I heard a radio flash," she said. "You are fugitives now."

"You going to let us in, or not?" growled Monk.

"I cannot refuse you refuge," she said. "Step in, please. Quickly!"

It was a two-room suite. The living room was not especially large, and a folding screen had been set before the window. That way no one could look in. Evidently, Vina Hawks Nansen had undertaken this precaution in the event of their arrival. The screen afforded a measure of privacy given that the window was open in order to let in the night air. In one corner, a small fan was stirring the hot air monotonously and without appreciable effect.

"This is a horrible turn of events," she said simply, wringing her thin fingers.

"It is," agreed Pat. "But let's get down to brass tacks. Ben Nansen is your brother, am I correct?"

"Yes, but how did you know—?"

"That's what I wanta know," inserted Monk, surprise pulling his brow lower.

"Deduction," said Pat. "Officer Dandy seemed very interested in getting a better look at Ben Nansen's profile when we were driving to the hospital. He had been looking closely at Miss Nansen before he demanded to see Ben Nansen's face better. No doubt he recognized a family resemblance, which I began to suspect when Dandy's actions called my attention to it. Now that I look you over more carefully, Miss Nansen, I can see that you have the same color eyes as Ben, as well as his prominent cheekbones."

Monk whistled off-key. "Well, what do you know?"

Pat braced Vina Hawks Nansen. "Do you know the present whereabouts of your brother?"

She shook her head. "I do not. Only that he is a prisoner once again. You see, after those gunmen carried us off, Ben and I were separated. I was searching for him when I came upon the two of you in the building that subsequently exploded."

"We will come to the question of how you accomplished that marvelous piece of escape work," advised Pat. "But first, how did you first happen along just as your brother accosted us?"

"Ben called me from a drugstore pay telephone, saying he had escaped from some horrible form of imprisonment and had made his way to the city of Tulsa. He begged me to come and pick him up. I was attempting to do exactly that when, evidently, he learned of your presence here, and decided to appeal to you."

"That's a load of deducting under the circumstances," observed Pat.

"It is what I surmised," said the blonde stiffly. "Had I happened along ten minutes sooner, I would have found Ben before he discovered you. It was simply circumstance that dictated what happened."

Monk interjected, "So how'd you escape those gunmen in the buildin' that went up in hellfire and smoke?"

Vina averted her deep brown eyes. "As you may have heard, I am a newspaperwoman. Sometimes my job requires that I contrive to get into locked places in search of leads. I carry a special hairpin in my hair at all times. It makes a handy lockpick. With it, I was able to open the door to the storeroom where the kidnappers placed me. It is nothing more remarkable that that, I assure you!"

"Show me this trick hairpin," challenged Pat.

The blonde hesitated. "I-I lost it along the way. But in seeking a way out of that building, I came upon the two of you, also prisoners. The rest you know."

"Bunk!" Monk exploded. "We were behind a door with no window. You hadda know we were in there because somebody tipped you off."

"And you knew all about that secret escape tunnel," reminded Pat.

A flush darkened Vina's pale face. "I overheard a gunman mention that they had taken you both prisoner," she said hastily. "I-I neglected to mention that fact. And I discovered that tunnel in my search for poor Ben."

"Nonsense!" snapped Pat. "You acted as if you knew a great deal about the place—and more besides. And why didn't you inform the police instead of risking your life in a blind search?"

"I wanted the story, as well as my brother," the blonde flung back. "And I did not wish to jeopardize Ben's safety if the police raided the location."

Pat and Monk scrutinized her, attempting to read the blonde's emotions. Her face wore strain like a marble mask, and her eyes had a haunted look.

Twisting her fingers together, Vina said, "I have given this matter considerable thought since I saw you both last. Information has also come into my possession, which changes the complexion of things."

"What sort of information?" pressed Pat.

"I would rather not divulge that at this time, but I have reason to believe that my brother will be released soon. I-I do not need your help any longer."

Pat laughed shortly. "Sister, you may not need *our* help, but we need *yours*. The streets are full of radio cars prowling for us. They're probably rooting around in our hotel room by now, and we have no place to go."

"You cannot stay here," Vina said shrilly. "It is quite simply impossible. I would be harboring outlaws. Fugitives from justice—accused murderers! I expect to marry Morgan Marrs in the Fall. He is a prominent newspaper owner in this town. And I'll be touched by scandal. It would ruin everything. Everything!" she finished anxiously.

"We wouldn't be in this fix if we hadn't stopped to help your brother," Pat Savage reminded.

Vina Hawks Nansen stiffened, then lifted her pale chin in a rather proud and slightly arrogant fashion.

"If you will both turn yourselves in to the police," she suggested coolly, "I am quite certain that the charges against you will be fixed up in short order."

"What makes you say that?" Pat asked sharply.

"My future husband is a powerful man in the city. He will see to it. I am confident in that. Please go. Throw yourself upon the mercy of the police, and mercy will be shown to you. Choose to run or fight, and no one can guarantee your safety. The choice is yours."

Monk was ambling around the hotel room, too nervous to sit down. At one point, his perambulations brought him close to a floor lamp that shone into his homely face.

Catching a glimpse of one of Monk's cheeks, Vina Hawks Nansen gave out a startled gasp. Both hands went to her mouth.

"What is it?" demanded Pat.

"Look at his face! There, on his right cheek. Look at it!"

Taken aback, Monk gulped, "What is that you say?"

Pat Savage came striding up, scrutinized him, then took Monk by the shoulders and spun him around until he was facing a wall mirror.

"Take a gander for yourself," she invited.

The homely chemist stared into the mirror, and then he saw it. A splotch. It sprawled across his right cheek, and resembled nothing less than a crawling scorpion. Not the bloody red mark that had been found on Ben Nansen's withered cheek, but a dirty-looking brown blot. It was as if blood had dried in the shape of a scorpion there.

Monk pawed at the patch, but it refused to rub off.

"How did this dang thing get there in the first place?" he howled.

No one had an answer for that and, inasmuch as the mark wouldn't rub off, Pat slapped Monk's hands down and said, "Leave it alone. We'll look at it later. Care to bet that it got on you somehow during our brush with those gunmen?"

"You mean those daggone Osage braves?" yelled Monk. "They done this!"

"I seem to recall one saying something about branding you when you were unconscious," Pat stated.

Monk made hairy fists of rage. "I'll wring their red necks for them. I'll twist their ears off, and make them eat them with onions."

"Time enough for that later," fumed Pat, adding, "Let's bid our fond adieus, and be on our unmerry way."

Monk hesitated. "What if this mark starts turnin' red?"

"I'll let you know if it does," promised Pat. "Let's get out of here."

They rushed to the door. Pausing at the open portal, Pat Savage said, "I am sure we will be in touch, Miss Nansen. We intend to get to the bottom of this black well of mystery."

"Please remember what I said," advised Vina Hawks Nansen with apparent sincerity. "If you turn yourselves in, it will go better for you."

"We'll let you know," said Pat, shoving Monk ahead of her and closing the door firmly behind.

THEY took the stairs down to the lobby, slipped out the back way and began moving through cramped and shadow-darkened alleyways.

"Beginnin' to feel like a dang alley cat," complained Monk. "I know this town like the back of my hand, but this isn't the way I like to navigate it."

"Hush," admonished Pat. "We need to think our way out of this mess. What if she's telling the truth? Do you suppose that turning ourselves in could be our best way out?"

Monk rubbed the back of his bristled neck worriedly. "If this wasn't a cop killin', I might be inclined to go along. But Tulsa police don't take kindly to cop killin's. We better stay on the loose until Ham gets here."

Pat arched an eyebrow quizzically. "Ham?"

Monk shrugged. "Forgot to tell you. When I was in that telephone booth, I called the shyster. He's gettin' on the next Tulsa-bound plane."

Pat sighed. "That means he should be here about this time tomorrow night. That's almost twenty-four hours from now. We're notorious now. What must we do in order to stay free that long?"

"No place to hide. We'll slip over to the Osage wilderness. They'll never find us there. That's where the local badmen go when they're on the lam."

"Well, Pretty Boy Monk," said Pat archly, "I'll admit it's better than spending the night in the slammer, but I'd like to be doing something constructive while I'm lamming."

They were walking along, struggling with their predicament, when suddenly ahead of them in the dim light appeared three men in plainclothes.

Their first thoughts were that these were detectives. They stood very tall in the shadows.

"Hold up, Pat," breathed Monk. "Looks like plainclothes cops."

"Do we raise our hands and surrender?" hissed Pat.

"If they really are cops, we should," said Monk. "But what if they're not?"

"Are you asking me?" questioned Pat.

"I'm just thinkin' out loud," admitted Monk uneasily, and then hoisted his long hairy arms. Pat copied the action.

While they were raising their arms in surrender, bright flashes of saffron exploded from the area of the midriffs of the faceless shadows blocking their way.

Gun thunder made the hot evening air quake.

The first blast of bullets was aimed in the direction of Monk Mayfair, who made an ugly *ugh!* sound and was spun around and driven back against a brick wall with sufficient force that the air went out of his lungs with a great gusty *whoosh!*

Pat yelled, "You boys aren't police!"

The shadowy figures did not respond to that accusation. Instead, they directed the muzzles of their smoking revolvers toward Pat Savage. Hard callused fingers began squeezing triggers as Monk slid down the brick wall to a seated position, a stunned expression on his wide features.

As he did so, his furry hands clapped at his clothes as if seeking to staunch the wounds that had brought him low.

Chapter XII

PLAN SINISTER

AFTER PAT SAVAGE and Monk Mayfair had departed the Gusher Hotel, Vina Hawks Nansen hurried to the window and attempted to watch them depart.

Her attractive face had turned pale with strain, and her cocoa-colored eyes held a frightened look, like that of a trapped animal.

As she watched anxiously, the door to the bedroom opened and out stepped a tall figure. A man. He was the bluff sort, firm of feature and steady of eye.

"I do not see them," she murmured, not turning.

A male voice, rich and a baritone, ventured, "No doubt they left the back way, inasmuch as they are fugitives from the law."

Vina turned, flung back harshly, "But they are innocent! You know that!"

"You did the right thing, Vina. There was no other way. Scandal cannot attach itself to you. Not with the bright and shining future that lies before us."

Vina took several halting steps and sank into the divan, burying her face in her hands. Her shoulders shook strongly.

"What future have I now? All seems so black that I despair."

"There, there, you did what you had to do. In order for the Chief to release your brother from thralldom."

Hot tears welled up in her eyes. "How was Ben dragged into this in the first place? I do not understand."

"I have been attempting to learn that myself. But the man I serve is reticent."

Vina's face came up and it was working with a kind of stiff horror. She jumped to her feet, making fists like baskets of delicate bone.

"The man you serve!" she blazed. "How can you call him that? He's not a man, but a devil. He does not even seem to be human. The things he does to decent human beings are beyond the pale. And you—you serve him? I cannot understand that."

The bluff man said patronizingly, "It will become clear to you over time. Very clear. But explanations must wait. Unpleasant things must be done. The master plan of Standing Scorpion is vast in scope. When it begins, he will levy tribute from all of Tulsa. The hour for this operation to commence is very soon— merely a matter of a day or two. With the funds raised, he will expand to nearby towns and cities, and before long all of Oklahoma will be under his thumb. All the oil wealth of this state will feed his lofty ambitions. Do not think for a moment that political power alone drives him. Tulsa is just the beginning and Oklahoma the base from which he will expand in all directions. Yes, it is a grandiose scheme that black gold will fund, but before he is done, Standing Scorpion will be recognized nationally as a great personage."

A strange fire burned in the flinty eyes of the man who spoke. He was, in contrast to young Vina Hawks Nansen, a mature individual. Silver touched his temples like budding wings. The face they framed was square and thickset. No doubt he had been exceedingly handsome when a young man. The passing years had diminished, but not obliterated, that fact.

"When you talk that way," said Vina Nansen, "it is as if you were another person entirely. Not the man I know. Certainly not the man I love. Were not the life of my brother hanging by a thread, I would break our engagement and flee from your side forever."

Publisher Morgan Marrs turned solicitous. "But where would you flee to, my dear? You can leave Tulsa, and even Oklahoma, but in time the power of Standing Scorpion will spread to all coasts and borders of this great nation. There will be no place to hide. So put that notion out of your mind. We are privileged to be small cogs in the building of a magnificent machine. A machine wielding political power and great influence. Trust me, I know. As publisher of the *Tulsa Trumpet*, I understand power in all of its permutations. That is why I am a willing servant to Standing Scorpion. A man of his stature will need lieutenants, and they must not be small men. His Indian braves serve him well, but they are thugs and cutthroats. Standing Scorpion needs sophisticated white men to be his instruments of influence. I count myself as the first among what will be a legion of advisors and power brokers."

"Oh, Morgan, I hardly know you now," sobbed Vina.

"When the time comes, you will put your pen to the task of painting word pictures to convince the general public that Standing Scorpion, whoever he may be, represents the future of this great nation."

Hearing these words, the blonde sank back to the divan and began turning her engagement ring around on her finger, saying, "My brother. Tell me about Ben. When will he be released?"

"Soon. Soon. It was an unfortunate coincidence that he fell into the hands of Standing Scorpion's braves. Ben Nansen was an out-of-work tool dresser, and he applied for work at the wrong place. It is fortunate that you were his sister, otherwise I would not have learned of his plight and gotten word to Standing Scorpion to release him."

Vina Hawks Nansen looked up. A dull light was in her chocolate-brown eyes now. "That is another thing I do not understand, Morgan. When Ben called me upon his release, he claimed to have escaped on his own hook. Men were searching for him."

"Yes," said Morgan Marrs. "Searching for him in order to restore him to you. It was an unfortunate chain of events that permitted your brother to escape on the eve of what would have been his release and restoration to his family."

"What family?" questioned Vina. "There is only Ben and me now that my mother is gone. As for my father...." Her voice trailed off as she shuddered uncontrollably.

"Do not fret about that, Vina, my dear," soothed the other. "After we are married, we will start a new family."

"How can you think about such a thing at a time like this? When my world is turning around me and I feel as if I am sinking into quicksand?"

As the woman spoke, her fiancé, publisher Morgan Marrs, loitered by the open window. Surreptitiously, he stuck out a hand, and flashed a disc in the moonlight.

This disc was about the size of a half-dollar, and silvery. Burned into its center was the many-legged symbol of the southwestern vinegarroon—a whip scorpion. This was done in red enamel.

In the bright Oklahoma moonlight, the scarlet scorpion shape showed clearly and distinctly to a huddled knot of men who were loitering across the street from the Gusher Hotel.

Seeing this sign, they melted down the street, intent and purposeful.

Turning from the window, Morgan Marrs announced, "I must be going now, Vina. I think you should stay at this hotel tonight. You'll be safer here. I will have a man guard you."

"I don't need any guard!" insisted the blonde.

"If those two easterners return, they could compromise your reputation," Marrs said solicitously. "They are fugitives, after all."

"What about fixing the charges against them? You promised you would try to do that."

"I *will* try. They must be taken alive. That part is up to them. Remember that, Vina. My hands are tied if they do not respect Oklahoma law."

Stepping outside the door, Morgan Marrs walked three doors down, knocked once sharply, and the face of an Osage Indian appeared in the opening door. He stood well over six feet in height. His nose was a broken beak in a flat face that had seen a great deal of physical punishment.

"Tall Turkey," he said. "I wish you to guard Vina through the night. See that no one disturbs her. Do you understand?"

"Is it the will of Standing Scorpion?"

"Yes, it is the will of your war chief. He does not wish any harm to come to my future wife. For she will be an important part of the new order."

Behind Tall Turkey, a hot breeze was coming in through an open hotel room window. And ordinary sounds of the city at night entered. The blare of honking car horns, radios blasting raucous music. Other discordant night sounds.

Mixed in with the common noises, there was a brief rattle of gunfire.

Both Morgan Marrs and Tall Turkey heard this. Tall Turkey grunted, "Sounds like gunshots."

The bluff publisher nodded curtly. "The Vinegarroon braves of Chief Standing Scorpion appear to have caught up with their quarry. There will be no further interference from the likes of Patricia Savage and Monk Mayfair."

Tall Turkey had the stolid expression of a Plains Indian. It did not flicker very much, but to one accustomed to the subtle alteration of facial expressions among his breed, it spoke volumes.

"That means Doc Savage might make trouble," he commented.

"I happen to know Doc Savage is out of the country. This has been reported in the newspapers. There will be no interference from Doc Savage until word reaches him."

Tall Turkey looked relieved.

"Now, if you will excuse me, I'm going to see to the disposal of the bodies."

Chapter XIII

COMPLICATED KNOT

PAT SAVAGE WATCHED Monk Mayfair floundering about in the dirty Tulsa alleyway, beating at his bullet-riddled clothes with rust-red paws.

To anyone who did not know the hairy chemist and his ways, it would seem as if Monk was engaged in a frantic and futile effort to put out the smoking bullet holes that perforated his loud coat jacket. Wisps of smoke were arising from the myriad points where the hot slugs had entered, but that was not the object of Monk's frantic flailing.

Pat Savage attempted two things at the same time—one of which was not noticed by the shadowy gunmen who were redirecting their weapons at her tense form.

Sealing her lips tightly, she held her breath. Then Pat scooted backward, throwing herself behind a trio of ashcans which were heavy with the powdery residue of a dozen coal furnaces.

The steel drums might or might not stop the bullets that were about to arrive, but even those that punctured the shells might lose their deadly force when they embedded themselves in the ash. The stuff was dense.

Pat's sudden gymnastics caught their assailants unawares. But one managed to squeeze off a snap shot. It struck one of the ashcans, knocking it over, spewing cold ashes in all directions.

Pat shifted behind the other cans, and placed both hands against their steel hardness, hoping against hope that she could keep them upright if she desired to live out the evening.

She continued holding her breath while Monk made smacking sounds with his flopping hands. There came a tiny sound, a kind of a crunching noise.

A second shot was fired, but it struck brick, producing flying chips, some of which tangled in Pat's bronze hair. Then, without another sound, the three men with big guns collapsed in the street, one by one.

One made a dull thud. Another fell backward with such violent suddenness that the back of his head collided against concrete with an ugly crunching noise. The third assailant simply twisted half about, collapsing as if he had been deflated somehow.

Pat peered up from behind the top rim of one ashcan and absorbed the sorry condition of her erstwhile foes.

Grinning, she rushed over to Monk. "Are you hurt?"

Monk growled. It was a very long and exceedingly fierce growl.

"Bulletproof vest stopped every one of them," he coughed out. "But I feel like I've been kicked by five or six mules."

"Let me help you up," offered Pat. But even her lithe strength was insufficient to hoist the burly Monk up from a seated position. The simian chemist weighed two hundred and sixty pounds and, if he could not get back on his feet of his own volition, the hairy chemist would not be moved until impelled to do so.

"That knockout gas worked like a charm," she murmured. "I held my breath until it became harmless."

Monk muttered as he sat there in a dazed state. "I couldn't remember which pocket I had the glass capsules in. I was carryin' them loose in case we got captured again. So I held my breath and beat at every pocket until I struck pay dirt."

The contents of the fragile capsules consisted of a potent chemical solution which quickly vaporized upon release and almost as rapidly combined with ordinary air to lose all potency. It was ideal for situations such as this one. Monk and Pat had only to hold their breaths for the requisite interval while the gas did its swift work on their unsuspecting assailants.

Pat regarded their vanquished foes sprawled in the gloom of the alley. "Well, those three are sleeping like Mary's little lambs. Let's take a look at them."

It took several minutes before Monk was in a condition to lever himself up on his bandy legs, and he had to use the brick wall for support until he got his senses organized.

"Holdin' my breath while the wind was being knocked out of me," he complained, "is an experience I'll try and skip next time."

Monk produced a flashlight, a spring-generator affair that he always carried. He gave the generator crank a few turns, then thumbed the button. A blinding ray of light fanned out, and they examined the faces of the sleeping trio in its intense glow.

"These boys look like they're straight off the Osage reservation," he said. "So they probably ain't plainclothesmen. Gotta be Standing Scorpion's killers. See how tall they all are—like the ones that grabbed us a while back? Osage grow taller than your average red man."

Pat knelt and began fishing out wallets and examining driver's licenses.

"This one is named Clyde Bottle. This other one here calls himself Billy Rae Eagle. Last one is Sonny Shield."

"Osage bucks," muttered Monk. "Let's grab their rods, since we don't have anything of our own."

Pat favored the homely chemist a dubious glance. "Are you crazy? There is no telling who these punks have killed recently. We don't want any more of our fingerprints on strange pistols, do we?"

Monk scratched at the rusty bristles atop his bullet skull.

"I guess we don't, at that," he mumbled.

"You must have struck the back of your head against the wall when those fellows blasted you," observed Pat. "You should know better than that."

"I am feelin' kind of dizzy," admitted the hairy chemist.

"Let me take a look at you."

Monk opened the skirts in his coat, and Pat unbuttoned his broad vest, revealing an undervest of light chain mail. The cloth vest had been punctured in spots, but the chain mail beneath it had successfully stopped every slug.

Reaching in with two slim fingers, Pat dug out one flattened pellet of lead and flung it away.

"You'll live," she pronounced. "But I wouldn't want to have your bruises."

Monk shook his head as if to clear it, and his eyes, which had a glazed look, began to show a clearer light.

"Those gunshots might've alerted somebody," he said. "We need to mosey along."

"Agreed. But to where?"

Before Monk could reply, around the corner of the building behind which they stood, the engine of a motorcar could be heard, followed by doors opening and clapping shut. Determined footsteps approached boldly.

One bluff voice said roughly, "Open up the trunk. We'll dump the bodies in there."

Pat looked at Monk and asked, "Whose bodies?"

"Ours, most likely. These Osage lads musta had a crew in reserve, waitin' to hear the sound of gunshots. Come on!"

One of Monk's long arms shot out, took Pat by the elbow and hauled her deeper into the darkness of the alleyway. They walked briskly and tried to make no sound.

"What if they catch up with us?" wondered Pat.

Monk guffawed, "Not a chance! When they find those boys layin' back there, they're gonna have to stuff them in the trunk to cover their tracks. It will keep 'em busy for a while. We gotta find some place to lay low."

Pat snapped her fingers suddenly. "I know! I'll call Harold Manton. He might have an idea."

Monk made helpless hand gestures. "You'll have to make the call. I'm as conspicuous as a horseshoe crab on a birthday cake."

They moved along the litter-strewn alleyways, crossing streets only where necessary. The occasional police radio car swept by. Each time one did, they froze in the shadows, yet somehow succeeded in not being spotted.

"This notorious outlaw business is for the birds," Pat complained.

"You'll get used to it," said Monk philosophically. "In my time, I've been wanted in half a dozen states."

Covering her luxurious bronze hair in a kerchief she fished out of a pocket, Pat found an all-night drugstore, slipped inside a telephone booth and asked the central operator to connect her with the office of Harold Manton in the Trumpet Building.

"Oil editor Manton," the man announced when he picked up.

"Three of Standing Scorpion's Osages just tried to rub us out," said Pat in her best gangster voice.

"You're still on the loose?"

"No telling for how long," whispered Pat.

"I'm impressed. There's a police dragnet out for you both."

"We noticed," said Pat wryly. "We're dodging and ducking our best, but it may be just a matter of time until they run us to ground."

"If you can find South Quincy Street, my place is there. I'll give you the number. I've got a spare key hidden in a tomato can buried on the south side by the tomato plants. You may let yourself in, but if you get caught, you're going to have to say that you broke in. And I'll have to prefer charges."

"Breaking and entering sounds like an easy rap to beat compared to what we're up against," said Pat. "But thanks."

"Before you go, one item of interest. That building where you were being held? It's owned by this very sheet."

"The *Trumpet?*"

"It used to be rented, but that market dried up," stated Manton. "I plan on asking my publisher all about it later."

"Good luck," said Pat. She hung up.

DRIFTING out of the drugstore, she slipped around the corner, then found Monk Mayfair waiting. Pat relayed the gist of the conversation she'd just had.

"Mr. Manton is a swell egg," she averred, concluding her account.

Monk grinned from ear to ear. "He's an Oklahoma boy, like me. Guys like him are one of the reasons Pretty Boy Floyd got away with all that bank robbin' as long as he did. Oklahomans don't turn rat on other Oklahomans."

"I hope you know where South Quincy Street is."

"Sure," said Monk, "but gettin' there will be a chore. We might wanna split up, in case one of us doesn't make it."

"If you don't mind," countered Pat, "I'd rather stick tight until we have to split up. I know the boys in blue are just doing their jobs, but the menfolk around here are pretty loose with their lead. And I'm not wearing anything bulletproof."

Considering the situation a bit, Monk said, "We can't make it on foot. A taxicab is out of the question." Then his tiny eyes narrowed cannily. "Follow me."

Monk led them to the maze that constituted the back side of the central Tulsa business district, and they moved through a residential neighborhood for a little bit until Monk came to a small used car lot that lacked a great deal in the way of class.

The small lot was crammed with jalopies and flivvers of the previous decade, and Monk managed to pry open the door of one old charger and get behind the steering wheel, where he began fiddling with the ignition wires.

The hairy chemist got the engine going so rapidly that Pat was astonished. Not so astonished that she failed to rush around to the other side and climb into the passenger seat.

While Monk tooled the unwieldy machine out of the lot without lights, Pat declared, "I didn't know you knew how to do that!"

"I told you I was kind of a hellion when I was a kid, didn't I?" grinned Monk.

The ancient engine sounded like a coffee grinder. It desperately needed tuning. But the flivver ran well enough, and they got out onto the street. Only when Monk felt it safe to do so did he switch on the headlamps.

The motor occasionally missed on one cylinder, but otherwise did not balk.

Pat said, "Harold Manton discovered that the old building in Broken Arrow is owned by the Tulsa Trumpet Corporation. It had been a rental property until the local economy went bust."

Monk's small eyes narrowed. "Wonder how that hooks up with anything?"

"Mr. Manton intends to ask his publisher that same question. But it would explain why Vina Hawks Nansen knew her way around the place—but not what she was doing there in the first place."

"The finger of suspicion is sure pointin' in some funny directions," muttered Monk.

They soon reached South Quincy, and found the correct house number. It was in the eleven hundred block. A neat brick bungalow of modest size but solid in appearance.

Pulling into the driveway, they slipped out, went around back and commenced rooting among the tomato plants, which had gotten quite high.

Their excavations soon bore metallic fruit. The tomato can became visible in the moonlight. This Monk unearthed. Shaking out the dirt caused a brass key to come tumbling out.

"Jackpot!" Monk enthused. He led Pat to the back door, and found that the key fit perfectly. Passing through the kitchen, they went to the parlor and sat there in the darkness, contemplating their worsening predicament.

"This," announced Pat, "is turning into a Gordian knot if I ever found one."

Monk observed. "Knots are meant to be unraveled. I prefer to use my teeth. If I can't pull the strands apart, I can sometimes bite through them."

"A Gordian knot is meant to be untangled, not chewed apart," reminded Pat.

Monk beamed in the darkness, saying, "I kinda like to use the gifts that nature gave me."

They found the console radio and turned it on, fished around until they got a news broadcast and, settling into comfortable chairs, listened in the darkness.

A running commentary by an excited announcer indicated that the police dragnet had expanded beyond Tulsa, but no sign of the accused killers, Monk Mayfair and Patricia Savage, had been uncovered. It was assumed by the chief of detectives that the two had fled the city environs. The search had been expanded to neighboring townships, and the police were confident that the two fugitives would be found and brought back for justice before dawn broke.

Although the radio volume was set low, it was loud enough to carry through the closed windows of the bungalow. Prudently, Pat chose not to open the casements despite the oppressive heat of the mid-summer night.

When footsteps rattled on the concrete steps leading up to the front door, Pat and Monk both lifted out of their chairs and craned their heads around, looking to see who it was.

The window blinds were only partly shuttered, and it was possible to discern something of the front of the home.

Monk caught a glimpse of a thin-limbed white-coated figure coming to the front door, but he moved out of view before the homely chemist could make out much of him.

Pat asked quietly, "Manton?"

"Couldn't see 'im clearly," replied Monk tensely.

The doorbell buzzed and the noise further jarred them, for they had been waiting for the sound of a key entering the lock, not the buzzing of a caller.

"What do we do?" asked Pat.

"I dunno," croaked Monk.

When the doorbell rang a second time and they still had not moved, the unknown caller began berating the door with his knuckles. An assertive voice called out, "I know you're in there. I can hear the radio. Open up, Harold."

Pat said quickly, "Slip into the kitchen. I'll handle this."

Monk stared at her as if she were contemplating jumping off a tall building.

"Go ahead," she urged. "Scat!"

Rearranging the kerchief masking her distinctive bronze hair, Pat snapped on a light as she glided to the front door.

Opening it boldly, she greeted, "Hello, who are you?"

The man who stood at the door was tall and sleekly dressed. Everything about him was lean—features, torso, limbs. Even his nose and eyes were narrow. He wore a seersucker suit, and a Panama hat that nearly matched the summery suit. A cigarette dangled from his lower lip.

Noticing Pat's pretty face, he essayed a friendly smile and remarked, "I might ask the same of you...."

"Well, you are the caller," countered Pat.

The man took off his hat, displaying thick brown hair that was shiny with some hair cream product. He introduced himself, saying, "Name's Ichabod Golden. Call me Ike. Friend of Harry's. I figured he would be home by now, and I wanted to share some gossip."

"Never heard of you," said Pat flatly.

"And Harold never mentioned you to me, Miss—"

"Gertrude Periwinkle," Pat said quickly. "Harold's cousin from back east. House sitting for a spell. What's your racket?"

"The same as Harold's. May I come in?" And he brushed past Pat as if the invitation had already been extended.

Tossing his hat toward a coat tree, the breezy fellow managed to hang it expertly from more than a dozen feet. It was an accomplishment that caused him to grin in a self-satisfied manner that made Pat uncharacteristically want to punch him in the face. Ike Golden was like that.

Having no polite alternative, Pat closed the door and asked, "I'm taking you for a newspaperman."

"That's very good, sugar," said Ike Golden, displaying pearly teeth that went with his white suit and hat. "I cover the oil beat for the *Daily Globe*. That's the *Trumpet*'s rival in town. But you probably know that."

"Peculiar, two rival reporters being so friendly," ventured Pat.

"Not so much," said Golden, throwing himself down into an easy chair and crossing his legs as if to make himself at home. "You see, if you're a reporter in Tulsa, you either work at the *Trumpet* or the *Globe*. And if you're on the outs with one editor, you can always walk across town and go work for the other. Me, I've been going back and forth between the Trumpet Building and the *Globe* offices for the last dozen years."

"I see," said Pat slowly. "What did you say was the purpose of your call?"

Golden's cigarette traveled from one corner of his mouth to the other, as if possessing a mind of its own. Smoke curled about his lean features. "This town is hot tonight—and I don't mean the weather. You got that Grabber Daly business blowing up. Now you have trouble at the *Trumpet*, or that's the rumor anyway. Something to do with the brother of the publisher's fiancée. Now I hear that a couple of Doc Savage's associates from back east are in hot water over the death of a police officer.

Been running around all day trying to get a line on this complicated web of intrigue, but every time I get hold of a strand, it just sort of melts in my fingers—if you know what I mean."

"No, I do not," said Pat frostily. "And I'm not sure when Harold will be home, by the way. Might be a long wait."

Ike Golden looked as if he did not have a concern in the world. "I've had a hard day, and I don't mind taking my ease. Chances are old Harold will fill my ears with more than I can handle." He smiled. "Should be worth the wait."

"Suit yourself," said Pat. "I was just listening to the radio."

"In the dark, I perceive. Do you like the dark?"

"It's cooler in the dark," returned Pat lightly. "Had you never noticed?"

"If you yearned for a nice breeze, you might've thrown open a window."

"Good idea," said Pat, going to a front casement. "I think I will." She had to walk around and behind the varnished end table in order to do so. As she moved toward the window sash, her golden eyes—which she had been keeping squeezed rather tight so their unusual hue was not so noticeable—went to one of the polished legs.

A telephone on a stand suddenly rang. Once. Twice. Three times.

Her eyes still fixed on the table leg, Pat hesitated.

Behind her back, Ichabod Golden stood up, fished a pale hand into his jacket coat and pulled out a stubby .38-caliber revolver that didn't look very large or impressive in his fist.

He aimed the weapon at the center of Pat Savage's back, approximately in the middle of her spinal column.

Without a word of warning, he squeezed the trigger slowly and carefully.

Chapter XIV

CLEVER WOMAN

A RATTLE OF gunshots came through the open window of the two-room hotel room suite where Vina Hawks Nansen passed the evening. An understandably nervous reaction caused the blonde woman to start and stand up from her chair.

Her fiancé, Morgan Marrs, had departed only a few minutes before, but not before introducing her to a rather bony and elongated Indian who called himself Tall Turkey.

"Those sound like gunshots," she said anxiously.

Seated in another chair, silently reading the sports section of the *Tulsa Trumpet*, Tall Turkey grunted, "Firecrackers. Sit down. Do not be nervous. All will be well."

Another report cannonaded and echoed outside, and this sound seemed to stiffen the spine of the blonde's previously vapid behavior.

Lunging for the telephone on a stand, she cried out, "I must call the police. Someone could be in trouble!"

Tall Turkey had been stolid and impassive in the Indian way as he guarded his boss' fiancée, but now red rage leapt into his dark eyes. He launched himself across the hotel room parlor, seizing hold of the instrument, violently tearing it from the woman's hand.

"How dare you?" she shrilled.

"Mr. Marrs says to keep you entertained and out of trouble. I cannot allow you to call the police."

"You red-faced roughneck!" Vina yelled. "I'll have you fired for this!"

Ignoring her, Tall Turkey reached down and wrenched the wires free of the ringer box and flung the tangle away.

The telephone was of the European type, with receiver and transmitter in one piece, and the instrument landed in the bedroom beyond the open connecting door. It rolled under the bed with a discordant clatter.

"Now you call no one!" he snarled fiercely.

Vina fixed him with angry, accusing eyes. "You're a beast. I don't know where my future husband found you. But the very sight of you makes me sick to my stomach."

The Osage did not take kindly to these words. His eyes began to cross a little, as if he were fighting back a rage that was building within him. Up until this point, Tall Turkey had been an unemotional companion. But now he resembled a human volcano on the verge of erupting.

From a pocket, the Osage produced a wicked-looking knife. It had a horn handle and its blade was like a stainless steel fang. It looked exceedingly sharp.

"My ancestors used to employ knives such as this one to take scalps and cut throats. Do not push me too far, woman. The blood of my ancestors runs very deep in my veins. If I lose control of my civilized parts, I will have your scalp and taste your blood, and surely be fired for my transgression. I prefer to hold onto my job."

Horror overspread the face of Vina Hawks Nansen, and she retreated from the threatening man, half-stumbled over a wooden chair, and suddenly seized it, lifting it high in such a way that the four legs of the chair were directed at the approaching Indian.

She had read that this was the best way to defend oneself from an attacker armed with a knife. A knife wielder would have a hard time getting past the chair and its projecting legs, if it was wielded properly.

"You stay away from me!" she yelled fiercely. "I'll brain you with this. I'll break it over your stupid skull!"

The vehemence of the blonde woman's threats seemed to pierce the red cloud of rage that was building up in Tall Turkey's brain. He seemingly shook off his mounting ire. His menacing stance melted away, and dark eyes lost their malevolent spark.

Thoughtfully, Tall Turkey pocketed the knife, slowly retreated to his chair, very calmly unfolded the newspaper and resumed reading the sports section as if nothing untoward had transpired.

Vina Hawks Nansen blinked twice, realized that the violent episode was over, and carefully replaced the chair on the carpet. Without a word, she retreated into the bedroom, firmly closing the connecting door, for she wished to hear the squeaking of the hinges should Tall Turkey dare enter.

She flung herself onto the bed and stared up at the ceiling. Slow tears began brimming from her brown orbs, and she wondered how her life had careened into such an unthinkable and precarious position.

After a while, contemplating the ceiling failed to clarify the situation in her mind, so Vina abruptly sat up, realizing that sleep would not come under the circumstances.

A small dresser crowded one end in the bedroom, and she went toward it, stared long and hard into the mirror as if its quicksilver reflective surface could hold some answers. But they did not. She saw her pale, bloodless features staring back at her, and it was as if Vina Hawks Nansen was looking at a stranger.

Distractedly, the blonde moved about the bedroom. Suddenly, she noticed wires running along the baseboard molding. They had been stapled there to hold them in place. She realized that these were in fact the telephone wires which led to the instrument that had been set up on the other side of the wall.

Remembering that the telephone had landed under the bed, she got down on hands and knees and, endeavoring to make no sound, reached under and fished it out.

Replacing the receiver on its cradle, she set the instrument on the carpet and sat down next to the wires.

Employing a nail file, she peeled the soft casing until she exposed the copper wiring. This was the electrical connection carrying juice through the telephone line.

On the other side of this wall, the frayed wires had been pulled free of the ringer box. These loose strands might be carefully reconnected by twisting them, Vina realized, and she endeavored to apply this tangle of copper to the exposed wires to test out her desperate theory.

She used the heel of the shoe that she removed from one foot to keep the wires pressed together so the current would flow back into the instrument.

Scarcely believing that the trick could be accomplished, Vina carefully lifted the instrument, and brought it to her ear.

A gasp escaped the woman's pale lips when she heard the distinct buzzing hum of a dial tone. It sizzled and popped, indicating the fragility of the reestablished connection.

Inserting a trembling finger into the "0" for operator aperture of the dial, she gave it a spin.

Almost immediately, there came a single ring and a voice announced crisply, "Hotel operator. How may I help you?"

"This is Miss Nansen in Room Three-ten," she said breathlessly. "Connect me with Mr. Harold Manton on South Quincy Street. Oh, please hurry!"

Although she whispered the words, the urgency of her situation made her voice shrill and this carried through the half-open door. The urgent syllables reached the alert ears of Tall Turkey who, upon hearing them, leapt from his easy chair, and crossed the room with grim determination. He flung wide the connecting door.

Dark eyes widened in amazement at the sight of Vina Hawks Nansen seated on the carpet, whispering into the telephone instrument that should have been entirely disabled, but obviously was not.

A weird rage came into the Osage's eyes and he fell upon her, yelling loudly, "I'll fix you! I will salivate you once and for all."

Whether Vina Hawks Nansen understood the meaning of the word or not, she let out a piercing scream that could be heard a block away.

No one hearing that shrill outcry would ever forget it.

Chapter XV

ANOTHER SCARLET SCORPION

AS PAT SAVAGE'S hand reached for the telephone, she kept her gaze on the varnished leg of the table. The table leg was so brightly polished it acted like a narrow mirror. This property had previously caught her attention, and now she employed it artfully.

Pat had been keeping an eye on Ike Golden seated behind her. She did not know whether to trust the man, but her intuition suggested otherwise. Pat always paid attention to her intuition. It had gotten her out of more than one scrape in the past.

Lifting the receiver to one ear, she pitched her voice low and asked, "Hello?"

The familiar voice of Vina Hawks Nansen came out of the diaphragm, punctuated by the popping and clicking of a bad telephone line.

In a voice twisted by fear almost to the point of unrecognizability, the blonde woman was pleading, "Please help me, Mr. Manton. I did not know who else to call. I fear for my life!"

Then another voice, cruel and masculine, snarled, "I'm going to salivate you! Do you know what that means?"

The resulting scream of shrill horror almost caused Pat to take her eyes off the varnished table leg. Fortunately for the bronze-haired girl, she retained her presence of mind.

She saw Ike Golden push himself out of the chair, reach a hand into his coat and produce a stubby nickeled revolver that gleamed in the lamp light.

Pat spun, then flung the telephone instrument at the man.

The Bakelite receiver failed to reach Golden's face, for it was arrested by its electrical cord, but Golden flinched in reaction, and his finger jerked on the trigger. The snapping bullet went wild, punching a hole in the ceiling.

Monk Mayfair came charging out of the kitchen, roaring his rage while Pat whirled smartly, took hold of the man's gun wrist, twisted deftly, and performed a judo maneuver that relieved him of his gun, his balance and, once he struck his head on the carpet, his ordinary senses.

Monk came to a skidding halt, blurted, "You didn't leave nothin' for me to do!"

Pat said rather superciliously, "He appears dazed, but not knocked out. You might remedy that particular omission."

"You wanna question him?"

Pat shook her head violently, "That was Vina Nansen on the phone. Sounds like she's in trouble. We better get over to her hotel."

"If you say so," said Monk, leaning down and applying his rusty knuckles to the point of Ike Golden's jaw. The knuckles landed with great force, and Golden's head rocked to one side. It was instantly clear that he would not be coming to any time in the foreseeable future.

Not wishing to leave anything to chance, Monk strode over to the drapes, pulled them down and energetically tore them into long strips, which he used swiftly to bind Ichabod Golden's wrists and ankles.

"That oughta hold you," he said with satisfaction. "Let's skedaddle, Pat."

They slipped out the back, got into their jalopy, and drove at the best speed possible for the Gusher Hotel, taking care not to run any stoplights or attract undue attention.

The fact that the machine was old and dilapidated no doubt aided their subterfuge. Fugitives preferred autos equipped with finely-tuned engines with which to make their escapes.

Beside that fact, according to the radio reports, the dragnet had spread outside of Tulsa. The law assumed that the now-notorious duo were no longer to be found within city limits.

They reached the Gusher, availed themselves of the back entrance and slipped up the stairs to the third floor.

Room 310 proved not to be locked. In fact, the door was open a crack, as if whoever had departed had fled in too great a haste to properly close and lock it.

Pushing ahead, Monk said to Pat, "I'll go first."

Given that Monk was wearing a bulletproof vest and Pat did not, the golden-eyed girl did not object.

The apish chemist slipped in, discovered that the light was on, and made a swift reconnoiter of the modest suite.

He found the telephone in the corner of the bedroom, and its condition told him at least part of the story.

Monk called out, "It's safe to come in, Pat."

The bronze girl entered, saw that the place was in a state of wild disarray.

Monk explained, "Somebody ripped out the telephone, but she managed to rewire it. Looks like she got caught in the act."

"Abducted?"

"What do you think?"

"I don't know what to think," admitted Pat unhappily. "A tough-sounding man's voice threatened to murder Vina. But I don't see any blood. Do you?"

Monk looked about. Animal-like, he sniffed the air, but decided he didn't detect any sanguinary odors.

Reaching into a pocket, the hairy chemist produced his spring-generator flashlight. Unscrewing the lens, he replaced the bulb with an ultra-violet filament. Reassembling the flashlight, Monk doused the ceiling lights and ran the invisible black-light beam around both rooms.

"If somebody washed up any murder blood, the black-light ray will bring out traces," he explained for Pat's benefit.

"They'd have to be mighty fast workers to do all that in the short time it took us to get here," reminded Pat.

The ultra-violet beam brought out no latent signs of vital fluid, however.

Monk shut off the flashlight and pocketed it.

"No blood and no body," mused Pat. "So where could she be?"

"Beats me," admitted Monk helplessly.

"Fetch me the telephone," requested Pat. "We might look up her fiancé. Even if he doesn't know, he would want to know what happened here."

"Good thinkin'," said Monk, reaching down with his overlong arms and picking up the instrument. He got the front desk, and said, "Get me an outside operator."

"Yes, sir," the hotel operator said crisply. When the phone company operator came on the line, he asked, "I want the address of Morgan Marrs. Make it snappy."

The address was quickly surrendered. Monk thanked the operator, then hung up.

"Guy's got a penthouse suite at the Metro Hotel."

"We're not going back to the Metro?" asked Pat. "We're known there! In fact, we're notorious!"

"Still got your room key?"

Pat fished around in a pocket and produced it.

Monk nodded. "Maybe we'll stop by and collect some of our stuff. Since we're fightin' kinda empty-handed right now."

"I like your thinking," said Pat brightly.

The flivver took them to the Metro, and they parked two blocks away, and around the side street. By now the hour was very late. Midnight had come and gone. There were few pedestrians. And even less automobile traffic.

Night was tolerably hot, yet slightly unpleasant. Their clothes were sticking to their skins, and both Pat and Monk felt the need of a cooling shower as they quitted their machine.

Approaching the lobby of the Metro, they heard the discordant sound of a flute.

Pat paused and asked, "Where have I heard that noise before?"

"Back when this all started—that time Ben Nansen interrupted our lunch. Panhandler was playin' a flute."

They hesitated before rounding the block. Pat slipped ahead and peered around the corner. There on the sidewalk squatted an Osage Indian dolefully piping away at his flute. A woven basket for loose change sat before his crossed legs. Both man and basket squatted upon a vermilion Indian blanket.

"I think that's the same panhandler," Pat said, turning.

"Lemme look," said Monk, shoving forward.

The homely chemist sidled up to the corner as Pat faded back to allow him peeping room.

The panhandling Indian could be seen in the light of the streetlamp, and his profile had that dry sandstone impassivity of his race.

"Don't look like the same bird," decided Monk. "The other one had a droopy eye."

Pat inserted, "I wonder what he's doing panhandling after midnight? It's very suspicious."

"And how," said Monk. Then his attention shifted toward an arriving sedan. The sedan pulled up before the entrance of the Metro Hotel. Due to the late hour, there was no doorman on duty, given that hotel guests were not much inclined to be out and about so late. The city of Tulsa closed early.

The driver's door came open and a man emerged from behind the wheel. He was tall and rangy, and the wide-brimmed hat on his head failed to conceal the carroty hair and open features of Harold Manton, oil editor of the *Tulsa Trumpet*.

"It's Manton," squeaked Monk. "What's he doin' here so late?"

Giving no heed to the panhandling flute-playing Osage Indian, Harold Manton strode confidently up to the glass doors of the Metro Hotel.

Pulling open one of the doors, he stepped in and, as Pat and Monk watched, the eyes of the Osage Indian followed him. As those eyes tracked the entering man, the flute moved with the rotating head and the sound of its music suddenly went still. The Indian's cheeks puffed out.

Harold Manton was holding the door open as he thrust his rangy body into the lobby, but suddenly he staggered, took a step forward, then two steps backward. Abruptly, he was sprawled out on his back while the heavy glass-and-brass door attempted to close but could not.

For Harold Manton's long body was blocking it. As they watched, burning crimson in the moonlight, a bloody sprawl of eight jointed legs, with matching pincers appeared. A downward squiggle of a thing suggested a thin red tail.

Like an unfolding flower of Hell, the crimson thing spread in all directions until it covered the entirety of the man's face.

The brand of the scarlet scorpion!

"For the luvva Mike!" squeaked Monk, fingering the brown mark on his own features. "That wasn't there a second ago!"

Chapter XVI

SINISTER SKEINS

HEARING MONK MAYFAIR'S grunt of astonishment, Pat Savage ducked her head around the homely chemist's burly body and wondered, "What wasn't there a second ago?"

And she saw it. The scarlet scorpion on Harold Manton's face. It lay there like a splotch of blood that had congealed into the semblance of a venomous creature. The long red stinger curled around his jaw line in a particularly gruesome way.

"What happened?" Pat asked huskily.

"I don't know," admitted Monk. "He threw open the door, then he staggered back. I didn't hear any gunshot. Heck, I didn't see anything. It just *happened!*"

Out of the corner of his eye, Monk noticed the Osage panhandler's hasty reaction to the sight of a stricken man collapsing just a few feet away. Hastily, he gathered up his basket and native blanket, and undertook to quit the vicinity.

Seeing this, Monk yelled lustily, "Hey, you! Stop right there."

Instinctually, Monk reached into his coat for his underarm holster with the intention of bringing out his superfiring machine pistol, and laying the fleeing Osage low, but his grasping fingers clutched only empty air.

"Plumb forgot," he squeaked. "I ain't got my dang superfirer no more."

The Indian cast a nervous glance over his shoulder, saw Monk crouching in the darkness like a gorilla, and fright seemed to seize his wind-burned features. In his haste to flee, he stepped off the curb, lost his footing, but scrambled to his feet, and kept on going.

Something clattered in the dark. The fleeing one hesitated, then resumed his escape. Diving into a waiting taxi, he urged the driver to leave the vicinity.

The taxi departed in haste, its sweeping headlights briefly illuminating the fallen object. It was the panhandler's flute.

Charging around the corner with Pat right behind him, Monk went to Harold Manton's sprawled form, while Pat scooped up the fallen flute and joined the simian chemist.

The oil editor was not breathing. They could see that right away. Perhaps it was the bright scarlet of the hideous bloom on his features, but his skin was deathly pale, as if all the blood had been drained out of it. That might have been an optical illusion. Possibly it was a trick of the moonlight. But both Pat and Monk were seasoned in the ways of danger and death. They recognized that Harold Manton was no more. Death had closed his eyes, whose lids were a ghastly crimson.

Standing up, Pat called into the lobby, "Summon an ambulance. This man has had a heart attack or something. Please hurry!"

Coming to his feet, Monk said thickly, "Ambulance ain't gonna help him none."

"I know that," hissed Pat. "But we can't just stand here and do nothing."

Behind the front desk, the desk clerk was frantically speaking into his telephone instrument, while pressing an electric push-button, obviously meant to summon the bell captain, or perhaps a hotel detective.

Seeing this, Monk said to Pat, "Here's our chance. In fact, it's now or never. Let's make a run for those stairs."

They made a beeline for the staircase, eschewing the elevators, for they did not want to be seen by the elevator operator.

They tramped up the stairs until they got to their floor and, as they worked their way down the corridor, Pat had a sudden thought.

"What if they rented out our rooms?"

"We'll find out soon enough," said Monk.

Going to Pat's door, Monk knocked briskly, paused, then applied one ridiculously small apelike ear to the veneer panel. There was no immediate answer.

A second knock failed to stir any occupant, so Pat fitted the brass key in the lock, twisted, and Monk shoved his way in.

Brushing the light switch with a thumb, he illuminated the suite.

The room was much as they left it, although the damaged window had been repaired, and it was obvious that a hotel detective, if not the local police, had searched the place thoroughly.

"Home, sweet home," breathed Pat.

"Don't get comfortable," admonished Monk. "Take a few minutes to freshen up and then we're goin' to the penthouse Morgan Marrs holds forth in."

"Why don't we just phone him?" suggested Pat. "If we barge in, he'll know we're back in the hotel. What's to stop him from siccing the law on us?"

Monk made thinking faces and finally decided, "Too risky. We'll have to go through the hotel switchboard. The call would be traced back to this room. If we show up at Marrs' doorstep, and things don't go our way, we can always retreat to this joint. Cops might not think to look for us here."

"Either way," said Pat, "it's a tangled web."

"Well," growled Monk, "where you find a tangled web, you normally have a master spider back of it somewhere. I aim to hunt him down."

Pat regarded the hairy chemist pointedly. "Do you mean spider, or scorpion?"

"I mean," grated Monk fiercely, "varmint."

An ambulance pulled up outside, and ambulance attendants bearing a wheeled stretcher hurriedly entered the lobby.

They did not see this activity from their hotel room, which did not face the front of the building, but they could hear it.

Someone was yelling, "We think he's dead."

"Let the docs decide that!" snapped an arriving interne.

Monk grunted, "Manton's dead, all right. Say, what's that you got in your hand?"

"This?" returned Pat. "The Indian dropped it."

"Give it here," requested Monk.

The flute proved to be just that. A homemade affair that looked as if it had been whittled into existence. Monk peered down the hollow tube, counted the holes running along the top, then remarked, "Nothin' special about it."

Pat frowned. "Except that it has collected our fingerprints," she reminded tartly.

Monk's face fell. "You think that means trouble?"

"Need I remind you that twice an Indian panhandler was piping away when a man fell down with a scorpion growing on his face?"

Monk looked aghast. "Well, this dang flute could hardly have anything to do with it, could it?"

"Just the same, better wipe it clean and hide it where no one will find it."

Monk set about doing exactly that, finally concealing the instrument behind a steam radiator.

"That's that," he announced.

Pat had stripped off the kerchief covering her head and studied her stylish bronze hair in a wall mirror. She made thoughtful faces.

"I have a peach of an idea," she exclaimed suddenly.

"Show me the fuzz," invited Monk.

"I'm going to dye my hair to make myself look like an Osage squaw and change into something less fashionable."

"Be my guest," said Monk. He was looking into another mirror, which reflected the brown scorpion tattoo discoloring his cheek.

Not liking what he saw, the apish chemist muttered, "Wish I had my portable chemical laboratory. I'd test this stain to see what the heck it is."

As she disappeared into the bedroom, Pat asked, "Why don't you pop down the hall and see if it's still in your room?"

"Nix," said Monk. "Cops probably confiscated it as evidence. And if I knock and some guest answers, they'll see my face."

"You're right," said Pat. "The jig will be up."

"But good," grunted Monk. "Got any cold cream? Maybe it'll take this stain off."

Pat dug into a travel bag and tossed the hairy chemist a flat jar. "Here. It's my own brand."

Monk caught it, unscrewed the lid and applied the cool white substance liberally. Then he asked Pat, "How long until it sets?"

"Give it five minutes and then wipe it off with a wash cloth. But don't get your hopes up too high. That brown stain isn't make-up."

Monk waited. Sounds of commotion continued to rise to their hearing. The body of Harold Manton had not yet been loaded into the waiting ambulance. No bell or siren had sounded, indicating that the machine was still parked in front of the hostelry. That in itself was foreboding. No doubt the rangy oil editor had been officially pronounced deceased.

After five minutes had elapsed, Monk shoved into the wash room and toweled off the cold cream. Whatever he expected, nothing significant resulted. The hideous brown mark remained visible.

"Danged if I know what this daggone stain is," he muttered. "But as long as it ain't turned red, guess I'll live."

"Maybe it's meant to incriminate you."

Monk examined his features carefully. "You mean it marks me as a henchman of Standing Scorpion?"

"Or as the head stinger himself," rejoined Pat.

Pat Savage came out of the bedroom. When she emerged, her hair was as black as night and lustrous as a mink stole. Her bronze skin was now a coppery-red, and transparent tape applied to the corners of her golden eyes gave them a narrower configuration, which also helped conceal their true color.

Seeing the transformation, Monk grinned and wondered, "What are you going to call yourself?"

"Betty Blaze," she said promptly, donning a pair of dark glasses to further conceal her unusual optics.

"The name sounds familiar," Monk mused, rubbing his jaw.

"I used this disguise and alias once back in Hollywood, remember? During that mystery involving those rust-colored clouds."

"The ones that came down from the sky and gobbled up people and machines like they were candy? Yeah, I remember now, you were passin' yourself off as a Hollywood extra." *

A determined look came over Pat's face. "Well, Betty Blaze is back and she's going down to the lobby and see what she can see."

Monk said, "I guess I'm stuck here, bein' as conspicuous as I am."

"Hold the fort," directed Pat, putting on a sun hat with a floppy brim so wide that its shade helped conceal her attractive features. "I won't be very long."

PAT took the elevator, and the elevator operator didn't seem to pay her any undue attention. There was no telling how long they could remain holed up in the vacant hotel room, but Pat hoped to be able to come and go without arousing any suspicion until they got on the trail of something.

Arriving at the lobby, she saw Harold Manton finally being loaded onto a stretcher, for conveying to the waiting ambulance.

---

* *The Desert Demons*

A man who appeared to be the hotel physician was packing away his stethoscope and other medical paraphernalia of his trade and was telling a police officer, "That poor fellow may be the latest victim of that paralytic condition which has been striking down citizens of Oklahoma in the last two weeks."

The cop nodded gravely, saying, "The thing they're calling Grampus paralysis?"

The doctor made a wincing face and said, "That is not the medical term. The newspapers are throwing that phrase around. I do not as yet know what this malady is. Only that the first victim appears to be old Nansen over in Oklahoma City. I understand he is very ill."

Hearing the name, Pat's eyes narrowed. "This is a new wrinkle," she murmured to herself.

The police officer queried, "What about that red mark on his face—the vinegarroon or scorpion, or whatever it is."

"That part I cannot explain," admitted the medico. "It does not appear to be a tattoo."

The cop was writing all this down in a notepad and he added, "According to this man's wallet, he is—was—Harold Manton, oil editor on the *Trumpet*."

"Well, you don't say!" marveled the physician. "You know, the *Trumpet*'s publisher lives in the penthouse suite of this very hotel. Someone should ring him up."

The desk clerk was hovering about with sick eyes and wringing hands. Overhearing this, he volunteered, "I will summon Mr. Marrs. He will certainly want to know about this."

Lifting the desk phone, he asked the hotel operator to connect him to the penthouse suite, and then listened intently as the telephone rang many floors above.

With a disappointed facial expression, the desk clerk hung up slowly and called over, "Mr. Marrs appears to be out. There is no answer."

Hearing this, Pat Savage drifted away from the newsstand where she had been leafing through an assortment of magazines while acting nonchalant. She kept her head tilted in such a way that her profile was blocked by the extravagant brim of her sun hat.

Pat decided that it was high time she returned to her hotel room.

As she walked briskly back to the elevator, the entrance door opened, and a familiar individual strolled in just as the ambulance attendants were wheeling the late Harold Manton out.

"What happened to him?" the new arrival cried out. He sounded stricken.

"Who's asking?" the cop challenged in a belligerent voice.

"Ike Golden, with the *Tulsa Globe*," proclaimed the new arrival, resplendent in his seersucker suit and matching Panama. The lean-faced reporter whipped out a notebook and pencil and prepared to write down the police officer's reply.

The announcement of Golden's identity seemed to change the police officer's truculent attitude, for he said in a mollified tone, "We don't know what happened to him. But the hotel doc here thinks it might be that Grampus paralysis that's been going around."

The reporter rushed over to the hotel doctor and began plying him with questions, writing down the answers in a rapid, scribbling hand. No one commented on the noticeable bruise discoloring the point of his jaw, where Monk Mayfair had kayoed him.

Pat Savage did not stick around to hear the rest of this exchange. Folding one side of her hat brim downward, she entered the elevator and asked the operator to take her back to her floor.

When Pat stormed into the room, she told Monk, "Ike Golden is loose! He just barged in, acting upset about Mr. Manton. But not so upset that he didn't start questioning everybody."

Monk frowned. "Wonder how he got loose?"

"Worry about that later," snapped Pat. "They called up to publisher Marrs in the penthouse suite. He didn't pick up the phone. The coast is clear for us to snoop around."

"What are we waitin' for?" asked Monk. "Now's as good a time as any."

Pat turned for the door again, suddenly stopped.

She elevated an eyebrow in Monk's direction so that it cleared her dark glasses.

"What," she asked suspiciously, "happened to your scorpionic tattoo?"

Monk grinned sheepishly. "I obliterated it."

"With what?"

"I kinda borrowed some of your make-up powder."

Throwing open the door, Pat warned, "Don't let Ham Brooks ever know you fell to wearing woman's face powder."

"I won't tell him if you don't," Monk grinned.

"Keep your nose clean and the thought will never enter my head."

Monk gulped. "That kinda sounds like a veiled threat."

"Nothing veiled about it…."

Carefully, they exited their hotel room, and took the stairwell to the second highest floor. There, they sought the fire stairs which would take them to the penthouse above unseen. The roof habitation was served by a private elevator, which could only be accessed by the owner. So that was out.

As Monk led the way, Pat asked, "Ever hear of a malady called Grampus paralysis?"

"Can't say that I have," admitted the homely chemist.

"Well, from what I heard in the lobby, it's been going around. And one of the first victims was a Mr. Nansen of Oklahoma City. What do you want to bet that this Nansen is connected to Ben Nansen and Vina Hawks Nansen?"

"I'll keep my change in my pocket," said Monk. "But around here, a grampus is another name for a vinegarroon whip scorpion."

"You don't say," mused Pat. "I wonder what the connection might be?"

They reached the roof and its well-manicured shrubbery grounds, drifted over to the penthouse door with the name "Morgan Marrs" on it. A nice breeze was blowing such that it was not so hot as it had been on the pavement level.

Monk asked, "What makes you think there's a connection to this mess we're in?"

"The hotel doctor thinks that Harold Manton caught this Grampus paralysis."

Monk's blunt nose wrinkled as he mumbled, "This tangled web we're caught up in is accumulatin' some funny new strands."

"I don't see what's funny about them," complained Pat. "In fact, they're downright sinister."

Then, to her horror, Monk Mayfair fell to knocking on the penthouse door as loudly as he could.

Chapter XVII

OZARK RUMORS

AS HE POUNDED the panel with one furry fist, Monk Mayfair used the opposite paw to depress the push-button doorbell ringer.

He made quite a racket doing so.

"Anyone home?" he yelled through the panel.

Pat hissed, "What are you doing? You'll rouse the other tenants! We already know no one is home."

"There might be a butler or some other flunky," squeaked Monk. "No sense takin' any chances if we're gonna bust our way in."

That made a certain amount of sense, so Pat let the apish chemist have his way.

Once Monk was satisfied that no one was about to answer the door, he took a pair of instruments like small darning needles from a coat pocket and inserted the points into the door lock, then began manipulating them in a complicated manner.

"Doc Savage teach you how to do that?" asked Pat, observing carefully.

"Naw," replied Monk. "I learnt this when I was just a shaver."

Pat remarked archly, "It's a wonder you didn't end up in jail instead of where you did end up."

"Watch your tongue. Endin' up in jail is lookin' likelier than ever."

"Sorry," said Pat, as Monk made the tumblers click. He tested the door; it fell open, and they entered on tiptoe.

Turning on the lights as they moved from room to room, they discovered a palatial mansion interior, as befitting one of the most powerful publishers in all of Oklahoma.

Morgan Marrs had done well for himself in the newspaper game. And the appointments and furnishings in the various rooms spoke to that. There were awards and framed letters of commendation on the wall of his den. Photographs with assorted Oklahoma politicians were also prominent. These items bespoke of a man who had given his life to public service in the newspaper field.

After they finished their exploratory tour of the luxurious digs, Pat said, "Well, it's obvious no one is home. Should we just plunk ourselves down and wait until Mr. Marrs' return?"

Monk thought speedily. "It's as good a place as any. No one's apt to look for us here. Marrs will wanna know about his missing fiancée, and he may be able to help with the murder charges against us. There's nothin' better to have at your side than the fourth estate—unless it's a good lawyer. And we got one coming our way, once Ham arrives."

They stood in Morgan Marrs' kitchen when this low exchange took place, so they were startled when they heard coming from the entryway a voice calling, "Hello? Is anybody home?"

Pat said, "That sounds like—"

"Ike Golden!" Monk growled. "What's *he* doing up here?"

"Let's ask him," suggested Pat, pulling out from her pocket the nickel-plated revolver she had relieved Golden of, back at deceased Harold Manton's home.

Pat pointed this weapon ahead of her as she stepped out into the parlor, Monk shoving in behind her.

"May we help you?" inquired Pat in a cool voice.

"What are you two doing here?" Ike Golden bleated, his painfully thin face losing two shades of color until it hovered close to the sugary hue of his seersucker suit.

"That's our question to *you*," countered Pat.

"I thought I'd get a quote from publisher Marrs about the murder of his oil editor, Harold Manton. I don't suppose you know anything about that, do you?" the reporter said, keeping his hands by his sides. The knuckle bruise on his chin looked like a small cluster of Concord grapes now.

"What makes you say that?" questioned Pat.

A crooked grin warped Golden's hungry-looking face. He said, "Manton was found with a scarlet scorpion sprawled all over his kisser."

"So we have heard," returned Pat calmly.

"I saw it up close," continued Golden, "and it looks a lot like the one that was on your friend's homely puss, except that it's brown, not red. Can you explain that?"

Monk grimaced fiercely. "We left you tied up at Harold Manton's place. How'd you bust loose?"

"Changing the subject won't help you," sneered Golden in a smug tone of voice. "The cops are looking for you both over that cop murder and now it's starting to look like you did for Harold Manton, too. What are you two up to? The public wants to know."

Pat stood her ground, keeping the reporter covered, but Monk, hearing this barrage of accusations, turned red as various expressions crawled across his wide face, making him look like a brick-complected gorilla.

"That's enough out of you!" he yelled, charging forward. "You're gonna answer our questions, like it or not."

Falling upon the man, Monk seized him by his coat collar and began shaking him the way a bull terrier shakes his prey.

Golden had no pistol, but a hand flashed into a pocket. It came up with one of those trick knives that resemble a black handle until you press a spring. Out popped a wicked blade. He began flailing about wildly, seeking to do some damage.

The steel edge took a sliver off of one of Monk's cauliflower ears, and the tip scored the pancake make-up covering the brown scorpion upon the hairy chemist's homely face.

"*Y-e-e-o-w!*" Monk yelled. Using a huge paw to knock the knife away, Monk sent the blade flying. Then he began slapping Ike Golden harshly, yelling, "Pull a knife on me, will you!"

Ike Golden was not built for battle. Monk's powerful blows knocked him backward. Growling his wrath, the apish chemist charged in, grabbed the reporter by his cottony coat lapels, and swung him around, flinging him into a waiting chair.

Colliding with the chair, Golden managed to land in a seated position—but the chair upset, and both toppled backward.

During this impromptu acrobatic performance, a fat envelope went flying from somewhere.

Seeing this, Pat Savage stepped in and scooped it up. It was thick with folded sheets of paper. As she began extracting these, Monk fell upon reporter Golden again, dragged him to his feet and found that the man had banged the back of his head when the chair upset. He was out cold.

"Dang!" Monk mumbled. "I smacked him too good."

"You better not have killed him, Monk," scolded Pat, eyes perusing the top sheets.

"Naw, he's just knocked senseless, is all. We'll have to wait 'til he comes around to get him to talk."

"We may not need him," said Pat thoughtfully, and she started handing sheets of paper over to the simian chemist.

"What's this stuff?"

"They came spilling out of his pocket when you sent him flying," supplied Pat. "The envelope was addressed to Harold Manton's residence, but the inside sheets were meant for us."

Monk was looking at the top sheet now, and it was addressed thusly:

> To my honored guests, whom I will refrain from naming to protect the innocent as well as the guilty:
> I have been using my connections around town to follow up on some of your questions.
> The moniker of Standing Scorpion is not known around Tulsa, but out in the Salem Plateau portion of the Ozark

Mountains, beyond where Oklahoma turns into Arkansas, it's a name to conjure with. No one knows much about this character, and what I've dug up smacks of superstition and hokum.

Standing Scorpion is known as the Ozark Ogre. He's a kind a bogeyman, and has a gang or a tribe or whatever you want to call it of Osage Indians—a shiftless pack of riffraff. Petty crooks and outlaws. They've been doing misdeeds out in the Ozarks where the police can't do much about them.

This Standing Scorpion is a mystery man. No one has ever seen his face. Nor knows his real name—if he has one.

This nebulous fellow, rumor has it, has been tied to the Grampus paralysis that has been popping up lately. You might remember the Jake paralysis people were suffering from a few years back from eating that Jamaican ginger patent medicine that was contaminated by bad alcohol. This is like that, although why it's called Grampus paralysis I have not been able to determine. Wealthy persons have been targeted, and I suspect that the facts are being covered up.

One of the first persons afflicted—although the newspapers have not reported on it much because of political pressure—is one Eric Nansen, a retired cattleman. Nansen lives over in Oklahoma City. Got a nice place there. If you can get away, you might stop around sometime. You should ask him about his daughter, Vina. And Ben Nansen, too.

I don't know how this all hangs together, but obviously it ties up in a big way.

I'm sending this to my place by messenger. Be sure to burn these pages after you read them. I have an appointment to see my publisher privately at his hotel later tonight. I'm going to lay some of this before him, and see if he can help out.

I don't have to tell you that this is a tricky situation for us all. There are considerable reputations involved, not to mention a lot of good families of Oklahoma, at stake here.

Best of luck.

THE long letter was signed simply, "H."

Reading this, Monk said, "That messenger must've come around, spied Ike Golden tied up inside the house, got in and set him free."

"Unquestionably," said Pat firmly. "Let's hope the messenger wasn't hurt. Luckily for us, Golden got hold of this message so that it found its way into our hands, anyway."

"That's a break for us," chortled Monk. "Let's hogtie this bozo again, and leave him for Morgan Marrs. Sounds like we might get someplace talkin' to this Eric Nansen."

"Agreed," said Pat. "You do the tying and I'll do the watching. We don't want any more visitors until after we've departed the premises."

The homely chemist scrounged around for some suitable bindings, and ended up having to scavenge several expensive ties from Morgan Marrs' bedroom. Most of these were silk. Monk tied them very tightly, cutting off the circulation to Golden's hands and feet, but he didn't let that consideration hinder him.

Monk stood up, surveyed his knot tying with satisfaction. Ike Golden would not be getting free without assistance. No doubt that assistance would be along before the night was over.

Eyeing the tightly-trussed reporter, Pat observed archly, "We appear to be leaving a trail of terror in our wake wherever we go."

Monk grinned, "We're regular Oklahoma outlaws. Now let's get goin'."

"We might take a detour to my room and gather up some essentials," suggested Pat.

"Fine by me," said Monk. "And while we're at it, we'll take along that vial Ben Nansen slipped us. We still don't know what that is, but it's gotta be important."

Exiting the penthouse, they slipped down the stairs and made their way successfully to Pat's hotel room, where Monk filled his pockets with assorted special grenades. After changing into a cotton summer dress that provided plenty of freedom of movement, Pat took along her make-up kit, with the idea of using it to keep up her disguise and conceal Monk's telltale facial disfigurement.

"Better powder your face before we go," suggested Pat, donning the floppy-brimmed sun hat once more.

Accepting a heavy-laden powder puff, Monk grimaced as he touched up his features, struggling to fight off a sneezing fit.

"How do you females put up with this stuff?" he demanded, handing the powder puff back to its owner.

"That bunk you hear about us being the weaker sex," returned Pat archly, "is just that—bunkum. And don't you forget it, buster."

It was still night, so they managed to slip out the back and reclaim their flivver, which the disguised Pat Savage piloted while Monk lay on the floorboards of the back seat, out of sight so that his conspicuous appearance—not to mention the half-concealed brown whip scorpion brand on his face—would not attract police attention.

Chapter XVIII

THE ONE WHO WAS STUNG

BETWEEN THE TULSA city limits and the state capital of Oklahoma City lie over one hundred miles of scrub oak amid rolling hills, with oil derricks and nodding pumpjacks as far as the eye could see.

Pat Savage drove west, beginning at the West Tulsa refineries, which seemed to be active even at this late hour. The smell of crude made the night air thick and unpleasant, like a warm rubber blanket enveloping the humid night.

Once they cleared West Tulsa, it was a straight run along Route 66.

Most of the machines abroad at this late hour appeared to be connected to the local petroleum industry.

A rusty old coupe equipped with a bit-rack got in their way. Pat passed it. Then she whipped the car around a loaded pipe truck that was lumbering along.

To pass the time, Pat made conversation.

"I always heard that this part of Oklahoma had become a boom town," she remarked to Monk, sprawled low in the back seat, "but I never imagined there would be so much drilling and pumping still going on since the business depression took hold."

"Heck," guffawed Monk, "it's startin' up again. They struck oil under the capitol building in Oklahoma City back in '28. Production has been goin' round the clock ever since. Times got tough a few years back, sure, but oil never goes out of style."

Pat drove just under the posted speed limit, but she feared for her tires and did not like the way the old flivver rattled and shimmied after bumping along the occasional ruts in the macadam road.

"You might," suggested Pat, "pass the time back there by saying a little prayer for this old jalopy. I'm not convinced she's going to make it to Oklahoma City."

"If I'm gonna pray," remarked Monk, "I'm prayin' that the cops don't pull us over. This is a state that goes to bed early, and we're tooling along pretty late."

"I'll just tell them I'm headed toward the state hospital to see my sick Aunt Penelope."

Monk grunted noncommittally.

"Have you ever heard of Eric Nansen?" asked Pat abruptly.

In the ill-lit darkness, Monk felt it safe to sit up. He scratched his bristled head and chin thoughtfully, then said, "Can't say that I have. If he's wealthy, that must say something about him."

As they drove along, an approaching state highway patrol machine topped the rise, its headlights blazing hot in their faces. Monk ducked from view.

Pat kept a straight face, counting on her Indian disguise to allow her to pass inspection. Oklahoma has probably the highest population of Native Americans of any state in the Union. Many owned automobiles. Especially since the oil boom, which had not discriminated. A lot of crude had been discovered on tribal land.

The state machine slowed slightly, and Pat squeezed her eyes so their striking gold tint did not show, her dark glasses temporarily set aside.

The driver of the official vehicle seemed satisfied, for he picked up speed and passed on by.

"It's safe to sit up, Monk," Pat declared.

The simian chemist took his time doing so, and when he did, he peered out the back window carefully, commenting, "You might get by in that squaw rig of yours, but between the scorpion on my puss and my general physique, I'm a marked man."

Pat nodded. "We should reach Oklahoma City around dawn. You just stay in the car while I palaver with Mr. Nansen."

Monk shrugged casually. "Suits me."

Pat ran slim fingers through her darkened hair and murmured, "This is all becoming more baffling every minute. What do you make of this Grampus paralysis business?"

Monk was a little while in answering. "This wouldn't be the first time that a campaign of murders hit Oklahoma, especially around oil."

"What do you mean?"

"Back a dozen or more years ago, they had what the papers called the 'Reign of Terror' up in Osage County. A lot of Indians had gotten rich when oil was found on Osage reservation land there. It was quite a mystery for a spell. White folks started killin' off rich Indians. They had schemed so that the oil royalty headrights the Indians owned would fall into their hands."

Pat frowned prettily. "I fail to understand how that might happen. How would the white people inherit?"

"On account some of these rich Osages married white women—and not all of them were honest. There are other types of swindles, too. You see, every Osage was entitled to his fair share of tribal oil royalties. That made for a powerful lot of rich Indians. So the more Osage bodies that piled up, the more suspicious the law became. Not everybody got convicted of murder, but enough of them did so that the Reign of Terror was stopped cold."

"You don't believe that this new reign of terror against wealthy Oklahomans has to do with oil rights, do you?" questioned Pat.

Monk grunted. "Search me. But some schemer is back of all this hell, and they're bound and determined to see you and me collect the blame."

"We *do* seem to be the scapegoats of the hour, don't we?"

"Yeah, we do. And the more I ponder it, the more I suspicion that the flute you picked up after that Osage panhandler high-tailed it was dropped on purpose so you'd snag it."

Pat sighed. "If this keeps up, I'm going to consider sanding my fingerprints smooth. Everything I touch seems to incriminate me."

Following that sobering thought, the two fell silent.

AS Pat predicted, dawn light began changing the eastern sky as they rolled into the outskirts of the city.

Milk delivery trucks were abroad, and an enterprising fellow with an ancient dun horse drawing a dilapidated old wagon was making his early rounds, calling, "Rags, rags, any old rags?"

Finding the home of Eric Nansen proved difficult. They had little enough to go on as matters stood.

Pat tooled around the suburbs until she found a filling station that was open for business, and pulled in.

While the attendant was filling the tank, Pat asked, "We're looking for the residence of a man named Eric Nansen, who lives around here. Would you know the address?"

"Sure," said the man. "Got a nice place on top of a hill. Drive south a little bit, turn off Main Street and you can't hardly miss it. It's got its own private road. It's marked Private Road. Cream-colored house with lots of windows and plenty of useless gingerbread."

"Sounds swell," said Pat.

The attendant grinned. "Mr. Nansen is a big wheel in this town. In fact, for a lot of Oklahoma. Rumor has it he's ill. No one's seen him in weeks."

"Thank you kindly," said Pat, paying the man and putting the machine into gear.

Following the filling station attendant's simple directions, Pat found the home of Eric Nansen. It was a palatial place, sitting on a low hill, and looked as if it was kept up the way a yachtsman maintains his prized boat.

As they moved toward the private road, a gray sedan pulled out of the side street and began following them.

Monk was seated in the back seat, and was in plain view. That may have explained what happened next.

The gray sedan fell behind at a decorous pace, but Pat noticed it in her rear-view mirror. She called Monk's attention to the trailing vehicle.

"It's too soon to decide that we're being followed," she imparted, "but I have a sneaking suspicion we're being followed."

Prudently, the hairy chemist did not turn around, for the rear window would have framed his pleasantly homely face perfectly. Instead, he asked, "Got a compact mirror?"

Pat handed it back, and Monk used this to look out the back window without having to turn around.

Two men were seated in the vehicle, its driver and a companion. In the early morning light their faces emphasized that reddish sunset cast that suggested that they were full-blooded Native Americans.

This was a common enough condition in Oklahoma, so Monk was not unduly alarmed. But he remained watchful.

Without warning, the trailing machine accelerated and endeavored to pass them.

As it did so, a sound rose up over the changing key of the pursuing motor. It was the sound of a flute being played badly.

Monk and Pat heard this, and Pat suddenly yelled, "Roll up your window, Monk!"

The homely chemist lunged for the crank, spun it with mad abandon. The window glass rolled up, and Monk spied the sedan pacing their flivver. The passenger was leaning out of his window, a long flute in both hands, its holes sealed by carefully-placed bony fingers.

Red cheeks puffed out, and something spat out of the flute's far end, to strike the window glass.

There was a thin crunching sound, followed by drooling liquid spatter on the other side of the thick glass that was suggestive of a scarlet scorpion unfolding itself like an ugly flower.

A few droplets of this stuff splashed into the interior of the back seat, but other than a faint smell of vinegar, nothing unusual happened.

"Standing Scorpion's boys!" yelled Monk. "Tryin' to run a whizzer on us!"

Wrenching the wheel hard, Pat forced the pacing machines to collide. Fenders clashed. Brakes barked. She swiftly ran the other car into the soft shoulder of the road. Monk wrestled with the door latch until Pat reminded, "There's no telling what would happen if you stepped outside, Monk."

In his anger, the apish chemist almost disregarded his better judgment. But the sight of the drooling liquid scorpion forming on the other side of the door glass stayed him.

Growling, he said, "Pass me back that revolver you got off that cheap reporter, Golden."

The nickeled revolver landed in the back seat. Monk snatched it up, kicked open the far door, and leaned on the high roof of the machine.

He emptied the cylinder into the sedan's rear tires, which exploded and hissed out trapped air. The sedan body settled at the back end.

Climbing back in, Monk shouted, "Take off!"

Pat complied, saying, "How did they know we were coming here?"

"The only person who could know that would have read Harold Manton's letter," Pat said tightly as the flivver shot ahead.

"That would be Ike Golden," said Pat.

"Or maybe Morgan Marrs. He would've come home by now, I think."

"That's right," said Pat. "He could have dragged the truth out of Golden. But Morgan Marrs couldn't possibly be tied in with Standing Scorpion, could he?"

"Well," muttered Monk, "somebody in the know was layin' for us. Knew we were coming here and aimed to stop us cold."

Pat said nothing to that. She concentrated on her driving. Soon, they were on the private road leading up the asphalt incline to the impressive home of Eric Nansen, the gingerbread of which smoldered in the sun's rising rays.

"Remember our plan, Monk," reminded Pat as the front driveway came into view. "You lay low and I'll pay Mr. Nansen a call."

"What are you gonna tell him? You can't call yourself Pat Savage. You'd get pinched."

"I'll think of something," reassured Pat. "Count on it."

Parking the ancient machine, Pat exited and walked up to the front door. There was a door knocker in the shape of a brass bull's head and a doorbell. It was early, so she used both.

Presently, a butler in full regalia appeared, looked her over rather disdainfully and observed, "Mr. Nansen is not expecting any callers at this hour."

"My name is Betty Blaze," said Pat swiftly. "I have important information about Mr. Nansen's daughter, Vina. She is in desperate trouble. Vina needs help."

The butler paled, and the skeptical light in his eyes grew sharp, and yet uncertain.

"Please enter. I will inform Mr. Nansen of your unexpected arrival."

"Thank you," said Pat politely, entering.

The interior of the home was impressive in an outdoorsy way. Trophy heads decorated the walls, as did antique weapons ranging from old frontier Peacemakers to percussion rifles. An enormous stuffed buffalo head presided over everything. In contrast to the weapons, it did not appear to be very old. This was the home of a rugged outdoorsman, a man of the West.

While Pat waited for what she hoped to be a formal intro-
duction, she studied her surroundings. They were tasteful yet
modern after the Western style.

SOON, a door opened and Eric Nansen appeared. When Pat
turned to greet him, a sharp look came into her eyes.

The man who rolled into view probably stood over six feet
tall when he was in his prime. He was far from his prime now.
He was also seated in a rather flimsy wheelchair of rattan and
wire wheels.

"Mr. Nansen, I presume?" Pat asked, putting out her hand.

Eric Nansen took it politely, saying, "Yes, and you are Betty
Blaze. I am told that you have word about Vina. I understand
that she is in difficulties."

"Extreme difficulty," corrected Pat. Then she related the events
of the last twenty-four hours, beginning with their first encounter with Ben Nansen, and Vina's mysterious intervention.

Pat was midway through that recitation when the man reached
under the horse blanket that covered his withered old legs. Up
came an astonishing sight.

It was an old percussion shotgun, its matched barrels truncated for use at short range. Eric Nansen pointed this relic up
at Pat, and rocked back the hammers of each barrel carefully,
warning, "Just because I have no hankering to shoot a lady,
doesn't mean I might not shoot one—if she deserved it."

Pat had nerve and kept it steady.

"Whatever do you mean by this?" she asked. Her voice was
thin, but without fear.

Eric Nansen stated, "That story you were telling me about
encountering my son and daughter, I have heard before, but it
involved a woman named Patricia Savage, who is supposed to
be a cousin of the famous Doc Savage. The same Patricia Savage
is now wanted for the murder of a Tulsa police officer." The old
man appraised Pat with unflinching gray eyes. "You say your
name is Betty Blaze, and you do not look like a white woman.

Therefore, you are either lying, or Patricia Savage wearing a disguise. Which is it?"

"Which answer will get me shot?" asked Pat.

"Why don't you tell the truth and find out for yourself?" suggested the withered old man.

Pat did not have to think about that. She was inclined to tell the truth, whenever practical. Also she did not really think the old gent would shoot her without better reasons than she was about to present.

"I'm Patricia Savage in disguise," she admitted.

"Where is your alleged accomplice in crime, Mr. Mayfair?"

"Hiding in the automobile we arrived in. He doesn't take to being disguised as well as I do."

Nansen studied Pat for a considerable part of a minute, and carefully reset the hammers, one at a time, then lay the old shotgun across his blanketed legs.

"I'm satisfied that you are telling the truth," he said quietly. "Continue your story, please."

Pat picked up her tale, told about the rescue by Vina from the building that had blown up and then the phone call in which Vina had pleaded for help.

"When we got to the hotel," concluded Pat, "she wasn't there any longer. We tried her fiancé's penthouse, but no one was home. We have no idea where your daughter is now, but I am certain that she is in terrible danger. Your son, as well."

"I have no doubt of that," said Eric Nansen. "Please call your friend in. And I will tell my own story in full."

Pat went out, collected Monk, and brought him in. Introductions were swift and to the point.

Monk was impressed by Eric Nansen's firm handshake.

"Three weeks ago," began Nansen, "a package arrived by express. I was not expecting a package. The butler brought it in and presented it to me. Right then, I was standing on my two good legs like a normal man would. Opening the box to find it was stuffed with ordinary excelsior, I naturally rooted around with my own hands. For my pains, I received the pungent rebuff of a venomous creature. A whip scorpion, to be exact."

"A vinegarroon!" exploded Monk.

"Exactly. Being an Oklahoma boy, Mr. Mayfair, you doubtless know that a vinegarroon is not a true scorpion, although it greatly resembles one. It lacks a proper tail and stinger, being equipped by nature with a whip of a tail and a mechanism by which it sprays acid at those who annoy it. As it did to me." The aged man shrugged elaborately. "That vinegary odor I smelled when I opened the box should have warned me. Although the acid spray was painful, and the creature easily dispatched by a hammer blow, in the days that followed I experienced a progressive weakening in both legs. Before long, I was reduced to being carted around in a wheelchair."

Various strong emotions crossed the old man's rugged features. He quickly asserted his self-control, however.

"Go on," invited Pat.

"At the end of the first week, in fact, on the one-week mark since the package arrived, an anonymous letter arrived in the mail. It demanded ransom. Not a large amount in comparison to my wealth, but enough to insult me. The person who wrote the demand letter said that if I tendered this amount to him, I would receive a cure by return mail and my troubles would be over."

"Did you pay?" asked Pat.

Nansen shook his head vigorously. "No, I did not."

"Why not?" demanded Monk.

"The chief reason was the ransom was so paltry," snapped Nansen. "It was an insult to my dignity. That led me to consider the possibility that the blackmailer—for that is what we should in all honestly call him—did not possess any such cure. I consulted with some of the finest physicians in the state—fine, upstanding men who were unable to fathom my condition. All insisted that whatever malady had hold of me, a cure was unlikely. So I held onto my money and I waited."

"When did your son disappear?" asked Pat.

"As far as I am able to tell, two months prior to my receiving the scorpion in the box. This troubles me greatly. For we had been quarreling considerably of late."

"About what?" prompted Pat.

"Ben never got over his mother's passing a few years back," said Nansen frankly. "He was still in school when Mrs. Nansen passed, and he took it hard. Dropped out of school, I'm sorry to say. Drifted some. Finally, he found work in the oilfields, worked his way up from roughneck to toolie."

Pat looked blank. "Eh?"

"He means a wrangler of oilfield tools," inserted Monk. "It's a tough job, but it will make a man out of you—if you can take it."

"Please continue, Mr. Nansen," invited Pat.

The old man had been fussing nervously with his blanket, but now his hands became still.

"Mr. Mayfair is correct. Ben got himself a good job, but I didn't see it that way. Made my pile in coal and cattle, years before black gold turned this state into a malodorous factory. Why, they drilled wells right beside the capitol building here in Oklahoma City. You'd think they'd show more civic pride, but that's what they did. Anyway, I criticized my son severely for joining the oil stampede and he up and quit that good job. Fell in with bad company, and things went from bad to worse, I fear."

"What kinda company?" asked Monk. "Crooks?"

"No. Shiftless, no-account Indians. Poolroom types. Call themselves the 'Tall Boys.' Fella named Tall Turkey organized them. Ben fell in with the Tall Boys, I suspect, out of misguided feelings toward his late mother."

Pat and Monk made puzzled faces.

Gesturing to a framed picture on a far wall of a comely woman with long, lustrous ebony hair and sharp eagle eyes, Eric Nansen said, "That is her. Natica Hawks when I asked her to marry me. A full-blooded Cherokee, she was. Ben took after her more than did Vina."

Pat started slightly. Natica Hawks was the alias Vina Hawks Nansen had used to rent a hotel room. The golden-eyed girl kept that morsel to herself, however.

Monk inserted, "You sayin' that maybe your son is tied into the gang that's dishin' out all this misery?"

Eric Nansen squared a stubborn chin. "I can't bring myself to believe it. But I will readily admit that the notion has troubled my otherwise dreamless sleep of late."

"And what did your daughter have to say about all this?" asked Pat.

Old Eric Nansen's Nordic-gray eyes grew frosty. "Vina was horrified at the thought, of course, and when I came down with this durn Grampus paralysis that is now sweeping the state, she pleaded with me to pay the ransom. But I am a stubborn man. I will not pay even a modest amount of money for a chance at nothing."

"How much did they ask for?" inquired Monk.

"Two thousand dollars! Can you imagine that? I am worth millions, yet all they asked for was two thousand dollars. This is why I did not take the demand seriously."

Monk frowned, commenting, "I don't think the acid spray of a whip scorpion would take away a man's power to walk. If it did, I'm not sure what the cure would be, myself."

Eric Nansen banged a fist on his leg and burst out, "My reasoning exactly. Hence my firm stance."

Pat had been silent, and now asked, "How well do you know your daughter's fiancé, Morgan Marrs?"

"Not well. But everyone in the state of Oklahoma knows of him. He's a fine, upstanding citizen. One I was proud to accept into my family. They are to be married in a few months, you know."

"Anyone have reason to want to bring harm to you and your family?" questioned Pat.

"You mean, do I have any enemies?" Nansen barked. "Of course I do! You cannot amass millions of dollars without creating enemies. But I have reached the stage in life where none of them has ever been able to touch me. Therefore, I cannot in my retirement imagine who could be reaching out from the past to harm me or my children."

Pat observed. "Sounds like we're at a dead end."

"What business is this of yours?" thundered the old man with a trace of ire.

Monk offered, "We sorta backed into this mess when your son glommed into us." The hirsute chemist produced the vial of clear liquid and displayed it prominently. "Know what this stuff is?"

Nansen shook his head slowly. "No, it looks like a bottle of ordinary water."

"Your son handed it to us," explained Pat. "He acted like it was important."

"Well," Monk said, "it's gotta be mighty important. People have tried to kill us to get it. We ain't figured out what it is yet, either."

"We'd like to get to the bottom of this," added Pat. "Clear our names. Get everything out in the open."

Eric Nansen said, "I will call Morgan Marrs and inquire after Vina. Please wait here."

The old man was gone ten minutes, and when he returned, his face was a sullen thundercloud of disappointment.

"Marrs does not answer. Rather early in the morning for a decent man not to be answering his telephone. This worries me."

"Then we've run smack into a brick wall," said Pat plaintively.

Various troubled expressions fought with one another on the old man's sun-seamed face. Finally, Eric Nansen looked up and studied them steadily for some moments in firm-lipped silence.

"Would you like to borrow a proper automobile?" he asked at last. "I can also supply you with any funds or weapons you might need to pursue the matter of my missing daughter and son. Are you game?"

Pat smiled in relief. "Then you're not going to turn us over to the police?"

"Hardly," snorted Nansen. "Full well do I know the reputation of Doc Savage. It is above reproach. I believe your story, and my suspicions are growing now that I understand that my daughter has also been drawn into the affair—whatever its meaning and origins may be."

"We'll gladly accept whatever help you can offer," said Pat. "We have a lot of territory to cover."

The old man spun his wheelchair around abruptly, barking, "Follow me, then."

Nansen led them to a spacious four-car garage which boasted a long black limousine, a sporty roadster the exact hue of a fire truck, and other fine vehicles.

Beaming, Monk said, "Let's take that ritzy roadster."

Pat frowned. "I would prefer something more discreet."

They settled on a tasteful touring car, and Monk helped himself to an assortment of rifles and pistols harvested from a trophy room where a wide array of hunting guns was racked on the paneled walls. In his day, Eric Nansen explained, he had been an avid hunter.

When he ambled out to the garage with his hairy forearms loaded with firearms, Pat eyed the apish chemist dubiously and remarked, "You look like you're preparing for war."

"The war's already started," said Monk. "I'm lookin' to finish it."

"Suit yourself," said Pat. "I don't imagine you found a Peacemaker in that collection?"

Monk grinned his broadest. "It's in the pile, and there's a box of cartridges in my pocket."

"Swell!" said Pat. Turning to Eric Nansen, she shook his withered hand again and said graciously, "Thank you very much for your assistance. You can be sure that Monk and I will do everything in our power to restore your daughter and son to their freedom."

"If you require a place to hide out, this is where you need to come," the oldster said firmly.

With that, Pat backed the touring car out, while Monk slipped the flivver into the garage where it would not be seen, and they tooled back down the private road.

Passing the parked gray sedan on the way, they saw that it had been abandoned. They did not stop to investigate further.

Monk said, "From the sound of things, Ben Nansen fell in with that outlaw band of Indians that's been operatin' out in the Ozarks."

Pat nodded. "Fell in, and then had a falling out. I'd still like to know who tipped off Standing Scorpion that we were coming this way."

"My money's on Golden."

"By all rights, he should have been clapped in the pokey once Morgan Marrs found him tied up in his digs."

Monk made a bland face. "Could be he is. How would we know about it either way?"

"We don't," admitted Pat. "But we are sure to find out once we get back to Tulsa."

Monk opined, "If we get lucky, maybe Golden is where we can get at him. Betcha we can wring some truth out of him if we squeeze hard enough. Like squeezin' lemons."

"If Ike Golden is still tied up in Morgan Marrs' penthouse," said Pat Savage firmly, "maybe Marrs has been kidnapped, too. If so, this tangled web keeps ensnaring folks connected with the Nansen family. Especially Ben and Vina."

"Somethin' to think about, all right," allowed Monk.

Chapter XIX

GASOLINE TRAIL

PATRICIA SAVAGE PILOTED the borrowed machine into Tulsa's busy downtown with its generous supply of modern buildings, many constructed in the architectural style called Art Deco, her narrowed eyes watching for blue uniforms and patrol cars every few yards.

Monk was hunkered down in the back seat once more. Fortunately, his rather truncated but powerful form permitted him to lay stretched out comfortably. It was often said of the gorilla-like chemist that he was half a man tall and about two men wide. That was an exaggeration, but not an implausible one. Monk was built like a squat box of muscles coated with wiry red hair.

As a strapping young lad, he had often gone skinny-dipping in his favorite swimming hole. One time, a hunter flung buckshot at him, mistaking Monk for a tailless baboon escaped from the local zoo. As a full-grown adult, Monk would easily pass as the so-called missing link.

Lifting his squeaking voice, he said to Pat as they tooled along, "I vote we just barge our way in, talk tough and act rough."

Pat shook her dark-haired head and said firmly, "This is *my* mystery. We're going to do things the Pat Savage way."

"Which is?"

"Let's see if we can't hunt up Vina Hawks Nansen."

Monk shrugged. "It's a fair notion, but I'd rather get my mitts on Ike Golden."

"Golden is likely in jail."

"You're probably right," allowed Monk. "O.K., we'll do it your way. Just this once."

"Razzberries to you," Pat sniffed.

Pat Savage soon pulled up at the front of the Gusher Hotel, where Vina Hawks Nansen had taken a room under the name of Natica Hawks, which they now knew to be the name of her late mother. The thought that the blonde young woman was half-Cherokee was somehow disquieting, given the proliferation of Osage Indians populating the baffling affair to date.

As they pulled up, a half-familiar tangle of melody came through the open windows. It was early morning, but the heat of the day had already commenced. It was building up to be another scorcher.

Parking and setting the emergency brake, Pat said, "I had better go in alone. You stand out like a wart on a banana."

"That crack strikes me as sorta unkind," mumbled Monk in an injured tone.

"Sorry, it just came to mind." Pat threw open the door and stepped out into the morning sun. After the breezy drive, it hit her like a furnace warming up.

The sounds of fragmentary melody sank in then. It was created by a flute, wielded by hands that were not very practiced.

Looking about suspiciously, Pat noticed the Indian seated on the vermilion blanket beside the hotel entrance.

Tawny eyes narrowed. This did not seem to be any of the same Indians who had lurked about on previous occasions, but another one entirely. But his regalia and basket and flute appeared to be identical.

Pausing by the running board of the machine, Pat said quietly, "I spy a suspicious red man. Can you hear him?"

"If that mangled melody is him," grunted Monk from his prone position, "I hear him just fine."

"Hmmm," murmured Pat.

"Same Injun as the other night?"

"No, this particular Hiawatha is a fresh face. But I don't like it."

"Why don't you head into the lobby and I'll keep an eye on him?"

"Deal," said Pat, starting off. She walked briskly for the revolving doors, then disappeared within. She made a point of not looking in the panhandler's direction.

Pushing himself up, Monk carefully peered out of the back window with one eye, and watched the Indian stand up, clutching his flute, then move in the direction of the revolving door.

As he walked, the red man did a strange thing. Two strange things, rather. First, he put something in his mouth, then he placed both hands on his instrument in a way that was peculiar. The fingers were spaced apart awkwardly and Monk could see that they were covering the holes that ran along the top of the flute.

The revolving door was still turning when the stealthy Osage—he was very tall in stature—slipped into one of the moving brass-and-glass quadrants, evidently stalking Pat Savage.

Kicking open the car door, Monk shot out like a cannonball, and raced across the sidewalk, moving as low as he could to avoid being seen. The sight of the apish chemist could hardly go unnoticed, but he made it to the entrance, slipping into the revolving door as the tall Indian shadow stepped out into the lobby.

Feet digging in, Monk forced the revolving door around and shot out the other side. The Indian was now directly behind Pat, who was striding through the lobby, oblivious to the fact that she was being shadowed.

Several expected things now happened at once.

Monk Mayfair was the only one who caught them all.

PAT SAVAGE arrived at the bank of elevators. She stood beside an electric fan on a tall standard that was blowing steady air for the benefit of waiting guests, and firmly stabbed the call button to summon the elevator. Just as Pat stepped back, the door rolled aside and she let out a gasp of surprise.

Coming out of the elevator were three individuals. A tall man they did not recognize, but who was well-dressed and imposing. He clutched a woman by one arm. She was pale and her hair was very blonde. A veil obscured her features, but there was no mistaking her stride. Vina Hawks Nansen. On the other side standing off a little, was the *Globe* reporter, Ike Golden, his pale Panama hat in hand.

They stepped off the elevator, noticed Pat Savage, but failed to recognize the golden-eyed girl in her Indian disguise of dark hair and reddish-copper skin.

It was at that moment that the trailing Osage Indian stopped in the middle of the spacious lobby and went into a crouch, the long reed flute, its holes capped by ruddy fingers, coming to his mouth. The man puffed a lungful of air through the tube.

Monk Mayfair was already bounding behind him, moving fast. One hairy fist slammed into the side of the Indian's head in passing as he leapt upon Pat Savage, clamped the other paw over her mouth and dragged her backward in the direction of the electric fan.

His face was now very red and it turned purple as he held Pat firmly before the blowing air.

The trio who had stepped off the elevator took in this unusual sight. Ike Golden started. "That's him! Mayfair!"

Galvanized by that yell, the tall and imposing individual all but dragged Vina Hawks Nansen through the lobby, Ike Golden trailing with alacrity.

Pat was pointing in their direction and trying to make sounds through Monk's clamping hand. She only managed to produce semi-whistling noises through pulsing nostrils.

"Keep holdin' your breath, Pat!" growled Monk. "This'll be over in a second."

Pat subsided, but her wide eyes were full of fear.

Monk took an experimental breath, and when he didn't keel over, he released Pat, saying, "I think that was a poison capsule he shot at you."

"Say again?" said Pat, steadying herself against one marble wall.

"That Osage I just clobbered. He trailed you in here. And I could tell he was fixin' to do something bad. Had something in his mouth. When he blew it out the flute, I had me a hunch."

"How did you know it was a poison capsule?"

"Lamp that wall," the homely chemist said hastily, jerking his head toward the bank of elevators.

Pat looked. Upon the marble sprawled a hideous red splotch of a thing, a bloody bloom suggestive of a scorpion with a thin, devil-like tail.

"Oh, my!" exclaimed Pat.

Monk grabbed her arm, saying, "We gotta get out of here."

The wisdom of Monk's sudden assertion was demonstrated when they heard the desk clerk yelling for the police over the telephone.

"It's the fugitive, Monk Mayfair!" he was howling.

Pat and Monk made a mad dash for the entrance and, using one of the ordinary glass doors, they sprinted for their parked machine, piling in with celerity.

A yellow taxicab was pulling away from the curb only a few yards ahead, and they could see Vina Hawks Nansen's veiled face looking at them with horror out the back window.

"She's been kidnapped!" yelled Monk.

"I'll follow them," Pat said, decisively throwing the car in gear.

"You can try," Monk growled, "but any minute now the cops are gonna be swarmin' all over this part of town. Not sure it's such a good idea."

"Well, we have to do something!" yelled Pat.

She flung the machine out into traffic, and was endeavoring to follow the taxicab, which had melted into traffic in such a way there was already a milk truck between them.

"That darn milk truck is blocking my view," complained Pat.

"I'm not sure that's such a bad thing," murmured Monk. "Given the circumstances. They saw me, even if they didn't recognize you."

Pat flung back, "So?"

"If they were smart, they would drive to the nearest police station, and step out, yelling bloody murder and pointing in our direction."

Pat shook her dark-dyed hair. "They wouldn't dare. It appears as if they were kidnapping Vina Hawks Nansen."

"Looks may not be what they seem. I got me a hunch the tall well-dressed dude was Morgan Marrs."

"Vina's fiancé? If that's true, maybe this isn't a kidnapping, after all."

"Who knows what it is," grunted Monk, picking through the assortment of weaponry in the front seat. "But if you see them take the next left, don't follow. That way lies the police station."

"We'll soon see," said Pat grimly. "I still say we witnessed a kidnapping."

At the next corner, the yellow cab wheeled left and came into view ahead of the trundling milk truck.

Monk said, "I told you so."

"We can't abandon Vina like this."

Monk thought swiftly, and then directed, "Take the second left, and we'll swing around. Maybe we'll get lucky."

They got lucky. They got very lucky. The yellow taxicab took them to a garage, where the trio claimed a limousine that had apparently been parked in the establishment.

When it slithered out, Ike Golden was behind the wheel, and in the rear compartment, they assumed, the tall imposing man who might or might not be Morgan Marrs, along with Vina Hawks Nansen, were safely ensconced out of sight. For the rear windows were curtained.

Monk said to Pat, "See if you can follow them without bein' spotted."

"I'll be as invisible as a gnat," promised Pat.

True to her word, Pat fell several car lengths behind. By ducking into side streets, they managed to follow along until it became evident that the limousine was leaving the city of Tulsa.

"Kinda looks like they're headin' north," Monk murmured.

"In that case," said Pat. "We're headed north as well."

"We'll soon be travelin' along country roads," cautioned Monk. "They're sure to spot us."

Behind the wheel, Pat frowned. "So what do we do? We can't just give up. Vina's life may be at stake."

"Probably is," muttered Monk. He was thinking swiftly. Rooting around, the apish chemist was going through the assortment of weaponry in the back seat and produced a .22-caliber target pistol with a very long barrel.

"What are you doing?" asked Pat, glancing into the rear-vision mirror.

The hairy chemist was rolling down the right side passenger window in the rear, and he stuck out his head, his long right arm holding the weapon.

"That limousine model has a mighty big gas tank."

"So rumor has it."

"I *know* it does. Ham owns one just like it. One time, I slipped some chemicals into the tank. They made the exhaust smell like a scared polecat was hidin' in there."

"Did Ham ever find out?"

"Not that he could prove it," allowed Monk. "But he harbored his suspicions." He lined up the long gun barrel, closed one eye and squinted with the other. "Maybe if I plink it just right, it'll start leakin'."

"I get it!" Pat said. "You want them to run out of gas somewhere. Just like Grabber Daly."

"Nope," said Monk. "Not exactly." Abruptly, he pulled himself back in without having fired a shot.

As their eyes met in the rear-view mirror, Pat looked perplexed.

"Dawdle along as far back as you can," directed Monk. "I'll tell you what to do when I have a notion to."

"That doesn't sound like much of a plan," Pat murmured dubiously.

Monk shrugged. "It's the only plan I got, and if you have a better one, spread it out on the dashboard for me to see."

"I figured on following that big limousine just as we are."

Monk snorted derisively. "We're sure to be spotted, if we haven't already been. But keep on goin'. I'll let you know when I get the notion."

Since it was morning, there was a lot of traffic on the road and they managed to stay with the limousine without incident. It ran six cars ahead, and sometimes seven. The limousine headed due north and did not waver.

The road naturally had its curves, and when it did turn, Monk said, "Fall back a lot."

"How much?"

"I'll tell you," said Monk, picking up the target pistol again.

Pat slowed the touring car, fell back by wrestling between two lanes of traffic. After a while, she could see the limousine ahead, showing clearly in the curve of the road. Monk had the pistol out the window, and said to Pat, "Tap your brake."

Pat braked briefly, and Monk fired once.

Nothing appeared to happen. At least, the limousine did not catch fire.

"Did you hit the gas tank?" wondered Pat.

"We'll know soon enough," said Monk, holding his bullet head out the window.

"Remember that you're a notorious fugitive," cautioned Pat. "I'm sure they've got wanted posters in the post office windows with your face plastered on them by now."

The unexpected thought caused the apish chemist to pull his head back in and duck low. He touched the part of his cheek where the mysterious brown scorpion stain lay beneath a thin layer of pancake make-up.

"Is that dang stain showin'?" he wanted to know.

"Just the tip of the stinger," reassured Pat. "If you don't shave, it might go away."

"If I don't shave," groaned the simian chemist, "I'll look even more like a sore thumb than I already do."

"Take your pick," clucked Pat. "Grow a beard or wait until that ugly tattoo fades."

"See if you can spot gas on the asphalt of the road," suggested Monk.

Traffic was moving again and Pat did her best. Finally, she announced, "I see a few drops of something that might be gasoline."

"O.K., find a place to pull over and we'll let them get some distance on us. If I did this right, we should be able to trail them to wherever they're going by the gas trail."

"Monk, you sound very confident for a man who isn't quite sure he hit his target."

"Well, I'm sure now," said Monk firmly. "I aimed to bark the gas tank the way Daniel Boone used to bark a raccoon by parting its scalp, but not breaking its skin."

Pat frowned in such a way that her darkened eyebrows knit together.

"Wasn't that Davy Crockett, not Daniel Boone?"

Monk shrugged. "Whichever one invented that trick shot, I copied it so that I just nicked the tank, not punctured it."

"If you pulled it off," proclaimed Pat, "it was the luckiest lucky shot ever. But if it works, I'll buy you a coonskin cap and call you Daniel Crockett!"

Chapter XX

TANK FARM

EVIDENTLY, NEITHER IKE GOLDEN, who was driving the long limousine, nor his passengers, were aware that their gas tank had been punctured and was leaking fuel.

The trail of gas droplets—which was intermittent to say the least—continued along for many miles as Pat and Monk followed it.

At Monk's suggestion, Pat had long since allowed the limousine to pull away and disappear from view, by which ruse the hairy chemist hoped they could lull Golden into a sense of not being pursued.

At one juncture, the trail veered onto a roadside filling station and Pat pulled in to make sure they did not lose it.

While Monk hunkered down in the back seat, Pat asked the attendant to fill the tank.

While the man did so, Pat initiated a conversation beginning with, "Some friends of mine are driving along this road. They're in a black limousine. Have they been by recently?"

The attendant was a friendly sort. He was only too glad to make conversation.

"Sure as shootin'. Came by about a quarter-hour ago. Filled up their tank. The driver was complainin' on account he thought he left town with a full tank."

"Imagine that?" said Pat innocently.

"Are you headed for Bartlesville, too?"

"That I am," replied Pat, thinking quickly. "How ever did you know that's our destination?"

"The big shot in the back of the limousine was complaining that they needed to get to Bartlesville before noon. He was pretty anxious about it, and the driver was sweating bullets as he tried to convince the big boy that they'd make it in time."

"Thank you," said Pat, paying the man a dollar and tipping him with a dazzling smile. She left the filling station rapidly, for it was already ten-thirty.

Once back on the road, Pat again picked up the trail of leaking gasoline. Now that the tank had been replenished, the line of dripping fuel along the roadway was more distinctly visible owing to the frequency of its drippage.

She asked Monk, "How far to Bartlesville?"

"It's a fair hike north," said the homely chemist, sitting up. "But we're sure to make it before noon."

"Anything to Bartlesville?" wondered Pat curiously.

"Oil town," shrugged Monk.

Pat laughed lightly and asked, "Aren't they all?"

Monk grinned. "Pretty much."

From Tulsa to Bartlesville, Oklahoma, near the border of the state of Kansas, was a hop of some fifty miles on a blacktop road that ran as straight as a string. It was that very straightness that had caused Monk Mayfair to direct Pat Savage to fall behind the black limousine, lest they be spotted.

As a tactic, it had worked well. As a stratagem, it remained to be seen.

The limousine followed the Bartlesville road for many miles, then turned east. It did not travel as far as Pat and Monk had expected.

Pat guided the machine to a gate, stopped, and got out to open the gate.

"I didn't think the Ozark Ogre would dare hide himself this close to Tulsa!" Pat exclaimed, surprised.

"What makes you think this is where Standing Scorpion hangs out?" asked Monk, peering about.

"Call it a hunch," said Pat.

"That's a hunch like you'd find on a desert camel. Cough it up."

"Oh," said Pat airily, "maybe I put two and two together. Vina looked like she was being abducted, and Ike Golden is probably a Standing Scorpion hireling. It only follows that she was being taken to his headquarters. Or one of them. Say, how far are we from Osage territory?"

"Next county over," said Monk. "So if this ain't a hidin' place, it's mighty convenient to one."

Reclaiming the wheel, Pat drove the car through the gate. They wound through low sand hills for a bit, then their surroundings changed remarkably.

Huge bulks reared up around them—steel crude oil tanks.

The Ozark Ogre seemed to have picked the center of a huge tank farm for his hidden headquarters.

Monstrous oil storage tanks stood about in orderly array. Each one of them was capable of holding fifty-five thousand barrels of crude, but they did not seem to be in use at present. There was no odor of petroleum hanging in the air, and the dikes encircling the metallic monstrosities showed no signs of leakage. Paint was scabbing off the tank surfaces and rust patches were creeping up from the ground.

"Abandoned!" Monk grunted explosively.

"All the more reason to suspect that it's a hideout," said Pat, stepping out of the touring car. She had the old Peacemaker six-shooter Monk had scavenged from Eric Nansen's impressive personal collection, and began loading it from the box of shells Monk offered.

Monk climbed out next, his hirsute fists bristling with matched pistols, and a double-barreled shotgun tucked under one arm. After pocketing the pistols, the simian chemist fell to loading the shotgun. Then he restored it to working order.

"Watch where you point that thing," warned Pat. "I've handled plenty of scatterguns in my life, and I know the kind of damage they can do."

Monk was searching the area with his small eyes. The tank farm nestled amid red-oak furred hills, where it would not be visible from the several approaches. Hence they had not realized the nature of the place until they had traveled up the gated road a fair ways.

"This would make a swell hideout for somebody," admitted Monk.

He was looking at the ground, as was Pat Savage. They recognized fresh tire tracks, along with a thin trail of gasoline droplets, indicating that the limousine had passed this way. There was no immediate sight of it. But the place was quite large. The tankage blocked most of the view to the north.

Cautiously, they advanced on foot.

As they made their way between the towering storage tanks, Monk noted further evidence that the place had fallen into disuse.

Irregularly shaped cooling ponds came into view, but they were not filled—were not even mud holes. The sun had baked them dry. These were impoundments normally used to cool hot process water, and sometimes to put out sagebrush fires.

A tumbleweed bounced along the bottom of one of the former ponds, looking like a brown animal seeking shelter.

"This place is a ghost town," muttered Monk, as he led the way.

Pat murmured, "I wonder if Standing Scorpion is somehow tied into the oil industry of Oklahoma?"

To which the hairy chemist replied, "Lots of Indians struck it rich out this way. Black gold has been found under reservation land, so it's a possibility, I reckon. But Standing Scorpion is no more of an Indian than I am."

"That," said Pat firmly, "remains to be seen."

As they moved in the shadows of one rusting tank, they started to wish that they had not discovered the tank farm in broad daylight. By night, no doubt, the place might have had its spooky aspects, but night shadows also would have sheltered them and made their slow approach less risky.

Before long, they heard voices talking rather loudly. These were muffled, as if they were coming from an enclosed space. But they were human voices and they were quite urgent.

"Must be coming from the pumping station yonder," decided Monk.

Pat looked about, frowned. "What pumping station?"

"There's gotta be one," affirmed Monk. "Them dry cooling ponds give that away."

For a moment, the homely chemist wavered in his resolve.

"What's the matter?" asked Pat.

"Might be there are guards picketed about. If we're spotted, we'd be in for a merry time chasin' around these storage tanks."

Pat nodded. Then she said, "I have a hankering to get closer and hear what's being discussed."

"Suits me," agreed Monk, suddenly looking up.

The storage tank in whose shadow they stood—indeed, every specimen hereabouts—was adorned with a spidery inspection ladder that ran all the way to the domed top.

"Are you thinking of climbin' this rusty monster?" asked Pat, seeing the expression on Monk's unlovely face.

"If I can get up there without bein' spotted," returned Monk, "I ought to be able to take in the whole layout."

"You could also get your ears shot off," reminded Pat.

"Could be," allowed Monk slowly, his eyes narrowing. Hefting his shotgun, he said, "Think I need a long gun for this operation."

"I suspect you're onto something," allowed Pat. "But if you're going up this ladder, I'm going up another. Two pairs of eyes from on high will see twice as much."

Monk asked, "You up to the climb?"

"I climbed my share of mountains in my own wayward youth," she insisted. "This is no different."

"Well, when you pick a ladder, pick one that ain't half rusted away. Otherwise you're in for a mighty long fall," warned Monk.

Retreating to the car, they each armed themselves with a Winchester lever-action rifle, caliber .44-40.

Pat Savage had wielded more than one of these in the past and she essayed a sly grin as she inserted bullets into the loading slot of the receiver. "This ought to do the job."

"Mebbe," said Monk, "but I'd still rather have my superfirer."

CREEPING back into the cluster of storage tanks, Monk found a ladder that looked substantial and gave it a vigorous tugging. It held. He waved Pat up.

Lashing the Winchester to her belt, she began her ascent. Monk watched anxiously from below. When the copper-skinned girl was halfway up the iron ladder, the apish chemist decided that she would make it to the top all right. He turned and went in search of a storage tank of his own.

Monk was soon climbing upward, his comically long anthropoid arms making a great contrast with his relatively truncated legs. He scrambled up the ladder like an ape in a slovenly suit of clothes.

Pat naturally reached the top first, and lay down prone on the dome.

Face showing some strain, she glanced over and waited for Monk to appear. When the hairy chemist's nubbin skull topped his chosen storage tank, he gave a reassuring wave and then plopped down flat on his stomach.

Standing up might have done them some good, but the vantage point they chose gave them a clear view of the brick pumping house. It looked as forlornly deserted as the rusting tanks, but the impressive black limousine was parked in plain view. There did not appear to be any guards, nor any other vehicle. This fact was slightly reassuring, but it told them nothing about what was going on inside the pump house.

The sound of voices had died down, so they listened patiently.

Before long, a woman's voice could be heard. It lifted, rose to the boiling sky, then echoed among the tankage.

"Oh! No, you cannot mean this. Not Ben. Please, do not harm him!"

The voice was unmistakably that of Vina Hawks Nansen.

While they were absorbing these words, the door to the pump house opened and four figures stepped out.

The one in the lead caused them to draw in sharp, surprised breaths. It was tall and garbed in flowing black silk. A purple hood so dark it was almost ebony concealed his head and on the chest glowed a vertical scorpion worked in scarlet, its thin, whip-like tail coiling menacingly. The twin eyes of the figure's hood gleamed like hellfire.

Chief Standing Scorpion!

Behind him, two equally-tall Osage braves were half-dragging a man they recognized. The foot-dragging fellow was unusually pale, as if he had been dipped in bleach. Even the wayward strands of his hair had a bleached aspect. He looked as if he had no strength to stand and walk under his own power, hence the dragging.

Pat caught Monk's eyes and mouthed two words: "Ben Nansen."

The homely chemist gave her the O.K. sign.

Both Pat and Monk could read lips fairly well and they fell into silent conversation.

Pat started it. "This was where they were keeping Ben Nansen prisoner. The question is what for?"

"Dunno," mouthed Monk. "But I don't like the looks of that procession."

"We could wing those two Indians."

"O.K. by me," replied Monk. "But what do we do then? It's a long way down to the ground."

"Let's figure that out when we hit solid ground," decided Pat.

While that seemed to be settled, Vina Hawks Nansen appeared. She rushed after her stricken brother, screaming loudly. "You cannot kill my brother! You cannot kill my brother! You promised that he would live!"

The exotic figure of Chief Standing Scorpion stopped stock-still and turned around majestically, so that the puffy cloth stinger decorating the tail of his hood became visible. It twisted in the hot breeze.

His sonorous words did not reach their ears, but both Pat and Monk knew that he was pronouncing doom upon helpless Ben Nansen.

For the two Osages resumed dragging the man away from the pump house.

A third Indian stepped out of the brick structure, seized Vina and hauled her forcibly back in. The old weathered door shut abruptly.

Turning again, Standing Scorpion continued leading his abbreviated procession. The trio was striding toward one of the dry-as-a-bone cooling ponds, and it quickly became evident that their intention was to dispose of his body therein.

That was when Monk and Pat Savage decided to take action. Working the cocking levers in their rifles, they jacked fresh shells into their respective chambers, and sought their triggers.

Monk fired first, and his shot caught one of the Osages in his right shoulder, spinning him about.

Pat Savage's bullet was half a second behind it. It caught the other in the ankle. The man actually jumped in place, and commenced hopping around, holding his injured foot and howling what was presumably profanity in his native tongue.

Both Pat and Monk next lined up on the bizarre tower of purple-black cloth that was Standing Scorpion.

But the figure was wily. He made a rush for the door. While their bullets chased him eagerly, all they did was spank up dusty red earth at his heels. His skirts were flying about, showing his beaded moccasins.

The door opened ahead of him, and the silken apparition vanished within.

The portal had barely slammed shut when Monk and Pat opened up again, peppering it in the hope of discouraging anyone else from exiting the pump house.

Dispensing with the lip-reading bit, Monk yelled, "Let's go!"

Pat had already disappeared from the storage-tank roof. She was moving down the ladder as fast as her trim figure permitted.

Nevertheless, Monk beat her to the ground, thanks to his nimble if freakishly ungainly limbs. They rendezvoused in the hot shadow of one tank and advanced together.

Monk handed over his rifle. "Hold this," he said as he started forward.

Before Pat could dissuade him, the apish chemist fell upon the Osage who was hopping madly about, clutching his bleeding foot. Monk slammed the howling one to the ground forcefully. A rusty-knuckled fist came crashing down, breaking the man's jaw and putting him to sleep for the rest of the afternoon.

The other Osage hightailed it into the cluster of storage tanks, disappearing from view.

Pat caught up with Monk. Working together, they dragged Ben Nansen to safety, hunkering down in the shadow of one hulking tank where they could peer around and keep an eye on the pump house.

"Standing Scorpion is holed up inside," Pat said breathlessly. "He can't stay in there forever."

"Sure, he can," reminded Monk. "He's got Vina. She's a hostage."

"So it's a stalemate, I guess," Pat decided.

Monk shrugged sloping shoulders. "Mexican standoff is more like it."

On the ground behind them, Ben Nansen looked like a ghost that was struggling to achieve some solidity on the earth. He was moaning. There was not much volume or force to his weak utterances.

"How many still in there?" asked Pat. "We nipped two Osages."

Nansen could hardly speak. It looked as if all the vital fluids had been drained out of his emaciated body. His words came with difficulty.

"Standing Scorpion. Vina. Ike Golden. Tall Turkey. Some other Osages."

"How many in all?" pressed Pat.

"About seven, counting Morgan Marrs. He's here, too."

"We're outnumbered," decided Pat.

Monk nodded. "But we've got the drop on 'em. Only one way out of that old pump station. That's through the doors and windows. They're sittin' ducks."

Feeding a fresh cartridge into her Winchester, Pat wondered, "How do we make them quack?"

"We'll wait 'em out."

"That could take all day," complained Pat.

"If you're up to knockin' on the door," suggested the hirsute chemist, "be my guest. But get ready to duck. Those holes we shot in the door would make pretty fair loopholes for anyone fixin' to shoot back."

Unhappily, Pat said, "I guess we wait it out, after all."

She and Monk sat down on either side of Ben Nansen, and the unfortunate man was so far gone he simply closed his eyes and lost all interest in his surroundings.

Monk looked him over sympathetically. His pallor was gruesome—something like unbaked pastry—and his head lolled as if his neck bones might be disjointed.

"Kinda looks like he needs a blood transfusion bad," mumbled Monk.

Pat shivered. "Don't say that. I don't believe in vampires."

"Where blood-suckin' vampires are concerned," admitted the hairy chemist glumly, "I'm startin' to acquire religion."

Chapter XXI

STANDOFF

THE BLAZING OKLAHOMA sun beat down upon them as the day wore on.

Pat and Monk were forced to drag Ben Nansen about the storage tank, following the shade cast by the climbing solar furnace.

"This is growin' monotonous," complained Monk. "We ain't gettin' anywhere fast."

"Well, it was your idea to wait them out," countered Pat. "Do you have a better notion now?"

"No," admitted Monk. Studying Ben Nansen, he said, "This guy needs cool water, or he's gonna up and die of thirst."

"One of us could carry him back to the car and take him to the hospital," suggested Pat.

"Yeah, but which one? And what happens to the one who stays behind? If they spot us goin', they're sure to come chargin' out, spoilin' for blood."

"You're right," admitted Pat. Then a thought leapt into her head. "What happened to that Osage who got away?"

"I've been keepin' an eye out for him, don't you worry none," reassured Monk. "He's probably hidin' out somewhere."

Setting her shoulders, Pat said, "Let's hope he's not a back-shooter."

It was afternoon now, and the shadows were starting to lengthen again.

An idea flaring in her brain, Pat said suddenly, "I'm going to try something."

"What?" asked Monk.

Instead of replying, the golden-eyed girl cupped her hands and called out, "Miss Nansen?"

There was a long pause. Finally, the voice of Vina Hawks Nansen called back, "I am here."

"We have your brother. He's alive."

"Oh, thank goodness! Please take care of Ben."

The woman sounded distressed in the extreme.

Monk decided he would join in the conversation. Lifting his squeaky voice to a dull roar, he called, "Hey, chief. You in there, too?"

There was a long period in which no answer came, then the sonorous voice of Chief Standing Scorpion floated out.

"You have angered me," he intoned. "Know that I am not only a war chief, but a powerful Vinegarroon medicine man, as well."

"Send the girl out and we'll parley."

"What are your terms?"

"What do you think? We got you covered six ways from Sunday. Send the gal out, and we'll talk it over."

"Hah! You dare not shoot while she is among us."

Pat made a face. "He's right about that," she confided to Monk. "We can't shoot up the place without fear of hitting her."

Monk's low brow furrowed. "I know it, and you know it. But sometimes guys who are in a tight spot, their thinking gets kind of rusty. I'm tryin' to rust up his thinkin' so he makes a fool move."

"Good luck," said Pat. "Standing Scorpion doesn't sound like anybody's fool."

Shrugging, Monk again called out, "I'll give you a few hours to think about it. Must be hot in that pumpin' station with the sun beating down like blazes. You're probably thirsty, too."

"We have water," retorted Standing Scorpion. "That is more than we can say about you."

"Have it your way," hollered Monk. "We got all day, and all night, too."

It was a boast, of course, but it proved to be prescient. As the sun started sinking a few hours later, they were still scooting around the shadow of the great empty oil storage tank. No lights showed in the pumping station as the sun dropped redly into the Western prairie.

"Now what do we do?" asked Pat unhappily. "It looks like we will be stuck here all night."

"Not me," grumbled Monk. "I'm gettin' hungry again."

Pat regarded him dubiously. "What do you propose we do now? Ben Nansen will expire without medical help and we've gotten exactly nowhere."

The simian chemist started going through his pockets, producing assorted items. "I've got a few smoke grenades, some more gas and a few other things. We'll shoot out some windows. Then I can sneak close enough to pitch in a couple smoke grenades to confuse them, then knock 'em all out with gas."

"Any time you care to commence operations," invited Pat, "I'll be sure to do my part."

"Give it another hour," decided Monk. "Another hour won't hurt us none and it's sure to wear them down some."

"Another hour then," said Pat, folding her arms impatiently. She was tired of gripping her Winchester for hours on end.

CONSIDERABLY less than an hour passed when they heard the sound of a motorcar engine starting.

Alarm came into Monk's eyes and Pat blurted, "How did they escape the building without being spotted?"

"I dunno," said Monk, springing to his feet, "but they have to drive that limousine this way in order to get out to the gate. We'll shoot out their tires when they run past us."

The limousine did not budge, however. The car-engine roar was not coming from the direction they thought. Instead, it was the sound of their borrowed machine!

By the time they realized this unhappy fact, it was too late. Pat and Monk leapt to their feet, and, weapons in hand, the hasty pair charged in the direction of the entrance.

The gate hung open. They had left it closed. Discouragingly, the tail-light of their borrowed touring car was visible in the gathering gloom, receding rapidly.

Lifting her rifle to her shoulder, Pat lined up its sights, and took a shot at one rear tire. She apparently missed because the vehicle continued on, undiminished in speed.

Monk took his chance, too, but all that he received in return was the hard spank of lead hammering against the steel construction of the touring car.

"How the heck did they get out of there without us spottin' them?" raged the homely chemist.

Turning around, they raced for the pump house, with the intention of claiming the limousine, and giving chase.

Reaching the long machine, Pat said, "Shouldn't we check the pump house first?"

"No time!" grated Monk. "We'll pick up Nansen on the way out. We gotta run them down."

Throwing himself behind the wheel, the hairy chemist found that the key was in the ignition, grinned fiercely, and gave it a twist.

The engine turned over immediately, but no sooner had he released the emergency brake than Monk discovered an unhappy reality.

Wrenching the wheel, he gave the engine gas—and it immediately sputtered and conked out.

"What the heck!" he complained.

Pat reminded him, "You nicked a hole in the gas tank a ways back, remember? This bus isn't going anywhere."

Holding back his wrath, Monk sprang out of the limousine and went charging around the pump house. He didn't hesitate. He got out his flashlight, spun the generator, and popped out a white-hot cone of light.

The homely chemist was flashing this about when he knocked in the pump house door, and discovered that the interior was empty of people.

"They've vamoosed!" he howled.

"But how?" Pat asked the thin air.

"Beats me," said Monk, but his flashlight beam soon disclosed something interesting. Amid a bulky mass of dull gray machinery in which polished brass gleamed, stood a round, black maw. Beside it lay a great metal fitting like a manhole cover and a sprinkling of loose lug nuts, along with the monkey wrench and other tools that had been used to remove them from their fittings.

The apish chemist began berating himself. "Am I a prize dope!"

"How so?" asked Pat, genuinely curious.

"This is a dang pump house. It's used to pump process water through the cooling ponds. The ponds are dry. Look at that aperture over here. They opened up one of the big pipes with a monkey wrench and crept through it to the cooling pond bed and then probably crawled on their bellies like snakes to our car."

"No doubt that Osage who was lying low in one of the dry ponds was collected on the way out," fumed Pat.

Exiting the pump house, they searched the vicinity, but discovered only a solitary Osage—the one whose ankle had been shattered by Pat's Winchester and whose jaw had been likewise broken by Monk's driving piston of a fist.

The Indian was showing signs of coming to, so Monk grabbed him by his shirtfront and began shaking him.

"Up, you! Wake up!"

The man slowly stirred, his eyes dull and listless. When he tried to speak, pain made his jawbone turn to fire and he cried out in his agony.

"You got left behind," explained Monk. "Nobody stayed behind you gotta protect, so spill some beans and we'll make a dang meal of it."

The Indian just looked at him dazedly.

Pat poked her head in view and got the fellow's attention. She asked a simple question: "Who is Standing Scorpion?"

"Tall Turkey," the man said in agony.

"Who is Tall Turkey?" demanded Pat.

"Vinegarroon medicine man. Powerful medicine man." Then pain made the man's brain short circuit or something, for he lost consciousness all over again.

Standing up, Pat said to Monk, "One of those Osages looked mighty tall for a red man."

"Yeah," said Monk thoughtfully. "Could be that was Tall Turkey, but I thought he was in view at the same time as Standing Scorpion."

"Now that you mention it, he was. Tall Turkey must've been another Osage."

Peering about the darkness of the tank farm, Monk changed the subject, "We're gonna have to figure out a way to get Ben Nansen to a hospital and ourselves back on the trail of Standing Scorpion, whoever the rascal is."

"That's a tall order," admitted Pat. Then she snapped her slim fingers. "And I think I know who will fill it."

Monk looked baffled in a comical way. "Who?"

"Let's hunt us up a telephone, and you'll see."

IT WAS a long walk in the dark to the nearest pay telephone and, fortunately, it was at a filling station. A drugstore would have been too chancy to enter.

Pat stepped in, closed the folding door and began dropping coins into the slot. She made call after call, and finally emerged with a satisfied smile on her attractive features.

"He should be here in less than an hour to pick us up," she announced triumphantly.

"Who?" blurted out Monk.

But canny Pat refused to enlighten the hairy chemist. She finally divulged, "You'll see."

True to Pat's prediction, approximately an hour later, a non-descript sedan wheeled into view and fixed them in the glare of its twin headlamps.

Rocking to a halt just a few feet from them, the auto came to a stop. And a slim but wiry figure stepped out from behind the driver's seat.

Before this individual could step into the glow, Monk Mayfair recognized him. He let out a howl that might have been a mixture of rejoicing and aggravation.

"Shyster! What're you doin' here?"

The man who stepped forward was attired in sartorial splendor. He carried an elegant black stick in one hand, and a runt pig under the other arm. The pig let out an excited squeal and jumped from the crook of the man's arm.

The porker rushed up to Monk, who stooped, picked it up and began throwing the shoat up and down in the air like an overzealous father with a toddler.

"Habeas! You made it!"

For the new arrival was Ham Brooks, one of Doc Savage's other associates, who had been summoned to Oklahoma by Monk himself. The simian chemist had forgotten that Ham should have arrived by this time, having taken a commercial flight west.

Turning to Pat, Monk asked, "How'd you get hold of this illegal eagle?"

"It was simple," said Pat brightly. "I simply called all the best hotels in Tulsa until I reached him."

"Slick!" Monk said admiringly.

After doffing his Homburg hat politely in Pat's direction while pointedly ignoring Monk, Ham drawled, "Inasmuch as you two remain fugitives, it is better if you got into the back seat and we will figure out our next move."

With suitable alacrity, they did so, Monk carrying his pet pig, Habeas Corpus, by one oversized ear. The pig seemed to enjoy the roughhouse treatment.

When their excited reunion settled down, Pat asked, "What do you think we should do next, Ham?"

"I would advise turning yourself in and making a clean breast of matters," advised the dapper lawyer.

"Nix!" snapped Monk.

"We are doing nothing of the sort!" flared Pat. "We're on the trail of something, and we are going to get to the bottom of it. We can turn ourselves in once we collect more fitting candidates for the electric chair. Otherwise it's the death house for us."

"That is a risky course of action," Ham said, frowning. "But let me hear your tales of woe before we get too far along."

"Before we go," Pat interjected, "I would like to check on Ben Nansen."

"Who is Ben Nansen?" wondered Ham.

Pat told him, "The poor fellow who started the unfortunate chain of circumstances that have made me and Monk notorious from Tulsa to Muskogee. We had to leave him, but the first call I made here was to the police. I told them where to find him, along with a suspicious Osage with a shattered jaw."

She stepped out of the machine and returned to the pay telephone.

Prompted by Pat, Monk added, "The Indian may be one of the Tall Boys gang."

Disguising her voice, Pat quickly ascertained that both men had been collected from the deserted oil-tank storage farm, and promptly transported to a local hospital.

"What hospital, please?" she asked.

After receiving a reply, Pat abruptly hung up, returned to the automobile and the trio went on their way.

Most of the ride back to Tulsa was occupied with filling in the dapper attorney. After hearing their account of the events since their arrival in Tulsa, Ham Brooks remarked, "Perhaps you are correct. Bringing in the real murderers may resolve things more swiftly than letting the slow wheels of justice grind you in its cogs."

"Our problem," declared Pat Savage, "will be getting back on the trail of the desperadoes. We know that most of the gang are Osage Indians. The publisher of the *Tulsa Trumpet*, Morgan Marrs, is somehow mixed in it, as is his fiancée, Vina Hawks Nansen. And so is Ike Golden, a reporter on the *Globe*. How all this fits together makes up a Gordian knot I can't mentally untie."

Ham considered all these facts carefully and finally decided, "We must find a suitable but secure hotel outside of Tulsa for our headquarters."

"Good thinkin'," squeaked Monk. "I could use some shuteye after bakin' in the sun all day long."

"There is only one problem," inserted Pat.

"And what is that?" asked Ham.

"The fact that Monk and I are fugitives from Oklahoma justice. And if you were caught with us, you'll probably land in the pokey for aiding and abetting two wanted outlaws."

Behind the wheel, Ham Brooks' firmly chiseled features paled. "I will have you know that I am not afraid to face Oklahoma justice, if it comes to that."

"You might lose your law license," reminded Pat.

If possible, Ham Brooks' pale face blanched even whiter. "That," he admitted reluctantly, "I am deathly afraid of facing."

Giving Habeas Corpus a thoughtful scratch, Monk imparted, "This is the dangedest mess we ever blundered into."

Pat regarded the apish chemist skeptically. "Seems to me I've heard you use those identical words in the past."

"Mebbe," grumbled Monk. "But this daggone mess is even more danged than any I can recollect at the moment."

Chapter XXII
SUSPECTS THREE

A TULSA HOTEL was out of the question for their night's lodgings.

Pat, Monk and Ham all agreed on that point. After that, however, their opinions diverged sharply.

"You two cannot be seen in the city of Tulsa," insisted Ham. "Even with Pat's disguise, Monk is too conspicuous. It would be impossible to sneak you into a respectable hotel without arousing police notice."

Monk made thinking faces. "I know of a seedy roadhouse out Ponca City way," he said. "Where we can rent rooms for the night—no questions asked."

"A roadhouse," insisted Pat, "is no place for a lady."

"And aside from that unassailable fact," inserted Ham, "no doubt the police dragnet is keeping a close eye on any such down-at-the-heels establishments."

While they were driving about, the elegant attorney questioned them about the affair to date.

Pat and Monk took turns telling the tale and the dapper lawyer stopped them frequently to ask probing questions.

One of the questions had to do with the mysterious panhandlers and their badly out-of-tune flutes.

"I fail to comprehend the significance of the flutes in regard to the death of Harold Manton."

"I already figured that out," said Monk. "The Osage who tried to murder Pat made a point of coverin' the holes in his flute with his fingers. That turned it into a kind of a blowgun. When I saw him stalkin' Pat, and sealin' the flute's top holes, I knew something sneaky was afoot."

Pat asked, "But how did you know he would be firing a poison pellet?"

"I didn't," admitted the hairy chemist. "But when the pellet struck the lobby wall, I saw a reddish gas or powder erupt. That's when I knew. That's why I pushed our faces in front of the lobby fan and told you to hold your breath while I held my own."

"Very clever, you ape," complimented Ham. "But that does not explain what felled Ben Nansen and Harold Manton in such a way that scarlet scorpions appeared on their faces."

"I ain't quite figured that out yet," admitted Monk. "But I'm workin' on it. I got one on my puss, but it ain't scarlet. It's plain brown, which is the normal color of a vinegarroon."

Monk and Pat were sitting low in the back seat, so Ham turned around to look. Studying Monk in the ever-changing light, he snapped, "I see nothing of the sort."

"That's because I covered it with—" Monk bit off his sentence, uncompleted.

"With what?" wondered Ham suspiciously.

"Oh, some stuff I found."

"Well, whatever the stuff is," retorted Ham, "I see nothing resembling a scorpion on your cheek."

A worried flicker touched Pat's attractive features. "I hope the authorities brought poor Ben Nansen to the hospital in time. He looked like he was just about done for."

Ham asserted, "When morning comes, I will check in on him. No doubt he has a great deal to tell us."

"According to Ben Nansen," offered Pat, "Standing Scorpion is an Osage Indian named Tall Turkey. Since all these Osage boys seem to be taller than the typical Indian, we don't know which one he is."

"I don't believe it!" snapped Monk. "When we first met Standing Scorpion, he was spoutin' Hollywood Injun talk, which no self-respecting Osage would ever mimic. I think he's a white man."

Hearing this, the fastidious attorney asked, "Who are the other suspects?"

Pat answered that. "Well, Vina Hawks Nansen ranked at the top of the list until Standing Scorpion dragged her brother out to be killed. That was no acting that we witnessed, Monk and I."

Contrarily, Ham pointed out, "But you do not know that the person wearing the hooded robes of Standing Scorpion in that instance was the same individual that you met before—never mind the real Standing Scorpion."

"A fair point," admitted Pat. "But Vina Hawks Nansen was not acting. She was terrified. That lets her out."

"Continue your inventory of suspects," advised Ham.

Monk took that one. "Well, puttin' Tall Turkey, whoever he is, aside for the moment, there's Ike Golden, the *Globe* oil reporter. He's mixed up in this pretty deep. We left him tied up at the penthouse of publisher Morgan Marrs, and now it looks like he's in cahoots with Marrs, or maybe—"

"Or maybe they joined forces!" crowed Pat.

"But why would they do that?" Ham wanted to know. "Golden works on a rival newspaper, does he not?"

"Yeah," admitted Monk, "but he used to work for the *Trumpet*, so he must know Marrs from those days. Golden told us reporters often switched sides when they got on the bad side of one editor."

"Golden is suspicious, all right," Ham allowed. "What about Morgan Marrs?"

Pat and Monk had to think about that for a while. Finally, Monk said, "We don't know much about him. He's engaged to Vina Hawks Nansen, and is a powerful man in the state. Why would Marrs be in back of this Grampus paralysis and all the intrigue that goes with it?"

"Powerful men sometimes desire even more power," advised Ham. "And what about the father of the two Nansen children?"

"He's out," said Pat swiftly. "He was the first victim of the Grampus paralysis. He's in a wheelchair now. And worried sick about his children. Mr. Nansen lent us a small arsenal and his touring car."

Ham frowned. "This would not be the first time a criminal mastermind pretended to be his own victim in order to allay suspicions over his guilt."

Pat said, "I don't see it, any more than I see Vina Hawks Nansen as culpable. I did before, but not now."

Then the barrister asked a question that was entirely unexpected. "Are we certain that Harold Manton is deceased?"

"Quite certain," said Pat. "We overheard a hotel doctor pronounce him dead in the lobby where he fell."

Ham stated, "Men have faked their deaths before. The reasons may be complicated, but not once they are brought to light. We should look into Harold Manton's background."

"He's the oil editor on the *Trumpet*," explained Monk, examining Habeas Corpus on his lap thoughtfully.

"Hmmm," murmured Pat. "Haven't a lot of the places where this Scorpion gang hangs out been oil property?"

"It *is* suspicious," allowed Ham. "Makes one assume the villain is connected to the local oil industry."

"That fits Manton and Golden both," muttered Monk. "What gets me is why was Manton killed? He was nosin' around on our behalf, but unless he stumbled across something important, I don't see why they killed him."

"Say, he *did* uncover the fact that the building where we were first imprisoned was owned by the Trumpet Corporation," reminded Pat. "That points to publisher Morgan Marrs, doesn't it?"

"Or Vina," inserted Monk.

Ham said, "It is clear to me that the mark of the scorpion is intended to terrorize the state of Oklahoma and further the aims of this Standing Scorpion person. Perhaps Harold Manton was killed as a convenience."

Pat was saying, "If you tie everything up together, it seems to go to the Nansen family, or Morgan Marrs. Of course those two threads are connected through the engagement of Marrs and Vina Hawks Nansen."

"This is gettin' us no place," blurted Monk. "And we ain't found a place to sleep or pass the night yet!"

Ham asked abruptly, "Where is the flute you confiscated from the second panhandler?"

"We left it at our old hotel room," said Pat.

"If it is a murder weapon, it is evidence," Ham reminded. "You did not leave your fingerprints on it?"

"No," said Pat. "Monk wiped them off."

Ham seemed to breathe a sigh relief. "At this point, there is only one murder weapon with your fingerprints on it. Is that correct?"

Pat and Monk exchanged uneasy glances in the dark back of the sedan. "Well," admitted Pat, "they got my six-shooter and Monk's superfirer. No telling what they've done with them by now."

Ham scolded, "You are so careless, the two of you! I would not be surprised if, before all of this is over, a dozen killings are charged to your names with the evidence of your fingerprints on a small arsenal of weapons."

In the end, they had to settle on the roadhouse. Monk directed them to it, while Ham went inside to secure three rooms.

It was the middle of the night, so there was only a sleepy proprietor, and he was only too happy to hand out keys without inspecting his new lodgers when Ham Brooks offered him cash in hand.

As they separated for the night, Ham told them, "Be sure to stay in your rooms until I knock for you. We will find a way to leave this place without being seen."

Running disapproving eyes over the lawyer's sartorial splendor, Monk Mayfair grunted, "Me and Pat can probably pass muster as locals, but in those dude duds you're wearin', people are gonna remember you."

Giving the head of his sword cane a polish with the palm of his gloved hand, the dapper barrister said, "I will have to endure that indignity, but I am sure that it will pass with time."

On that note, they retired for the evening.

Chapter XXIII
SEARCH PLANE

THE MORNING BROUGHT many surprises. None of them pleasant.

Ham was the first to awaken, and the thing that roused him from sleep was the buzzing of an airplane flying low.

Looking out the single window of his rather dilapidated room, the dapper attorney saw that the buzzing was produced by a scarlet-and-black airplane. The striking aircraft seemed to be flying about aimlessly, and this fact made him wonder if it was a police plane, searching for fugitives. It was equipped with pontoon floats, making it an amphibian—an unusual sight in arid Oklahoma.

Ham was sufficiently alarmed that he dressed hurriedly, and went to Monk Mayfair's room, knocking lightly at first and then with increasing force, for Monk's snoring indicated that the homely chemist was deep in slumber.

Monk shuffled to the door and opened it a crack after ascertaining the identity of his caller. Habeas stuck out an inquisitive snout as well, snuffling sleepily.

Ham said, "There is a suspicious plane flying about in the sky."

Monk dry-washed his face absently. "Well, what's suspicious about it?"

"It is flying about in a rather aimless fashion, and seems to be circling the immediate vicinity."

Listening, Monk remarked, "I don't hear any buzzin'."

Entering, Ham Brooks pushed him aside and went to the window. He shoved this up and stuck his head out. The sound of the low-flying airplane's buzzing was no longer to be heard.

"It appears to have departed," Ham decided.

"That's exactly what we should be doing. After breakfast, that is."

"You dare not eat breakfast here, looking like the slovenly ape that you are," admonished Ham. "Remain in your room, and I will talk to Pat."

"O.K., but I'm gettin' breakfast one way or another. I'm famished."

Knocking on Pat's door, Ham was pleased to discover that the copper-complected girl was already up and waiting patiently for the others to rise.

"I slept in my clothes," she explained. "The sooner I'm out of this joint, the happier I'll be."

"There was a suspicious plane circling the area," advised Ham, "but it's gone now. It may mean nothing. I think you and I should go over to the hospital and look in on Ben Nansen."

"What about Monk?"

"We can't drag him around in broad daylight. He will scare dogs, small children, and attract the law."

"No argument there," said Pat. "Let me get my things."

They stopped at Monk's room on the way out to apprise him of their plans. The simian chemist looked miserable. "What about my breakfast?"

"You will have to wait," said Ham primly. "We will not be long."

"Hurry up. My stomach only knows one time: Hungry o'clock."

THEY got to the hospital without incident and presented themselves as concerned friends of Ben Nansen.

This did not arouse any undue suspicion, for the police apparently had not yet identified the man.

"Unless you are relatives or otherwise connected with the patient," the head nurse said firmly, "I am afraid you cannot see him."

Proffering his business card, Ham said, "I am an attorney. I have been retained by his father, the esteemed Eric Nansen of Oklahoma City, to represent Mr. Nansen in the unfortunate events in which he has been embroiled. It is important that I consult with my client."

The nurse examined the card and glanced at Pat, who was still tricked out as an Indian woman. "Who is this?"

"Natica Hawks, Ben Nansen's half-sister," said Pat swiftly.

Amazingly, this bald if not preposterous imposture passed muster. They were escorted to the patient's room without further delay.

A concerned-looking physician was examining Ben Nansen. Color had not yet returned, and the young man's unhealthy pallor was stark and frightening.

After presenting himself, Ham inquired, "How is my client coming along?"

"It will be touch and go over some time," said the doctor. "This man's blood has been drained from him to an unnerving degree. We are giving him transfusions, and that is helping. But I am afraid that there will be many more."

"What could have caused such a distressing condition?" demanded Ham.

"Numerous puncture marks were discovered on the man's arms and legs," supplied the doctor. "It appears as if his blood was siphoned over an extended period of time. But for what purpose I cannot conceive."

"Do you mean to say," pressed Ham, "blood has been systematically drained from his body?"

The medico nodded somberly. "It is a miracle that he is alive. But he is in no condition to talk."

Ham frowned. "I see. What about the fellow who was brought in with him?"

"The Indian? His jaw was so broken we had to wire it shut. Apparently, his education is lacking. He does not know how to write. So it will be many weeks until he can communicate—unless it's in smoke signals."

"Thank you, doctor," said Ham. "We will return at a more opportune time."

Exiting the hospital, Pat said to Ham, "When we first encountered Nansen, he mumbled about being used to feed something."

"Something? What do you mean—something?"

"That is all we got out of him. That his blood was being used to sustain something horrible. How that connects with this horrid mystery, I confess I have no idea."

As they drove back to the roadhouse, Pat noticed something in the sky. Shading her disguised eyes, she studied it closely.

"What color did you say that suspicious plane was?"

"Scarlet with black trim. Why?"

"Because I spy such an aircraft in the west."

The elegant attorney was so concerned that he pulled over to the side of the road, got out onto the running board and shaded his eyes with his right hand. He held his sword cane in the left. He swept the Western skies with dark, intelligent eyes.

"I cannot for the life of me," he murmured, "tell if that is the same plane or not. But it is flying in the same aimless manner, as if it is searching for something on the ground."

They watched the aircraft for some time. It ambled in their direction and, as it neared, they noticed that it was buzzing very low.

Now it was Pat's turn to frown. "I do not like the color of that paint," she remarked.

"Nor do I," agreed Ham. "There is something sinister about that combination of colors."

"That's not what I said," Pat corrected. "The color is the same blood-red shade as the scarlet scorpion mark on the faces of the two victims, Ben Nansen and Harold Manton."

"Coincidence, probably," mused Ham.

As the aircraft dropped low and glided overhead, they could see on the underside of one wing an insignia. The wing was scarlet. In the center of it was a black crest, the disk encompassing a scarlet scorpion sporting a thin trailing tail.

"Did you see that?" Pat yelled.

"I did," grated Ham. "That aircraft is somehow connected to Standing Scorpion. I would bet my life on it."

"Well, toss my life into the pot while you're at it," said Pat darkly. "They're either looking for us, or they're up to no good."

Settling back behind the wheel, Ham snapped, "We had best collect that perpetually hungry ape, Monk. Something sinister is afoot."

Monk was only too glad to be collected from the roadhouse, especially when he heard about the scorpion emblem on the wandering amphibian.

As they slipped the apish chemist out the back way and he jumped into the back of the waiting car, Habeas Corpus concealed under his coat, Monk ventured an idea.

"I don't think they're searchin' for us," he said.

"Of course they're looking for us!" snapped Pat. "Practically all of Oklahoma is looking for us."

"Standing Scorpion wouldn't be lookin' for us in a sky wagon marked with his own brand. He's up to something else."

"Why do you say that?" asked Ham impatiently as they pulled away from the roadhouse.

"Call it a hunch," said Monk. "But I think we should borrow us a plane and go chasin' after that black-and-blood bus."

As a suggestion, it was not much. But as a plan of action, it excited the imaginations of both Ham Brooks and Patricia Savage. They instantly decided that it was an appropriate course of action.

"Ham, take us to the nearest airport," instructed Pat. "We'll go upstairs and have a close look at that scorpion plane."

"We are entirely out of clues," returned Ham grudgingly. "It is as good a plan as any other."

Monk said, "The Tulsa airport is about forty miles south. I'll show you the way. Hope you got a spare supermachine pistol."

"It just so happens that I brought one along," admitted Ham.

"I don't suppose you have any extra mercy bullets that will fit a six-shooter?" asked Pat forlornly.

The dapper attorney shook his head. "We will have to recover your grandfather's revolver when we smash this conspiracy, whatever it may be."

"I'm glad someone in this automobile is an optimist," murmured Pat unhappily.

Chapter XXIV

SKY SCORPION

SEVERAL PROBLEMS WERE encountered acquiring a rental aircraft at the Tulsa Municipal Airport.

First and foremost was the fact that Pat had previously hired a small plane out of this field. That was the bus that had caromed off an oil derrick near Tumbleweed Station in Seminole. They had not yet had time to make good on that aircraft, and their faces were no doubt burned into the memory of the airport operations manager.

The other was that the airport seemed to have acquired more than its fair share of police officers.

Several radio cars were parked conspicuously. Officers were walking about in a very attentive manner.

"Uh-oh," said Pat. "The law is present in force."

Monk muttered, "They're probably keepin' an eye on the airport in case we try to get away by plane."

"There is nothing to stop *me* from renting an aircraft," reminded Ham. Picking up his walking stick, he told the others, "I will park in a quiet spot and make arrangements. Remain here, and keep your heads down. Especially keep that infernal pig from squealing. I will return once I have secured a suitable airplane."

Ham exited the vehicle, then walked swiftly and smartly to the operations shack. They were all business. It took him some twenty minutes to conduct a transaction, and when he exited, he appeared to be smiling.

Crossing the tarmac, the dapper barrister entered a tin-sided hangar. Before long, a plane motor could be heard warming up.

The aircraft in question came bouncing out of the hangar, dragged along by its nose propeller. It was a subdued green, with cream trim and wings.

Piloting the bouncing ship onto the tarmac, Ham lined up the nose on the main runway and made ready to take off.

"After you," urged Monk, grabbing Habeas. "We'll make a dash for the plane. By the time the cops notice us, if they ever do, we'll be in the air."

"Sounds risky," mused Pat.

It was. But not for Pat and Monk. They left the machine, and began making their careful way toward the aircraft, Habeas Corpus tucked in the crook of one of Monk's apelike arms, concealed by his coat.

While they were doing that, a police machine suddenly appeared from nowhere, and rocked to a jouncing stop in front of the whirling propeller.

"The jig's up," squeaked Monk.

"What jig?" wondered Pat, who was walking behind the burly Monk and failed to notice the sudden arrival of the police.

Four police officers surrounded the aircraft, their service revolvers drawn. Every muzzle was pointed at the cockpit of the plane.

"Come out of that thing with your hands high!" yelled one officer.

Ham hesitated. The officer fired a warning shot into the sky. Ham's hesitation melted.

The door popped open and the elegant lawyer stepped out, his sword cane held high. It was a mark of his personality that he never relinquished the stick if he could possibly avoid doing so.

"I surrender peaceably," he announced, loudly enough that they heard.

"Drop that stick!"

The dapper attorney again hesitated. A sharp-shooting officer blasted it out of his surprised fingers. The expression on Ham's sharp features was priceless.

"I will have you know that I am Theodore Marley Brooks, noted New York attorney and an associate of Doc Savage himself," shouted Ham indignantly.

"Are you also an associate of Monk Mayfair and Patricia Savage?"

Ham swallowed before he answered that. "I am," he admitted frankly.

"That makes you what we call a 'known associate.' So we're taking you in for questioning. We want to know their whereabouts. And don't tell us that you're in Tulsa by accident."

"Of course I am not!" rejoined Ham waspishly. "I am looking for them, just as you are."

"We'll sort this out at the station house," said the lead officer. Ham was promptly placed in handcuffs and forced into the back of a radio car.

The vehicle took off, siren wailing, while the other officers fanned out in search of Ham's automobile, which they assumed would be parked in the general vicinity.

While they were about their business, the green airplane sat on the tarmac, the propeller still turning, none of the police officers possessing the knowledge of how to turn off the motor.

"They have Ham," moaned Pat. "What a terrible, terrible turn of events."

Monk snapped, "It'll be worse if they get us. C'mon!"

Releasing Habeas so he could trot after him, the simian chemist raced for the aircraft, whose door still hung open. Pat was hard on his heels, thinking that she stood an excellent chance of being gunned down before they could reach the aircraft.

But, miracle of miracles, they made it. They piled in. Monk seized the controls first, barely beating Pat to the punch. He pulled the door shut, released the air brakes, and sent the plane scooting down the hot tarmac.

"I," said Pat huffily, "entertained hopes of piloting this bus."

"If we don't make it," the homely chemist growled, "you can say I forced you to come along."

The aircraft picked up speed, tail lifting.

"Don't think for a moment I am mollified," Pat said crossly. "Because I am not!"

"Just hang on!"

The little green-and-cream ship vaulted into the sky before the police got themselves organized.

The officers flung a flurry of lead in the general direction of the fleeing bus, but did no damage.

In the cockpit, Pat and Monk congratulated themselves on their successful escape.

Their grins of relief soon sloughed from their faces as they realized they had added another charge to the growing list of felonies against their good names.

"We're ruined!" Pat said miserably.

"We've been ruined before," retorted Monk. "We got more trouble than the Texas Rangers, but we'll get out of this mess. Watch and see."

"Poor Ham," said Pat. "He came all this way just to land in handcuffs."

"Aw, that shyster will talk his way out of any trouble they pile on him. He rented this airplane fair and square. It's not his fault if we stole it."

"No, but it paints him as an accomplice of yours truly."

The apish chemist banked in the direction they had last seen the sinister scorpion ship flying, grunting, "We'll worry about that fix once we run down that danged scorpion plane. Ain't that right, Habeas?"

But the shoat failed to reply.

Monk had perfected a ventriloquial trick whereby he made it appear that the porker responded in a comically cartoon voice. He had been getting ready to try it for Pat's amusement, but the first words died in his thick throat.

"Blazes! Where'd he get to?" blurted the gorilla-like chemist.

"I thought he was with you!" snapped Pat, looking about the cabin.

"He was right at my heels the whole time we ran for the plane," Monk returned in a sick squeak. "But I ain't seein' or hearin' him."

"Could he have failed to hop aboard?"

"Must not have," groaned Monk. His wide face fell.

"Oh, cheer up, Monk. Habeas will be all right. He takes after his master. Tough to the core."

The hairy chemist said nothing. He turned his attention back to his flying, small eyes anguished.

PATRICIA SAVAGE had the borrowed six-shooter in hand, and was checking the action.

"This is a similar shooting iron to the one that belonged to my grandfather," she was saying in an effort to distract Monk's mind from his troubles. "Only this one has a trigger and a gunsight."

Monk corrugated his rather small brow.

"I know you like to fan your granpappy's six-shooter," he said, "but it seems to me I've seen you work it with a trigger, too."

Snapping the gate back into its frame, Pat said, "I put a trigger into it a time or two, but I always end up taking it out. Since I usually carry my six in my purse, and the trigger can snag on cloth like nothing you ever saw. I prefer to fan my grandfather's old pistol anyway."

"Don't that make it harder to hit the target?"

"Exactly," said Pat firmly, squinting one eye while she looked down the barrel with the other.

Monk frowned deeply. "I don't exactly follow."

"If I can hit what I am fanning at with a smoke wagon, I can't hardly miss when I squeeze the trigger."

"I get it," said Monk, face brightening. "You're a dead shot either way."

Shoving open her passenger-side window, Pat let in some of the hot rushing Oklahoma air.

"You catch up with that scorpion plane," she said tightly, "and I'll perforate it properly."

"We want to force it down and grab that pilot, not kill anybody," reminded Monk.

"Oh, I'll force it down," Pat said airily. "Just catch it first."

Monk was endeavoring to do exactly that. He had the throttle flat out, and the propeller was eating up air miles.

In no little time, they spotted the tiny ship. It was an ungainly red pelican of a thing buzzing the city of Tulsa.

"I wonder what he's looking for?" murmured Pat.

"Maybe he's not lookin' for anything," suggested Monk carefully.

Pat swiveled her head and asked, "What else could he be doing but searching?"

In another moment, they found out.

The scorpion plane began to execute a series of acrobatic maneuvers that at first made no sense.

Banking, it twisted around, performed a flashing chandelle, then twisted upward again, as if seeking its ceiling.

After a minute or two, puffy white smoke squirted out of the scarlet-and-black scorpion aircraft's tail assembly.

"He's smoking," said Pat excitedly. "Maybe his engine is cutting out on him."

Monk shook his head violently. "That's not trouble smoke; it's too white."

Then to their mutual amazement, a letter formed in the sky.

It was the letter "S." It was followed by a "U," then a pair of sloppy "R"s, and then a somewhat better composed "E."

In due course the word "SURRENDER" was spelled out in puffy white letters.

"Skywritin'," growled Monk. "He has a lever in the cockpit and he releases the smoke to form the lines and curves, cutting it off when he needs to."

As they approached at top speed, the "S" in "SURRENDER" began to fall apart just as the "R" at the end of the word was being completed.

Then, the plane looped about and up and made a shape that was not a letter. Crisscrossing it longitudinally eight times, the pilot managed to make a credible cloud that resembled a scorpion, even if it was not perfect in its configuration.

Monk exploded, "Blazes! He's just told the city of Tulsa to surrender and he signed it with the mark of the Vinegarroon tribe, of which there ain't no such thing."

"Surrender?" said Pat. "What does that mean? Surrender what? Surely, they're not trying to take over the entire city."

"Terrorize it, most likely. That Grampus paralysis is already spreadin' and this is Standing Scorpion's way of lettin' folks know he's causin' it to happen."

"Nervy of him, isn't it?" Pat drawled.

Monk shrugged sloping shoulders. "It'll make a conviction easier once the law catches up with him."

They were close enough now to get a good look at the plane. It was striking in its design. This was an all-metal commercial ship of a type they recognized. Only a few years out of date, but the red-and-black paint was fresh and made the ship look as if it was fashioned out of enamel. On the tops and bottoms of the wings on either side of the fuselage burned the emblem of the whip scorpion, worked the way a cockade was emblazoned on a World War-era biplane.

"Standing Scorpion is not one to hide his light under a bushel, is he?" murmured Pat.

"Let's see how good a pilot this egg is," suggested Monk.

He had altitude on the scorpion ship, which was flying low enough so the letters could be read from any point in the city. Dropping into a howling dive, Monk made a point of flying past the right wingtip of the scorpion bus so closely that the pilot jerked hard left, not knowing what manner of thunderbolt had nearly collided with him.

Monk pulled out of his dive, and climbed after the scorpion craft. That was when the dance of death began.

Neither ship was a military aircraft, so there was no chattering of wing-mounted machine guns or any of that melodramatic stuff.

Instead, Monk's plane and the scorpion ship rolled about and dodged one another, performing loops, snap rolls and other aerial acrobatics.

As a pilot, Monk was more than a daredevil. He liked to take chances, and he took them now.

Coming up from behind, he laid his ship above the scorpion plane's empennage. The pilot looked back, and saw the other ship nearly on top of him, pacing along, propeller dipping lower as if to chew into the upper fuselage like a buzz saw.

The two planes were so close that the pilot dared not bank or roll lest there be a violent collision. Monk was counting on that.

"He's rattled," said Pat with tight satisfaction.

Monk grinned. "See how much more rattled you can make him."

"Don't mind if I do," allowed Pat, sticking her head and one gun arm out of her cabin window.

Lining up on the scorpion cockade, she began riddling it as if it was a bull's-eye. Wrapping the second joint of her thumb around the hammer, she rocked it back and let it go.

The first slug perforated the cockade's right pincer, and the enemy plane gave a little jump. Then Pat punched a hole in the second pincer and, after switching about a little, severed the whip-like tail from the main body of the image.

From his control cabin, the pilot had a perfect view of this remarkable example of aerial marksmanship. He could not help but be impressed. He was, in truth, dumbfounded.

Taking a chance, he dropped his plane into a dive, and went into the "falling leaf" series of side-to-side swinging stalls that look so dangerous when witnessed from the ground, but are an example of a practiced pilot in full control of his aircraft.

"Follow that cab—I mean, crate!" laughed Pat.

Monk obliged, sending his own plane screaming down. When the scorpion ship came level and was flying only a few hundred yards above the ground, Monk brought it about and slightly behind the opposite wing. Pat started shooting up the other scorpion insignia, alternating between trigger pulls and the cock-and-release method of fanning. This time she shot out its beady eyes in quick succession. At least, she made holes where eyes should have been since the emblem lacked those distinctive features.

Seeing this second example of trick shooting, the pilot decided he had enough.

Turning tail, he flew north, in the direction of the Osage.

Pat crowed, "That spooked him!"

Monk vowed, "Not as much as I'm going to spook him when I get my mitts on his neck."

Then the apish chemist settled down to follow the plane wherever it went.

The pilot showed every indication of being content to wing north, letting the trailing ship follow at its own pace. But he was not without tricks of his own.

TWO aircraft crashed through hot blue sky without anything coming of it.

Forty minutes along, with the scrub oak hills of the Osage unwinding beneath their wings, the pilot suddenly lifted his ship, and throttled back his engine.

This caused the gap between the plane's tail and the howling propeller of Monk's ship to close. The homely chemist let it close, curious as to what the pilot was up to.

Before long, he had an inkling.

From somewhere in the tail of the ship, a substance began spraying, forming a spreading bloom the hue of blood. It was soon coating their windscreen. But the stuff was powdery, not liquid.

Pat frowned. "Is he making smoke again?"

The hairy chemist studied the red residue collecting on the cockpit windscreen and said, "Better close that window—quick!"

Pat did so, then asked, "What do you suppose that is?"

"Dunno, but it can't be good. It's not fogging up or coatin' the windscreen so I can't see, but I'll be blamed if I know what the blasted stuff is."

As they watched the powder swim about, it had a slightly oily quality without being any recognizable petroleum product.

Then they became cognizant of a bitter odor.

"Vinegar!" exclaimed Pat.

"Vinegarroon acid," corrected Monk, whose chemically-sensitive nose knew the difference.

After a few minutes, the pilot must have thrown a lever or a petcock because the aerosol substance ceased to spew out of the plane's tail. The scorpion pilot then continued on his way, making no attempt to evade the pursuit plane.

This part of the Osage had a few playa lakes, which are lakes that are formed in the shape of a horseshoe or some similar meander. They looked as if someone had taken a section out of a winding river and plopped it onto a dry area.

Passing two such formations, the scorpion plane began losing altitude.

"Those funny-looking lakes make me think of the whip tail of the Vinegaroon scorpion," remarked Pat.

"Probably coincidence," said Monk, but his dubious tone of voice suggested otherwise.

The scorpion plane continued its slow descent and it soon dropped toward what appeared to be a private airfield graded out of a flat section of the Osage, which was otherwise hilly country furred by red-oak brush.

There was something that might pass for a small operations shack or guard house. But it was no shack. Instead, a solitary teepee stood sentinel adjacent to the airstrip. There was not much to it—being merely a cone of cowhide draped over a framework of lashed sticks. Decorations upon its sides were daubed in vermilion, but unreadable from the air.

The scorpion plane came in flat, its air wheels struck the red earth and made puffs of dust which turned into long strings of dust as it rolled along with the bumpy dirt airstrip.

Pivoting on one braking wheel, the pilot turned the lurid aircraft about before he ran out of runway. It was a close thing, however. The runway was barely long enough to accommodate the cabin ship.

Monk overflew the runway, and brought his own plane sweeping around, while Pat studied the surrounding terrain. No other habitations showed for miles around.

"I gather we should simply land," she murmured. "It will be two to one."

Monk made a face. "I don't like the looks of that wigwam."

"Circle around. If there's anybody inside it, they should come out to greet the pilot."

The simian chemist did exactly that, circling three times. But no one came out of the lonely teepee and the pilot did not exit his aircraft.

Shrugging burly shoulders, Monk lined up on the rugged runway and brought his own craft down more expertly than had the scorpion pilot.

Braking near the other ship in such a way as to block it from taking off again, Monk threw open his door, while Pat did the same. They came out brandishing their weapons, and approached the scorpion plane from either side.

"Come on out of there!" yelled Monk. "And grab for a cloud while you're doin' it."

From the other side, Pat lined up on the propeller, unloosed a single hunk of lead that caused it to go spinning. That settled the pilot's uncertainty.

Unlocking his door, he stepped out, dropped to the ground and placed his hands over his head to show that they were empty.

Pat came around to join Monk and they both got a clear look at the pilot. He was very tall and his hair was a rather dusty mop that shown blackly in the afternoon sun.

"Another Osage buck!" exploded Monk.

Pat let the Indian get a good look at the hole from which bullets would jump out of her six-shooter and asked the fellow, "Would you be one of the Tall Boys?"

"I would," admitted the Osage pilot. "What is it to you, squaw?"

The description took Pat slightly aback until she remembered that she was still disguised as an Indian maiden.

"Just asking," she commented. "No particular reason."

"What was that red junk you sprayed at us?" Monk demanded. "The stuff that got on our windshield."

"Scorpion vinegar," said the Osage. "Powerful bad medicine if it gets on you."

"Well, it didn't," said Monk. Turning to Pat, he said, "I'll keep an eye on this Tall Boy while you check out the plane."

"Good idea," said Pat, climbing aboard. She made a thorough inspection of the interior of the craft. It was spacious. There were several pressure tanks bolted to the floor in the rear. She looked them over and decided one was the smoke-generating apparatus used for skywriting and the other must have been the aerosol spray the Osage styled "scorpion vinegar." Beyond those items, there was nothing else of interest.

Climbing out again, Pat said, "We ought to analyze whatever is in that vinegar tank, but otherwise I don't see anything resembling a clue—or whatever I might have been looking for."

Monk said, "We'll do it later. After we give this aborigine the third degree."

The Osage grunted contemptuously. "I've been sweated hard by the cops. There isn't anything you can do to me that hasn't already been done. And I'm still standing."

"Then you don't mind me tryin'," growled Monk.

The Indian was wearing a hat. The band was black and red and sported stylized scorpion designs. A feather jutted jauntily up from the band. It looked like a hawk's feather. Pat was studying it and decided to remind the Osage Indian of her skills at marksmanship.

Lifting her six-shooter higher, she squinted down the barrel, rocked back the hammer and the Osage started to tremble a little bit.

"Are you fixin' to shoot off my hat?" he asked nervously. "If that's so, it's my favorite hat. I'll take it off."

"Why don't you do that?" suggested Pat in a thin voice as she closed one golden eye.

The Indian hesitated, but then he reached up with both hands and attempted to doff the battered hat.

The hat was in the process of coming off the Indian's head when Pat loosed the bullet that clipped the hawk's feather from the band.

The Osage jumped, almost fell backward, dropped his hat and, when he felt it safe to look again, he saw the greater portion of the hawk's feather flutter down to land gently on the dented crown.

The queasy look that came into his dark orbs made them think that he did not quite believe what his eyes registered.

Appraising Pat with newfound respect, he commented, "Annie Oakley ain't got nothing on you."

"I'm more the Calamity Jane type," retorted Pat. "And when you put your eyes back in your head, you can start talking turkey."

The Indian blinked. "Funny that you would say 'turkey'...."

"Why is that?" demanded Monk.

The Osage shrugged negligently. "Oh, it is nothing. A little joke."

Pat studied him suspiciously and asked, "You wouldn't be going by the name of Tall Turkey, would you?"

The Osage opened his mouth as if to reply, and then shut it suddenly.

A new voice came from behind them and growled, "Naw, he wasn't thinking that kind of turkey. He had in mind a turkey shoot—which is what we're about to have with a pair of bushwhacked palefaces if you don't drop your armament."

Monk and Pat froze. Another new voice added sharply, "And if you turn around, we'll shoot more than a hawk's feather off your sorry heads."

The tall Osage pilot managed a kind of twisted smile as he said, "You might as well hand over your weapons for safekeeping. My blood brothers might try to shoot them out of your hands, and they're not really accurate shooters that way. Liable to knock off a few fingers trying."

Faces falling, Pat and Monk reluctantly dropped their weapons to the dirt. Without being asked, they brought their hands slowly up to the level of their shoulders and then went higher when another voice barked, "Why don't you two try reaching for a higher cloud since it was your idea in the first place?"

When Monk got both paws as high in the air as his rounded shoulders would permit, somebody came up behind him and clubbed him with the butt of a Winchester rifle.

The gorilla-like chemist fell forward, his broad face landing in the red dirt of the Oklahoma soil that had birthed him.

Pat Savage regarded the homely chemist, and suddenly held her breath. She had a hope that perhaps Monk had fallen in such a way that some of the gas grenades that he habitually carried in his pockets might have shattered.

When none of the Osage Indians who had emerged from the teepee's hide flap lost consciousness, Pat resumed breathing normally and said in a sullen tone, "Well, I guess I'm your prisoner then."

"There are worse things," remarked the Osage pilot offhandedly. "Maybe we'll get around to showing you a few of them," he added meaningfully.

"I don't like the sound of that," admitted Pat. "Could you be more specific?"

"We'll let you know when we come up with something specific," said the pilot, picking up Pat's six-shooter and pointing at her casually.

"Heap smoke wagon," he remarked, hefting the antique firearm.

"Try not to lose it," requested Pat. "I promised the owner I would return it."

"And who is that?"

"Eric Nansen. Ever hear of him?"

"Any kin to young Ben Nansen?"

"His father."

The Osage burst out laughing. The laugh was nasty, not mirthful. Pat suddenly wished the Indian would choke on the dusty air so she wouldn't have to listen to it any more.

Shifting the gun barrel toward the sun-baked teepee, he said, "Let's go and see what's in store for you."

Noticing for the first time that the vermilion symbols decorating the primitive teepee suggested crawling scorpions, Pat ventured, "If it's all the same to you, I would rather not."

This only brought more ribald laughter from the towering Osage.

Chapter XXV

MYSTERY SHOTS

MONK MAYFAIR AWOKE to a pounding in his thick skull and the gurgle of moving water directly beneath him.

The hairy chemist's return to consciousness was a slow, throbbing ordeal. He was more preoccupied with his concussion than his surroundings. Monk had an inordinately thick skull. Over the course of a rough-and-tumble life, numerous hard objects had collided with it. Principally gun butts and leather blackjacks. None of it had ever done him any permanent harm, but that was a testament to the thickness of his brain case, not any lack of effort on the part of those applying various implements of destruction against his person.

Monk let out a low bellow that would have reminded a farmer of a milk cow in distress.

The groan didn't do his headache much good, and when Monk attempted to lift his head, he paused, a peculiar expression overtaking his homely features. He found that he could not move his arms to assist himself into a seated position.

By now his small eyes were open, but not much light was available by which to see anything of significance. So Monk used his ears. They told him that moving water lay below the hard surface upon which he lay spread-eagled. There were pungent smells about him, and these were also familiar. The predominant one smacked of rotten eggs.

"Crude," he mumbled.

This was not a reference to his surroundings, for he could not perceive them. Having been familiar with oilfield operations over many years, the homely chemist recognized the smell of crude oil. The distinctive odor was all around him.

This brought an alarmed look to his simian features.

"Sure hope I'm not soaked in the stuff," he muttered darkly. "If I am, one match strike or spark and I'm a goner."

Monk spoke aloud, half by habit but also in the hope that there might be another person dwelling in the darkness with him. If there was, that hypothetical individual failed to announce himself.

Monk tried to sit up, but something was weighing him down. His arms were particularly heavy, and he struggled with his mighty muscles to jerk them about.

As he did so, frustration made his features work. Perspiration broke out on his forehead anew. While insensate, he had been sweating steadily, for his clothes felt soaked. It was very hot in the confines of this dark space, wherever that might be.

Eventually, the apish chemist's eyes became accustomed to the gloom, and he saw that his arms were weighed down by lashing them to a pile of long tubes of steel weighing forty pounds each. Heavy rope had been tied to his ankles and forearms and looped through the tubes in such a way that he was weighed down by the accumulation of metal.

Between his groping fingers and his improving vision, Monk recognized the tubing as pipe collars of the type used in and around oil rigs to join lengths of oil-carrying pipe.

This provided him with his second clue where he was imprisoned, the smell of crude oil being the first.

Monk tried rolling over, but got no place in particular. For his legs were similarly tied and weighted down.

The sound of water rushing and purling below the floor helped to complete the picture that was growing in his anxious mind.

"Danged if I ain't stuck in a derrick house someplace."

Monk knew that the likeliest spot was the Arkansas River, where numerous riverbed derricks had been erected in years gone by. Piles driven into the river bed provided the support on which these tireless rotary rigs stood.

The Arkansas wound through a large tract of Oklahoma, so this specific location could not be arrived at by guesswork.

The popular conception of an oil derrick is a spidery tower of iron framework. But many of the older derricks had been constructed of wood and were still in good working order in this era of metal rigs. What is more, the lower portions were sometimes housed-in to protect the bull wheel, calf wheel, walking beam and well casing, as well as the drill floor.

During his days as a tool dresser—which is another way of saying an oilfield blacksmith—Monk had been inside many such housed-in old wooden derricks. Once he had assembled these clues in his mind, the hirsute chemist felt less anxious about his predicament—although it was hardly a reassuring prospect to contemplate.

At a loss for anything more constructive to do, Monk began digging his heels into the greasy floor and by this means slowly and laboriously propelled himself toward one corner of the derrick house.

He grunted with each exertion, for he was also pushing approximately five hundred pounds of iron tubes along with his muscular bulk. Some of the cuss words he picked up back in his youthful pipeliner days came back to him and he used them liberally, for the exertion was tremendous.

When the bristled top of his head encountered a thick derrick leg in one corner, it did not do his headache any good.

"Blazes! If I have a concussion, it's a ring-tailed beaut."

Monk lay there and let his headache settle down. He attempted to scheme his way out of this present predicament.

Perhaps it was a growing sense of desperation, or simply the concussion making his mental processes less reliable than normal, but the simian chemist contemplated a risky prospect.

In pushing himself along, his back had counted the iron spikes in the wooden flooring, and the boots Monk wore happened to have hobnails. It might be possible, he realized, to bring one into hard contact with the other, resulting in the creation of a spark that would ignite the greasy layer of old crude befouling the drilling floor.

If the blaze was slow-moving, its flames might burn through the ropes holding the pipe collars to his bandy legs. Monk would experience some burns, but he might be able to free his legs and by anthropoid strength, push himself upright, giving him a chance to hurriedly exit the derrick house.

The main question in his mind was if there were a lot of crude or just residue? It occurred to Monk that this rig was likely a stripper well—one that had been exhausted, or nearly so; otherwise, it would have been in operation at this hour. So it stood to reason that the oil was old stuff that had sunk into the wood over time. No doubt it was still flammable.

Monk fervently hoped that he never got to that desperate place in his mind where he decided to find out.

On the other side of the derrick house lay the enclosed belt house. This is where the calf wheel controlling the band wheel and sand line lay under the walking beam. Beyond it was the motor shed, housing the engine that drove the whole works.

From this direction came the steady press of soft-sounding footsteps.

Figures moved into the gloom, and a hand brushed a light switch, which action filled the place with yellowish illumination.

An inordinately tall figure stood in this unpleasant light.

Most of it consisted of purplish-black fabric, but the eyes were weird red cutouts, and on the chest was stitched an appliqué depicting a scarlet whip scorpion, its thin tail coiled like that of a rattlesnake.

It was Chief Standing Scorpion. He stood regarding Monk Mayfair in an ominous silence, as if awaiting the apish chemist's reaction to his unexpected appearance.

When Monk stubbornly refused to react, the uncanny figure hissed out, "Where is the brand of the Vinegarroon tribe, the mark of my proud people?"

"Never mind that!" snapped Monk. "Where's Pat?"

"We buried her in the Osage, where her body will never be found. She is of no use to us. But you, bearing the vinegarroon mark on your ugly face, will be found where we fling your corpse, the mark of guilt revealed for all the world to see."

A grinding rage filled Monk's next words, "If anything has happened to Pat, I'll break every bone in your body, and don't think I won't!"

"You will do no such thing, for you are powerless in my toils," intoned Chief Standing Scorpion. "And very soon you will be dead. For the mark that was laid upon you was a seed planted to sprout on this very day. Once my pilots fill the skies over Tulsa with the vinegar breath of the scorpion which produces what the newspapers are calling Grampus paralysis."

"So that's your scheme. You're gonna make people sick."

The hooded head nodded in a soft rustle of fabric and the muffled voice said, "Make them sick, only to make them well again. For a price. A reasonable price."

"What's reasonable about it?" asked Monk, playing for time.

"Many will succumb; some may die. The survivors will surely pay. Pay for a cure. They will pay what they can afford, but so many will pay that they will make the Vinegarroon tribe rich. After Tulsa pays up, we will move on to other places. Ponca City. Seminole. Sand Springs. Sapulpa. Oklahoma City. And once Oklahoma has paid its dues, we will move on to Arkansas and beyond."

"That's crazy talk," said Monk disgustedly.

"It is powerful medicine, and I control it."

Stepping forward, Standing Scorpion leaned in. With a single glove, he dipped his fingers in crude oil, and used them to wipe the side of Monk's face where the brown scorpion mark had been laid. The application of crude turned the layer of pancake make-up into a moist substance that was easily sloughed away.

A hiss of satisfaction escaped hidden lips and Standing Scorpion added, "You will taste the bitter vinegar of the whip scorpion before you die."

"Taste this!" growled Monk, and bit the gloved hand hovering near his mouth.

The looming figure reacted violently, giving out a screech of pain and pulling back hard.

Monk's teeth were strong, but terror of them enabled the sinister figure to pull his hand free, leaving the black silk glove in Monk's mouth. He spit it out contemptuously.

"Why did you do that?" demanded the other.

"That's so I can identify you later by teeth marks," said Monk without fear.

"For you, there will be no later," snarled Standing Scorpion. "I go now. My followers will see you to your unpleasant demise."

With that, the towering mystery figure turned and disappeared into the slot immediately under the walking beam and vanished into the belt house, making very little noise in departing.

THERE was a long interval in which Monk resumed his struggles with the numerous pipe collars, and although he turned the air hazy blue with his frustrated profanity, the anthropoidal chemist failed to extricate himself.

Sounds of footfalls came again, and through the dark slot came two persons.

Monk recognized the first by his seersucker suit and Panama hat, and his squeaky voice proclaimed, "Ike Golden!"

"At your service," sneered the oil reporter, doffing his hat elaborately. He stepped aside to allow a second figure to enter.

The second figure was very tall, and Monk did not recognize him in the yellow light.

An Osage Indian. A bony cadaver with a flat face and a broken beak of a nose, he carried in one hand one of the long flutes that had dealt out mysterious death twice in his presence.

"Who the heck are you?"

The Indian declined to reply, and he fished into a coat pocket and removed something which he inserted into one end of the flute.

Ike Golden commented, "Maybe by now you figured out how this gimcrack works."

"Sure," said Monk. "The flute passes for a blowgun once you seal the holes with your fingertips. It only works at short ranges, but that's enough if no one's expectin' sudden death. Capsules are shot out of it, but I don't know exactly how the scorpion mark is made."

"That's a tricky little thing to explain," said Golden as the Osage quietly positioned his fingers over the flute holes.

Monk said, "I figure the capsule contains some kinda red stain or something."

"A dye," explained Golden. "A dye filled with the stuff that causes the Grampus paralysis, as well as a trace of vinegarroon acid. Sometimes it's strong enough to kill, but usually it will just leach into a man's skin and slowly rob him of his leg power, kind of like polio, I guess you could say."

"Guess it sort of makes sense," said Monk, eyeing the grim-faced Osage, who had yet to speak. "But I can't figure out how the scorpion mark is created."

"The capsule gimmick is rigged so that it splashes outward in a certain way that forms the scorpion shape. It's not a perfect scorpion every time, but people's imaginations kind of fill in the rest. The one we're about to lay on your kisser doesn't have to look much like a scorpion at all. You've already got the mark." Golden peeled thin lips to expose his pearly teeth. "And now you're going to get the works!"

Chuckling to himself, Ike Golden added, "Go ahead, Tall Turkey. Let him have it."

"So you're Tall Turkey," said Monk.

The Osage named Tall Turkey nodded without bothering to speak.

"Ben Nansen told us that you're really Standing Scorpion," said Monk pointedly.

This casual remark caused Ike Golden's eyes to fly wide and his narrow jaw to drop. Turning to the Osage, he demanded, "What's this? You—Standing Scorpion?"

Tall Turkey's stiff features did not alter in any way. It was an imperturbable mask.

"Pay him no heed," intoned the Osage. "He is loco from too many blows to the head."

Turning back to Monk, Golden asked, "Where do you get that?"

"Ben Nansen swore to it," supplied Monk.

The homely chemist's eyes went to the Osage's feet and commented, "When I first laid eyes on Standing Scorpion, he was wearing a pair of beaded moccasins that don't belong to any Oklahoma tribe. I knew they were fakes. Dime-store stuff. The Standing Scorpion who was in here a few minutes ago didn't wear any moccasins. He had on white man's kicks. And he wasn't talking like a comic-strip Injun, either."

Jaw sagging, Ike Golden looked down at Tall Turkey's feet, and saw that he wore ordinary shoes. They were so coated with a yellowish dust that it was difficult to discern their underlying color.

"Like those?" demanded Golden.

Before Monk could respond, Tall Turkey snarled, "Do not listen to that fool! We came here to do a job. Let us be about it."

While all this was sinking into Ike Golden's brain, Monk made his move. It was not much of a maneuver. But he had been preparing for it.

By shifting his shoes, Monk had found one of the iron studs in the floor planking and brought one of the hobnails in his sole into contact with it. Pulling back against the dead weight of the iron pipe collars, he gave it all his might.

A spark resulted. It flew up into a tiny arc and came down to expire after a brief moment.

"What are you doing?" Golden demanded.

"Tryin' to start a conflagration," gritted Monk fiercely. "How do you like it?"

"I like it not at all! This place is soaked in crude! Don't you know what will happen if you ignite it?"

Monk grinned, and his deep-set eyes took on a crazed light.

"Sure, I do. But if I'm goin' out, I'm takin' you birds with me." He hauled back his leg for another attempt.

Seeing this, Tall Turkey brought the flute-blowgun to his snarling lips while Ike Golden leapt in to seize Monk's hobnailed shoe.

Monk was ready for Golden, and when the slender man fell upon his leg, the hairy chemist put all his might into a round-house swing.

Despite the prodigious weight of the pipe collars, Monk managed to brain the reporter just as the capsule left the other end of the flute.

Whether by accident or design, Ike Golden's head rocked backward, intercepting the capsule. It struck the side of his lean face just in front of his left ear.

The capsule broke, shattered. Spreading outward, the splash of red dye formed the crude likeness of a blood-colored scorpion, which inexorably infiltrated his hair with its spreading insect-like limbs.

Seeing this, Tall Turkey's dark eyes flashed with rage, and as the frenzied reporter pawed at his face in his death agonies, the Osage grimly drew forth another deadly red capsule.

He was in the act of inserting this into the flute, when the long tube went flying from his hands.

The sharp crack of a shot shook the interior of the derrick house. Cursing, the Osage whirled in the direction of the report. He never completed the turn, for another shot rang out, striking him on his left shoulder and spinning the Indian in the opposite direction.

Teeth grating, Monk tried to sit up, but between the pipe collars and the dying form of Ike Golden sprawled across his legs, he could not budge.

His eyes went to the narrow slot under the walking beam and someone crept closer until the barrel of a small automatic pistol poked into the yellow light. It moved about like the weaving head of a cobra preparing to strike, then the tiny bore ceased moving, and pointed directly at the spot between Monk Mayfair's puzzled eyes.

Chapter XXVI

DERRICK DOOM

AFTER MONK MAYFAIR had been knocked unconscious at the Osage landing strip, Pat Savage found herself
staring down the barrel of the borrowed six-shooter that had
been taken away from her.

The antique gun waggled at her and the Osage pilot said,
"Don't move until we hear back from the Chief."

"Should we search the sky for smoke signals?" suggested Pat,
arching a skeptical eyebrow.

"Nope," replied the pilot curtly. "We got us a ham radio rig
for that. A twenty-meter outfit, modern as can be."

Several of the Osage Indians retreated into the cowhide
teepee that served as an operations building, but also apparently housed a radio shack. Studying her surroundings carefully, Pat finally spotted the aerial strung between a nearby red
oak tree and the grouping of dead branches sticking up from
the teepee's open smoke hole. It had not been visible from the
air.

The Osage cohort were on a "ham" radio outfit for several
minutes until one came out and called over, "Plane is going to
come for her."

"What's wrong with this crate?" demanded the pilot. "It's
got plenty of room."

"They're sending the duck plane," said the radio man.

"Does that mean what I think it means?" asked the pilot.

"No telling. Maybe, maybe not."

Keeping his weapon trained on Pat's exquisite form, the pilot said, "O.K., I guess it doesn't make much of a difference."

"It does to me," retorted Pat. "What did you mean by that earlier remark? 'Does that mean what I think it means?'"

"You'll see," said the pilot. "Now button your lips and go sit in the plane. Unless you want to catch heatstroke."

"No, thanks," said Pat, climbing back into the plane. Once inside, she whirled and yanked the door shut, then threw herself into the pilot's bucket. Her intention was to fling the plane about and take off, even if she had to do so in a hail of hot lead.

Pat never got that far; the expected hail of bullets started before she got the motor going.

First one and then a second air tire were shot, and the plane settled on its left wing, then collapsed upon its right wing.

"I knew it looked too easy," grumbled Pat.

Spewing profanity, the Osage pilot banged on the cabin door with the butt of the six-shooter, yelling for Pat to come out.

"If I step out, you'll probably shoot me," retorted Pat.

"My orders are not to shoot you if I can help it."

"Maybe," allowed Pat, "but that was before I made you shoot out the tires of your plane."

"If you don't come out right now," the other grated harshly, "I'll start shooting out the window glass. That stuff can really cut skin when it gets to flying."

Pat gave this prospect some thought and decided that she had very little to gain by remaining at the controls, even if quitting the plane meant that her remaining life was measured in minutes, not days or weeks or months.

The copper-skinned girl stepped out with her hands over her head, and awaited the pilot's angry response.

"If I could shoot you, I would," he asserted.

"Your chief doesn't want you to," reminded Pat nonchalantly.

"Could be he wants the pleasure all to himself," gritted the pilot through set teeth.

The other Indians had boiled out of the pale teepee to see what had happened and they were berating the Osage pilot in no uncertain terms about his carelessness in permitting Pat Savage to get the better of him.

The pilot took it. He had no other choice. He had balled things up pretty thoroughly.

"Now where are we going to get replacement tires out here in the Osage breaks?" one demanded of him.

The red man's face was brick-red by this time and he hung his head and shoulders and looked like he wanted to expire on the spot. Shame rode his previously stoic features.

"Maybe we can patch them up," suggested one man.

"With what are we going to re-inflate the tires—a bicycle pump?" sneered another. "We don't have one of those, either."

"This will sure set the plan back a few days," grumbled another. And, hearing this, Pat Savage had to repress a smile. She may not have managed to escape, but it looked as if she had hurled a sizable monkey wrench into the whole diabolical works.

When the argument finally settled down, the pilot marched Pat into the plane, sat her down and trained the six-gun on her, but all the fire and bluster was out of him. He was thoroughly ashamed of his actions. He seemed to lack any ire toward the girl.

TWO hours passed before the so-called "duck plane" arrived. This was a cabin seaplane. The color scheme was black, and trimmed in scarlet—the opposite of the skywriting amphibian. Otherwise they were similar ships—good for long-distance hops. The clumsy-looking craft bounced along the rocks and finally came to a stop, its propeller still turning.

Another Osage stepped out, heard the story of Pat's misadventure stolidly, and ducked into the large cabin plane to pull her out, practically doing so by the hair.

"Smart girl, huh?" he said. "But you're not gonna get the better of *me*."

"I may have learned my lesson," said Pat in an abashed voice. She wasn't actually that deflated, but she thought it would throw off the new arrival.

Instead, the man brought out one of the long flutes.

Pat flinched. "Hold on a minute. What are you planning on doing?"

"Marking the merchandise," said the other laconically. Holding the flute so that it was level, he inserted a red pellet in one end, brought it to his lips and carefully sealed the holes.

Not every hole sealed properly, for when he gave a puff, not very much happened except a thin musical note escaped from the flute's open end.

Pat decided to run. She half turned, managed three paces then was struck in the side of the face by a pellet that exploded less than an inch from her nose.

In her mind, she had visions of a spray of red painting her face with the scorpion's sinister silhouette, but in reality a strange odor crept into her nostrils. Swiftly, she lost consciousness, and fell to the red earth of the Osage gully.

Pat did not hear the man who brought her low tell the others, "Pick her up and heave her into the plane. I've got a schedule to make."

WHEN Pat Savage awoke, it was many hours later. It was very dark in the space where she found herself. Her hands were bound behind her back. Luckily, her legs were free, although one ankle was tied to the Sampson post, which restricted her movements without making her completely helpless.

A strangely familiar voice asked, "Are you awake?"

The voice was feminine and it took a moment for Pat's head to clear. She inquired, "Who is speaking?"

"Vina—Vina Hawks Nansen."

Pat peered around, and all was gloom. "Where are we?"

"An old oil derrick on the Arkansas River. I was placed here hours ago. When they brought you in, my heart quailed."

"Mine is merely sinking," said Pat ruefully.

She sat up, discovered that the floor planking was greasy with crude oil and stopped breathing through her nose in an effort to keep out the rotten-egg smell.

"Did they bring my friend, Monk?"

"No. They did not mention him. There are just the two of us here."

Pat got tired of breathing through her mouth, took in a short breath through both nostrils and decided it had been a poor idea. The dense smell of crude made her feel as if her tongue was coated with the stuff.

Paying attention to her surroundings, she detected the rushing of water beneath the floor.

"You say this is an oil derrick. Funny how Standing Scorpion always seems to have a hideout connected to the petroleum industry in Oklahoma."

Vina said, "I believe that is because of Ike Golden. As a former oil editor, he would know about places that are not in use."

Pat frowned. "I did not know that about him. I thought he was a common reporter."

"He had been the oil editor on the *Trumpet* until Morgan fired him, hiring Harold Manton in his stead. Yet Morgan remained close to Golden. I suspect that the firing was a ruse, one that enabled Golden to serve as Morgan's spy at the *Globe*."

"The plot thickens," remarked Pat dryly. "That explains why Morgan Marrs failed to turn Golden over to the law after we left him tied up in his penthouse that time. They were in cahoots!" A frown made her tanned chin dimple. "But why would Marrs go to all that trouble?"

"The *Trumpet* has not been doing well. Not for years. I have no doubt that Morgan feared for the future of his newspaper."

"This puts a fresh complexion on Harold Manton's murder," Pat mused.

"My own suspicion is that Mr. Manton was looking into matters too deeply and asked the wrong questions of the wrong person."

"Yes, but of whom? The last we heard of him was he had made an appointment to talk with his publisher."

A gloomy silence followed.

"Did you hear me, Miss Nansen?" asked Pat.

A defeated sigh broke the silence. "Yes. I might as well admit that my fiancé appears to be mixed up in this matter in a way I do not understand. Harold Manton was prying into Morgan's affairs in a way that was alarming to Morgan. Particularly upsetting to him were the questions pertaining to that building over in Broken Arrow from which I effected your escape—the place that exploded so suddenly."

"I never fully accepted your explanation for being there in the first place," Pat stated.

"I—I will now admit that I was tricked into helping you escape," said Vina. "Morgan convinced me to do this, and I now believe that the purpose was to put you and Mr. Mayfair in positions whereby you would be arrested. No doubt Standing Scorpion thought this would help avoid the wrath of Doc Savage."

Pat nodded. "Harold Manton was no doubt eliminated because he got too close to the truth about his boss, poor fellow," she suggested. "That building tied Standing Scorpion in with the *Trumpet*. Say, is there any member of your family who is not enmeshed in this sticky web?"

The distraught blonde turned away, and her voice shrank in a kind of weary anguish. "Please do not ask me to explain further. I am distraught about all this."

Pat changed the subject without delay. "You might be interested to know that we took your brother to the hospital. They are treating him."

Relief flooded Vina's voice. "That is the first good word I've heard about Ben."

"Your brother also told us who he believes Standing Scorpion really is."

"Yes, he is an Osage Indian named Tall Turkey. He is a—"

"He is what?" questioned Pat.

"I have seen him around my fiancé, Morgan. It was Tall Turkey who accosted me in the hotel room when I was being held prisoner, that time I telephoned Harold Manton for help in the hope that he could rescue me without alerting the authorities. Mr. Manton is—" she caught herself—"was exceedingly loyal to Morgan."

"How do you know Tall Turkey is the head skunk of this outfit?" demanded Pat.

Pat could not see Vina Hawks Nansen in the darkness, but her hesitation filled the silence that followed.

"What I have concluded stems from the many things I have witnessed."

"What is Morgan Marrs' connection with all this?"

"That," said Vina, "is something I am still trying to fathom."

"Not a very satisfactory response," commented Pat.

"It is not a very satisfactory situation I find myself in," admitted the blonde woman in a miserable tone of voice.

The silence which followed was interrupted only by the purl and rush of water around the unseen support pilings beneath them.

"I wish I knew what happened to poor Monk," murmured Pat finally.

"I do not know what they intend to do with us, but the guards I overheard seem to believe that we are being held here temporarily until we can be taken to another location."

"Do you have any idea where?" pressed Pat.

"No, I do not," Vina said firmly. "But it is my impression that the great scheme is now underway, but there are problems with it. Whatever Standing Scorpion intends, his plans have not been going smoothly."

"You can thank Monk and myself for that. We've been flinging monkey wrenches everywhere we go. A few have rebounded to bounce off our skulls in return," she added wryly.

"It is my impression," said the blonde woman after another silence, "that Standing Scorpion has a headquarters far from here. One where he oversees operations in safety. It is my fear that we are going to be taken to that headquarters."

"You would think," said Pat, "that for all the trouble we've caused everyone, they would just do away with us and be done with it."

"I have wondered about that same thing myself," admitted the woman. "But just as my brother was useful to them in some weird manner I cannot fathom, we may also be marked for similar treatment."

Pat shuddered in the darkness despite herself. "I don't believe in vampires. At least, I didn't until I met your brother. The last time I saw him, it looked as if almost all the life had been drawn out of him."

"Poor Ben," said Vina. "He was simply a soul who lost his way—then nearly lost his life."

Pat returned to a subject that continued to bother her. "Do you have any concrete reason to believe that Tall Turkey is Chief Standing Scorpion?"

The woman hesitated before replying. "It is my surmise, and nothing more. I will confess that to you now."

"Yet your brother seemed convinced of it," reminded Pat.

Vina's voice grew distant. "My brother has seen things while being held captive, which no doubt make him better informed than I."

That appeared to be the extent of the woman's fund of knowledge on the subject and she fell pensively silent. Only her breathing could be heard in the gloom.

Pat was looking around, saw a pencil of pale light, and scooted over toward it, ignoring her bonds.

Applying a narrowed golden orb to the hole, she spied two items of interest. One was the black-and-scarlet seaplane moored to another riverbed derrick. Beyond that stood another wooden derrick, which was also enclosed at the lower portion. It was set on stubby pilings, and a wooden walkway connected both oil rigs to one another, so that an inspector could move from one to another without having to resort to a boat or swimming.

Pat continued to watch. Before long, a solitary individual emerged from the other derrick, and came walking along the rickety catwalk. It was a tall fellow, with the dark hair and impassive features of an Osage Indian.

"It appears that company is headed our way," Pat told the blonde woman.

"Perhaps they intend to move us finally," hazarded Vina.

"I spy the amphibian that brought me here tethered to another derrick. No doubt someone is going for a ride."

"Anything would be better than this horrid cell," said Vina with just a hint of despair in her voice.

The Osage entered through the cobwebbed gear shed. He used a stubby flashlight to illuminate the faces of the two female captives.

"You two are being moved," he stated firmly.

"Whither, if I might ask?" inquired Pat.

"Do not ask," said the Osage. He produced a folding buck knife from his belt. "I will cut the fetters around your ankles so that you may stand and walk. Do not run. If you fall into the river, you will drown."

Holding the flashlight in one hand and the knife in the other, he knelt, sliced away Vina's bonds, then came over and did the same for Pat Savage.

After that was accomplished, he helped first one and then the other woman to her feet. Both women were unsteady.

Stowing away the buck knife, he reached into another pocket and pulled out a pistol so small that it was almost swallowed by his large wind-burned hand.

"Not much kick to this gun," he remarked, "but it will put a pellet where I point it. Remember that. Now march."

WITHOUT a word of complaint, they allowed themselves to be marched out of the housing and into the dark and grimy gear room, then onto the walkway which was very long and quite rickety. It had been built a good while ago and, while it stood firmly on its pilings, individual planks had warped and become loose.

Vina led the way, with Pat following and the Osage gunman taking up the rear.

Studying the surroundings with her canny eyes, Pat considered going for a swim and taking her chances. But she decided they were not good, given that her wrists were bound too tightly to overcome. Also, the prolonged heat of summer had taken its toll on this section of the river. The sluggish water had retreated from its banks, and did not appear to be very deep in the center of the channel, where the pilings stood in support of the oil rigs.

Vina walked with great care, for she found the planks under her feet less than reassuring. Pat managed to quicken her pace and very soon she was directly behind the blonde woman.

"Keep moving, you two!" warned the Osage. "But I got my eye on the both of you."

Pat decided to take a chance. It was a long one. But she took it because she did not care to entertain the prospect of another airplane flight to an unknown destination and uncertain fate.

When Vina hesitated before stepping onto yet another rickety plank, Pat used one foot to trip her by hooking said foot around the blonde's ankle.

With a sharp exclamation of surprise, Vina Nansen Hawks fell to the planking. The guard came rushing up, expostulating vociferously.

"She fell!" cried Pat. "Oh, please help her."

"Get out of my way, squaw!" yelled the Osage, endeavoring to push Pat aside.

Employing the same foot, Pat tripped the Indian. He went down hard. With the other foot, she gave him a resounding kick and he went flying, breaking the fragile and flimsy rails of the wooden walkway. He made a noisy splash entering the river.

"Find your feet, Vina!" yelled Pat. "Make a dash for that other derrick."

Vina Hawks Nansen struggled to her feet. It was no easy task, but she managed it. The woman began running hard.

Pat dropped to her knees, and saw that the Osage's .22-caliber automatic had landed on the planking. But she could not get to it with her hands bound behind her back.

Squirming about, Pat found a place where a plank had split, making a long sharp tooth which stuck up. Hooking it with her bonds, she started sawing wildly.

She made good progress while the Osage splashed around in the muddy water. But then the wood fang split. Pat found another ragged piece of wood, and continued the frantic operation.

The cords began to part, and Pat next found a protrusion strong enough to catch, and then she was straining mightily against her bonds. They broke. Swiftly, her hands were in front of her and she was pulling off the remaining ropes.

In the next instant, the .22-automatic was in her right hand and she was training it on the floundering Osage.

"You don't look much like a swimmer," she called out. "You might want to make for dry land before I bark you with this thing."

The Osage's face took on a look of wrath, and he resembled a man ready to climb the piling and reclaim his weapon.

Pat stroked the trigger and sent a slug snapping past his right ear. Showing better judgment than his temperament indicated, the Osage turned about in the water and swam for his life.

Pat caught up with Vina Hawks Nansen when she reached the other oil derrick, which proved to be deserted.

Searching it, she discovered that yet another drilling rig stood beyond—also connected by a ramshackle catwalk. This third derrick stood seven hundred feet away. From it came a commotion that carried across the rushing river water.

"Could mean trouble," barked Pat.

Then came a squawling that was inarticulate yet recognizable to the golden-eyed girl.

"Monk!" she said shrilly. "Sounds like he's in trouble. You wait here."

Without waiting for a reply, Pat Savage tore out of the oil derrick housing and flew across the catwalk, making speed, but exercising reasonable caution lest a plank drop out from beneath her flying feet.

Walking up to one of the gear housings, she crept in, letting her eyes adjust to the gloom and then moving toward the housed-in section surrounding the well casing.

There, an Osage Indian was about to murder Monk Mayfair.

Bringing the .22-caliber pistol up to her face, Pat sighted carefully and shot him in the shoulder with satisfying results. The Osage did a little twirling jig on skipping feet.

Stepping in, she trained the tiny weapon about the interior, spied Monk's unlovely visage and said, "Looks like I got here just in time!"

"Pat!" yelled Monk, giving out a whoop of joy. "They told me they buried you out in the Osage."

"If they were smart, they would have done exactly that. I found Vina. She's a prisoner too. Now come on. We've got to get out of here."

The homely chemist attempted to raise his muscular arms, but the weight of the pipe collars made that impossible.

"It ain't that simple, Pat," he said miserably.

"I can see that," said Pat, approaching. "Maybe I can find a tool to get that stuff off of you."

"You'll need a blowtorch," grunted Monk.

Then beyond the plank derrick-house sides came a snarling sound, followed by the racket of an outboard motor. The excited sounds of men yelling were mixed with this bawling.

And from the other direction came the sound of Vina Hawks Nansen crying, "Miss Savage! Our escape has been discovered!"

Pat and Monk exchanged anxious glances and Monk squeaked, "Better make tracks, Pat. Forget about me. Get the girl away while you can."

"Nothing doing," flared Pat. "I'm making my stand here with you."

"Don't be that way!" cried Monk. "No sense all of us gettin' drilled with holes."

"If there's any holes to be drilled," said Pat seriously, "I aim to drill my fair share of them. Now settle down and let me think. As my grandfather used to say, we're not licked until the last scalp is taken."

Chapter XXVII

RIVER RUCKUS

PAT SAVAGE WAS looking about the riverbed derrick's interior when she noticed the slumped form of Ichabod Golden lying in a heap alongside the well casing head in the center of the floor.

"Dead?" she asked Monk.

"Like yesterday's news. We can scratch him off the list of suspects. He's not Standing Scorpion. But that Tall Turkey is around here somewhere."

Pat fell to searching the man's body, looking for additional weapons. She found one. It was a serviceable heavy automatic. She frowned. The golden-eyed girl much preferred revolvers, the bigger the better. But she could handle an automatic. She jacked back the slide, and a single unspent shell popped out.

Removing the magazine, she found four additional shells, inserted the one in her other palm into the magazine and then reloaded the weapon.

"I feel more confident now that I have something like a cannon to work with," she said firmly.

Turning to the slot leading to the catwalk, she called over to Vina Hawks Nansen. "Better take this. You may need to protect yourself."

Pat tossed the little .22-caliber and the woman caught it in both hands. Vina's hands were now free. She had severed her bonds on the same sharp splinter Pat had used.

"Guard the way in," ordered Pat. "I have to free Monk."

The blonde nodded tightly.

Returning to the derrick housing, Pat said to Monk, "I was hoping to find a knife on him. No such luck."

"Did you check his socks?"

"Socks?" Pat echoed.

"Sure," returned the homely chemist. "Some smart guys like to tuck a small pistol or a spring-snap knife into their socks where they can get at it in a pinch. Hardly anybody searches a man's socks."

Returning to Golden's body, Pat felt of the man's hose, which was kept up by green garters. Her fingers found a bulge on the inside of the right calf. Pat pulled out a black object with a silver button on it. She depressed this and the blade snapped open with sudden violence.

Satisfied, she returned to Monk Mayfair and began sawing away. The knife was designed as a stabbing tool more than for cutting, but it had an edge. That edge quickly dulled as Pat worked at the heavy line.

She got one arm free at last. Monk snatched the blade from her fingers and started working at the opposite wrist.

"Think you can cut through them all?" she asked the apish chemist.

"Or croak tryin'," muttered Monk.

The squawling racket of an outboard motor had become very loud by this time.

"You keep working," urged Pat, putting an eye to a knothole and seeing the approaching motorboat. It was a trim affair of polished mahogany, boasting two separate cockpits and a powerful quad motor in the rear.

At the wheel in the forward cockpit was hunched no less than Chief Standing Scorpion, his outrageous purple-black hood flattening to his face in the slipstream. Behind him in the other cockpit stood two Osage braves, bearing Winchester rifles.

One of them yelled, "There's the girl! On the catwalk."

A voice that must have been coming from the hood lifted harshly, saying, "Don't harm her! Take her alive."

That proved to be easier said than done because Vina Hawks Nansen lowered the .22 automatic and, aiming carefully, snapped off a single shot that shattered the windshield of the motor boat.

The tiny pellet went on through and nicked one Osage in his muscular thigh, causing him to drop his Winchester and clutch wildly at a fountain of blood that suddenly appeared.

The other Osage jacked a round into his rifle chamber and looked as if he were determined to return fire.

Taking hands off the wheel, Standing Scorpion whirled in a flourish of purple silk and slapped the rifle down.

"What did I just tell you!" he screamed. "If you want to shoot something, fire into that derrick housing. You might get lucky."

Hearing this, Pat Savage took one dark eye from the knothole and hissed, "They're about to open up on this place."

Monk had almost cut through his right wrist bonds, but still had a long way to go until he stood erect and free.

"Can you make good use of that knothole?" he asked.

"Shoot through it? I'm not sure I can hit anything."

"Try to scare them off. Buy us some time."

Nodding determinedly, Pat placed the muzzle before the knothole, angled the automatic around experimentally, and squeezed the trigger with care.

The heavy pistol jumped once, ejecting a smoking shell, and there was more yelling from the approaching motorboat.

Applying one eye to the knothole, Pat saw consternation aboard the boat as Standing Scorpion, regaining control of the wheel, caused it to shear violently to the left, creating a boil of muddy water.

"I don't think I hit anyone," she told Monk. "But I sure spooked them."

"Good. Now spook them out of their skins."

Pat Savage gave it her best. She let fly with a couple more rounds, producing further consternation.

Squawling, the motorboat gouged up churning waves, and by this means Standing Scorpion managed to run his powerboat around the pilings to the other side of the rickety old derrick.

Pat yelled to Vina on the catwalk, "See if you can't contribute your share of hot lead."

The blonde woman took careful aim and her tiny weapon cracked once again. Nothing much resulted—except that the speedboat kept twisting and turning as its pilot desperately sought to avoid the seeking lead.

"Keep working," said Pat to Monk. "I'm going to see what I can accomplish from the catwalk."

While Monk furiously cut away at his bonds, Pat worked through the gear house, and stepped out into the blazing light of the catwalk.

Turning her head, she saw something for which she was not prepared.

STANDING SCORPION had chopped power to the motorboat. The craft continued on, propelled by momentum. From somewhere on the floor he had produced a Thompson submachine gun and was wrestling it up into position.

Seeing this, Pat's face paled and she yelled to Vina, "Make a break for the other derrick house. That's a Tommy gun!"

Vina did not hesitate. She broke into a dead run, firing one wild shot behind her. The weapon made a spiteful snap, but damaged no one.

Pat was lining up on the hooded figure, looking for a spot where she could do some damage, but not inflict a fatal wound. Her hesitation almost proved fatal to her, however.

The machine gun muzzle came up and commenced chopping the catwalk with its chattering storm of lead. Planks jumped up, broke in two. Wood rails split, and splinters flew everywhere as the deadly stream of slugs began inching in her direction.

Retreating to the enclosed drilling rig, Pat reached Monk's side and dropped flat on the greasy floor, breathing heavily.

Standing Scorpion proved free with his lead. He chewed up the catwalk with energetic abandon. The sound of the Tommy gun was a throaty stutter.

"Blazes!" exploded Monk. "And I still have a ways to go."

Just then, the Tommy gun erupted and once more the snarling sound of wood being dashed into flying flinders came unmistakably to their ears.

Frighteningly, the vicious stream of lead moved in their direction and the derrick house started coming apart with great violence all around them.

Seeing this, Pat threw herself to the ground and yelled to Monk, "Flatten!"

Monk didn't need to hear it twice; he had already thrown himself backward and was lying prone.

Tommy-gun lead stormed about, shattering the headache post, banging off the bull wheel and doing assorted other types of damage to the complicated guts of the old oil rig.

This went on for what sounded like an eternity, but was probably less than thirty noisy seconds. Then came a pause.

"Hand me another ammunition drum!" Standing Scorpion yelled. "Then get yourself organized and join in the shooting party."

"They're going to drill us," Monk muttered.

"That was going to be my job," fumed Pat. "Is there another way out of this contraption? You know these oil rigs."

"Not unless you can bust a hole in the floor."

Pat examined the oil-soaked floor. The planking was heavy and solidly constructed. It had to be in order to support the structure, which towered over a hundred feet.

"If my teeth were stronger and sharper," Pat murmured, "I could make like a beaver and do exactly that. The river is our only chance, but if we rush for the catwalks, they'll cut us to pieces."

Monk was growling, the way he did when he was angry or frustrated. And then his small eyes gleamed with an idea.

"Pat! Fish around in my watch pocket. There's a packet of pills there."

"Don't tell me you have a headache."

"Take them out. Put one in my mouth and swallow the other one yourself."

Kneeling, Pat found the watch pocket and brought out a little tin container of pills. When she slid open the lid, her golden eyes brightened.

"Aren't these—?"

"Exactly," said Monk. "You got the idea. Now I want you to go to the opposite corner, frisk Ike Golden again."

"What for?"

"See if he's got a cigarette lighter."

Pat wasted no time scooting over to the body. The late Ichabod Golden had indeed carried a cigarette lighter, and Pat brought it over to Monk, saying, "What do you want me to do with this?"

"It's risky, but some of these ropes around my legs have soaked up some crude. Try to light them afire."

"But your legs will burn!" protested Pat.

The recharged Tommy gun resumed chattering again, and the derrick house commenced rocking and shaking as dust filtered down from the higher section containing the crown block.

"They're tryin' to burn us right now," Monk pointed out. "We gotta take this chance."

Grimacing, Pat snapped the flint wheel, produced a flame and gingerly applied it to several spots on Monk's ankle ropes.

Then she stepped back, watching in horror as a yellow flame danced and spread.

Monk stared at the spreading fire with worried eyes. "Now find another patch of oil and light that up, too. Heck, light every one you can."

Horror made the copper-skinned girl's voice twist. "Do you want us to burn alive?"

Another stuttering burst of Tommy-gun lead all but drowned out the terrified question.

Biting her lower lip, Pat went in search of flammable patches of oil and found two. They were close together. She applied the flame and had to jump in order to avoid her own clothes catching fire.

Oil smoke soon filled the interior. Monk and Pat held their breath as the place filled with noxious fumes.

The Tommy gun continued punishing the derrick housing, and the whole rig started to lean and groan.

Monk was pulling at the bonds of his ankles, trying to keep his fingers from being burned and yanking furiously so that the ropes parted while the greedy flame ate away at the cordage.

In this way, the simian chemist got both ankles freed, and sprang to his feet. Then he did something that seemed to suggest he was possessed of a species of madness that comes upon some men when they face imminent destruction.

With the derrick crumbling under the lash of machine-gun lead and dirty smoke billowing from every crack and crevice, the hairy chemist attacked one of the derrick legs which supported the structure.

His gorilla-like strength, combined with the weakness of the aged structure, caused the rig to rock and groan. Before Pat could demand that he stop, the old wooden frame began coming apart.

With a violent commotion of breaking wood and falling beams, the entire derrick collapsed into the river, its pieces all but burying the ancient pilings that supported it.

STANDING on the mahogany bow of the stalled speedboat, the hooded figure dressed as Standing Scorpion ceased firing and said, "That finishes them. Nothing could live through that destruction."

Still, they carefully watched the water's muddy surface, waiting for air bubbles that would betray the fact that their enemies still lived. No such bubbles reached the surface, however.

Handing the still-smoking Tommy gun back to one of his Osage Indians, Standing Scorpion said, "Start the engine. We will get the girl and fly back to our stronghold."

This proved to be no easy task, for Vina Hawks Nansen was still armed.

The Osage who had been wounded by the .22 slug had tied a vermilion neckerchief around his thigh, staunching the flow of gore. As the motorboat putt-putted toward one still-standing oil derrick, he stepped onto the bow, jacked another slug into the chamber and called out, "Come on out with your hands up, lady. Do it now and I won't send you to the bottom of the river."

It was some moments before Vina gingerly emerged, pale of face and trembling. Her upraised hands were empty.

As Standing Scorpion guided the motorboat toward the shattered catwalk, he didn't gun the engine until it warped alongside the portion that was an open gash.

"Jump down and no tricks!" he called up.

Vina did not jump down. She climbed down and landed in the back of the boat, where there was a third, auxiliary cockpit.

She was carefully searched, and then Standing Scorpion demanded, "What happened to your pistol?"

"I threw it away. What good is it against a machine gun?"

Rustling, the hood nodded. "You are very wise for a white woman. Sit down and be quiet. Soon you will behold with your own eyes the headquarters of the future power over the nation, the den of Chief Standing Scorpion."

Throwing the throttle into reverse, the hooded figure sent the boat boiling backward, then turned it around and made for the black-and-scarlet seaplane secured to an oil derrick further upriver.

Had there been any other witnesses, they would have seen very clearly that someone awaited the search party in the amphibian. That person stuck his head out and waved at the others to hurry up.

Vina saw the face, and her trim little jaw trembled.

"Morgan!" she breathed, her shoulders sinking in defeat.

At the wheel, Chief Standing Scorpion regarded her with his hell-red celluloid eyes and remarked, "That your fiancé is a blood brother to the Vinegarroon tribe is not a new thing to you."

"No," admitted the blonde woman. "It is not new. It is just that every time I am confronted by the truth, it takes another piece of my soul out of me."

From behind the ebony hood, the hidden lips of Standing Scorpion chuckled maliciously.

"Your soul," he breathed, "now belongs to me. For I have great use for you, white woman."

Sobbing, Vina Hawks Nansen buried her face in her arms and did not budge until the two Osage braves lifted her up into the waiting arms of her fiancé, Morgan Marrs, who regarded her with flinty, unforgiving eyes.

Someone untethered the mooring rope, and pushed off.

After all concerned had climbed aboard, the amphibian came to life. It made a loud racket as it backed away from its derrick mooring, swung about, and started racing along the coursing river, picking up speed as it charged into the prevailing wind.

The aircraft took off with an abruptness that threatened to tear off its wings.

But they held. The ship quickly found its altitude, then turned toward the east, its roar fading into a steady moan that was soon heard no more.

Chapter XXVIII

OZARK TRAIL

THE LONELY SECTION of the Arkansas River where several oil derricks were arrayed in a loose chain following the muddy watercourse was not close to any city or settlement.

Smoking quietly, the wooden derrick that had collapsed into the riverbed continued to burn for some time, its wildly canted summit sinking even deeper as flames licked at the portion that stood above water, slowly swallowing the working platform derrickmen call the monkey board.

The amphibian anchored to an undamaged rig upriver had long since departed with a moaning that was quickly lost among the willow trees baking forlornly in the heat.

Thus there were no witnesses when Pat Savage popped her head up in the sluggish confluence, looked about, and saw that all was deserted.

Taking a deep breath, she dived again, fought her way down to the mud-obscured river bottom, and felt around until she found Monk Mayfair. The hairy chemist was struggling with one of the heavy pipe collars. Amid the tumbling down of the rig, one leg had somehow become wedged into the tube, and Monk was having trouble sitting up properly to get at it.

Seeing the copper-skinned girl through the swirling mud, Monk pointed at the problem, his eyes wide.

Displaying surprising strength, Pat helped extricate the leg, and the apish chemist pulled free. Together, they swam to the surface, there to tread water as they searched their surroundings.

"Thanks, Pat," Monk gulped, spitting out river muck.

"It's darn smart of you to always carry some of those trick oxygen pills Doc Savage invented," commented Pat.

Monk grunted, "I never go anywhere without 'em. Not only do they let you breathe underwater, but if you hold your breath and pinch your nostrils, poison gas can't harm you—unless it's the kind that works through the skin pores."

Pat nodded vigorously. "That was the hard part of playing possum for me. I'm not used to those things. My poor lungs kept wanting to breathe, and I had to force them to hold still. It's a very queer sensation, as you know."

There was no sign of the seaplane, but the racket of it leaving had transmitted down through the sluggish waters of the Arkansas River, so they knew it had departed, presumably taking away all parties concerned in the affair.

"Looks like they nabbed Vina again," moaned Pat.

Monk asked, "Did you get a good look at the ones in the motorboat?"

"I did. It was Standing Scorpion and two of his gunmen. I didn't recognize the two Osages, and that creepy hood of his kept me from seeing the face behind it."

"Think it might've been Tall Turkey?"

Pat shrugged casually. "It sure wasn't Ike Golden."

"If they ever find his body in that tangle down there," allowed Monk in a callous voice, "it'll be long after the fishes finish nibblin' on him."

They swam to the riverbank, crawled up its mucky embankment, and sat among the weeping willows and the scrub brush, letting their clothes dry in the Oklahoma sunlight.

Pat had managed to hold onto her automatic, and she was drying it in the sun, hoping it would function properly if need be.

After a while, she pointed the blunt muzzle into the air and gave the trigger a firm yank. Receiving an unimpressive click, she tried again and again until convinced that the mechanism had gotten fouled by mud. Pat tossed the weapon into the Arkansas River, where it disturbed a cruising catfish as it sank from sight.

"We are," she said wryly, "smack up against another dead end."

"Yeah," agreed Monk. "No tellin' where they hightailed it off to."

"I overheard Standing Scorpion say something about a stronghold."

Monk felt of his face, which by now had grown a ration of beard stubble that was encroaching upon the scorpion brand on his cheek. "Probably off in the Ozarks."

Pat sighed. "We could start there, I reckon."

Monk made a simian face. "The Ozark range stretches from eastern Oklahoma clear on through Arkansas and a hunk of Missouri. It's mostly mountainous brush and wilderness. Take us a year to go through it all, even if we knew what we were looking for exactly."

Pat frowned. "At least we had the satisfaction of interrupting their master plan, whatever it was."

Monk cautioned, "Don't get your hopes up too high. They'll find other planes to do their dirty work with."

Suddenly, the hairy homely chemist said, "Did you happen to notice Standing Scorpion's shoes?"

"Not really," said Pat. "That ridiculous robe hangs right down to his uppers, and he was standing in the cockpit of the motorboat. Why do you ask?"

"When he pronounced death on me in the derrick house, he wasn't wearin' his beaded moccasins, but ordinary store-bought brogans."

"What color?"

"They were kinda a dusty yellow."

"Yellow shoes might be a clue if we can find the owner," admitted Pat. "But I don't see how we're going to do that without transportation of our own."

Studying the homely Monk's rather battered features, Pat remarked, "That scorpion mark is showing on your face again."

Monk grumbled, "I'm a marked man. No tellin' what the law will do to me if they ever catch up."

The waterlogged pair lapsed into dejected silence while they contemplated their diminishing options.

Pat ventured hopefully, "I don't imagine that, being a local boy, you know where we are?"

"I don't recognize this stretch of the river," admitted the apish chemist. "And the Arkansas runs a mighty long ways, like I told you. I figger we're still in Oklahoma, though. But it would help to know where the nearest town lies—otherwise we could be walkin' a long ways for nothing."

"I am in no mood to wear out my shoes walking along this riverbank without anything more to go on than the vague promise of eventually stumbling upon civilization," decided Pat.

So they sat, watching the demolished oil rig burn itself out. Finally, the smoking summit fell apart, and vanished from their sight.

They continued to squat there as the hot Oklahoma sun dried their clothes, which it soon did. This improved their comfort and appearances, but not their general dispositions.

Before long, Monk began going through his waterlogged pockets. His simian features wrinkled into the semblance of an old catcher's mitt.

"Gone!" he gulped.

"If it's your dignity," sighed Pat, "you'll find it with mine—wherever that might be."

"Naw, it's that bottle we've been carryin' everywhere—the one Ben Nansen tossed at us back at the beginnin' of this screwy shindig."

Pat made a cross face. She dropped her chin back into her cupped hand, as if to keep it from sinking to the ground—an unmistakable outward indication of her crestfallen mood. "All of our progress has been circular, where it hasn't gone strictly backward."

"It musta been important," Monk grumbled. "But now we'll probably never know why."

"Oh, I don't know," Pat said airily. "I understand all questions are eventually answered in the afterlife."

"Lotta good that'll do us," grunted the gorilla-like chemist.

After a while, a farmer happened along, apparently attracted by the airplane racket and the black smoke rising from the smoldering oil derrick.

Monk quickly smeared river mud on his homely features to disguise the scorpion mark while Pat stood up to greet the new arrival.

"A passel of trouble here, I see," the man remarked. "Do you folks need help?"

Pat said, "We could use a lift into the nearest town. We were exploring that derrick when we caused a spark and it caught fire."

The man made a downcast face and said, "Those old wood rigs should've been torn down a long while back. All they are is nuisances. Sure, I can give you a lift. Come along."

The lift got them as far as a rough-looking town called Denoya. There the man let them off and wished them well, but it was plain that he did not care for Monk and Pat and their disheveled appearances. Pat still played the part of a copper-skinned Indian woman. Monk looked as if he might be a typical Oklahoma oilfield lease monkey who had fallen on hard times.

By this time, it was becoming dusky and Monk and Pat stood on a deserted street corner, contemplating their next move. Whatever it might be was not obvious to them. For they had no means of transportation and no prospect of acquiring any, short of downright theft.

"Is it too much to hope that you're carrying anything in the way of money?" wondered Pat.

Monk yanked out the lining of his pockets. "They glommed my wallet, and every cent I had."

"I imagine we are going to have to steal another automobile if we are to make any progress," Pat said unhappily.

Monk looked bereaved. "I wouldn't want to steal a hard-up workin' man's motorcar," he admitted.

"Maybe we can scrounge up a bicycle built for two," said Pat.

They wandered around town until they came to the local creamery, where the milk trucks were parked, awaiting the next day of dawn deliveries.

"One of those might do," suggested Pat.

"It might, at that," agreed Monk.

Without hesitating, he climbed the wire fence, dropped down to the other side and tried various truck doors until one popped open.

Grinning, Monk climbed in, ducked down and began his fiddling. The simian chemist was soon rewarded by a throaty grinding signifying the turning over of the motor. Releasing the clutch, he wheeled the machine up to the padlocked gate, and then slowly pushed the truck's blunt nose ahead until the straining gate came off its heavy hinges.

Reaching down, Pat dragged the gate out of the way so Monk could drive out onto the street. He threw open the other door and Pat climbed inside.

"Where to first?" asked Monk, his humor returning.

"The hospital where Ben Nansen is being treated," said Pat without hesitation. "Maybe I can slip in and have a word with him."

"If he ain't croaked by now," grunted Monk pessimistically.

BEN NANSEN had not died. In the intervening hours since he had been taken to the hospital, he had been poked and prodded by a battery of doctors, and been the recipient of two blood transfusions. Those, as well as a hearty meal, had begun to put color back into his ghost-pale features.

The sparkle of life had returned to his dark eyes. As night approached, he sat up in his hospital bed for the first time, taking notice of his surroundings.

One of the things he noticed was the nurses. They were very pretty. As a shift changed, different nurses made their rounds, and every time one looked in on him, he attempted to make brave conversation. His efforts were feeble.

Night had fallen when the latest nurse happened by, wearing the crisp white uniform of her profession. She appeared to be a Native American, although on that score Ben Nansen was not quite clear. She had the dark hair and her skin was a nice shade of copper, and she was pleasant to look upon.

"How are you feeling?" she inquired, stepping in and closing the door gently behind her.

"Better," he said, his voice cracking a little. It was evident that he was far from being well.

The Indian nurse looked at the chart at the foot of his bed, nodded once and remarked encouragingly, "The doctors seem to be doing an excellent job with you."

"I feel human again," admitted the young man.

"What did they do to you—the ones who reduced you to looking like a human ghost?"

The question caused Ben Nansen's sunken orbs to retreat slightly, and he appeared to hesitate only due to remembered pain, not an unwillingness to talk.

"They drew blood from me, several times a day; they used it to feed something in the next room."

"Did you get any idea what it was?"

"I fear to say."

"Go ahead. I won't scoff."

"From time to time, they brought in the red vinegarroons," he related. "If you've ever seen one, you know they grow as long as two inches and are a dull brown, like old leather. These specimens were larger. They were as red as if they had been dripped in blood—or something the color of blood."

Ben Nansen shuddered, and the attentive nurse pulled his covers up to his chin.

"Go on," she invited.

"They… they hinted that these creatures were the offspring of a giant queen vinegarroon spawning in the next chamber. And my blood was being fed to this monster whip scorpion to sustain her." Nansen closed his dark eyes. "I never saw the queen. Only the babies."

The nurse nodded. "It sure sounds horrible. Where was this place?"

"High in the Ozarks, over in Arkansas."

"That covers a lot of territory," the nurse remarked casually. She was fussing about the room, not doing anything in particular, looking busy, but in fact conducting a clever interrogation.

Ben Nansen continued. "They took me there and held me for a week. I was certain I was going to die. But something happened that caused them to bring me back to Oklahoma. There, I escaped, got to Tulsa and almost rendezvoused with my sister, Vina."

"Vina Hawks Nansen?"

The pale patient sat up abruptly. "Yes, yes, you know her?"

"Not as well as I would like," admitted the nurse. "But I have some bad news for you. The people who abducted you now have Vina in their clutches. By all reports, they have taken her to their stronghold in the Ozarks."

A long groan escaped the cracked lips of Ben Nansen, and he seemed to shrink into his mattress in his helpless grief.

"Vina… I should never have fallen in with those damn no-account Osages…." The young man turned his pained features to the wall.

The nurse leaned over and whispered, "The authorities would like to know where that stronghold is. Have you any idea of its exact location?"

Nansen stirred to life slightly. "Only in a general way. It is a great sandstone castle of an affair fronting a lake. It is one of those lakes that is shaped like an 'S' and resembles an abbreviated river more than a lake, but it is not a true river."

"I see. What part of the Ozarks is this?"

"It lies," said Ben Nansen, "on the Salem Plateau."

"Thank you," said the nurse, declining to reveal her identity. "I am sure something will be done to rescue your sister. Now you just lie back there and continue your recuperation."

"Thank you. Oh, nurse. I didn't catch your name."

"Betty," replied Pat Savage. "My name is Betty Blaze."

"Cherokee?"

The nurse smiled cheerfully. "No. I belong to the Savage tribe. We're a whole lot wilder."

With that, Pat Savage slipped out the hospital room door, made her way through the maze of corridors that comprised the hospital and hurried through the night to the waiting milk truck where Monk Mayfair was hunkered down, all but out of sight.

Clambering in, she said, "I hope you know where the Salem Plateau lies."

"Sure, I do. What's out there?"

"A castle on a lake."

Monk made a face. "No wonder they took off in a seaplane. We're gonna need one, too."

Pat made a different face. "We have been holy heck on other people's aircraft ever since we hit Tulsa. I don't know that we could snag another one successfully. They would probably shoot us on sight if we showed up at the Tulsa airport."

"I don't think they got any amphibian planes out there, anyway." Monk frowned deeply. "I gotta figure out a place where we can nab one."

"Do you have any ideas?"

"We'll have to improvise," said Monk. "Try a couple of the lakes hereabouts and hope we get lucky."

"Getting lucky is not something we have been very successful at of late," reminded Pat in a tight voice.

Putting the truck into gear, Monk growled, "If we're gonna clear our names, we gotta get to manufacturin' our own luck. Startin' now."

Chapter XXIX

STRONGHOLD

MONK MAYFAIR'S BOYHOOD in and around Tulsa proved not to have been wasted.

He drove the borrowed dairy truck back to the Arkansas River, and concealed it from view in a stand of red oak trees and bedraggled weeping willows. This was necessary due to frequent brushes with prowling police radio cars. They dodged seven of them in the course of leaving the vicinity of the Bartlesville hospital.

Each encounter was hair-raising. Monk was entirely too conspicuous, his scorpion facial tattoo notwithstanding. And inasmuch as women drivers were not ordinarily employed to drive milk trucks, Pat was equally conspicuous.

"No sense gettin' pulled over," he explained to Pat. "We got this far all right."

On foot, they walked the banks of the Arkansas River until they found an unsecured canoe, which they borrowed, Pat remarking, "Murder charges aside, we are piling up quite a rap sheet of damaged or stolen property."

Monk shrugged, setting the canoe in the water with his freakishly long arms. "A lot of lives are at stake. We can't be too particular about how we get from here to there, never mind keepin' ourselves out of the calaboose."

"We'll just have to make good on all of these things, once we clear our good names," said Pat, climbing in after Monk.

"Speak for yourself," grunted Monk. "Back in Tulsa, my name's worse than mud."

Trying to look as natural as possible, they paddled down the central channel of the Arkansas until Monk steered in the direction of a thin tendril he recognized as Shell Creek. The tributary meandered west of Tulsa and fed into a large body of still blue water, which soon came into view.

When the small canoe finally reached the lake, Monk broke out in a huge grin. "This is turnin' out to be easier than I thought. I didn't recognize the stretch of the Arkansas where we were, but we got lucky."

The hairy chemist seemed to have a definite objective in mind, for he followed the southern lake shore a fair distance.

Some small buildings, and a larger one, came into view ahead.

"Where are we?" asked Pat.

Monk grinned. "Shell Lake. I used to go fishin' here, me and my old hound dog, Ponto. Back when I was a shaver."

Abandoning the canoe, they walked to the collection of buildings. The big structure was erected close to the lake shore and proved to be a hangar that housed a seaplane. The hour was too late for much to be doing about the place, for sunset was upon them. The drive from Bartlesville had been necessarily circuitous, which had cost them considerable time.

The shadowy pair made for the hangar.

A husky man wearing a flying helmet was using a small tractor to haul from the water a small two-place monoplane equipped with floats. A wheel-cradle was in place under the floats. The plane was hardly new, for its construction consisted of doped fabric over steel tubing. The old ship had a rattletrap quality about it. Its tandem cockpits were of the open variety.

The tractor made considerable noise. The man on it had his head turned, ascertaining the seaplane entered the hangar properly. No one else was around.

The pilot never heard the approaching footsteps—had no suspicion of their presence until fingers closed about his throat like iron bands of gripping bone and sinew. The fellow was lifted bodily off the tractor. One of the apish chemist's hands held the man helpless as a baby while the other threw the tractor out of gear.

The fingers loosened on the man's throat long enough for him to speak.

"What are you going to do with me?" the fellow whined.

Monk replied nothing.

"Oh, jeepers!" the pilot squawked. "Can't you say something, buddy? What's the idea of grabbing me?"

Monk's fingers tightened. Carrying the pilot out at arm's length as though he were a caught fish, the simian chemist took the man into the hangar. A sharp rap of knuckles against the fellow's jaw made him unconscious.

A darkened corner of the big structure absorbed the two figures. A grim sort of quiet fell, during which a close observer might have seen the long gorilla arms of Monk Mayfair moving in rapid motions, hog-tying the unconscious pilot.

The observer also would have sworn it was the same pilot who came out of the darkened corner. But a look under an old plane wing in the corner would have disclosed the real pilot, bound and tightly gagged.

The seaplane had been hauled to the hangar tail-first. Monk disconnected the tractor from the wheeled float-carriage, then clambered into the rear cockpit, Pat Savage having claimed the front one.

"That went according to plan," she noted.

"Let's mosey before somebody spots us," grunted Monk.

They donned leather flying helmets, along with aviator goggles to protect their eyes from the punishing slipstream. Pat keyed the ignition switch, and gave the electric-inertia starter a spin.

The motor caught with a bilious, uneven sputter, exploded erratically a few times, then began to roar. Pat took plenty of time warming up the cylinders. She did not like the sound of the engine.

Roosting crows cawed enthusiastically, inaudible over the crashing exhaust. While the needle which indicated engine temperature came to life and crept sluggishly around the dial, Pat watched the lake surface.

Exhaust stacks continued popping erratically and disgorging brown smoke. The balky engine warmed cantankerously, then began to run more smoothly.

Pat opened the throttle. The seaplane bumped and rumbled along for a couple of hundred feet before the vibration of the old crate settled down.

Drawn by the air-clawing propeller, the craft rolled down the slipway into the broad lake. The wheeled carriage was left behind as the twin pontoons floated. Light as a duck, the plane heaved over the wavelets. Soon it began smashing through them, then went on step, touching the water only every few yards.

Cautiously, Pat levered back on the control stick. The float-plane got off.

Slanting upward abruptly, it took the air. Without bothering to circle for altitude, Pat held the sluggish craft straight ahead, with the sunset horizon smoldering behind her.

The pontoon plane went booming out to the east, heading for the Ozarks.

The ship proved to be airworthy, despite its general condition. It held its altitude as night clamped down and stars appeared one by one, followed by the slow, majestic rising of the lunar orb.

Noticing the yellowish hue of the doped-fabric fuselage, Monk leaned forward so Pat could hear his words. "Can't say I care for the color of this old bus."

"What's wrong with it?" called back Pat.

"Nothin' much. It's just that we've had some bum luck with yellow planes lately."

Pat laughed. "Just hang on and say a little prayer to Pegasus. I'll get us there."

For all its lack of modernity, the aircraft was speedy. In less than an hour, it was banking low over the border of Oklahoma and Arkansas. After that, the seaplane flew along for a time.

The arid scrub brush of eastern Oklahoma soon turned into the soaring heights of the western Ozark Mountains. This section shone spectacular in the starlight. Lushly forested with pine trees and oaks, it was dotted with little lakes and streams that meandered like molten silver past limestone bluffs to vanish into shadowy, primeval rock crevices.

As they thundered along, Monk Mayfair discovered a folded newspaper in the rear cockpit. It was an evening edition, so it carried the latest news.

Over the steady howl of the slipstream and engine racket, the homely chemist began reading to Pat Savage the latest news. He had to shout.

"It says here that Tulsa got hit pretty hard with that red stuff sprayed by the Scorpion airplane. People are gettin' sick in droves. A lot of them can't walk already. Kinda like polio got loose somehow. Sounds like an epidemic!"

"All the more reason to cut that high-and-mighty Standing Scorpion down to size when we catch up to him," vowed Pat.

"What are we going to use for weapons? We keep losin' every firearm we lay our hands on."

Pat said nothing. She had no hopeful answer for that.

Suddenly, Monk let out a yell, "According to this, Ham Brooks is up on charges! Accessory after the fact of murder."

"Whose murder?"

"Jim Dandy's, among others. They can't hang that charge on the shyster. He was in New York when that cop got his."

"Accessory after the fact," reminded Pat, "probably means that he's accused of aiding and abetting a fugitive from justice."

Monk grunted. "Well, he *is* guilty of that. I sure hope somebody is takin' care of Habeas. I should never have asked Ham to bring him along."

"Your pet pig," said Pat pointedly, "is the least of our troubles now."

Monk continued reading and found an inside page with an interesting item.

"The cops are still lookin' for Grabber Daly and his stooge. But they're gettin' nowhere now that it looks like the police have bigger fish to fry than him."

"Such as ourselves?" asked Pat.

"Yeah, probably," snorted Monk. "The tables sure have been turned on us. The cops were huntin' that no-good lease grabber on our account and now he's runnin' free and we're one skippin' step ahead of Oklahoma justice."

Studying the Ozark Mountains and their green-furred peaks turning argent beneath the twilight stars, Pat reminded, "Well, we're in Arkansas now, aren't we?"

Monk looked over the padded combing of his cockpit and said, "Yeah, looks like it. This is wilder country than the Osage. If we get lucky, we can stay on the loose a long time out here."

"What I meant was," interjected Pat, "we've crossed state lines. That makes us fugitives from Federal justice."

"Hadn't thought of that," mumbled Monk, too low to be heard.

The apish chemist folded the newspaper and stuffed it down beside his seat and continued studying their surroundings. Now that they had made it safely into Ozark territory, it was the hairy chemist's job to navigate. He knew the terrain, at least generally. Pat did not.

Reaching forward, Monk tapped Pat on one shoulder and then the other, signaling her to bank left or right. It was easier that way than shouting. They had done enough of that, exchanging ideas on the mess they were in.

Time passed, and the rather ramshackle floatplane continued along. Night had finally fallen, and the climbing half moon rose resembled a wedge of luminous ice. It made them feel cool to look at it.

Finally, Monk called out, "Salem Plateau dead ahead. Fly straight for a while, and then start searchin'."

Pat lifted a hand in acknowledgment and banked left. She put the rickety fabric plane through a series of swooping turns, leveled off, and they both got busy swiveling their heads and sweeping their gazes, looking for the queer lake that fronted the stronghold of Standing Scorpion.

Anxious golden eyes continually went to the fuel gauge. They had plenty, but every hour that passed drained their tank. Too, the copper-skinned girl was acutely aware of the distressing fact that she was piloting a plane that was equipped with twin pontoons, but no landing gear. When the time came to set down, it would be upon water, otherwise prospects were bleak for a happy landing.

EVENTUALLY, their efforts were rewarded. An S-shaped lake shimmered in the moonlight. Monk fished out a pair of binoculars that happened to be pocketed in the rear cockpit.

Searching, he noted an amphibian plane moored to a float consisting of a long tongue of sheet metal supported by floating oil drums. There did not seem to be much to the lake except that. But one side of it butted up against a rough rise.

Tapping Pat on the shoulder, Monk leveled a furry forefinger. Pat took the binoculars from him and applied her optics to the eyepieces.

One look was enough to satisfy her.

While they circled the lake at a distance, the amphibian stirred to life. Sparks and smoke gushed out of the engine bayonets, and it was soon scooting across the surface of the lake, trailing a growing fan of wake.

"Trouble comin' up!" yelled Monk.

"Swell!" enthused Pat. "I've been spoiling for a fight."

The copper-skinned girl banked the plane, and decided to let the seaplane give chase.

The pilot of the amphibian readily obliged. Shooting up into the night, he achieved the correct altitude and began chasing the other aircraft. Pat recognized the ship as the cabin plane that had been moored to a river derrick back on the Arkansas River. It was black and scarlet, the ebony portions suggesting something charred.

The pursuing plane was newer and had a better motor, and it soon overhauled the rattletrap floatplane.

"Hang on, Monk!" yelled Pat, throwing the aircraft into a climbing loop, twisting the wings about. The pursuing pilot was startled to discover that his quarry was now a vicious buzzsaw coming up on his empennage.

He did not like that, and immediately worked rudder and ailerons and sent his own craft turning and diving.

The two aircraft commenced chasing one another about the sky, engines howling, fabric rattling, wings straining at their roots. But no greater violence resulted.

"Nobody's armed!" shouted Pat. "So that's good."

Monk shrugged and yelled back, "Not so good if we want to force him down."

"I might have a notion about that," Pat called back.

Before she could put that notion into action, the other plane came sweeping down from above, and vaulted past their heads low enough that they ducked in spite of themselves. The open cockpits made them feel extremely unprotected.

From the rear of the red-and-black ship, a billow of reddish smoke erupted.

"*Whoooeee!*" yelled Monk. "Bank hard!"

Pat did. She threw the old rattletrap plane off to the left, gritting her perfect teeth. The floatplane lurched sickeningly as it struck a down current, giving them a bad scare on top of their jangled nerves.

The hell-red powder or vapor—or whatever it was—never reached them, but a pungent, vinegary odor blew toward their faces. Monk recognized it.

"Vinegarroon acid!" he burst out, pinching his blunt nose shut. Instinctively, Pat did the same.

As they boomed along, they were acutely aware that their open cockpits made them especially vulnerable to the bitter stuff. On the other hand, whipping slipstream and their speed guaranteed the scarlet bloom could not get to them as long as they didn't fly into a cloud of it.

The pilot did his best to pirouette around, climb and dive, and attempt to get in front of them so he could fill their lungs with the red peril vapor.

Pat Savage would have none of it. She did more with the old plane than the enemy pilot did with his new sky wagon. Twisting, climbing, banking hard, she kept one step ahead of him.

"These wings had better hold!" howled Monk.

"Do we have parachutes?" Pat yelled back. "I forgot to look."

Startled at the thought, the homely chemist looked about his cramped cockpit. His ugly features lit up.

"I found one!"

"Hurray for you," barked Pat. "We can share it!"

"I got me an idea," Monk said suddenly.

Fishing around in his cockpit, Monk grasped a wrench that was tied down to the floor. He got it loose, tapped Pat on the back of her helmeted head with it.

Turning, Pat saw Monk brandish the heavy tool. She got the idea.

Giving a thumb's up sign, she swiftly executed a banking turn that brought them above the other ship.

"Stay even with him!" called Monk.

Pat did her best. She put the ramshackle ship through its paces, holding her own against the more modern craft, which jockeyed wildly.

Monk stood up in his rear cockpit, turned his upper body about against screaming slipstream. When he felt the time was right, he dropped the wrench onto the rocking plane below.

He missed the fuselage, but not by much. The wrench struck the leading edge of the right wing, which caused the ship to jump and buck like a hornet-stung horse.

The other pilot struggled to get his amphibian under control, and after he did, he shook a furious fist out a window at them.

"Got his attention!" crowed Pat.

Monk grinned. "That'll teach him to spray us with that scorpion vinegar."

The black amphibian attempted a snap roll, but Pat sent her bus scooting around, and the maneuver availed the spooked pilot not at all.

"Doc sure taught you good!" chortled Monk. "You're flyin' rings around him. And he knows it, too!"

In the end, the outmaneuvered aviator gave up and headed for home base.

Settling her own ship level, Pat followed him at a careful distance, holding her plane a thousand feet above the other craft.

Pat circled warily as the seaplane alighted on the snaky lake and skimmed over to the float, scuttling to its mooring with scarcely diminished speed. Dark figures rushed out to secure the craft.

During this operation, concealed floodlights opened up on the settling craft, illuminating the rocky cliff overhang. What it showed was a wonder.

For the sandstone cliffs had been carved out into a castle-like structure, most of which was embedded into the sheer face of the cliff.

"Lookit!" shouted Monk.

"I see it!" said Pat. "But what is it?"

MONK studied the thing for a while in the bobbing floodlights, and decided that some ingenious person had caused the sandstone cliffside to be carved into shapes that were remindful of various Indian habitations. The central structure was like a lodge house, and like the turrets and battlements of a medieval castle, wikiups dotted the half roof projecting from the cliff. Other features led them to believe that a natural cavern had been used as the basis for the stronghold, and the fanciful castle façade carved around it.

The metal dock resembled a shining drawbridge projecting from the cave mouth, adding to the sense of the castle-like fortress.

Dark figures gathered on the narrow ramparts and watched them curiously.

"That Standing Scorpion," remarked Monk begrudgingly, "sure has some grandiose ideas. I ain't never seen anything like that set-up in my life."

"It's probably not safe to land," remarked Pat.

"Probably not," agreed Monk. "On the other hand, we can't have much fuel left, and this joint is what we were lookin' for, so we might as well take a long chance."

"I'm with you," said Pat, throwing the stick forward to depress the ship's snout and sending the baying propeller toward the rippling lake surface. A narrow stretch of lake offered room for a safe descent. She came in at a shallow angle.

Pat calculated wind direction from the spindrift thrown from wavelet tips. There was a warm crosswind. There was no time to turn the nose into the wind. Neither was there room.

She leveled out, watched alertly until the plane was inside the slot of an opening, then worked her feet briskly on the rudder bar to fishtail from side to side and lose additional flying speed.

The air currents were bumpier than she had anticipated. The plane dropped like a plummet, struck with a force that nearly wrenched her head from her shoulders. A torrent of cold water and dirty foam cascaded up on either side of the fuselage, drenching them.

Pat and Monk rubbed slosh from their goggle lenses.

After the pontoon floats struck water, the fragile ship bounced a time or two, then settled in, momentum pushing the old rattletrap plane along.

Keeping the motor gushing air against the empennage for taxiing control, Pat herded the little amphibian shoreward. After she pinched off the throttle, momentum pushed them toward the float.

Pat snapped her goggles up on her forehead. The craft sloughed into a sluggish drift less than a score of yards from the moored amphibian.

It was while they were coasting toward the float that they noticed men rolling large drums out of the dark cavern mouth.

These were brought up to the edge of the lake, opened in some fashion, and liquid began pouring into the lake.

"Those look like aviation fuel drums!" thundered Monk.

After a moment or two, it became obvious that's exactly what they were, for the stink of aviation fuel soon reached their nostrils. Matches were struck, thrown into the lake water and, with a great gush, the spreading fuel ignited.

As flame rushed across the lake surface, seeking them, Monk howled, "Try to get her off!"

Pat Savage gave it her best, but the engine was cantankerous, and it was still banging and coughing when the licking flames crawled toward them.

Over on the other side, the black seaplane was in motion, and the pilot was trying to get his crate off the lake surface before it was also involved. But there was no time. He succeeded in beaching the craft half out of the water, however.

Night turned into a red and yellow nightmare as the lake became engulfed in fast-moving fire composed of shimmering, spreading hellfire.

By the time the conflagration reached their pontoons, they knew they had no chance, but Pat still fought hard to restart her motor. Features grim, she adjusted the choke. Then she spun the engine with the electric-inertia starter. Still spinning it, she threw the ignition switch.

The cylinders caught with a wheezing, angry bellow. The plane wobbled sluggishly, got under way. The engine was firing confidently now. There was plenty of room for a take-off. Pat realized that she would have to take off cross wind, but that was the least of her concerns.

Propeller whirling wildly, the little floatplane started on its run. The craft gathered momentum.

"Hang on!" she called back to Monk.

Mouth agape, the hairy chemist clung to the cockpit combing and ducked his bullet head as low as he could while simultaneously swiveling his head to take in the immensity of the spreading fuel fire.

Pat worked the stick back and forth, trying to get the pontoons off the lake surface. But they were the old-style V-bottom floats. Not very efficient since they lacked built-in steps. Monk tried rocking in his seat, hoping to break the suction holding them down.

With that first rocking movement, their spines congealed.

Unfortunately for Pat and Monk, leaping flames now swirled all around them. Too late to turn, they realized they were doomed.

As their struggling aircraft charged into the leaping inferno, they saw the doped fabric on their wingtips catch fire and curl—and they knew that even if they got into the air, they would shortly crash like a fiery comet.

Face fierce, Pat frantically worked the rudders, seeking to slow their course. But it was too late for that, too.

"Ditch! Ditch!" yelled Monk. "It's our only chance!"

At the last instant, Pat cut the ignition switch in defeat.

Together, they threw themselves out of the aircraft, diving for the water, passing through myriad tongues of fire and disappearing beneath the burning lake surface.

No longer under control, the rattletrap floatplane continued scooting along, but its wings were soon ablaze, and the undercarriage smoked ominously. It kept going like a juggernaut of fire until it inevitably reached the lake shore, where it collapsed in a blazing ball of fabric and tubular structure.

The propeller went spinning away somehow, having gotten detached from its engine mount.

Fuel oil burned for over an hour, during which time nothing emerged from the lake's incandescent surface.

Safely beached, the all-metal black amphibian survived the conflagration unscathed.

Eventually, someone stepped out of the tall cavern mouth with a Thompson submachine gun and, as the impish yellow flames settled down, a tall figure emptied the ammunition drum randomly into the water to make sure.

The sharply staccato sub-gun finally finished its stuttering song. After that, there was only the oily smoke and a great empty silence.

"Tell the Chief they've been scalped right down to their skull bones," the Tommy-gunner shouted over his shoulder.

Chapter XXX

TERROR THRONE

FROM A NOTCH of a window cut into the ornate-carven sandstone cliffside, Vina Hawks Nansen watched in horror as the flaming lake slowly ceased burning, turning into a great smoky smudge pot as the last of the surface oil burned off.

The vertical window was too narrow to permit her to leap, for she would have done exactly that had it also not been barred, so great was her grief and horror.

"They had no chance," she moaned, turning her face away from the dying conflagration.

"None whatsoever, dear," intoned a deep voice behind her.

Whirling, the young woman blanched at the sight of her fiancé, publisher Morgan Marrs. And the disgusted revulsion in her chocolate brown eyes was impossible to conceal.

Below, the last chattering of the Tommy gun snarled out. Then all fell silent.

"It was necessary to guarantee that they did not somehow survive," said the publisher gravely. "Not that there was any doubt."

"You previously believed they had died in the burning oil derrick on the river," reminded the woman.

"I do not know how they managed that miraculous feat. Neither does our master, Standing Scorpion," admitted the publisher. "But this time their fate has been sealed."

"All of our fates will be sealed—once the law catches up with us," Vina said dispiritedly.

A self-conscious laugh, not much more than a chuckle, passed the publisher's firm lips. He stood with one hand in his coat pocket, and kept it there.

"After today," he said, "we are well on our way to *becoming* the law of the land. I have been listening to the radio reports. Tulsa is in an open panic. Citizens are fast succumbing to the Grampus paralysis, and flooding area hospitals. After a day or two—no more than three—they will be begging for the cure."

"And there is no cure," moaned Vina.

Morgan Marrs shook his head solemnly. "There you are mistaken, my dear. For there is a cure. We will wait three days. Long enough for the doctors to pronounce the paralysis incurable, then we will offer a cure, for a reasonable sum of money. Greenbacks and gold will pour in, to fund our next wave of terror."

"Wasn't the power of being a publisher enough for you?" the woman snapped back angrily.

"No, I'm afraid not. Especially with my newspaper failing. The rival *Globe* is overtaking us rapidly. It was fortunate for me that I fell in with Standing Scorpion and we pooled our assets toward the great revolution."

Indignant disdain flavored the blonde woman's rebuttal. "What you call a rebellion is simply terror and extortion. And you know it!"

"Consider how this country was founded," Morgan Marrs said suavely. "The red man was crushed under our heel, and the bravery of our soldiers and settlers was praised and promoted. Once we begin our march to power, high praise will fall upon Standing Scorpion and those who supported him in the early days of this revolution."

The publisher paused. His flinty eyes grew sombre.

"It is not by accident that you have been pressed into service in our important cause," Marrs averred. "You are perhaps the most widely-read newspaper columnist in all of Oklahoma.

Under my guidance, you will pen the early accounts that will sway the American people to our cause."

Vina Hawks Nansen's cocoa eyes widened in shock. "You cannot mean this!"

Marrs nodded. "I selected you, and groomed you toward this task. For no revolution can succeed without positive press relations to convince the common people that the new way is the best way—the way of the future."

"Press relations!" flared Vina. "I can think of a more fitting word: lies!"

Marrs shrugged negligently. "Call it what you will. Your facility with a pen is unmatched. It will sway emotions and so mold minds."

Fists hardening into pale bones, Vina said tightly, "I will not proselytize for you. Never! I wish I had never met you!"

She had taken firm hold of the diamond ring around her finger and now she ripped it off, flinging it toward him, heedless of the blood she had caused to flow from the skin-scrape created in doing so.

The ring bounced off the publisher's rather florid tie, and he bent to pick it up.

"You'll wear this again," he said coolly, "once your head is clear. When the great march to power is no longer stoppable."

Trembling, Vina husked, "Did you ever love me?"

Morgan Marrs hesitated slightly, and then admitted frankly, "You were selected for your writing skill, but you will make a fitting wife. Once you settle down to your new life."

Vina Hawks Nansen stood framed in the narrow barred window, and the look on her face was one of fury. Her lips parted and she appeared poised to hurl biting invective in her former fiancé's face.

Came a knock at the door, and Marrs turned to open it.

A tall Osage Indian stepped in. "Standing Scorpion wishes to speak with the squaw."

"Watch how you talk about my future wife, Red Crow."

The Osage did not blink. Nor did he apologize. Instead, he repeated the invitation, choosing his words more carefully.

"Chief Standing Scorpion wishes to speak with the white woman."

Nodding, the publisher stepped aside, and waved his fiancée to follow the tall Osage brave.

"No doubt this will be an important palaver," said Marrs. "Follow this man, and we will speak again later."

Vina Hawks Nansen refused to budge from the window. The Osage stepped up and seized her by the arm, squeezing hard enough to make her wince, then walked her out of the room as Morgan Marrs watched her depart, his features stiff and his flint eyes unmoved by the woman's suffering.

Vina was escorted through corridors that were hewn from native sandstone and illuminated by hurricane lanterns and long candles set in niches spaced along the way. She walked with her features held rigid, her feet whetting the bare floor as she resisted being forced along.

IN time, she was brought to a chamber possessing qualities of a dressed cave. It lay deep within the face of the sandstone cliffside, and was barred by a door of spike-studded oak.

There was a peephole in the door cut in the shape of a whip scorpion, with its tail curled tightly. A hot red light burning on the other side made the many-legged void smolder malevolently.

Without a word, Red Crow flung the door open. The Osage squeezed his eyes tight as he walked Vina in, then left her there, closing the heavy door.

The place, after she entered, almost hurt her eyes. From several points scarlet spotlights blazed, turning the entire chamber into a blood-red nightmare.

Her own eyes narrowed to knife slits, Vina Hawks Nansen attempted to peer through the red atmosphere, and realized that the garish lighting was magnified by strategically placed mirrors. The entire effect was disorienting in the extreme.

"I cannot see a thing," she said tightly.

"Be patient, white woman," a voice intoned.

In time, her eyes became accustomed to the weird red glare.

The first thing that resolved itself before her blinking brown orbs was a great fan of eagle feathers. This proved to be a traditional war bonnet that had been affixed to one wall in such a way that it formed a barbaric halo around a figure seated upon a throne set upon a raised dais.

The throne was carved of hickory wood and the armrests fashioned like the pincers of a scorpion while, from the hard back, a similar object curled up and forward. It was the jointed stinger of a scorpion's tail.

Chief Standing Scorpion sat on the throne, his hooded head just beneath the arching stinger. Ebony-gloved hands gripped the pincer armrests. The red glare made his purple robes glow a queer violet, as if ignited by an otherworldly flame.

The fabric hood started twitching as he spoke.

"The Savage girl and the gorilla man are now dead. You have no hope of rescue. Do you understand this?"

"I understand that you're a fiend!" she snarled back.

Standing Scorpion did not seem to take offense, for he continued his sonorous speech.

"It has been explained to you—your role in the future of my enterprise."

Vina's eyes blazed. "And I've explained that I want no part of this madness!"

"You say this now, and your sincerity rings in your voice. Standing Scorpion respects this."

"That means nothing to me," spat Vina. "You're a killer. I've already informed Morgan that I refuse to participate in any of it. Refuse, do you understand?"

The other seemed unperturbed by the woman's defiant out-burst. "I understand your words. You make them plain. Do you fail to understand my power? It is the power to rob men, women and children of the use of their legs. To make them immobile. To take from them the thing that separates them from the beasts of the forest and the vermin of the desert. The ability to stand upright and walk like humans."

Vina Hawks Nansen said nothing to that.

Chief Standing Scorpion resumed his diatribe.

"When the city of Tulsa pays tribute to me, we will move on to Oklahoma City, Enid and Lawton, then spread outward to Arkansas, Missouri and Texas. Municipalities will pay because the cure will prove so potent that no one could deny its value or efficacy."

Curling her lip in contempt, Vina snapped, "I told Morgan I did not believe in any such cure, and I say the same to you. The finest doctors could not cure my father. How could you?"

Standing Scorpion laughed softly, causing his hood to puff out in front of his mouth.

"Look around you. It is in these caves that I discovered the agent that causes Grampus paralysis. The doctors who treated your father suspected it was a virus, but could not cure it. They have considered that it might be a form of bacteria, but that, too, they could not cure. Their error was in their thinking. The Grampus paralysis is caused by a mold—a mold which, when inhaled, infiltrates the nervous system and brings about the desired—or should I say *undesirable?*—results. That mold grows deep in these chambers. It is red. Almost as red as these walls of rock about you."

"You are a liar!" Vina Hawks Nansen charged. "Are you forgetting that my own brother insisted that his blood was drained to feed something horrible? That could only be bacteria, or perhaps a germ agent."

"Or perhaps nothing at all," returned the weird figure in purple and scarlet. "Your brother was released to tell his story of being drained of blood to feed something he never beheld. That was to confuse the medical authorities. If they were looking for something that was a bacteria or a germ, they would not suspect a mold. And so they could not stumble across a cure."

His gloved hands slipped into the folds of his robe and withdrew two vials, one which contained a red substance and the other which appeared to be ordinary water.

"In my left hand is a specimen of the mold," he explained. "I have only to throw it at your feet, causing the glass to shatter. You will inhale it and be infected with the Grampus paralysis. In my other hand is a vial similar to the one your brother stole from me. This is the cure. One sip, and forty-eight hours later the unshakable paralysis will depart the afflicted one."

"You are horrible—horrible," the woman shouted defiantly. Fear lashed her voice, however, and she was stepping backward with every word.

"I ask you one more time: Join of your own free will, and I will pocket the red vial, as well as the clear bottle, for neither will be necessary in this instance. Refuse, and be reduced to the same pitiful state as your father...."

"Monster! You robbed my father of his vitality. You drained the blood from my brother merely to confuse hard-working medical professionals. You are a vile monster, I tell you!"

"Choose!" thundered Chief Standing Scorpion.

Her back coming into contact with the closed door, Vina Hawks Nansen stopped, her face stark in the room-suffusing crimson glow.

"You should have searched me better," she hissed. "When I was captured, I concealed my gun."

"Impossible!" Standing Scorpion insisted. "You were frisked by your fiancé."

The blood draining from her features, Vina Hawks Nansen reached into her hair, as if to tear at it in her anguish. Instead, she dug around in the gauzy blonde mass until she found the tiny .22-caliber automatic hidden there.

The pistol flashed into view. She laid the sight on the seated figure, who suddenly reared up in defiant anger, a silken tower of garish purple whose celluloid eyes and whip scorpion emblem burned a lurid red.

"You would not dare fire that thing at me!" he flared.

Without hesitation, Vina squeezed the trigger—and the result made the entire chamber explode in an impossible way.

The momentary flash of gunpowder and saffron tongue of flame emitted by the pistol forced the defiant woman to squeeze her eyes shut.

A jangling sound filled her ears, followed by a crashing cascade of sharp noise. It rang for a long time before quiet returned.

Vina opened her eyes. The hellish glare was still there, but the throne and the man who stood before it, including the war bonnet wall hanging, had vanished!

Not believing her eyes, the blonde leapt toward the scarlet glow and discovered that what she thought was a wall was in fact a great mirror that now lay broken upon the floor, its jagged fangs and sharp square edges each reflecting the hot glow like separate furnaces.

A low, breathy exclamation escaped her parted lips.

Spinning about, Vina Hawks Nansen looked around wildly to behold the actual throne that the mirror had reflected to fool her. It had been behind her all along!

From somewhere in the chamber someone or something hissed venomously. It made her think of a whip scorpion getting ready to strike....

Chapter XXXI

SHOCKING SURPRISE

AFTER THE LAST of the oil skim had burnt off, a blackish-gray residue of malodorous smoke continued to hang over the queer lake fronting the sandstone castle that was so fantastic-looking in the Arkansas moonlight.

This low-hanging pall blocked all lunar rays from penetrating to the lake bottom; consequently, it was dark as pitch there.

Catfish and bass swam about the waters, unaffected by the pooling flames above, although their agitated manner suggested that they were disturbed by the unnatural phenomenon.

Lying on his back in the silt, Monk Mayfair stared again at the luminous dial of his wristwatch and saw that the safe period of time since taking an oxygen pill after diving from the flaming floatplane had nearly elapsed.

The hairy chemist figured he had nearly five minutes left, and was considering stirring, seeking Pat Savage, who had also consumed one of the lozenges before dropping into the water.

The remarkable thing about the pills was that they so saturated the human body with life-giving oxygen that it was entirely unnecessary to breathe. Consequently, no air bubbles had escaped Monk's tightly-compressed lips for nearly forty minutes, for he had taken a triple dose of the lozenges, and the effect upon his imagination was marked.

It was the most perfectly natural thing in the world to inhale and exhale during respiration, but Monk had carefully avoided doing that since it was temporarily unnecessary.

No sooner had the thought entered his mind than it was about time to surface. The unsettling rattle of the machine gun penetrated the still waters, and a handful of lead slugs chopped deep into the lake.

One came perilously close to Monk, but it had been deflected by dense lake water upon entering, and lost almost all of its force before it sank to the bottom.

That was enough for the homely chemist. Gathering himself up, he began scrambling on all fours along the silty surface, until he encountered one of Pat's legs.

Pat clutched at Monk's hairy forearms and, by squeezing the other's arms, they reassured each other that both were intact.

Grasping the girl by her wrists, Monk gave Pat a boost to the surface, then began kicking after her.

When they surfaced, the pair immediately took stock of their surroundings.

There was not much to take stock of. Oil smoke hung like a black haze, obscuring almost everything. Monk undertoned, "Don't breathe yet. This is bad stuff."

Pat said nothing, squeezing Monk's hirsute wrist to indicate that she understood.

There was no more rattle of gunfire, so Monk started pulling Pat in one direction. To his surprise, she began pulling him in another. She did so with such urgency that the apish chemist decided to follow along.

Before very long, they were treading water and coming up out of the lake, walking hunched over so as not to be spotted from the weird sandstone castle.

By this time the oxygen pills' potency was growing thin.

Pat began hacking slightly, but managed to put out low-toned words. "We're near the cliffs; let's make for them."

The sandstone cliffs had formed an arc around one limb of the tranquil lake, and Monk allowed himself to be led toward them.

The air cleared, and visibility became more practical.

Monk saw that the towering sandstone cliffs at one end of the castle cut into its face and from this vantage point he could see that the castle was really more of a façade than an actual structure. It had been hewed out of the cliff face, and no doubt behind it lay caves and hollows that provided the true habitation that served as the headquarters for Chief Standing Scorpion and his Osage band.

Reaching the base of the cliff, they climbed it carefully, discovering a narrow stony ledge only a few feet above the waterline. It was barely wide enough to stand upright upon its narrow surface.

Monk hissed, "It widens in front of the cave mouth yonder. Follow me."

Inserting themselves into cracks and crevices, they paused often in the stillness to make sure they were not spotted, and so approached their objective.

It was very late and there did not seem to be any guards, the one with the Tommy gun having withdrawn into the great maw at the base of the castle's façade.

Peering about, Monk muttered, "Are you game for bustin' in?"

"Busting in," rejoined Pat, "and busting right out again. We're going to rescue Vina Hawks Nansen and pull the pinfeathers out of Chief Standing Scorpion's tail."

"I'll settle for pulling off that dang hood. I still think he's a white man."

"He's tall," reminded Pat. "He could just as easily be an Osage Indian."

Monk grunted, "Back at the oil derrick on the river, I took a bite out of his right hand. His glove came off. It was hard to see in the dark, but he might've been a paleface. Anyway, he's got my teeth marks on his mitt. That'll give him away for sure."

"Good thinking," complimented Pat.

"And another thing," added Monk. "He was wearin' yellow shoes."

"Speaking of shoes," whispered Pat, "we better take ours off if we intend to sneak around like Comanches on the warpath."

The pair removed their footgear, jammed them into handy crevices and began to slip back down to the hard ledge fronting the lake.

With elaborate creeping caution, they made their way to the great arch of an entrance, which appeared to be nothing more than a natural cavern, one of many such which dot the Ozark landscape in Arkansas.

There were no guards, no doors—simply a gaping black mouth that was arched at the top and naturally flat at the bottom.

"Are you game to try this?" Pat hissed.

Monk rubbed his rusty knuckles, each in set turn, and growled, "I'd like to see somebody stop me."

So the unlikely duo entered, walking boldly but soft-footed.

They had not very much time to imagine what lay beyond the black cave mouth. Had they given it any thought, their imaginations would not have prepared them for what they encountered.

The antechamber of the place was a natural cavern, rather high, nearly twenty-five feet at its ceiling. Limestone stalactites hung down like threatening teeth, but the stalagmites that grew up from the base of the cave floor had been shattered by sledge-hammers or some similar tool and hauled away. A litter of limestone shards was stacked in a gloomy corner deep within.

The floor of the place was therefore smooth. In fact, it appeared to have been worn smooth by the tread of countless feet over generations of use.

Monk grunted, "This joint's been occupied long before Columbus ever landed."

"Monk, look!" whispered Pat.

In the center someone had carved out an outline of a many-legged whip scorpion, which was notable by its thin tail, coiled like a rattlesnake.

The workmanship looked fresh. Otherwise, it might have been mistaken for a Native American petroglyph such as those that are found on cliffs in Colorado's Mesa Verde pueblo settlement, or other parts of the southwestern United States.

From out of a crevice, something small and scarlet moved, and they saw that it was a living whip scorpion, except that it was an unusual crimson hue. The red was powdery and unnatural.

Pat hissed at the thing in alarm. It lifted its pincers defensively.

Monk stooped, grasped a small stone that his foot had encountered, and heaved it at the many-legged creature.

The rebounding rock drove the vermilion vinegarroon back into its den.

"This must be the cavern of the Vinegarroon tribe that Chief Standing Scorpion boasted about," Pat remarked, low-voiced.

Monk snorted derisively, "If there is anything to that screwy yarn, I'm gonna join 'em as a blood brother. I still say it's a lot of hokum."

As they moved deeper inside, moonlight became thin and then frighteningly indistinct. They had no flashlights.

They spotted a pair of steps to the right that were cut into the side of the cavern. These wound up out of sight.

"Somebody sure went to a lot of trouble to make this place," said Monk, pointing toward the natural staircase.

Creeping in that direction, they came to the bottom step. Monk looked it over carefully, then remarked, "The steps are old. Maybe I spoke too soon."

"Eat your crow after it's baked," said Pat. "Are we going up, or not?"

Listening a moment, they heard very little. This emboldened them to start climbing. Their bare feet aided their stealth. As they moved up into the high reaches of the stairs, rudely-dressed walls pressed all about them.

The steps came to an abrupt halt, and they stood on a plat-form. Above them, illumination glowed. It was pale stuff and they decided that it might be created by candlelight or some similar non-electrical means.

The light showed a rude ladder made from dry sticks, and lashed together with dried leather. There seemed to be no way up to the lighted region other than to climb the ladder, so Pat went first while Monk studied the rickety contraption, his apish features worried.

Once Pat reached the next level, Monk followed, climbing carefully, fearful that his two hundred and sixty pound weight would be too much for the primitive ladder. But it held.

When they reached solid flooring, they discovered what would pass as a chamber hewn from the sandstone and dusty with age. Its walls were covered in carvings, many of which were scorpionic in nature. These looked ancient.

"Reminds me of a *kiva*," mumbled Monk.

"A what?"

"A chamber used for religious ceremonies," explained the hairy chemist. "The Hopis and some others built them. Mostly, they were underground, and you reached them by a hole equipped with a ladder like the one we just climbed. They called the floor a *se-pah-poo*." Monk's blunt nose wrinkled. "Could be this place was inhabited long ago, and updated by Standing Scorpion and his gang."

A corridor bisected the ancient chamber, allowing one to enter and exit via opposite walls.

"Which way?" asked Pat.

Monk shrugged wordlessly. Each direction looked similar. A rude passageway that curved out of sight until either termi-nus was lost to view.

Having no better clue, they moved left, picking their way carefully, listening with all their might.

Niches had been cut into the walls every few yards and in these, simple kerosene lanterns furnished fitful illumination.

The natural ceiling was sooty from collecting the wispy grayish-black curls of smoke arising from the little metal chimneys. From the look of these deposits, the place had not been inhabited for very long—only months perhaps.

"This place is like a burrow," whispered Pat. "Do scorpions burrow?"

"Sometimes," returned Monk. "Mostly they like to hide under rocks."

They came to a spur of the passageway that cut deep into the cliff, and the smell coming from within made them cough and gag a little. It was a fetid, moldy odor like nothing they had ever before smelled. They decided not to explore the tunnel further, but kept moving along the main passage.

The absence of habitation amazed them, for they imagined the castle would be teeming with the minions of Standing Scorpion. Yet they encountered no one in their perambulations.

"Could be the Vinegarroon tribe don't amount to much," cracked Monk.

"Let's not underestimate them, or overestimate our prospects," cautioned Pat. "We have not exactly covered ourselves in glory to this point."

Further along, they heard muffled shouting, then a man's voice lifted in vibrant outcry.

"You would not dare fire that thing at me!" he screeched.

Then came the muffled report of a small-caliber pistol, followed by the *crash-jangle* of breaking glass.

A woman's scream followed and the timbre of it was familiar.

"C'mon!" yelled Monk. "That sounded like Vina!"

PELTING down the hall, their bare feet slapping undressed sandstone, they came to a heavy door. In the center of the panel, at eye level, a scarlet scorpion burned so brightly they could barely stand to look at it directly.

"Blazes!" Monk barked. "Looks like the portal to Purgatory!"

"Don't let that stop you!" blazed Pat, throwing herself at the heavy iron handle.

The simian chemist sprang into the hot, intimidating glare after Pat flung open the door.

Once the portal opened, there erupted a hissing susurration that sounded as venomous as a viper preparing to strike.

Standing in a glimmer of red light, surrounded by shards of broken mirror that reflected even more of the harsh red glare, stood Vina Hawks Nansen, a smoking .22-caliber pistol in her hand.

Turning, she said in a shocked voice, "I shot him, but-but he wasn't there."

"Who?" demanded Pat.

"That beast! That horrid beast. He is somewhere in this horrible red light."

The hissing came again, followed by a puff of air. Then something struck the door beside Pat Savage's head.

Turning toward the striking sound, she saw as if by magic a scarlet scorpion form against the panel.

Monk reached over, grabbed her by the mouth and nose and pulled her away, yelling, "Don't inhale! Nobody breathe. That stuff is poison!"

Came another hissing, and another scarlet scorpion came to life with an ugly *splat* of a sound. This time it struck Monk on the shoulder. He flung off his shirt, exposing the magnificently red forest of hair that covered his apish chest.

"Come out and fight like a man!" he yelled at the red glare.

"He is no man, but a beast," moaned Vina, swinging her automatic this way and that, looking for the source of the venomous hissing.

The brutally scarlet glare made it almost impossible to see clearly.

Moving fast, Pat claimed a piece of the mirror, and held it before her like a shield.

Another warning hiss and another scarlet scorpion appeared on the surface of the shimmering shard of quicksilver.

Pat flung the jagged glass wildly in the direction of the hissing. With a hasty rustle of skirts, their assailant withdrew deeper into the regions of red sandstone glare.

"He went that way," advised Pat, stepping up to Vina Hawks Nansen and claiming the automatic. "I'll bet I'm a better shot than you. Let me have that."

The woman surrendered the weapon without protest.

"Dare you follow him?" she asked dully.

Pat considered. "Not without knowing what I'm blundering into. Let's retreat to the passageway, where we can see what we're shooting at."

They did so, finding the mellow light of the passageway with its tapers and lanterns more to their liking. It took some time to blink away the persistent red afterimage burning in their hurting optics, but when they did, they felt more confident in their hunting.

"He probably didn't come this way, so let's keep pushing on," suggested Monk.

"Stay behind us, Miss Nansen," Pat cautioned. "There's liable to be hot lead flying, if not far worse things."

Pat and Monk in the lead, they pressed further into the sandstone phantasmagoria.

The passageway had been curving to the right, but now it gave a twist to the left which confused them.

This direction brought them to another chamber, which was on the left. A Navajo Indian blanket served as a curtain. They pushed in carefully.

When they entered, their jaws fell open and their eyes grew wide.

THE place looked a little bit like a makeshift laboratory, such as might be seen in a horror movie. Two packing crates were set in the center of the chamber, separated by about four feet of space. On one reposed a wire cage, and the cage held living things.

Approaching cautiously, Monk soon recognized them.

"Whip scorpions!" he grunted. "A mess of them."

The apish chemist looked them over and saw that they were the specimens common to the American southwest. All were a dull leathery brown and as he hovered by the cage, scuttling around, one whipped its flagellate of a tail and the acrid odor of vinegar burst outward.

"Be careful!" warned Pat.

"Scorpion acid can't harm you," scoffed Monk. But when he turned his attention to the other crate, he became very quiet.

For there stood a rectangular container of glass, such as might be seen in an aquarium. It, too, was swarming with vinegarroon scorpions, but these were different. All were a blood red. Even their thin, devilish tails. Their hue was powdery and disquietingly unnatural.

"Looks like one of the critters we spied on the way in," he muttered uncertainly.

"Why are they so queer-looking?" wondered Pat uneasily.

"Dunno," admitted the homely chemist. "But I'd steer clear of that container. They ain't been put under glass without good reason."

Vina Hawks Nansen contributed one comment before they resumed their exploration.

"The vinegarroon that sprayed my father was also a bright red."

"Wish I had a can of gasoline and a match," muttered Monk. "I'd burn those red devils up quick."

"Better not to fool with them," warned Pat. "Should they get loose, we'll be the ones in for a hot time."

In one gloomy corner was tucked a camp cot, as well as a clutter of medical equipment such as might be used to draw blood from a man.

The cot was occupied. A human form lay under a sheet. The white cloth draped this individual from head to toe, as if he had expired. They saw the tubes that had been used to draw the victim's blood away into glass bottles that stood about the floor, brimming with bright vital fluid.

Carefully creeping forward, Pat and Monk got on either side of the sheet. With a nod to one another, they pulled back the covering together.

Of all the faces they expected to behold, this was probably the most unexpected of all.

Although he was pale to a degree that was chilling, his face dead and waxy, both Monk and Pat recognized the unfortunate man who lay dead on the camp cot.

"Finbar Collins!" gasped Pat. "What is *he* doing here?"

"Dunno," blurted Monk. "Looks like they siphoned the blood out of him just like they did with Ben Nansen. But how'd he get here in the first place?"

Since the dead man could hardly give any answer, they replaced the sheet and quit the room of grisly horror, returning to the corridor.

"Who was that man?" asked Vina.

Pat replied tightly, "Assistant to a man named Alec Daly, alias 'Grabber.' But I cannot understand what he's doing here."

Monk scratched his head thoughtfully and remarked, "I can't figure it, either. But we still gotta find the lodge spirit of this place."

"Tall Turkey," said Vina. "It could be no other."

Neither Pat nor Monk replied to that. They were withholding judgment on that score.

Moving along, they came to another unexpected sight. A trail of blood—a great deal of it. The blood splatters went from one slit in the right wall to another chamber on the opposite wall, which was also barred by a wooden door.

They studied the splatters and concluded that the injured party had crossed from the right chamber to the left, for there were red half-footprints in the welter of gore, and these conveyed a direction.

Pat lifted her automatic to the height of her lowest rib, while Monk got on one side of the door and prepared to heave it open.

At a nod from the golden-eyed girl, the hairy chemist threw the door open and Pat leapt in.

Almost immediately, she struggled for words.

Entering cautiously, followed by Monk, she walked up to a prone figure in a purplish-black robe whose front was emblazoned with a vertical scarlet whip scorpion. The hooded individual had evidently fallen on the spot where they found him. He was lying in a pool of blood that was fresh.

In the center of the stomach protruded a large shard of mirror. The glass fragment was sunk in deep. Seeing this, Pat Savage went as pale as her coppery complexion permitted.

"Oh, no!" she moaned. "Do not tell me that I killed him when I threw that shard."

Behind her, Vina Hawks Nansen intoned, "He deserved it, the monster."

Pat Savage failed to register those words amid the sudden roaring in her ears. She took a step backward, the tiny automatic trembling in one fist.

Unimpressed by all the blood, Monk stepped forward, reached down and pulled off the ugly scorpion-tailed hood.

A shock greater than any they had experienced before awaited that revelation.

With his face staring up, eyes widened in death, mouth agape, was none of the many individuals they suspected of being Chief Standing Scorpion.

Instead, it was another nemesis entirely. A fellow they believed had fled into the Osage—if not for parts even more far distant.

Pat Savage moaned low in her throat. She tried to get the name out, but her tongue would not obey her. So Monk Mayfair gave voice to the thought that had stunned her disbelieving brain.

"Grabber Daly!" he exploded. "Who would've thought it?"

Chapter XXXII

CLOSING IN

THEY STOOD STARING down at the dead face of Alec "Grabber" Daly, the lease hog who had fled Oklahoma justice only a few days before.

They were in shock. Their faces told that story.

Vina Hawks Nansen asked, "Grabber Daly? I—I can hardly believe it myself."

Monk muttered, "Mebbe he up and went pump-wooly."

Pat looked at him blankly.

"In oilfield lingo," he explained, "it's the same as goin' loco. Comes from workin' too many leases out in the hot sun."

Pat Savage got a grip on herself and her eyes sparkled as she firmed up her chin.

"Well," she said tightly, "I, for one, do not believe this at all. It makes absolutely no sense. Grabber Daly is no more Standing Scorpion than I am."

Still stooping, trying to keep his bare feet out of the spreading pool of gore, Monk was studying the encrimsoned shard of glass protruding from the dead man's stomach and stood up abruptly, long arms swinging.

"I don't believe that hunk of glass you threw had enough force to impale him that way."

Pat blinked. "What do you mean, Monk?"

Pointing, Monk said, "Look how deep it went in. Somebody drove it into him to cover their tracks."

"But who would do that?" wondered Pat. "If Daly is Chief Standing Scorpion—even if he isn't—what would the other man's motive be?"

The homely chemist looked baffled, at a loss for a sensible answer. He scratched at the rusty stubble that had partly obliterated the brown whip scorpion adorning one cheek.

"Danged if I know!" he confessed.

Frowning, Vina Hawks Nansen asked, "Would it not be possible that when I shot at the mirror, thinking I was shooting Standing Scorpion, a different shard of glass struck him?"

It was a plausible explanation and Pat, stepping around the pool of blood, studied the shard of glass critically from several angles before deciding, "No. That is the same piece of glass I threw." She shook her head decisively for emphasis.

"No one could've gotten all this way with that hunk of glass stuck in him," insisted Monk. "There's no way that you killed this guy, Pat. Someone else did this, then dragged Daly here. Somebody tryin' to cover their tracks."

"Well, who is left?" demanded Pat. "Tall Turkey, of course. And Morgan Marrs." Turning to Vina Hawks Nansen, she asked, "Is your fiancé in this stronghold?"

"Yes, he is. And I must finally confess to you that he is in league with Standing Scorpion. Morgan admitted as much to me. I have known this for some days now. But I can scarcely still believe it. There is no point in denying it now."

Pat addressed the shaken woman and demanded, "Your brother stated that Standing Scorpion is actually Tall Turkey. What do you say?"

Vina Hawks Nansen looked away distractedly. "I don't know *what* to say. I don't know what to *think!* Morgan admitted to me that he works for Standing Scorpion, but he has never told me who the man really is."

"Well, he *must* know," snapped Pat. "He can unravel this mystery for us. Let's hunt him down."

"Haven't we had enough bloodshed?" cried the blonde woman.

Monk growled, "Not nearly enough to satisfy me. Not until we mop up this place. Now let's get to it."

Exiting the chamber of death, they worked their way along the passage, and discovered at the terminus another rickety ladder leading to a higher region of the complex stronghold.

They went up this, poked around in very thin light, and the unpleasant odor they had encountered in the lower passage slowly crept into their nostrils. Moving toward it, they tread carefully, pinching their noses shut, and feeling an overpowering urge to cough and even retch.

The impulse to turn away became stronger the deeper they ventured.

Finally, they came to an unusually large door set in the sandstone cliff face. A gleaming brass key jutted from a keyhole that was as large as the type formerly used in castle dungeons in times gone by.

There was no guard and no peephole, so Monk took hold of the key, gave it a twisting wrench, and received a squeak and squeal of mechanism in return.

He pulled open the door gingerly and recoiled violently. The stink that struck him in the face caused him to slam the door shut and retreat, coughing and hacking.

"What is it? What did you see?" demanded Pat.

Monk's coughing fit took a while to subside. When he finally got control of himself, he said, "There's a long cave in there, with walls as red as cinnabar. Looked like mold, the awfulest-smelling mold you could ever inhale. Would like to have died from the smell of it."

Vina Hawks Nansen said, "That is the secret of the Grampus paralysis. Standing Scorpion told me that much. It is not a germ, bacteria or virus. It is mold. A poisonous mold that grows in this cave. By some means they implanted the matter into capsules, which they spit at their enemies. Paralysis follows, and if the concentration is high enough, death is unavoidable."

Pat blinked. "What about the blood that was drawn from your brother to feed something horrible?"

"A ruse," explained the blonde woman. "Calculated to throw medical experts off the scent. The blood that was taken from Ben had nothing to do with the Grampus paralysis."

"Clever," said Pat. "Now, since this is a dead-end, let's search in a fresh direction."

They retreated to the ladder, worked down to the lower level, and went in a different direction from their original route.

THEY soon encountered a room in which cowered a man.

It was evident that the man had been hiding in there, and was in a fearful and agitated state. For no sooner had they approached the door than it burst open. The fellow stepped out, crying out, "I surrender! I surrender!"

Pat trained her tiny automatic upon him and demanded, "Put your hands up. We're collecting donations for the law."

Behind her, Vina gave out a strangled cry of anguish. "Morgan…!"

Indeed, it was the publisher of the *Tulsa Trumpet,* Morgan Marrs. He was very pale and the expression on his mature countenance was that of a shattered man.

"I am at your mercy," said the newspaperman dully. "I have no resistance left in me. Now that Standing Scorpion is no more."

"What makes you say that?" asked Pat suspiciously.

"I came across his body. He had been impaled horribly via a piece of the great mirror he uses to protect himself when granting an audience. Somehow he had been killed by his own clever device."

Pat paled anew.

"Don't listen to him, Pat," inserted Monk. "You had nothing to do with that."

"Nevertheless," admitted Morgan Marrs, "Standing Scorpion is dead, and without his genius, his master plan lies in tatters. I am prepared to surrender myself to the authorities and take my medicine."

"This is too easy," said Pat, waggling the gun at him.

"You got that right," growled Monk. Advancing, he began staring at the newspaper publisher's shoes, which were brogans, gleaming yellowish in the pale light.

"Those are the same shoes Standing Scorpion wore back at the oil derrick," he said fiercely.

Morgan Marrs looked down at his own feet, blinked several times stupidly, then said evenly, "Everyone who spends any time here picks up the yellow dust. The shoes are not actually yellow, but coated with yellow residue."

"Is that so?" returned Monk. "Let me see the backs of your hands. Rotate your wrists. Don't drop your mitts, just rotate your wrists."

"Whatever for?" asked Morgan Marrs, hesitating.

Pat flared, "Just show us your hands!"

Shrugging heavily, the publisher slowly turned his wrists. As he did so, from seemingly nowhere there came the unexpected blast of a machine gun and everyone scattered from the scene, dropping to the sandstone flooring to avoid flaming lead.

Vina Hawks Nansen stood stunned, having retreated to a wall. So Monk rushed to tackle her legs and push her down as another blast of .45-caliber lead chopped up the sandstone walls all around them.

Lifting her head off the floor, Pat Savage lanced her sharp gaze in the direction of the stuttering sub-gun.

At a curve of the wall, a tall man stood cradling the vicious weapon. He was an Osage Indian. His face was indistinct in the light, but Pat was able to make out some details.

It was broken-beaked Tall Turkey! Grinning savagely, he squeezed the trigger of the Tommy gun again, this time directed at Pat. But the copper-skinned girl beat him to the punch. She fired once, almost without aiming.

A single lead pellet caught him high in the shoulder and spun him around, making the Tommy gun chatter wildly as he twisted in reaction to the stinging bullet.

The recoil of the powerful weapon caused it to tear out of the man's hands, and it fell to the ground, going silent, but smoking prodigiously.

Yelling fury, Monk leapt from the ground, and sprang upon it, taking firm hold of the deadly weapon. Elevating the muzzle, he depressed the trigger, causing fistfuls of sandstone to break and shatter and drop all around the Indian.

Cursing, Tall Turkey retreated around the curving bend.

Wildly, Monk gave the Tommy gun a shaking. It rattled metallically, indicating that there was perhaps a quarter of a drum left—fewer than a dozen shells.

Turning his head, he bellowed, "That was Tall Turkey! I think."

"Yes, Tall Turkey," confirmed Vina Hawks Nansen, clambering to her feet. "He must be Standing Scorpion. Of that, I have no doubt."

Cradling the Tommy gun, Monk braced publisher Morgan Marrs, demanding, "What have you got to contribute to this fandango?"

Morgan Marrs was shaking like a strong tree in a stronger gale. "Tall Turkey is Standing Scorpion."

Monk's jaw dropped open. "Don't hand me that! You said he was dead."

"I—I believed so when I came upon his dead body," the publisher said shakily. "But I failed to remove his hood to ascertain his identity. Now that I see him standing before me, I acknowledge my hasty error. Make no mistake. Tall Turkey is the architect of evil. I will testify to that in court. And if you carry me out of here safely, I would use everything in my power of the press to clear you and Miss Savage of the murder of the police officer in Tulsa."

"Sounds like a square deal," decided Pat. "I say we take him up on it."

"O.K.," muttered Monk. "But no more double-crossin'. We had enough of that. Now march, you!"

Chapter XXXIII

TREACHERY

AS THE GROUP moved toward the ladder leading down to the castle's cavernous entrance, Pat Savage rattled off a series of questions.

"Is there really a cure for the Grampus paralysis?"

Morgan Marrs replied swiftly, "Yes, yes, there is. I carry a vial of the serum on my person at all times."

The publisher produced the vial in question. Seeing this, Monk bellowed, "That looks like the bottle we had before it got away from us!"

"If you mean the one that Ben Nansen carried off," Marrs stated, "yes, that was another dose of the cure."

"You better hope we can get this to Tulsa before anyone dies," warned Monk. "Otherwise it's the hot seat for you."

Morgan Marrs nodded heavily. "I must have been mad to think that Standing Scorpion's grandiose schemes could ever succeed, but I was driven by desperation over my own precarious financial position." Turning to his fiancée, he asked, "Vina, can you ever forgive me?"

The woman turned her face away. Her lips moved, forming the word "Never." But she did not utter it. Nor did Marrs perceive the unspoken denial.

"Is there really a Vinegarroon tribe?" pressed Pat.

"No. Tall Turkey is an Osage, as are his boys. They made up that story inspired by this cavern, which is filled with whip scorpions, as well as the deadly red mold. An unknown Indian tribe lived here long ago, but must have been driven out by the accursed mold, which has been growing and spreading through-out the cave system for generations untold. We all talked up that story to add luster to the legend, as well as to obscure the author of it all, which is Tall Turkey himself."

Monk clucked, "Pretty fancy schemin' for a bunch of Osage bucks."

"Tall Turkey and his Tall Boys grew ambitious from their modest start as a gang of hooligans," replied Marrs.

They came to the *kiva* hole, but it was clear that Tall Turkey had beat them to it. For the ladder was no longer there. Looking down, they saw it lay flat on the surface below, well out of reach.

"We're stuck here," Monk barked.

Training her automatic on Morgan Marrs, Pat demanded curtly, "There must be another way down."

"There is, but it's through a passage that comes off the great mold chamber. It would be exceedingly deadly to attempt to traverse it."

"Are you saying it can't be done?"

"I am saying it cannot be done safely. And our bargain is that you bring me safely out of this castle so that I can live out the remainder of my days—even if my admitted guilt forces me to do so in the penitentiary."

Monk laughed dismissively. "You'll be lucky if iron bars is all Oklahoma deals out to you."

"I know that now," said Morgan Marrs miserably.

Pat was thinking and mused aloud, "When Standing Scor-pion escaped that maddening room of red glare, he must have done so through a secret exit. Do you know anything about that, Marrs?"

The man shook his head gravely. "No, I do not. That was Standing Scorpion's private throne room. I never got to see the inner workings of it, only that he employed an arrangement of mirrors, rather like that of a stage magician, to protect himself in the event of a mutiny by his Tall Boys."

Monk said, "Let's investigate. It may lead us somewhere."

Returning to the chamber of broken mirrors, they pushed through the ominous red glare, being careful with the broken shards that lay scattered about, most underfoot, but some leaning against sandstone walls and dangerous to the touch if their skin came into contact with the edges. They were exceedingly sharp.

"Nothing cuts like glass," reminded Monk. "There's been enough bloodshed already."

Pat grinned fiercely, "That's saying something, coming from you."

"I don't mind spillin' a little gore," said Monk amiably, "but I've seen enough in the last hour to do me 'til Christmas."

Vina Hawks Nansen said nothing to this. She was very pale—although one could not see that in the hot red glare of the throne room.

Picking through the debris, they discovered the secret exit—a slanted mirror was arranged in such a way that it reflected its opposite wall, concealing an unbarred notch of a doorway.

Shouldering ahead, Monk poked his head into the notch, looked both ways and whispered, "Coast looks clear."

The others followed him. Pat brought up the rear, keeping her gun trained on Morgan Marrs, whom she did not at all trust.

They found themselves in a passageway that appeared to parallel the one they had previously reconnoitered, but there was no way of telling for sure. But this was a different tunnel.

Leading with the Tommy gun, Monk looked both ways and sniffed the air. There was the faintest suggestion of the night air to his right, and so he waved Pat in that direction.

They came at last to a set of steps that was carved in the sandstone wall face, leading downward. This crude staircase had no interrupting platforms requiring makeshift ladders to reach them, as had its opposite on the other side of the castle-like cavern.

Warm night air drifted up from below and they could smell water. Also some of the lingering oil smoke continued to waft upward.

Monk grinned. "Looks like this leads all the way down to the cavern where we entered."

Pat smiled in relief, saying, "It's a clear shot to the amphibian if we don't encounter trouble."

They started down, Monk leading and Pat taking up the rear, and almost immediately encountered trouble.

The steps were a remarkable engineering achievement. A great deal of man-hours must have been expended to excavate them. For they were cut such that there was a wall on either side of the steps. It was really a kind of slanting downward tunnel equipped with dressed steps.

Picking their way down this required that they feel their way, there being no light source anywhere, except at the base and from the point at which they entered.

It was thus spooky going, for there was only the sound of their bare feet and the rough texture of the sandstone walls under their fingertips and brushing their shoulders. Descending the staircase required a great deal of trust and balance, but finally they made it to the cavern cathedral and its smooth floor and fanged stalactite ceiling.

Monk naturally emerged first. He swept the chamber with the muzzle of the submachine gun and was soon satisfied that there were no ambushers lying in wait.

"Hurry up," he called back.

As the homely chemist stood guard, Vina stepped into the thin light, followed by a nervous looking Morgan Marrs. Once they were on flat ground, Pat Savage came next, her small automatic picking up reflections of moonlight.

Almost immediately, the newspaper publisher whirled and produced a short length of reed tube from an inner coat pocket. This he brought to his lips and expelled a short vicious breath in Pat Savage's direction.

Her eyes just becoming accustomed to the moonlight, Pat was searching the cavern for any sign of lurking trouble when she felt the hurtling capsule come in contact with her right cheek.

Recoiling, she brought up searching fingers to her face, and encountered a powdery residue, which told her that she had been marked by the surprise scarlet scorpion that had brought death and disease to so many. A faint whiff of vinegar stung her quickening nostrils.

SMOTHERING an outcry, Pat leveled the pistol at her assailant, but Morgan Marrs dropped his blowgun in haste. From another pocket, he produced a small vial filled with red powder.

With his other hand, he seized Vina Hawks Nansen about the neck, throwing her in front of him as a shield. Lifting the red vial, he warned, "If you fire, I will shatter this bottle and the entire chamber will be filled with the red mold of the Grampus paralysis."

Monk yelled, "You do that, and I'll blaze away with this baby!"

Marrs stiffened. "It appears that we have a standoff."

Pat had staggered back against the sandstone cavern wall, and was staring at the red powder on her fingertips. Her eyes went to Monk Mayfair.

"Don't forget there's a cure!" he called encouragement.

Marrs scoffed. "Yes, this is a cure. But you have to obtain it first. The only way you can do that is by letting me go. I will take the seaplane and my fiancée, and you will tend to Miss Savage. For I will leave my vial of the serum behind once I am assured of safe passage. That way we will all live to fight another day."

Hearing these words, Monk Mayfair began growling deep in his barrel chest. The ferocious animal sound swelled and filled the cavern.

That meant he was very, very angry. Pat Savage being marked by the scarlet scorpion had done that to him. Monk was mentally berating himself for not frisking the newspaper publisher before this. Also, he remembered that he had not seen the back of Morgan Marrs' right hand, and could not do so now the way the man had seized Vina Hawks Nansen.

"I don't much like that deal," snorted Monk.

The newspaperman reminded, "Do not forget that you can still capture Tall Turkey, who is Standing Scorpion, if you remain behind."

Monk retorted, "I ain't so sure he *is* Standing Scorpion. I kinda figured *you* for being the head skunk. This outfit needed more brains than an Osage gunman might have, not to mention more money and influence. You had both."

"Nonsense!" hurled back the publisher. "I have told you the truth. Tall Turkey is Standing Scorpion. I was in league with him, yes, but it was a conspiracy of the like-minded. You might almost say we were partners."

Monk said nothing to that. His angry eyes were watching Pat Savage, and the girl seemed to have forgotten the .22-caliber automatic, for it hung loosely at her side. Her eyes filling with horror, Pat rubbed the livid sprawl of scarlet from her pretty face, using her kerchief.

"Is this—is this the fatal form of the mold?" she asked weakly.

"No," Morgan Marrs reassured her. "The fatal form is a higher concentration of the deadly stuff. You will merely lose control of your legs over the coming days. What I hold in my hand would be fatal if I shattered the vial. So stand aside, Mayfair, and let me depart, or I will consign us all to the deepest of hells."

Monk Mayfair knew when he was beaten. Lowering the muzzle of the Tommy gun, he stepped aside and said, "I'm no back-shooter. Go—but don't let me ever catch up with you again."

"Never fear, I have no intention of letting you do so. Once I have departed this place, you may take possession of Tall Turkey and do with him as you wish. He is the one the law really wants. He is Standing Scorpion. Be satisfied with him."

"Not hardly," said Monk, "but have it your way. I can't stop you. Yet."

"I must be content with that. Come, Vina. It is time to go."

Before Morgan Marrs could drag his reluctant fiancée out into the open air, a new voice spoke up. It was angry, surly, and it echoed and rebounded among the stalactites fanging the cathedral ceiling.

"Treachery!" the new arrival yelled. "Do my ears deceive me? You betray our friendship, you, Morgan Marrs, blood brother to Tall Turkey?"

Twisting around, keeping one arm wrapped around Vina Hawks Nansen's throat, the startled publisher searched for the source of the accusing voice.

It came from the other side of the great cavern, and the staircase that had led up to the second level of the pseudo-castle.

There stood Tall Turkey, his bent-nosed face an ugly mask of wrath. Behind him flocked a knot of Osage Indians. Every hand bristled with weapons—pistols and automatics, and a few buck knives. One man clutched an upraised tomahawk.

"How can you desert me to fall into the hands of our enemies?" he thundered.

Morgan Marrs stared at the new arrivals, and his mouth sealed into a firm slash of resolve.

"I have nothing to say to you," he said grudgingly. "The great plan has come apart. There is no rescuing it while these two live."

The inference was obvious. Monk swiveled the Tommy gun's cold muzzle in the direction of Tall Turkey and his Tall Boys.

"Anybody who figures he can take us," he warned, "better think a second and third time. I got more lead in this drum than you boys have in all of your popguns combined."

It was a bold lie, but the Osages did not know that. Another stalemate impended, this one more complicated than the previous one.

All eyes were on Tall Turkey and his Osage gunmen.

Tall Turkey was saying, "If you want to know the truth about Chief Standing Scorpion, it is not what it seems. Above our heads lies the body of a man who stumbled into the Osage fleeing justice. We seized him and his confederate, knowing that no one would look for them in this desolate place. It was our plan to arrange matters so that it appeared that Grabber Daly was Standing Scorpion. But he was not. He was merely a useful tool. A wanted criminal on whom we could hang our crimes."

"Keep talkin'," encouraged Monk. From out of the corner of one eye, he noticed Pat Savage moving stealthily.

"Chief Standing Scorpion is a myth," continued the Osage gang leader. "A creature we concocted, Morgan Marrs and I. A figure of menace designed to conceal the truth, but also to act as a bogeyman to instill terror in those we sought to conquer. You asked who Standing Scorpion really is. It is not Grabber Daly. It is not Morgan Marrs. It is not I, Tall Turkey. Standing Scorpion is whoever wears the robes and hood of Standing Scorpion!"

"Hah!" snorted Pat. "The truth will out!"

Tall Turkey went on. "Principally, that is Morgan Marrs and myself. We shared that role, knowing that it would confuse all others, including our own followers, who could only suspect the truth."

Vina Hawks Nansen gave out a shriek of alarm. Her sparking brown eyes went to Morgan Marrs. "You? You are Standing Scorpion? All this time? Why, when I shot at you in those horrible robes, I meant to kill you. I almost killed you, Morgan. Almost killed my own fiancé! How could you put me in such a situation? How could you?"

Morgan Marrs appeared to be taken aback by the vehemence of his fiancée's shrill accusations. He looked as if he wished to defend himself, but words failed him. His tongue was a heavy weight in his mouth.

In that moment of mental and physical paralysis, Pat Savage lunged like a coppery-bronze tiger, fell upon her opponent's wrist and wrestled from him the vial of red mold that could kill everyone in the cavern were it to shatter.

Just then, all pandemonium broke loose!

Chapter XXXIV

DEATH AND COMPANY

BENEATH THE STALACTITE ceiling of the dim sandstone cavern, a great many things happened at once.

Pat Savage wrested from Morgan Marrs the vial of blood-red mold and, during the brief struggle, the newspaper publisher was forced to release his fiancée, Vina Hawks Nansen.

Gathered at the staircase on the opposite side of the cavern, Tall Turkey and his cohorts let out a resounding war whoop and charged.

Monk Mayfair bellowed out one of his own, then leveled the clumsy Tommy gun at the stalactites dangling above their heads. Hauling back on the firing lever, he directed a spray of bullets at the fanged ceiling.

Inevitably, the limestone columns broke, shattered and cascaded down. Few struck anybody. But one unfortunate Osage was hit on the shoulder. That was enough to knock him flat. Seeing their fellow brave knocked out of action, the others beat a hasty and disorganized retreat.

Tall Turkey was another one who had been struck a glancing blow, but the piece of limestone barely staggered him. He produced a six-gun and he leveled the weapon at Morgan Marrs, snarling, "Death for you, paleface betrayer!"

He fired once, and the publisher was struck in the left hip with such force that the bullet turned him completely around. Marrs staggered, weaved, and his flinty eyes took on a strange, disbelieving light.

Vina Hawks Nansen screamed at the sight, for red fluid swiftly soaked through the man's trousers.

The prospect of imminent destruction can do strange things to a man's brain. Morgan Marrs may not have believed that death was upon him. Possibly he was merely enraged that his erstwhile confederate had shot him.

Strange grunting sounds coming from deep within him, Marrs withdrew a blowgun tube from a coat pocket, calmly inserted a red capsule and, before anyone—least of all Pat Savage—could stop him, he let fly in the direction of Tall Turkey.

The Osage leader attempted to duck. By some freak of luck, Morgan Marrs' aim was bad. As a consequence, the capsule struck the ducking Indian square in the forehead. Blooming like a weird flower, a scarlet scorpion commenced to unfold. Tall Turkey staggered.

This caused the Tall Boys to go berserk. Howling, they charged the publisher, who was calmly inserting another capsule into his blowpipe, his face ghost-white but determined.

Amid this noisy ruckus, a new figure stepped from the staircase down which Pat, Monk and the others had descended.

He was not noticed at first, but Vina Hawks Nansen happened to catch a glimpse of him out of the corner of one widening orb. Her frightened gaze falling upon the new arrival, she let out a scream.

"Look!" she yelled.

All eyes turned in her direction. Vina was pointing at the man standing at the foot of the staircase.

The new arrival was very tall. From head to toe, he was robed in purplish-black regalia. Upon his chest burned an upright whip scorpion. Eyeholes in the hood that concealed his entire head gleamed catlike in the moonlight. The red of the eye holes exactly matched the scarlet scorpion on his chest.

"What the heck!" Monk yelled.

"It can't be," blurted Pat. "Not *another* Standing Scorpion!"

"The *true* Standing Scorpion!" proclaimed Morgan Marrs in an elevated voice. A laugh of macabre humor escaped his twisted, bloodless lips.

"What gives?" growled Monk, tiny eyes jumping from Morgan Marrs to the new arrival.

The publisher's tall form shook with a weird hilarity, as if possessed by devilish imps. His eyes were wide, wild. "Yes, I lied to you. I was lying all along!" His laughter rolled forth in mad waves.

Then the Tall Boys fell upon him, using knives, clubbed guns and even a tomahawk someone wielded. The tomahawk blade was made of shaped stone. It struck Marrs on one temple and the sound made by the brutal blow was an ugly crunching.

Seeing this, Vina Hawks Nansen let out a thin, twisted wail and all but collapsed, weaving on her feet.

"Any more bullets in that typewriter?" Pat asked Monk breathlessly.

"Enough to settle a few of these Indians," Monk said grimly. He elevated the muzzle, depressed the trigger, and a last burst raked the limestone ceiling, causing another cascade of stalactites.

This latest avalanche struck no one, but got everyone's attention.

Tall Turkey was standing over the fallen form of publisher Marrs, and in his hand was a well-worn single-action Frontier-era six-shooter that Pat Savage instantly recognized.

"My grandfather's six!" she said fiercely.

Pocketing the red vial, she leapt upon the Osage, gave his gun wrist an artful twist—and sent him sprawling on the sandstone floor, the antique six-gun firmly in her hand now.

Leveling it at the remaining Osages, she rocked the fanning spur back with an audible click and warned, "If this dog barks, somebody'll get bit. Any takers?"

None, but a few of the braves looked poised to spring at her at any moment.

One snarled, "Bronze squaw cannot shoot us all."

"Maybe not," retorted Pat. "But I know ways to perforate a man so that he remembers me to the end of his days."

Grimacing, the Osage band held back, and Monk's small eyes went to the purple-costumed figure behind them.

"If Morgan Marrs and Tall Turkey took turns bein' Standing Scorpion," he wondered, "who the heck is *that?*"

"Why don't you find out?" suggested Pat.

"Good idea," said Monk, throwing down the exhausted Thompson gun and storming in the robed figure's direction.

Gloved hands fluttered hastily. Out from under the generous robes came one of the flutes that doubled as a blowgun.

"On second thought—" squeaked Monk, hesitating.

"One false move," intoned the robed figure, "and the brown scorpion on your face will acquire a companion."

"Say that to *me*, won't you?" Pat spun smartly, fanned the hammer once—and the blowgun jumped out of the man's gloved hands, neatly cut in twain.

Pat made a show of blowing gun smoke from the long barrel, remarking, "Annie Oakley, step aside for your betters!"

Grinning fiercely, the simian chemist finished his charge, took hold of the figure by his robed arm and stripped off the right-hand glove, exposing reddish skin.

"No bite mark," he barked. "What gives?"

Pat advised thinly, "Take a look at Morgan Marrs. His right hand has a nice set of toothy red indentations. I'll bet they match yours."

Monk came over, took a good look and saw that it was so. "So you were the Standing Scorpion back at the oil derrick."

Morgan Marrs was staring up at the ceiling, and life was ebbing from him. The fading light in his stricken orbs told that story better than his next words.

"One of them," he coughed out.

"If you live," snorted Monk, "you're gonna sit on the hot seat. You'll be *Squatting* Scorpion."

A weird smile curved the publisher's writhing lips, and he pointed a finger ceilingward. It trembled. "None of us will live. Look above you."

They couldn't help it; they all had to look. Even the Osage braves.

Over their heads, but off to one side, the broken bases of the stalactites resembling the blunted teeth of a monster that had been punched hard by another monster hung poised and threatening. That in itself was of no concern. The remaining stalactites appeared firmly fixed in place. It was the other thing.

Rilling down from the cracks in the ceiling came a trickle of matter. The matter was crimson. The trickle they noticed was not isolated. There were other places where the red mold was sifting down. A bit of drifting red haze showed as the mold spores became airborne.

As it happened, the concentration of the stuff was falling upon the Osage braves led by Tall Turkey. It was turning their dark hair a powdery red and they began pawing at it. The stuff turned their dull red hands a bright scarlet. Only now did they realize that it was not merely sandstone dust or limestone grit coating them.

When they understood that it was the deadly red dust, their eyes grew wide and they began to curse in their native language. Their cursing grew vehement.

An argument broke out among them and soon grew vociferous. Panic leaped into the eyes of the assembled confederates of Chief Standing Scorpion.

Seeing their chance, Pat and Monk pulled Vina Hawks Nansen and the robed Standing Scorpion toward the cavern mouth. They did so without words, or calling attention to themselves.

Shouting to quiet the others, Tall Turkey pointed at the moonlit lake and started issuing urgent orders.

The panicky knot of Osages made a break for the lake, apparently thinking that they could wash the stuff off in its waters. They ran pell-mell toward the sandstone-ledge beach, and plunged in.

There ensued a great deal of vigorous splashing and diving. Very quickly, it settled down as the Osages sought to dive deep in the lake to cleanse their bodies of the horrible dust of doom.

Monk said to Pat, "Let's get a move on. While they're fussin' about, we can take off in the plane."

Hauling Standing Scorpion—or whoever he was—by one purple shoulder, Monk led the way, Pat taking up the rear with Vina Hawks Nansen.

The blonde woman glanced back at her fiancé. A spreading red cloud of mold spores was swiftly enveloping him, coating his pale face in the rusty pall.

As Morgan Marrs began coughing out the smothering stuff entering his lungs, his body gave a great series of racking shudders, then fell still.

No one looked back after that. They were too busy escaping the spreading cloud of crimson.

The amphibian plane had been restored to its float anchorage, looking none the worse for wear other than a few streaky scorch marks. The craft was spacious enough to carry all four of them. Monk undid the single mooring line. They got on board, shut the cabin door and made certain that the windows were closed tight, while Pat laid aside her cherished six-shooter and got the motor turning. The engine ran smoothly, building up R.P.M.

Monk looked out to where the Osage Indians were attempting to save themselves. Moonglade on the lake surface was agitated, but soon it died down.

"How are they doing?" asked Pat as she jazzed the throttle.

"Not so hot," said Monk. "I don't see a single head in the water."

"You don't mean—?"

"I dunno what I mean. Maybe they drowned, maybe the mold spores got them. But the lake waters look like they're settlin' down."

The amphibian was nosed into the wind, which was blowing across the lake, and therefore in the wrong direction. Pat yanked the throttle open several times with the stick over and one rudder bar shoved forward. She got the plane about, partly closed the throttle, and let the wind swing the plane about once more.

Face composed, Pat Savage sent the plane scooting ahead. It cleared the float, skimmed across the lake surface, got on step, and vaulted into the air without balking.

Soon it departed the lake and they stole one last look backward. Pat aligned the baying nose due west, in the direction of the Oklahoma border, noting that the aircraft had plenty of fuel to reach Tulsa.

Behind them, the great dark mouth of the castle slowly exhaled a pall of crimson that shimmered with an eerie beauty in the lunar light. Despite its unearthly glamour, they knew it was deadly to human life.

"Even if those Osages come up for air," muttered Monk, "they're gonna be breathin' that evil stuff. So they're all goners."

Vina Hawks Nansen sobbed, thinking of her late fiancé, who had already succumbed to such a fate.

"Not *all* goners," reminded Pat. "We still have our prisoner, whoever he is."

ONCE Pat leveled off the climbing ship, Monk jumped out of his seat, snapping. "Let's see who you are, guy!"

He laid a frighteningly strong paw on the man's shoulder and tore off his hood by its puffy stinger appendage.

The face that was revealed was one they had seen before. It was one of the Osage Indians who had participated in the struggle back at the beginnings of the whole affair. His left eye drooped noticeably.

"Who are you?" Monk demanded.

"Name's Red Crow," admitted the Osage sullenly.

"Where do you figure into this shindig? Straw boss, maybe?"

The man shrugged resignedly. "Just another one of the Tall Boys. Nobody special."

"Just a punk, huh? What are you doing in that rig?" asked Monk, shaking the fellow.

"I was high in the Wikiup—we called it that—when I heard a commotion below. I could hear what was going on. All that shouting commotion traveled up the staircase. So I thought fast. I threw on one of the spare Standing Scorpion costumes, figuring to try and break things up. Didn't work out so good, I reckon."

"I reckon not!" exclaimed Pat from the pilot's seat.

"So you're not Standing Scorpion?" said Monk.

The crestfallen Osage shook his head, "That was Morgan Marrs and Tall Turkey. They took turns in the outfit, so as to confuse everybody. It worked pretty good for a while. Nobody knew who was who."

Pat turned her head and studied his face in the cabin lights, noted his drooping left eye. "Aren't you the Indian who pretended to be a panhandler, the one who killed Harold Manton?"

The man's head-shaking turned vigorous. "You got me confused with my cousin, Blue Crow. He did that. I was the one who waylaid Ben Nansen, who *didn't* die."

"Why was Nansen attacked?"

"The Chief had to let him go because Miss Nansen was kicking up such a fuss," the other related. "But things went haywire and I was sent to throw a scare into him before he could tell his sister anything useful."

Pat turned her attention back to her flying. "I see," she said thinly. "We know that Ben Nansen had a quarrel with his father and, out of spite, joined up with the Tall Boys gang. But we don't know why they fell out, or why he was subjected to such terrible torture."

"That's a long story," the Indian replied. "Sure, Ben joined us. We all worked the oilfields. That's how we first got acquainted. But he was never really one of us, on account of Ben was a Cherokee, not Osage, and only a half-breed at that."

"Don't say that to Jim Thorpe," cautioned Pat.

Monk snorted, "So you were just stringing' him along?"

Red Crow shrugged. "Sorta, yeah. Well, Ben had been bad-talking his old daddy so much that it gave Tall Turkey an idea. We were about to start our reign of terror in Oklahoma, and needed to announce Standing Scorpion to the world, you might say. We'd been building up such a reputation folks in Arkansas got to calling him the Ozark Ogre. So Tall Turkey told Morgan Marrs that old Eric Nansen would make a pretty fancy first victim and mailed him a vinegarroon scorpion that had been dipped in the weird red mold we discovered in the cavern."

"I see!" said Pat. "Mr. Nansen got sick because he touched the whip scorpion, not because it sprayed him!"

"That's right. We planned to ship out a pile of the spore-dusted vinegarroons, except one of our boys up and got sick boxing them up. He was like to have died, except that we had already concocted the cure serum. Tall Turkey did that, by the way. That wasn't his real name, either. He was born Billy Roan into one of those oil-rich Osage families and had gone to medical school before going bad. Flunked out, is what I hear. Too much red-eye whiskey. But Tall Turkey had enough medical knowhow to figure out why the red cave mold affected the nervous system, and how to cure a man. He also came up with the idea of making a solution out of the mold and ordinary scorpion vinegar that could be poured into a glass capsule and shot from blowguns."

"Go on," invited Pat.

"Yes, we are very interested in your story," added Vina.

"Anyway, when old Ben found out that his father was the first victim of the Grampus paralysis, he sorta went berserk. Turned on Tall Turkey and threatened to expose us all. Guess he wasn't so sour on his old man, after all. Well, Morgan Marrs couldn't have that. So we made him a prisoner."

"I take it Ben Nansen didn't suspect Morgan Marrs was back of it all?" suggested Pat.

"Nope. We let him think Chief Standing Scorpion was Tall Turkey. He had no reason to suspect otherwise, not with us holed up in an ancient Indian pueblo full of vinegarroons." The Osage chuckled to himself. "Ben thought he had joined a modern Indian uprising. We made him an Osage blood brother. Shot the works with a big ceremony. But I guess there's stronger types of blood…."

Vina Hawks Nansen interrupted, "But why did my—why did Morgan Marrs agree to make my father his first victim?"

"Forgot to mention that part. Morgan Marrs cottoned to Tall Turkey's idea because he didn't much care for your father, Eric Nansen. Wanted to have you all to himself. His notion was to inflict the Grampus paralysis, collect the first ransom, then use your newspaper column to publicize Nansen's capitulation. But it backfired when your daddy refused to pay."

Vina nodded. "I understand now. My father insisted that I not write about family for print."

"Balled up the whole works, you and your daddy did," clucked the Indian. "That and all the problems mailing the mold-infected vinegarroons to other victims. After a few did pay up, and the authorities hushed it all up, Marrs hit upon the idea of spraying Tulsa by air and going into the wholesale extortion business. You late arrivals gummed up that part when you damaged the skywriting plane."

"All in a day's work," commented Pat brightly. "Tell me how Grabber Daly and Finbar Collins got mixed up in everything."

"Them two?" Red Crow gave a short, contemptuous laugh. "We found them wandering about the Osage. They broke into our teepee at the dirt airfield we got out there. They saw the skywriting plane with the vinegarroon on its wings, and that sealed their fates. We flew them to the Wikiup and started draining their blood with the idea of cutting them loose once they were half-dead to add to the atmosphere of horror."

Vina interjected, "Explain how Ben managed to escape."

"He didn't. I mean, he tried once. But we caught him before he got very far. That's when they commenced siphoning out his blood and feeding him that wild yarn about using his juices to feed a giant scorpion queen. Miss Nansen had been raising Cain about her missing brother so bad she came all the way to Tulsa to look into the matter, since that was where he had been living. It kinda got on Mr. Marrs' nerves, so he ordered Tall Turkey to cut him loose. Old Ben thought he'd escaped on his own hook, but it was all arranged. We figured that when Ben showed up in Tulsa, half-dead from blood loss, he'd sorta be our advance agent for the terror that was hatching. Kinda get the devil ball rolling right, you know?"

"So why did you try to kill him?" Pat demanded.

"I did no such thing!" the Indian blazed. "You get that straight in your mind. My job was to hit him with the paralysis, not kill him. We thought it would get to working on his tight-fisted daddy's mind, maybe cause him to shake loose with some of his money. That was all planned in advance, too." Red Crow paused, then let out a soft sign of resignation. "What wasn't planned was that we discovered that Ben had gotten away with a bottle of the cure serum after the fact. My job was to infect Ben and grab back the serum. But you two shoved your beaks into it, and this led to a merry chase after the aluminum tube containing the serum. That spooked Morgan Marrs into think- ing that Doc Savage might land in Oklahoma, and start clean- ing up. He didn't want that. So he hit upon the idea of brand- ing Monk Mayfair with a scorpion mark to throw police suspicion on him."

Pawing at his bestubbled face, Monk demanded, "What is this stuff, and how does it come off?"

The Indian shrugged helplessly. "Search me. Aren't you a chemist? Maybe you can figure it out eventually."

Monk began growling in low frustration. His small eyes narrowed, and his fist bunched up, causing Red Crow to wince under its iron-tendoned pressure.

It took a few minutes for everyone to absorb this account.

"What was the motive for Harold Manton's murder?" asked Pat after a long silence.

"He was asking the wrong questions of the wrong parties," Red Crow said sullenly. "So he had to go."

"We figured that part out, already," Monk commented, releasing the fellow. Returning to his seat, the hairy chemist added, "Well, consider yourself dang lucky. You're the only one who survived out of the whole bunch."

"Not so lucky," the man said miserably. "I guess they'll plant me in the electric chair."

"Sure they will," said Monk without sympathy. "You got it coming, don't you?"

Red Crow hung his head and said nothing. The drone of the motor was the only sound for a while. The air was not very bumpy, so there was little jouncing in the cabin.

Pat Savage said, "If it's any consolation, we may be joining you."

The Osage looked puzzled. Then it hit him. A crafty light came into his eyes.

"You talking about that Tulsa copper that got killed?"

"That's what we mean," said Pat wryly. "The police think we did it."

"I happen to know that it was Tall Turkey who fired the fatal shot. He did it out of spite, because he doesn't like cops. No better reason."

Pat turned, her tawny eyes alight.

"Are you willing to testify to that in court?"

"Not without something in return."

Monk lifted out of his seat, seized the man's shoulder with one hand, and his throat with the other. His brutally strong fingers tightened. "I'd think that over," he warned. "We don't have to turn you over to the Tulsa police. We can dump you out into any lake we come across. Heck, we might not even bother pickin' out a lake."

Red Crow lost his belligerent arrogance. His dark eyes became filled with a creeping fear.

Before he could speak, Pat Savage said, "We happen to know a very good lawyer. We might be able to convince him to accept you as a client."

Monk said, "Sure. Ham will be only too happy to represent this sorry bird. Only you'll have to promise to testify on *our* behalf," the apish chemist added.

"I never heard of any Tulsa lawyer named Ham," the man gurgled.

Monk told him, "Ham Brooks don't hail from Tulsa. He comes from back East. But he's in Tulsa now. He'll take your case—once we spring him from the hoosegow."

Red Crow looked puzzled, "What's he doing in jail?"

"Never mind that," said Monk, relinquishing the man once more. Sitting back down, he said, "You tell your story to the cops and Ham will cut us loose. Then you'll just have to take your chances with the judge."

The Indian did not look very comfortable, or at all very reassured, either. "I don't think my chances are very good."

"You can fry or you can sit in jail a very long time," reminded the homely chemist.

"And we will help you with the latter, if you don't care for the former," advised Pat firmly.

"I hear jail isn't so hot, but it's better than the hot seat," Red Crow finally admitted.

The cabin fell silent again. After a bit, Pat Savage asked Vina Hawks Nansen, "How are you holding up?"

"I feel as if a nightmare has ended."

"It will have ended for the people of Tulsa, and for your father and your brother once we bring back the cure."

"Hey!" said Monk suddenly. "I forgot about that. Morgan Marrs had some of the stuff."

"Had," said Pat brightly. From a pocket she pulled the vial of colorless liquid that they all recognized.

Monk howled, "Where'd you get hold of that?"

"From Morgan Marrs. While I wrestled the red vial out of his hand, I slipped my other hand into one of his coat pockets and palmed this little item. After I was struck by the blowgun capsule, I took a tiny sip. So far I feel fine."

"Do you think it is enough to cure all those afflicted?" wondered Vina.

"Only the competent doctors can tell us that," admitted Pat. "But even if it isn't, they might be able to figure out what it is and make more of the stuff."

Vina let out a great heaving sigh of relief. "That means my father will walk again, doesn't it?"

Pat nodded. "No reason to think otherwise."

Vina shuddered suddenly. The shuddering wracked her body for some time before she settled down.

"You are safe now," reassured Pat sympathetically.

"Yes, safe now. But I was just thinking what would have happened had Morgan Marrs and the others gotten their way. I would have been married to him and a slave of their mad scheme."

Pat asked, "Did you love him?"

Vina Hawks Nansen was a long time in responding. Her mouth sealed in a firm line. Finally, she intoned in a very low murmur, "Less and less as time went by."

They left it at that.

Chapter XXXV

QUARANTINE

TO THEIR PROFOUND surprise, Ham Brooks met them at the Tulsa Municipal Airport.

The dapper lawyer was wearing a morning coat and carried his elegant black stick, which he twirled jauntily. Ham never traveled without a spare, and this cane no doubt replaced the one broken earlier by a sure-shot lawman. Ham was surrounded by a contingent of stiff-faced Tulsa police officers who were waiting with open handcuffs in hand.

It was morning again, and the sun drenched everything in a brilliant glow. Monk had radioed ahead, offering to surrender peaceably, and so they were not surprised to see the welcoming committee in blue.

When the amphibian plane finally slowed to a stop and Pat Savage shut down the motor, Monk gaped at the unfriendly-looking welcoming committee and gulped, "Blazes! Will you lookit that. Somebody sprung Ham!"

Pat Savage said dryly, "Knowing Ham, he sprung himself."

That proved to be exactly the case. They opened the door and filed out with their hands in the air—all except Vina Hawks Nansen, who identified herself as the daughter of Eric Nansen, prominent Oklahoma millionaire and the former fiancée of publisher Morgan Marrs.

Once she had given her pedigree, the police declined to handcuff the blonde woman and she told them, "Miss Savage and Mr. Mayfair are innocent of all charges, and this will be proven via unimpeachable witnesses."

The police were not quite convinced, but Pat said to the blonde woman, "Thank you, Miss Nansen."

Along with Red Crow, Pat and Monk were promptly handcuffed and stuffed into a police car, after which they were whisked off to Tulsa Police headquarters, Ham following in a taxicab, and Vina accompanying the lawyer.

It was the early part of the morning and it was already as hot as a coal furnace going full blast.

The accused were fingerprinted and booked for capital murder and assorted felonies and misdemeanors, and were promptly haled before a stern judge for a preliminary hearing, where the charges against the pair were solemnly read.

These included the capital crime of murder in the first degree in the death of officer James Dandy and inciting a reign of terror throughout the state of Oklahoma, general mayhem, criminal coercion, and wholesale extortion. Also cited were a long list of lesser infractions ranging from theft and destruction of property, including a few petty charges such as bank robbery that made Pat and Monk swap baffled glances, for they knew nothing of these crimes.

Ham Brooks presented himself as their attorney and opened his remarks with a long oratory about the good works of Doc Savage, the impeccable reputation of Patricia Savage and, begrudgingly, the accomplishments of one Andrew Blodgett Mayfair, "alias Monk."

The hairy chemist muttered under his breath, "Did you have to put in that *alias* part?"

Ham suppressed a satisfied grin and continued his oratory.

"My clients have informed me, your honor, that not only have they smashed the grisly menace hanging over Oklahoma, but they have brought with them a cure for the Grampus paralysis." Producing the vial Pat had captured, Ham added, "I request of the court that this bottle be introduced into the record as evidence."

The judge asked, "How does this relate to the matter presently before this body?"

"This vial contains sufficient serum to cure all non-fatal cases of the so-called Grampus paralysis," replied the dapper barrister. "Let me recommend that this specimen be rushed to the city hospital so that administration of this precious remedy may commence without delay."

The judge ordered a bailiff to take charge of the bottle, and to have it conveyed to the proper medical authorities immediately.

Satisfied that he had won the judge's sympathy, Ham went on to explain that, although Monk Mayfair's face was branded by a sinister brown scorpion, this had been a clumsy attempt to frame him for the depredations of the mythical Chief Standing Scorpion.

The pistol that had been used to slay officer Dandy was also entered into evidence, and Ham made a vociferous attempt to have it thrown out, inasmuch as it could not be tied to the defendants, Pat having wiped it free of all fingerprints.

The judge refused to do any such thing, and the hearing proceeded.

At the end of it, the Osage Indian named Red Crow made his confession.

The court sat in stunned silence as the Osage related the identities of the true master minds behind the Grampus paralysis epidemic.

"I am confused," admitted the judge gravely. "Which of the accused is the brain back of these outrages against the good citizens of Oklahoma? Morgan Marrs or Tall Turkey?"

"Both of them were in cahoots, your honor."

"And where are these master criminals now?"

Red Crow considered that question. "Up yonder, I reckon."

"Eh?"

"Dead," explained Red Crow. "You can find their bodies out in the Ozark mountains, if you care to bury them proper. Otherwise, they ain't much good for nothing no more."

"The same holds true for the late Alec 'Grabber' Daly and his business associate, Finbar Collins," added Ham.

Eyebrows lifted throughout the packed courtroom, and the judge had to bang his gravel to settle the rising of excited voices.

"Were they in on this, too?" he demanded.

"No," replied Ham somberly. "Merely additional victims."

The courtroom exploded. Rival reporters rushed for the exits, keen to file their sensational copy, then reversed course when they realized there was yet more to the story.

Pat and Monk spoke their pieces. After they concluded, a rousing cheer rose up in the courtroom, and hats went flying joyously everywhere.

Since he was a Tulsan, Monk Mayfair received most of the shouted acclaim.

"*Y-e-e-o-o-w!*" he exclaimed, grinning broadly, "I'm a daggone hometown hero again."

"Don't let me ever hear you tell my cousin that you and you alone saved the day," Pat warned through a frozen smile.

"Don't let Ham know I had to use your pancake make-up to cover my face," Monk gritted back through clenched teeth.

"Deal."

After the judge heard it all, he declined to proceed with criminal charges against either Patricia Savage or Monk Mayfair and immediately released them on their own recognizance, but advised the vindicated pair to remain in Tulsa as material witnesses in the upcoming trial of Red Crow, who appeared to be the sole survivor of the Tall Boys outfit—discounting the gunman with the wired-up jaw recuperating in a Bartlesville hospital.

"I assure you that the defendant will receive a speedy trial and you will not be inconvenienced any more than is necessary," the judge told them. "For justice will be meted out Oklahoma style—which is to say, swiftly."

As the sullen Osage was led off to jail and photographer flashbulbs popped madly, reporters broke for the doors again. Some surrounded Vina Hawks Nansen, who answered their questions as best she could through her gracefully contained grief.

ONCE the courtroom had cleared, Monk and Pat and Ham exited the courthouse through a back door in order to escape the press. Pat was smiling with relief, happy at the imminent prospect of removing her Indian disguise.

"That was fast work, Ham! How did you ever get free?"

"After I was apprehended," allowed the dapper lawyer, "I presented myself to the court and announced that I would represent myself."

Monk grunted, "I thought you once told me that any lawyer who ever represented themselves had a fool for a client."

Ham winced, then composed his sharp features. "Possibly I did. Yet you see the end result of my efforts. I was immediately released from custody, and told to remain in Tulsa until the matter was settled."

"What did you tell the judge?" asked Pat.

"It is complicated," said Ham primly. "But by the time I finished, the judge saw his way clear to my release. Also, we studied at Harvard Law School together. In the same graduating class, as a matter of fact. That may have colored his ruling." The elegant attorney cleared his throat politely. "Slightly."

"Ah-hah!" shouted Pat. "The truth comes out!"

"I knew there was a catch!" yelled Monk. "Lawyers! They always stick together!"

Changing the subject, Ham declared loftily, "I imagine you both need rest and refreshment. I took the liberty of securing hotel rooms for you at the Metro."

"And how!" exclaimed Pat. "I could sleep for a week."

"Me, too," grumbled Monk. "My dogs are tired, my noggin hurts and my back aches." Suddenly, he turned to Ham and demanded, "Where's Habeas Corpus? Last time I saw him was back at the airport."

"Habeas?" Ham murmured distractedly. "Where have I heard that name before?"

The apish chemist grabbed the dapper lawyer by his silk tie and tightened it fiercely.

"Spill, you!"

"We might try the dog pound," suggested Ham. "Unless they sold him to a farmer for bacon."

Using both hands, Monk tightened the knot and Ham's face began to grow purple. Coolly, he gave his cane a flick, and the barrel dropped off, revealing the glittering sword blade, which he laid atop Monk's left ear, a cauliflowered mass of cartilage.

"Unhand me, you missing link," he grated. "Or I shall remove that ear and fry it up for your breakfast."

"Talk straight," said Monk fiercely.

Begrudgingly, Ham confessed, "You will find that walking flea factory waiting in your hotel room. But mark my words, if he chews up any furniture, you will find the damages on your room bill."

Monk let go of the tie and the dapper barrister stooped to reclaim his cane barrel. After snapping the two halves together, the pair resumed walking as if nothing had happened. Their long friendship was like that. They had been described as the best of enemies and the worst of friends.

"I guess we're stuck in town for a while," observed Monk philosophically.

"There are worse places to pass the time," allowed Pat. "Besides which, we have to find a lawyer who will draw up the purchase agreement on that farmer's acreage." Glancing in Ham Brooks' direction, she asked, "Is that up your legal alley?"

Doffing his silk hat gallantly, Ham said smoothly, "I will be happy to draw up any agreement you wish—in return for a dinner engagement."

"Nix!" snorted Monk. "Pat and me have gone through a lot together. She's havin' dinner with me."

"I am having dinner with neither of you gentlemen," reminded Pat firmly. "I already promised that nice telegrapher Johnny Deal, whom we met over in Seminole, that I would have dinner with him once I was free. After Ham draws up the purchase and sale agreement, we are going to drive out there, where I intend to claim my forty acres. Then I'm going to be rich."

"*If* you strike oil," reminded Monk.

"I changed my mind," said Pat. "I might like Tulsa to visit, but I don't want to spend too much time here. I'm going to sell that land to one of the big petroleum companies and pocket the difference after all."

"That sounds reasonable," allowed Ham. "What do you intend to do with your gains?"

Pat looked thoughtful. "I might sink it into a new racing plane. There's a Miami-to-Rio-de-Janeiro air race in the Fall. The prize money is ten thousand smackers. I might enter that race and see if I can beat all comers."

Ham frowned. "That is a deucedly long flight."

"And plenty dangerous," added Monk. "Are you sure you wanna tackle it, Pat?"

"Right now the only thing I'm sure of," said Pat in a tired voice, "is sleep. And plenty of it!"

"Ditto," said Monk. Rubbing his scorpion-branded cheek, he added, "And I gotta hunt up my chemical laboratory and figure out how to rub off this daggone mark."

Pat suddenly went pale.

"I don't have time to sleep!" she said suddenly.

"Why not?"

"I acquired one of those red scorpions myself. I don't know if I took the proper amount of serum. I must rush over to the hospital and get in line in order to receive my proper dose of the cure."

They lost no time piling into a taxicab, which whisked them off to the hospital and a long argument over Pat's case.

The place was packed to the rafters with anxious Tulsans demanding a share of the serum—whether they had been infected or not. They had to shove their way in and wait an hour before anyone talked to them.

"We have a number of persons insisting upon receiving treatment, who have evinced no symptoms," the medico stated firmly.

"This is different," Ham asserted forcefully. "This woman happens to be Patricia Savage, cousin of the renowned Doc Savage."

When the head physician digested this morsel, his attitude changed markedly.

"The woman who brought back the only known cure?"

"That's right," barked Monk. "I was there with her."

"In that case," said the doctor sternly, "you must all go under quarantine until you have been certified by the Board of Health as free of the malady."

"How long will that be?" questioned Pat sharply.

"Less than a month, I judge."

Monk groaned. Pat sighed. For his part, Ham Brooks pointed out, "That may be about as long as it will take to clear up the legal end of this entire matter. I will do whatever I can to urge the court along, of course."

"You will do no such thing!" snapped the hospital physician. "I am placing you under quarantine as well. Now that we know a mold spore is to blame for this Grampus paralysis, utmost caution must be exercised."

Ham immediately objected. "But we are not contagious!"

"Not in the customary way, no," allowed the medico sternly. "Inasmuch as mold spores can become dislodged from an exposed person's skin or clothing, and thus become airborne, the pernicious mold could travel from person to person as readily as would a communicable virus."

Ham purpled. He squeezed the barrel of his cane so hard his knuckles whitened.

Sighing again, Pat remarked, "It should beat marinating in jail, shouldn't it?"

Monk scratched his bullet head. "Depends on the food," he muttered.

Ham sniffed, "With your appetite, there may not be sufficient meals for everyone."

"I just thought of something!" Monk yelled.

"What is that?" Ham asked.

"Who's gonna feed Habeas while we're stuck here?"

The elegant attorney turned scolding. "You should have thought of that before you had me bring that insect to Tulsa."

Monk snapped, "Somebody had better call the hotel and request room service for that hog. Otherwise he'll eat the dang furniture."

"If he does," reminded Ham, "you and you alone are responsible for the damages."

Pat rolled her golden eyes ceilingward. Addressing the physician, she said, "Let me request a separate floor away from these noisy gentlemen. Better yet, you might wish to quarantine the two of them apart from each other. Less violence that way."

In the end, owing to the congested state of the facility, they were confined to the same room, separated only by hanging sheets.

Monk and Ham argued so much that Pat Savage threw her shoes over her sheet, one at a time, hitting no one but making her feelings plain to all.

"Next time I find a mystery to call my own," she warned them, "I intend to fly strictly solo!"

About the Author
LESTER DENT

LESTER DENT—SIX FOOT two, weight 210, age 32, born in La Plata, Missouri. Was brought to Oklahoma, to a farm near Broken Arrow, when four months old, which practically makes him an Oklahoman.

My dad, with the usual Dent luck, sold his Oklahoma farm a year before oil was struck on it, and went to Wyoming. As a small boy, I was taken across Wyoming in a covered wagon.

I lived on a cow ranch in Wyoming, have been a prospector, farmer, teacher, and a telegraph operator, winding up by doing my last telegraphing on the *Tulsa World* in 1931. I studied law at Tulsa University law school, nights, with an outstanding lack of success.

While working a night telegraph job—the "early" from midnight until eight in the morning in Tulsa—I got started writing. The impulse to write arose from a combination of two things— greed and shock.

The shock came when I reported, by accident, an hour early for work one afternoon in the offices of the *Tulsa World*. There I found another telegraph operator, who was also not supposed to be on duty, bent over a typewriter. The other operator wore an intent expression. I inquired why. The other operator explained that he was writing a fiction story. The resulting dialogue went something like this:

"A what? You're writing a what?"

"A fiction story," the other operator said patiently.

"Haw, haw!" I said. "Imagine a telegraph operator trying to write!"

"Look," the other operator said.

He then turned over, for my inspection, a check lying on the desk. It was for three hundred and some odd dollars, and payment for a story the operator had sold.

The result was that I started writing. I turned out thirteen stories, some of them book-lengths, and all came back with a perfect record of consistency. The fourteenth story sold to *Top-Notch Magazine,* a pulp, for $250.

A few months later, a large New York publishing house, after reading the first story I sent them, telegraphed me to the effect that, "If you make less than a hundred dollars a week on your present job, advise you to quit; come to New York and be taken under our wing, with a five-hundred-dollar-a-month drawing account."

After telegraphing friends in New York to inquire around about the publisher's sanity, I went to New York. That was in 1931.

I have written hundreds of stories since. I have been rated as one of the world's leading writers of the type of fiction which I specialize in—adventure and detective yarns for the pulp magazines.

Five years ago, I started writing an entire magazine about a character called "Doc Savage." The magazine, using the same character each month in a story, was so successful that within two years there were almost twenty imitators in the field.

I still write Doc Savage—a 60,000-word story each month. A 60,000-word yarn is a full book-length story. The Doc Savage stories are also put out in low-priced books, and the magazine is translated monthly into several foreign languages and published abroad in Spanish, French, German and Scandinavian tongues. For writing Doc Savage, I use the pen name Kenneth Robeson.

I have also sold to most of the pulp magazines extant, among them such magazines as *Argosy, Black Mask, Crime Busters,* etc.

I write rapidly, having averaged 200,000 words of published fiction a month over a period of two years at one time, and rarely dropping below a hundred thousand words a month. During the past four years, I have not had a rejected story in the pulp field, due to the fact that most of the stuff is written to contract or on order.

I write mechanically, to a formula, a story blueprint. A writer's yearbook—*Writer's Digest Yearbook* for 1936—published my mechanical plot formula for a 6,000-word short detective story. Over two hundred writers wrote in that they had sold their first story by writing it to the formula.

A considerable amount of my stuff is dictated.

While writing, I have prospected for gold in old Mexico, Death Valley, Colorado, Arizona and elsewhere. I have done exploration work in South America and the Caribbean. I am a member of the Explorers Club in New York City.

I spent almost two years on my own schooner, treasure hunting in the Caribbean, finished up with that about a year ago. I did not find any treasure.

I guess I'm more Oklahoman than anything else, having lived there longer than anywhere else by about five years. I spent six years in the midcontinent oilfields. Have worked on pipelines, leases, pumping stations, drilling rigs, etc.

At the present time, I am probably on the Atlantic liner *Queen Mary*, with my wife and secretary, bound for Europe.

—Lester Dent, 1938

About the Author
WILL MURRAY

WILL MURRAY HAS had three ficti-
tious heroines storm through his life
to date.

The first he encountered back in 1962 when
his Third Grade teacher, Mrs. Dunn, offered
the class a crack at a set of Hardy Boys and
Nancy Drew mysteries to read during class
time. For some reason, the eight-year-old
turned his nose up at the Hardy Boys but
devoured *The Secret of Red Gate Farm*, followed
by *The Secret at Shadow Ranch*, and several
other entries starring the legendary girl sleuth whose exploits
commenced in 1930 and continue to this day.

Murray failed to suspect it at the time, but this was his first
exposure to classic pulp-style fiction, for these were vintage
editions written in the early 1930s. And Carolyn Keene's style
would imprint upon his impressionable mind literary precon-
ceptions that would resonate seven years later at the ripe age
of 15, when he purchased his first Doc Savage adventure, *Dust
of Death*. Stylistically, both series were in the same vein. The
psychological similarities between Nancy Drew and Doc Savage,
the Man of Bronze, are also quite compelling. Where Doc
Savage is a multi-talented superman, Nancy was an accomplished
supergirl. Both were paragons of virtue.

By the time Murray discovered Doc Savage, he had long since

put Nancy Drew behind him. It was when he read his second Doc novel, *Death in Silver,* that he discovered his second imaginary crush. For that story introduced him to Patricia Savage, Doc Savage's capable cousin, who coincidentally was roughly the same age as Nancy Drew during that same Depression decade.

Will Murray never imagined writing any Doc Savage novels—much less Patricia Savage sagas—back in those days. But after he started the Wild Adventures of Doc Savage, readers began clamoring for a companion series, the Wild Adventures of Pat Savage. It took a while for Murray to get around to it, but when he did, he produced *Six Scarlet Scorpions,* which promises to be only the first of Pat Savage's solo adventures.

You might wonder who the third crush was. Back in the early 1990s, with the legendary Spider-Man artist Steve Ditko, Will Murray created the Unbeatable Squirrel Girl for Marvel Comics. She is nothing like Nancy Drew or Pat Savage, yet she has somehow managed to captivate a new generation of readers. As of this writing, several young Hollywood actresses are vying for the opportunity to play her on the screen, big or small.

While the world is wondering who will portray Squirrel Girl, Will Murray is pondering who might play Patricia Savage, when the inevitable and long-anticipated Doc Savage movie finally materializes.

About the Artist
JOE DeVITO

JOE DEVITO WAS born on March 16, 1957, in New York City. He graduated with honors from Parsons School of Design in 1981 and continued his study of oil painting at the city's famed Art Students League.

Over the years, DeVito has painted many of the most recognizable Pop Culture and Pulp icons, including King Kong, Tarzan, Doc Savage, Superman, Batman, Wonder Woman, Spider-Man, *MAD* magazine's Alfred E. Neuman and various characters from World of Warcraft. Throughout, his illustrations have displayed an accent toward dinosaurs, Action Adventure, SF and Fantasy. He has illustrated hundreds of book and magazine covers, painted several notable posters and trading cards for the major comic book and gaming houses, and created concept and character design for the film and television industries.

In 3-D, DeVito's sculptures include the official 100th Anniversary statue of Tarzan of the Apes for the Edgar Rice Burroughs Estate, The Cooper Kong for the Merian C. Cooper Estate, Superman, Wonder Woman and Batman for Chronicle Books' Masterpiece Editions, several other notable Pop and Pulp characters, including a Doc Savage statue executed for Graphitti Designs, based on DeVito's own cover to Will Murray's *Python Isle*. Additional sculpting work ranges from scientifically accurate dinosaurs, a multitude of collectibles for the Bradford Exchange in a variety of genres, to various awards and larger-than-life statues.

An avid writer, Joe is the creator of *Skull Island*. Exclusively authorized and endorsed by the Cooper family, *Skull Island* is the first King Kong/Skull Island origin story since Merian C. Cooper created King Kong. DeVito has also created and is developing an all-new, eon-spanning paleo action-adventure tale called *The Primordials*. He is also the co-author (with Brad Strickland) of two novels, which DeVito also illustrated. The first, *KONG: King of Skull Island* (DH Press), was published in 2004. It is based on Joe's original Skull Island creation, as is an upcoming new series, starting with the eponymously named *Skull Island*. Also co-authored by Joe and Brad, *Merian C. Cooper's KING KONG* was published by St. Martin's Griffin in 2005. DeVito has contributed many essays and articles to such collected works as *Kong Unbound: The Cultural Impact, Pop-Mythos, and Scientific Plausibility of a Cinematic Legend* and "Do Android Artists Paint In Oils When They Dream?" in P*ixel or Paint: The Digital Divide-In Illustration Art.*

Of his *Pat Savage* painting, Joe notes:

> We mined *three* different Doc archives on this one, each about 30 years apart. We drew inspiration from original pulp sources for the look of the villain, a great James Bama shot gleaned from his photo sessions with Steve Holland from the '60s to augment the pose and lighting effects, and from my cover for *The Jade Ogre* from a quarter century back (it is strange referring to my own work as being from 25 years ago!).
>
> Walter Baumhofer's *Czar of Fear* magazine cover from November, 1933 inspired the plum purple color scheme for the villain, with the actual hood textures being a cross between it and the Bama shoot. Of course, the bell of the '33 cover was replaced by the much cooler scorpion in Will's story. We all liked the feel of the mist-like arms I first painted in *The Jade Ogre* and felt it would be a great homage to use the same ef-

fect in this painting for the scorpion claws and tail stinger. Also borrowed from the photo shoot for the *Jade Ogre* cover was Pat herself, though in this painting I redrew her features quite a bit to emphasize her toughness (but not too much so). When I blended everything together, the resulting composition and color scheme had a respectful nod to the past while being firmly rooted in the present and beyond. Going forward, should Pat find her own series, I think we're off to a great start in establishing a wonderful look for the thrilling Wild Adventures to come!

www.jdevito.com
www.kongskullisland.com
FB: Joe DeVito-DeVito Artworks

About the Patron

DAVE SMITH

LIKE MOST ADOLESCENT boys of the 1960s, Dave Smith was into comic books. Even before the 1966 *Batman* TV show aired, Dave had already filled his young mind with reruns of the old George Reeves *Superman* TV show. He began reading comics in the late 1950s and has been on the hunt ever since. He lived only a few blocks from downtown Anaheim and would ride his bike to his favorite drugstore selling the latest comics. Then in the late '60s, he stumbled upon Doc Savage and the awesome James Bama art that initially attracted him to the Bantam reprint books. Dave remembers starting with *The Man of Bronze* (you have to start with #1, don't you?) which engrained the origin story deep in his psyche. He still recalls reading *Brand of the Werewolf* and *Resurrection Day* early on. The paperbacks' copyright dates led him to discover the actual pulp magazines from which they originated.

Dave remembers the day when a used bookstore opened up in downtown Anaheim. He peered into the front window for the first time and saw on a pegboard display some old comic books. These weren't just old, they were really old, like from when his dad was young—titles such as *Superman* #14 (January, 1942), *Green Hornet* #23 (March, 1945), *America's Best* #14 (June, 1945) and many others. This new bookstore was The Book Sail and would be a life-changing place for this young boy. Dave started hanging around and learned all he could from the owner, who taught him about not just old comics, but pulp magazines and rare books. The first pulp magazines he ever saw were a run of *Amazing Stories* back to #1. Eventually, he was hired in 1969 to work for the store at age 14.

Dave also remembers his first hunt for a *Doc Savage* pulp magazine. He had heard about this one particular story called *Up From Earth's Center* where Doc goes to Hell… well, maybe. That sounded intriguing to him and he started searching for that issue. Dave eventually discovered an outstanding copy at a comic book convention in Anaheim, CA. In retrospect, it's interesting that the first *Doc Savage* pulp he ever bought turned out to be the final issue of the run.

Dave learned all he could about the history of comics and pulps, as well as all the characters and authors who started out in the pulps. He educated himself about the various artists and why some were more desirable than others. He also absorbed the traditions of being a book dealer and made many connections. He learned the art of negotiation, buying wholesale, and how to meet the needs of customers. He enjoyed speaking with collectors and helping them find what they were looking for. Sounds simple, right? Finding those last few pulps to finish a collection for a customer is not easy, but it's one of the more satisfying parts of the job for Dave. Finding scarce and rare items for people has become a very important part of the business even to this day and it's almost as much a thrill as filling in holes in his own collection.

Dave worked for The Book Sail on and off from 1969 to 1978, then opened his own comics store in Garden Grove, CA, in 1979. Fantasy Illustrated went from a 500 square foot storefront a mile and a half south of Disneyland to an 800 square foot unit, allowing him to create a pulp section. Dave remembers one of his first big buys was a beautiful run of early *Docs*. He kept the really high grade *Red Skull* because of the striking cover and he still has that pulp to this day. Alas, most of the rest of the run was sold to pay bills and living expenses. Ah! The bitter world of being a collector-dealer.

Over the years, Dave has published 30 mail order catalogues in the Comic, Pulp and Paperback fields, publishing his last one in 1999. That was about the time he switched to selling on eBay as the source of most of his mail order business. That last catalogue Dave recalls fondly as the one that introduced the Yakima Pulp Pedigree collection to many pulp collectors.

A while later, he met his future wife, Kelli. She was an attorney becoming burned out as a public defender. She wanted to get into another area of law, but didn't quite know how to go about starting her own office. Since Dave knew how to run a business and had been self-employed most of his adult life, they worked out a plan to open up their own law office. Dave went back to college and earned an advanced Paralegal certificate. A month after his 2005 graduation, they opened a law office. Today Dave works part time as a paralegal and office manager but the rest of the time buys and sells for Fantasy Illustrated. But it's clear Dave doesn't look at it as work. When you're passionate about something, it really isn't work, is it?

Currently, Dave spends a copious amount of his time buying and selling pulp magazines. In his spare time, he is a writer on the subject of pulps and also sharing what he has learned in the decades of running his own businesses. He has written for *Blood 'N' Thunder* and also publishes his own fanzine: "Dave's Clubhouse" for PEAPS (Pulp Era Amateur Press Society). After decades of collecting, dealing and chasing down all kinds of pulps both for himself and his customers, Dave now owns two complete sets of the *Doc Savage* pulps: a personal set he has been working on and upgrading for decades and one for sale or trade. What a great life!

www.fantasyillustrated.net

TARZAN®

Return to Pal~ul~don

"This first authorized Tarzan novel from the sure hand of pulpmeister Will Murray does a fantastic job of capturing the true spirit of Tarzan, not a grunting monosyllabic cartoonish strongman, but an evolved, brilliant, man of honor equally at home as Lord Greystoke and as the savage *Tarzan the Terrible*."

—*Paul Bishop*

$24.95 softcover
$39.95 hardcover
$5.99 ebook

WORDSLINGERS

AN EPITAPH FOR THE WESTERN

☞ WILL MURRAY ☜

Will Murray's Wordslingers is not only the first in-depth history of the Western pulps, it's one of the best and most important books on the pulps ever written, perfectly capturing the era, the magazines, and the writers, editors, and agents who helped fill their pages. Pulp fans will be fascinated by the rich background provided by hundreds of quotes from the people involved in producing the Western pulps, while writers will benefit from the discussions of characterization and storytelling that prove to be both universal and timeless.

—*James Reasoner*

$29.95 softcover
$39.95 hardcover
$8.99 ebook

ALTUS PRESS · THE NAME IN PULP PUBLICATIONS

Available at AltusPress.com and Amazon.com

THE
ARGOSY
LIBRARY

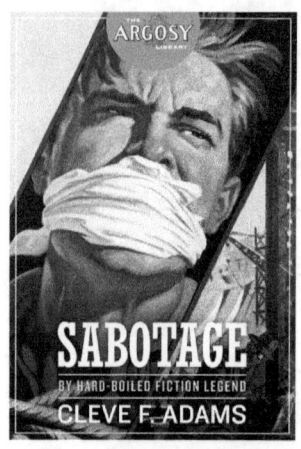

SABOTAGE
BY HARD-BOILED FICTION LEGEND
CLEVE F. ADAMS

CHAMPION OF
LOST CAUSES
BY WILLIAM F. NOLAN
MAX BRAND

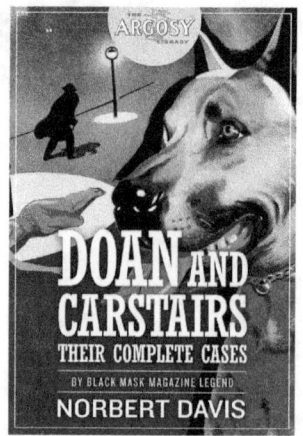

DOAN AND
CARSTAIRS
THEIR COMPLETE CASES
BY BLACK MASK MAGAZINE LEGEND
NORBERT DAVIS

THE KING WHO
CAME BACK
BY THE AUTHOR OF THE RAMBLER
FRED MacISAAC

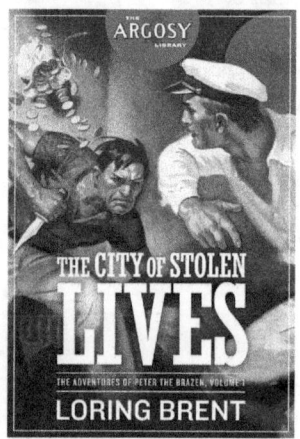

THE CITY OF STOLEN
LIVES
THE ADVENTURES OF PETER THE BRAZEN, VOLUME 1
LORING BRENT

THE RADIO
GUN-RUNNERS
BY SCIENCE FICTION LEGEND
RALPH MILNE FARLEY

BLOOD
RITUAL
THE ADVENTURES OF
SCARLET AND BRADSHAW, VOLUME 1
THEODORE ROSCOE

THE SCARLET
BLADE
THE RAKEHELLY ADVENTURES OF
CLEVE AND D'ENTREVILLE, VOLUME 1
MURRAY R. MONTGOMERY

THE COMPLETE CABALISTIC CASES OF
SEMI
DUAL
THE OCCULT DETECTOR, VOLUME 2: 1912–13
J.U. GIESY AND JUNIUS B. SMITH

SOUTH OF
FIFTY-THREE
BY THE AUTHOR OF THE TORCH
JACK BECHDOLT

THE ARGOSY LIBRARY ™

SERIES 2 INCLUDES:

* BRAND * BRENT * ADAMS *
* MacISAAC * ROSCOE *
* GIESY & SMITH *
* BECHDOLDT *
* MONTGOMERY *
* FARLEY *
* DAVIS *

THE BEST FICTION
FROM THE FRANK
A. MUNSEY LINE

THE ALL-NEW *WILD* ADVENTURES OF
DOC SAVAGE

Doc Savage:
The Desert Demons

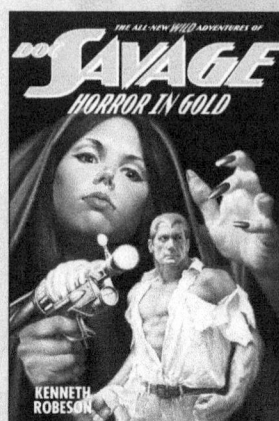

Doc Savage:
Horror in Gold

Doc Savage:
The Infernal Buddha

Doc Savage:
The Forgotten Realm

Doc Savage:
Death's Dark Domain

Doc Savage:
Skull Island

ALTUS PRESS · THE NAME IN PULP PUBLICATIONS

Available at AltusPress.com, AdventuresInBronze.com, and Amazon.com

THE ALL-NEW *WILD* ADVENTURES OF

DOC SAVAGE

THE SINISTER SHADOW

The Man of Bronze comes face to face with his strange opposite—the mysterious midnight avenger known as The Shadow! His mocking laughter is heard over radio airwaves, his thundering guns clean out the darkest dens of the Underworld. But is he a force for good, or evil? Doc Savage faces his greatest challenge yet....

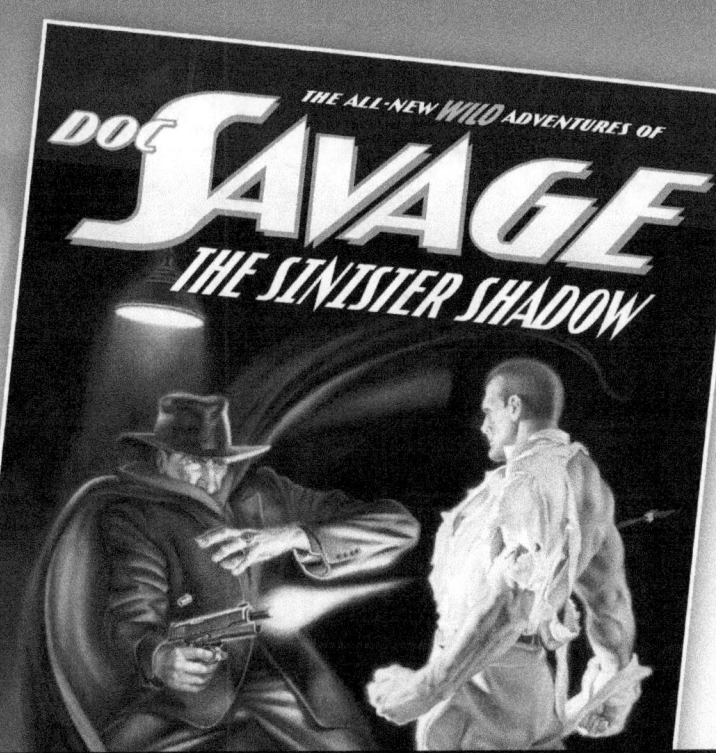

Deluxe Signed Hardcover: $39.95 | Softcover: $24.95 | Ebook: $5.99

Available at www.adventuresinbronze.com or www.altuspress.com

Published under license from Advance Magazine Publishers Inc. d/b/a Condé Nast.

DOC SAVAGE

LIMITED EDITION FINE ART PRINTS!

WWW.JDEVITO.COM

www.ingramcontent.com/pod-product-compliance
Lightning Source LLC
Chambersburg PA
CBHW070322030726
47505CB00004B/1058